Rapture—and peril—await beyond a kiss...

A SEASON BEYOND A KISS

Also by Kathleen E. Woodiwiss

Ashes in the Wind
Come Love a Stranger
The Elusive Flame
The Flame and the Flower
A Rose in Winter
Shanna
So Worthy My Love
The Wolf and the Dove
Petals on the River

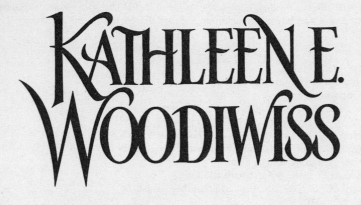

KATHLEEN E. WOODIWISS

A SEASON BEYOND A KISS

AVON BOOKS NEW YORK

AVON BOOKS, INC.
An Imprint of HarperCollins*Publishers*
10 East 53rd Street
New York, New York 10022-5299

Copyright © 2000 by Kathleen E. Woodiwiss
Cover illustration by Glenn Harrington
Interior design by Kellan Peck
Published by arrangement with the author
Library of Congress Catalog Card Number: 99-94874
ISBN: 0-380-80793-9
www.harpercollins.com

Library of Congress Cataloging in Publication Data:

Woodiwiss, Kathleen E.
  A season beyond a kiss / Kathleen E. Woodiwiss.
    p. cm.
  1. South Carolina—History—1775–1865—Fiction. 2. Charleston (S.C.)—Fiction. I. Title.
PS3573.O625 S4 2000
813'.54—dc21   99-088712

First Avon Books Trade Paperback Printing: March 2000

AVON TRADEMARK REG. U.S. PAT. OFF. AND IN OTHER COUNTRIES, MARCA REGISTRADA, HECHO EN U.S.A.

Printed in the U.S.A.

OPM   10 9 8 7 6 5 4 3 2 1

To my oldest sister, Evelyn.
When I was a child,
she was like a second mother to me.
I love her dearly.

—KEW

A Season
Beyond A
Kiss

1 ✑

Near Charleston, South Carolina
July 29, 1803

ℛeluctantly Raelynn Birmingham roused from slumber and lifted an eyelid to peer menacingly toward the open French doors through which drifted a distant, repetitive pounding. The sun had barely weaned itself from its earthly breast, yet a clammy warmth, augmented by a brief downpour during the night, had already stolen into her second-story bedroom. In spite of the portent of unbearable heat and humidity, Raelynn considered her chances of getting a few more moments of sleep . . . *if* she could bestir herself from the chamber's stately four-poster long enough to close the portals. Through most of the hours of darkness just past, she had tossed in restless frustration upon her lonely bed, tormented by sensual longings her handsome husband had awakened within her, cravings that were as yet unappeased after almost two weeks of marriage. If not for the untimely intrusion of a predacious blackguard, who, with his hired rabble, forced his way into the plantation house on her wedding night, and the barrier she had personally set between her bridegroom and herself a day later after hearing a young wench accuse him of siring her unborn child, Raelynn had no doubt that she would have now been sharing not only her husband's bed but all the pleasures to be found in matrimony. Truly, in this case, ignorance might have led to bliss if not for a girl named Nell.

The idea of remaining ensconced in bed didn't seem nearly so appealing when Raelynn realized she had been perspiring enough to have dampened her batiste night-gown. It clung to her with maddening persistence until she was driven to pluck the garment away from her bosom and fan herself with it, creating a billowing motion that forced a light current of cooling air over her moist skin. It brought instant relief, but, at best, it would last no longer than her efforts.

Her lengthy yawn bordered on a recalcitrant groan as she crawled from the bed and tottered drowsily to the washstand. There she poured water into the porcelain washbasin and cupped the liquid to her face, hoping to put her doldrums to flight. The benefits proved just as fleeting, and no less groggy, she lent her attention to brushing her teeth.

Foreseeing a lingering lethargy unless she regained some small portion of the sleep she had lost, Raelynn pondered her chances of subduing the noise to create a more restful mood. In such a quest, she wove an unsteady path to the French doors, but upon reaching the glass-paned portals, it dawned on her that if she closed them, the room would then become stifling. Her bedchamber was one of four opening out onto the veranda that stretched across the back of the house. Only Jeff's larger chambers next door and the bedroom at the opposite end of the structure had combinations of windows and French doors. The middle two only had a double set of the latter.

When presented a choice between suffocating within the confines of a hot, stuffy room and suffering through the noisy hammering, Raelynn decided forthwith that she could tolerate the racket far better than the unbearable alternative. Far removed from England's moderate weather, she was now ensconced in Oakley Plantation House, located in the Carolinas where she had been warned prior to her arrival that temperatures could soar to sweltering degrees in the summer, especially in the latter months of the season. It was not a place to lightly dismiss the discomfort and hazards of rising temperatures.

A disconcerted sigh escaped Raelynn as she leaned a shoulder against the jamb and swept her gaze beyond the white balustrade bordering the outer limits of the gallery. Some time after the rain, a thick haze had crept over the land. Even now, it seemed to isolate the manse in a world of its own. Wreathed by the milky vapors, a row of huge, sprawling live oaks created a vague rampart of blurred darkness across the spacious back yard, obscuring everything beyond them as they separated the main grounds from the servants' quarters, a collection of cabins, ranging in size from small to large, that resided in the shade of other lofty trees. Raelynn had no need to probe the mists to locate the area from whence the din arose. She knew as well as anyone living on the plantation that behind the third tree a new structure was presently being erected for the black housekeeper and her small family. Less than a fortnight ago, charred ashes and blackened timbers were all that remained of Cora's home and possessions, yet, as late as yesterday afternoon, Raelynn had seen pitched rafters rising above the new timbers that now formed the outer shell of the structure.

Making no attempt to stifle another yawn, Raelynn lifted her long, auburn tresses off her neck. In such climes her hair had proven as heavy and warm as wool, and in view of the heat yet to come, which only promised to worsen as they entered August, she could only foresee added discomfort unless she started braiding the thick mass before retiring at night.

In preceding years, when her father had been respected as a loyal subject and emissary of King George the Third of England, the name of James Barrett, Earl of Balfour, had drawn swarms of guests to her family's London estate. For those lavish affairs her personal maid had coifed her hair with an artistic flare, the beauty of which had drawn raves from friends and guests who had lavishly praised not only the styles, but the rich color and lush texture. In gracious response she had acknowledged their compliments, lending little consideration to her maid's talents or toils that, even on a diurnal basis, had seen the auburn tresses arranged in more sedate, yet no less charming modes.

That was *then*. *Now* Raelynn had to care for the unruly mane herself, making her fully conscious of the arduous task just keeping her hair clean and reasonably subdued in a chignon. Merely combing out the tangles after every washing was an ordeal, one which had recently led her to consider the benefits of reducing its length by at least half, but she had refrained, not at all certain how her husband would react to such a change. Considering the formidable wall she had erected in her marriage with her refusal to yield herself to the intimacy involved in a marital union, she dared not tweak Jeffrey's temper any more than she had possibly done already. Her sire would have had a bloody fit if she had had the audacity to do such a thing while he had still been alive, and she couldn't say with any assurance that her husband would tolerate such a deed any better. Though in preceding weeks she had glimpsed Jeffrey's unyielding tenacity only once, and that during his confrontation with Nell, she had nevertheless been left with the impression that there were definite limits to what Jeffrey Birmingham would tolerate. As yet, she had not dared test that extent herself, certainly not after her request for separate beds, for to do so had seemed a definite pathway to folly.

Deliberately Raelynn turned her thoughts away from that sensitive subject, and in an attempt to stretch and tauten her muscles, she twisted this way and that several times before bending forward and pressing her palms flat upon the floor. Upon rising again, she arched her back as far as she could go, and then repeated the exercises.

On the voyage from England, steerage had been packed nigh to overflowing with passengers, and there had been little space to walk about in the dark, dank hole to which the less fortunate had been consigned. Any movement beyond the limited area her mother and she had been allotted had usually entailed bothering others, which they had both been reluctant to do. Her inactivity throughout the whole of those three months had left a lingering stiffness that, even now, was still noticeable immediately following her initial departure from bed. Still, Raelynn considered herself fortunate to have survived the poor conditions and the scarcity of food; her mother hadn't.

"You're up early, my sweet."

Straightening with a gasp of surprise, Raelynn glanced back along the veranda from whence the deep, male voice had emanated and found her husband strolling leisurely toward her. Apparently he had ventured past the open French doors of her bedroom while she had still been asleep, no doubt to observe the progress of the carpenters from the far end of the portico, a favorable spot from which to view the building site. He wore no shirt or shoes, only sleek taupe trousers that accentuated the muscular trimness of his hips and waist. His short, raven hair was wet and wildly spiked, evidencing a recent washing that was further confirmed by the linen towel hanging about his bronzed neck.

Perhaps it was just another dreamy fantasy she was having about the man who had whisked her out of the path of a swiftly approaching four-in-hand shortly after they had collided quite by accident on a boardwalk in Charleston, but Raelynn thought he looked especially virile this early morning hour. No doubt his abbreviated garb lay at the root of such a premise, for the man had been gifted with a most excellent physique. His shoulders were remarkably wide, his arms admirably wrought with lithe muscles, his darkly furred chest broad to just below his male breasts, from there tapering downward nicely along firmly fleshed ribs. She knew well enough that beneath those crisply tailored trousers, his hips were narrow enough to be envied by a woman. He was an active horseman and, on a regular basis, sparred with several of his close friends merely for the sport of it. As a result, his muscles were well honed to a vibrant hardness.

Though his hair was as black as ink, he was not a man who was naturally swarthy or excessively hairy. His chest and loins bore the heaviest matting, his forearms and long, lissome legs only a light layer, his back and shoulders none at all.

His features were noble: his jaw crisply chiseled beneath warmly burnished skin, his nose lean with a subtle aquiline curve, his chin slightly cleft. Whenever he smiled or thoughtfully pursed his lips, twin indentations appeared in his tautly fleshed cheeks as a vague form of dimples that, along with the beauty of his darkly translucent green eyes, never failed to capture the attention of young ladies everywhere. His lop-sided way of grinning could be termed lethal in regards to stripping away a woman's resolve. Raelynn had found herself no less susceptible and, many a time, had been forced to fortify her wits lest she, too, fall prey. In all aspects, her husband was an exceptional specimen of the male gender.

If she had been a wife in actuality, Raelynn would have yielded to a strengthening desire to sweep a hand over that firm expanse of sinew, muscle and crisply curling hair that constituted his chest, much as she had done on their wedding night when she had first viewed him without hindrance of clothes and had been awestruck by his manly grace and beauty. But then, it would hardly have surprised her to discover that since that time she had become more than a little besotted with and perhaps even a bit prejudiced about a certain Southern gentleman named Jeffrey Lawrence Birmingham.

"Jeffrey, you startled me," she scolded with a nervous little laugh. It didn't help her composure one whit knowing that behind that charming mask of refined masculinity there could be lurking a disreputable rake bereft of any concern for how carelessly he used smitten young maids for his own ease and pleasure. Even after witnessing the altercation between Jeff and Nell, Raelynn realized she had cause to fear that she, too, was becoming just as susceptible, for it seemed lately that she could think of nothing else but those brief moments she had spent in his arms.

His white teeth flashed briefly in a wayward grin. "Did I now?"

The way his eyes flicked over her in a sweeping glance left Raelynn feeling as if she had just been stripped from head to toe. It was enough to bring a brighter glow to her cheeks and leave her voice less than steady. What was worse, it aroused within her a yearning for his husbandly attention and fervently wishing she could forever banish the memory of Nell to the four winds. "You're usually gone by this hour of the morning, aren't you, Jeffrey?"

"Aye, but my bookkeeper wanted me to look over the accounts for my shipping company, and I just finished them this morning. It's always tedious work, and I decided to spend a few leisured moments relaxing before making the trip into Charleston." He canted his dark head at a contemplative angle. "And what of you, my pet? Are you normally up this early?"

Raelynn blushed, knowing that in contrast to his

early morning risings, she probably seemed like a sleepyhead. The French doors of her bedroom were usually left open all night to allow the cooler air to enter its confines. Though no sound had disturbed her, she had roused from sleep enough times to have become cognizant of the fact that it wasn't at all unusual for her husband to roam the gallery just before or shortly after daybreak, leaving her no other choice but to assume that he was well acquainted with her habit of sleeping fairly late. "The hammering woke me."

The hand she clutched to her throat trembled slightly, in part from an inexplicable excitement that his presence never failed to evoke within her, and, perhaps in similar degrees, from a troubling suspicion that she was weakening like some mindless twit to a libertine's subtle wiles. If she had her wits about her, she wouldn't wait around for him to rend her heart. She'd turn tail and run. It was pure folly to subject oneself to temptations that with each passing day were becoming more difficult to resist. Indeed, the only thing that had thus far kept her from avidly pursuing a consummated marriage was the niggling fear that Jeffrey Birmingham wasn't nearly as honorable, noble or gentlemanly as he seemed on the surface.

More often of late, her heart seemed torn asunder by two choices, both of which at different times seemed rational. One was driven by a growing desire to become his wife in actuality; the other, based on fear and suspicion, to abscond with her virginity intact before she fell victim to his deceit. Yet when she mused on the latter option, a miserable emptiness settled within her vitals, leaving her feeling drained, and she'd find herself struggling against a volley of tears, both strong indications of his affect on her and her reluctance to leave him.

The tumult raging within her seriously jangled her nerves, and as much as she would have preferred otherwise, Raelynn feared that she was behaving like some bedazzled young miss infatuated with an older man. Jeffrey was indeed that, being a score, ten and three, and her senior by four and ten years, which made her even more wary of his appeal. What could a mere girl do to fortify herself against the persuasive charm of a man of experience?

Certainly a few moments in his presence could leave her hopelessly flustered in spite of the small collection of handsome, young aristocrats who had once vied for her attention in England, but in retrospect those eager gallants seemed hopelessly immature and foppish now that she had a more worthy subject with whom to compare them. It was indeed a rare man who could claim the equal to Jeffrey's gentlemanly allure, notable physique, and stunning good looks. And she wondered *why* she was becoming so vulnerable? Surely by now, a simpleton could have figured out the reasons!

In spite of the precautions with which she had sought to fortify herself, it was a hard fact for her to face knowing that her fascination with the man had deepened in the short span of time that they had been married. Her attraction had obviously been bolstered by his manly charisma and striking physical appearance. Nevertheless she was wont to wonder at times if the situation she had created for herself had somehow strengthened his appeal. Basically, by the same restrictions she had decreed for him, she was allowed to look but forbidden to touch and handle. Such limitations were comparable to a delectable sweetmeat being teasingly dangled just beyond the reach of a young child. The more it remained out of range, the more fervently it was coveted.

Raelynn's cheeks warmed once more beneath the heady intoxication of those smoldering emerald orbs as they glided leisurely over her meagerly clad form. It was a well-worn path upon which her own memories trod, back to that moment wherein Jeffrey Birmingham had braced himself above her to complete their marital union.

Before that single night of frustrated pleasure, she had never even glimpsed a naked man, much less lain equally devoid of clothing within his arms. Yet if she had been called upon to describe that stirring vision of a princely groom clothed in nothing more than the natural raiment of a man, she would have painted a most winning, detailed likeness of a tall, young god in the prime of life and in the heat of passion. Her eyes had feasted upon his manly beauty, and even after Nell's accusations, she had only to close her eyes to form a mental image of his face and form.

Jeff's lips curved roguishly aslant, displaying the tantalizing depression in one of his cheeks as he paced forward with measured tread. Had he been stalking a wary doe, he could not have been more careful *or* deliberate. "Should I be whipped for a scoundrel for startling you, madam?"

"No, of course not, Jeffrey. How absurd." Raelynn stared up into those luminous orbs, saying nothing more until she realized she was grinning back at him with a total lack of aplomb. The fact that she now felt completely alive and alert made her mindful of the potency of the strange elixir exuded by the man. "I mean, you make me feel . . ." She searched for a word or phrase that would adequately describe her disarray and yet leave no derogatory image of a love-struck chit. How could she, with trite comparisons, explain the blissful aura that at the moment seemed to encompass her?

She certainly had no wish to reveal the mental upheaval she was suffering because of their marital dilemma. By dint of will she had managed to withhold herself from his amorous attentions, yet it hadn't been easy by any means. Having been taken to the very brink of consummation, she had then been unable to relegate those sensually stirring memories to the realm of oblivion. She had seen him as a bridegroom fully aroused, and thereafter, a battle had raged within her for possession

of her mind. In spite of the difficulty she had in control-
ling her own growing curiosity and desires, the chasm
between them had continued to widen, especially after
he had begun distancing himself from her. Many times
during his absence, feeling lonely even in the midst of
so many servants, she had caught herself savoring recol-
lections of those titillating adventures in his arms. Now
she had no need to conjure images from the past. He was
standing before her, barely a step or two away, close
enough for her to feel the aura of his manly magnetism
as keenly as if it were of tangible substance.

"Make you feel like what?" Jeff queried, his lips once
again sliding upward at a corner.

Unable to contain her own grin, Raelynn cast a coy
glance upward. For the life of her she couldn't deny the
way her senses seemed to soar to bracing heights in his
presence. "Wonderful."

"Wonderful?" The emerald eyes probed hers, searching for the precise import of her flirtation. Jeff was wary.
He had lost himself in the fervent heat of those darkly
lashed, blue-green orbs once before, and he had taken
great delight in sweeping his young bride to their marriage bed, only to have been halted on the very threshold
of fulfillment by the entrance of a rowdy band of brigands, who had whisked his bride away to the warehouse
lair of Gustav Fridrich. In giving chase after a leaden ball
had creased his scalp, which had led the miscreants to
think that they had killed him, he had rallied his brother
and a collection of friends, including Sheriff Rhys Townsend, who, along with his deputies, had met him in
Charleston. The lot of them had stormed the building in
which the German and his army of callow toughs were
holding Raelynn captive, and though they had proven
victorious over the ruffians who had outnumbered them,
Jeff had later been frustrated by Rhys's announcement
that Fridrich couldn't be arrested for the simple reason

that Raelynn's uncle, Cooper Frye, had tricked the man into believing he had bought her.

Only a few hours after his wife's safe return to Oakley, Jeff had found himself encountering a different sort of aggression. Accusations from a former hireling had left his bride less than confident of his integrity and fearful of becoming intimate with him. Thus, what he had fervently hoped would be the beginning of a loving, passionate marriage with a woman who had seemingly made his dreams a reality, had become instead a titular relationship.

Through the next pair of weeks, the two of them had lived in polite but stilted congeniality, eating and conversing together but sleeping apart, she in her room and he next door in his. It was an arrangement that Jeff had tolerated, but only by the grit of his teeth. Indeed, there had been moments wherein he had found his gentlemanly forbearance sorely strained. His wife was far too beautiful and alluring for him to nonchalantly endure her nearness. In a quest to put some distance between them, he had spent long hours away from the house, directing his attention to his many business affairs: his shipping company, his lumber mill, his horse-breeding operations, or overseeing the earlier harvests with his foreman. To some degree, his attempts had helped to abate his concupiscence, but coming home to her had been tantamount to being hit with a sledgehammer in a most vulnerable area.

"Wonderful in what way, my sweet?"

Raelynn lifted her slender shoulders, not willing to divulge the full extent of the feelings he awoke within her. One moment she was fraught with anxiety over what she might suffer yielding to him; in the next she could not fathom continuing on in their marriage another moment longer without becoming his wife in truth. "Just wonderful."

"Madam, in that regard, may I say how wonderful

you look this early morning hour," he murmured, his eyes carefully probing the delicate fabric that all but flaunted her womanly form.

Mindful of her husband's proximity in a variety of different ways, not the least of which was his close attention and the scent of his cologne mingled with an underlying essence of soap, Raelynn suffered another attack of nervous jitters, which, beneath the flame burning in those dark, crystalline depths of emerald green, might have equaled those of a fox-cornered hen. As observant as Jeffrey was, she was sure that any smile from her lips would have been construed as an invitation, encouraging him to test her restraint, leaving her to face the quandary of whether to ignore Nell's accusations or to accept his advances with open arms. Torn between that which she had hotly craved in the dead of night and the more arduous travail of keeping up a cool facade of offended wife, Raelynn could not at this point predict what her answer would be. A small, inner voice counseled aloofness and separation; certainly wisdom cautioned that she hold this man at bay until confident of his merit as a gentleman. Nevertheless her young body yearned for the thrilling excitement that she had experienced far too briefly. Brought up sharply by the conflict raging within her, leaving her mind roiling in indecision, Raelynn cried out in silent anguish, *What to do? What to do?*

In spite of the tormenting vacillation she was encountering, Raelynn sought with casual comments to safely anchor a ladylike amenability, in that way hoping without undue hardship to escape the moment of temptation. "Your men are moving right along with Cora's new cabin, Jeffrey. Why, at the rate they're progressing, the structure will be finished by the end of next week. I'm sure you must be aware of how anxious Cora and her family are to get into a home of their own again."

She broke off suddenly, realizing to her abashment that a dignified serenity was not what she was imparting.

Indeed, she seemed to be chattering on like a mindless ninny, hardly conscious of what she was saying. How in the world could she even come close to a cool-headed logic when those probing green orbs all but devoured her? Every time his gaze flicked over the cloyingly damp cloth veiling her bosom, she was brought up short by a memory of those brief moments of passion wherein his tongue had moved with tantalizing slowness over her soft nipples. It was quite exhilarating to realize that even now that particular recollection had the strength to arouse a hungry yearning in the core of her womanly being.

Jeff stepped even closer yet, his gaze dwelling upon the delicate pink crests teasingly displayed by the diaphanous fabric. Having anticipated the pain that had promised to lay him low each and every time he yielded to a manly propensity to indulge in a visual appreciation of his wife's beauty and winsome form, he had abstained from that kind of self-abuse by limiting the time he spent with her. Even when he had been forced by the demands of protocol to conduct himself in social good manner and escort his young wife to functions which had required their attendance as a couple at weddings, christenings and similar affairs, he had sought to remain distantly detached and had only glanced at her when he had been compelled to and then, only briefly, a contrivance which had allowed him by dint of will to maintain his gentlemanly forbearance. Although she had looked no less than enchanting every time they had gone out, she had hardly been clothed then in a filmy thing that left nothing to his imagination. Whether due to her softly swelling bosom or the intriguing shadow vaguely hidden beneath her nightgown, his attention was firmly ensnared. Such enticements were too much for any man to ignore, much less one who had found himself hard-pressed by a lengthy abstinence and ever-goading passions. He could only hope that this time her generous display amounted to an invitation and that she was actually coaxing him to do more than just look.

"Aye," Jeff finally agreed, "it won't take any time at all for my men to finish the cabin."

Raelynn was herself besieged by a growing tension, the like and depth of which in her maidenly innocence she had never experienced before. After the miserable night she had just spent, the merest thought of withholding herself left her devoid of any hope of finding a sensible remedy for her situation. She had definitely grown tired of that transparent guise of an offended wife denying her husband for no other purpose than to obtain irrefutable proof that he was nobly pure. When she was harried by fierce longings of her own, she certainly didn't feel all that saintly herself. Jeffrey *was* her husband, she mentally argued against a chiding conscience. He had not only viewed everything her nightgown now displayed, but he had also handled her with all the familiarity a newly espoused husband is wont to lend his bride. The fact that she was standing there, submitting herself to his probing gaze, all but screamed for him to take her.

Still, he was very much a stranger to her, her pragmatic self argued. Nigh to two weeks ago they had met for the very first time after she had broken away from her uncle. Yet when Jeffrey had proposed that very selfsame hour to save her from Cooper Frye's devious plans, she had felt no qualms about accepting. It had only been afterwards that she had questioned her wisdom in speaking the vows with him so quickly. As much as she had struggled to thrust them from her mind, Nell's accusations had continued to rake their cloven claws across her memory, undermining her aspirations to be joined to this man in body as well as in name. It was the idyllic standard to which most married couples conformed, and it was only natural for her as a young wife to yearn for marital union. Indeed, there were times when those unsatisfied longings left her feeling much like a broken ship washed up on a beach.

Cognizant of her own weakening resolve even in the face of harrowing images of Jeff seducing Nell, Raelynn felt as if she teetered precariously on the sharp precipice between commitment and rejection. More than anyone she recognized the fact that she had to find a way to end her shilly-shallying and settle her mind on a prudent decision, for she was beginning to suspect that her awakened passions were now pulling sway over all the rational arguments she could put forth.

Idle chitchat seemed essential to ease the struggle roiling within her and, at the very least, to end the lengthy silence between them. Yet she blushed in discomfiture, knowing that it was merely a sham to hide what was really going on in her woman's brain and body. Truly, her husband might have been shocked if he'd have been able to discern the scope of her imagination, for at times it seemed most vivid. "Cora's new cabin appears twice as large as the old one, Jeffrey. She'll enjoy having so much room."

Jeff tilted his head wonderingly as he tried to find a reason for the vivid blush now infusing his wife's cheeks. The fact that she was garbed in a gossamer creation and had made no effort to fly out of his reach gave him cause to think that he could woo her into his bed, if not this very moment then perhaps very, very soon. Yet she seemed as nervous as a young chick looking into the greedy beak of a hunting hawk. He suffered no doubt that she had been far less tense when she had voiced her decision not to go to bed with him.

"Considering my housekeeper's fondness for children, 'tis highly unlikely that Clara will be an only child," Jeff surmised, leaning near to sample his wife's fragrance. It was a very delicate, enticing essence, reminiscent of a fresh bouquet of spring flowers. "It seems reasonable to assume that in a few years Cora and her husband will be needing quarters as large as the one that's presently being built for them."

Raelynn's jitters had come back full force as she felt Jeffrey hovering near, and just as before, her tongue began racing off in nervous haste as she sought to hide her unease. "Your rescue of Clara was certainly admirable, Jeffrey, but it's my most fervent hope that I shall never have to witness such a daring feat again. When I saw you running into that burning cabin with only a split wooden barrel shielding you from the flames, I was certain you'd be cindered right along with the house and the child." She smiled up at him nervously as he straightened. He didn't meet her gaze, but seemed oddly intrigued by the drawstring that kept her gown snugly closed at her throat. "Truly, with everything that happened during the first days of our marriage, perhaps you can understand how grateful I am that in these past weeks I've been able to enjoy the serenity of your plantation. My greatest fear is that it's only a lull before a storm. I know in time Gustav will try to avenge himself for the shoulder you shattered in spite of the fact that Olney Hyde was really the one at fault."

"I wish I could remember shooting the scoundrel," Jeff murmured and ran his fingers reflectively over the scar that had been left in his scalp after Olney had shot him, an incident which had immediately caused his own pistol to discharge a leaden ball into Gustav Fridrich's shoulder. "Such a memory might help ease my irritation over the circumstances that have allowed Fridrich the liberty to continue his chicanery and, in spite of the warrant Rhys issued for Olney's arrest, the fact that that young whelp is still wandering freely about somewhere."

"You can be assured that Kingston hasn't forgotten any of the particulars of that incident," Raelynn replied with a faint laugh and then scolded herself for not being more dignified and serene. Her husband was completely self-possessed, which in comparison to her uneasy fits and starts left her feeling as awkward as a bumbling chit. Even so, she rushed on, unwilling to give him time to dwell on her discomfiture. "After suffering through the trauma of thinking that Olney had killed you, Kingston was nearly rolled back upon his heels when you revived. The story seems quite humorous when he tells it, but I recall the horrible dismay I suffered far too vividly to even think of laughing over that dreadful incident."

The only remaining impression Jeff had of those moments immediately following his return to consciousness was his butler's slack-jawed astonishment. That singular memory would likely abide with him for the rest of his life. "I seem to remember Kingston saying something about an angel. I suppose he thought it was some kind of miracle when I regained consciousness."

"It *was* a miracle! If that shot had been any lower, Jeffrey Birmingham, you'd have had a large hole bored through your head, and I'd be standing here no less than a widow."

The corners of Jeff's mouth twitched with humor as he toyed with the delicate ribbon dangling from the bow at her throat. "I wonder how many virgins in the last hundred years have been left bereaved by the untimely demise of their bridegrooms. I doubt there have been many."

A soft, fluttering sigh escaped Raelynn as he leaned forward and brushed his lips against her cheek. From there, soft kisses trekked a leisurely descent along the creamy column of her throat. Cautiously she laid a trembling hand against his steely chest and closed her eyes, nearly swept away by the languid caress of his mouth. Beneath her palm, his heart nearly matched the swiftly thumping rhythm of her own, attesting to his growing involvement in his game of seduction. "I can't imagine that our situation is all that unique, Jeffrey."

"Surely other men would think so, my sweet," he murmured, having wondered many times in the last fortnight if he was the only husband in creation whose wife was still a virgin.

Jeff marveled at her willingness to accept his warming attentions, yet he was still wary of being rebuffed. Lifting his head, he searched her face for what emotions might be revealed in that sublime visage and was again impressed by her unparalleled beauty. The texture of her creamy fair skin was as lush and smooth as satin. A rosy blush infused her cheeks, brightening her aqua eyes until they seemed to glow with a brilliance of their own behind the thick, sooty lashes. Her nose was pert and slender; her soft mouth winsomely curved and much in need of kissing. In all of that wondrously fair countenance, Jeff could detect no slightest hint of diffidence. Though her eyelashes fluttered downward as she shyly avoided his gaze, she remained well within his grasp, encouraging him to test her resistance as well as that of the silken cord.

A small gasp escaped Raelynn as she felt the nightgown sliding away from her throat and the placket widening between her breasts. "Jeffrey, please . . ." Her whisper was hardly more than a soft exhalation of a breath. Once more she found her wits scattered, her attempts to appear composed hopelessly frustrated. Certainly what spilled forth in a hasty rush from her lips had no real relevance to what she had craved in her lonely bed. Though outwardly her statement conveyed something else entirely, it had much to do with her own incertitude over the circumstances in which she had been cast. "I don't know if I'm ready for this."

Jeff managed a stiff smile as he straightened to his full height. He had expected her to put him off, and though it was not at all to his liking, he was hardly one to fly into a raging fit when he didn't get his way. Still, if he could ascertain anything from her sudden nervousness, he'd be inclined to think that she wasn't nearly as cold and aloof as her words had led him to believe.

A more careful testing of her rejection seemed in order, yet just as needful was a careful soothing of her qualms if he had any hopes of breaking through the thin barrier she had erected between them. It seemed prudent to continue his manly assaults on her senses, but in a more subtle fashion. In that endeavor, he turned her attention to another matter which in recent days he had begun to consider. "How would you like to accompany me to Charleston today, madam, and order a new gown?"

Astounded by his invitation, Raelynn stared up at him as if he had just told her the moon had fallen from the sky. Only when their combined presence had been requested at social affairs had he relented of his ongoing aloofness and escorted her to the port city. During those outings, he had been very much a gentleman, yet she hadn't been able to shake the feeling that he had also been anxious to put those events behind him, if for no other reason than to retreat from her presence. But then, considering what she had demanded of him, she could hardly have blamed him.

As for ordering a new gown, she couldn't imagine the cost of the finery he had already purchased for her. Without a doubt, her new attire was of a quality that only the rich could afford. Still, after being forced to endure both his stilted reticence and lengthy absences, she wondered how he could be so magnanimous as to suggest that she was deserving of any gifts. "More clothes, Jeffrey, after everything you've already given me?"

His naked shoulders lifted in an indolent shrug. "It's only right that we should give a ball in honor of our marriage to allow our neighbors and my acquaintances from Charleston to meet you, madam. Considering the length of time it has taken me to find a suitable mate, the event should be a grand occasion to attest to my delight in finding a bride so fair. Such an affair warrants a gown as dazzling as yourself, and only my friend, Farrell

Ives, can design one worthy of that distinction. He'll make you the envy of nearly every lady in the area. . . ."

The blue-green orbs glowed at the pleasurable idea that she would at last be able to make a wifely claim on Jeffrey Birmingham in front of his collection of friends and acquaintances. She was especially eager to demonstrate her ownership to all those well-garbed ladies she had seen either eying him covetously from afar or, at closer range, smiling up at him invitingly. During those functions wherein he had done his husbandly duty by escorting her upon his arm, she had maintained a poised reserve, having sensed in him a polite, but stilted detachment that had discouraged wifely overtures, but he could hardly distance himself from her at a ball celebrating their marriage. "I needn't wear a sumptuous gown to elicit jealousy from all the maidens who've apparently tried to harness you into marriage in the past, Jeffrey. I believe I became a full-fledged recipient of their envy the day we were wed."

"You exaggerate, Raelynn," Jeff protested with a dubious chuckle.

"Were you not at the vanguard of the most sought after bachelors in the area?" she probed, struggling to convey a teasing mood. It was difficult to be lighthearted about all the other women who were enamored with him, for the thought of them made her think of Nell's accusations, which always provoked her curiosity as to how many other women might have had him as their lover. "Or have I wrongly laid the blame for the cause of the dejected stares that winsome young maidens are wont to cast your way whenever we're in their midst? Is it merely disappointment I see, Jeffrey, or some stronger passion that likens itself to shrewish jealousy?"

"If you arrived at that conclusion because of Nell, my dear, please allow me to assure you . . ."

"I try not to think of that little hussy any more than I have to, Jeffrey Birmingham, and I'd thank you not to remind me," she replied with far more sincerity than humor. "Kingston has definitely lent me an earful while ranting to Cora about Nell's audacity to accost you in your own bed. It's rather strange the way your butler's conversations always shift to that little chit the very moment I come within hearing. Evidently he thinks you're innocent of Nell's accusations and entirely free of any blame in getting her with child." Raelynn wished she could be so confident. Still, the corners of her mouth curved upward enticingly as she settled a playfully baleful glare upon the handsome man. "If I were of such a mind to be suspicious, dear husband, I'd think you've been coaching Kingston behind my back."

"I'll have to caution the man about being more discreet in the future," Jeff observed drolly, sweeping her with another divesting perusal. He cupped a hand against her throat and watched her eyes grow increasingly limpid as he brushed a thumb caressingly along the underside of her finely boned jaw. No smallest trace of reluctance or aversion could he discern in her expression. Indeed, if he could perceive anything from the softening of her expression, he'd be inclined to think she relished his touch as some splendid enjoyment. To test his theory more fully, he bent near and pressed a lingering kiss against her temple. A trembling sigh escaped her, encouraging him to slide his palm downward along her throat until he reached its base. Her nightgown had fallen away from that graceful column and posed no hindrance as he swept his hand outward across her shoulder, deliberately pushing the garment toward her arm. As he neared the creamy precipice, he flicked a glance upward and found her soft lips parting in a way that likened itself to sensual pleasure. It took no more than the lightest brush of his fingers to sweep the cloth over the edge.

A gasp escaped Raelynn as she quickly clapped a hand to the valley between her breasts, barely catching the falling nightgown, in so doing thwarting her husband's efforts to lay bare all the delights hidden beneath the fabric. Yet when Jeff noticed the depth to which her breasts were now exposed, his disappointment ebbed forthwith. Nothing more than a strip of gossamer cloth formed a shallow covering for one creamy orb, while the other lay fully exposed, allowing him a delectable view of a delicate pink crest. He vividly recalled when he had first savored the intoxicating nectar from those pale peaks and was now equally desirous of lending them his fervent attention.

Jeff bent low with bold purpose, causing Raelynn's breath to catch in her throat as she became aware of his intent. She shivered in anticipation and then, as his open mouth came upon her nipple, almost dissolved in bliss. A fiery torch stroked across the pinnacle, setting off a barrage of delectable sensations within her loins. Her whole being awakened to a heightening excitement as his tongue slowly traced around the delicately hued areola, and still she watched as if nothing more than a distant spectator. Vaguely she was aware of several things, the sharp contrast between her own fair skin and his warmly burnished features, the tantalizing depression in his cheek that came and went, the magnificent eyebrows she yearned to trace. Still, it was difficult to focus on anything but the waves of bliss that kept washing over her, growing stronger and more thrilling with each passing moment until she came nigh to dissolving in his arms.

His long, lean fingers ascended upward beneath the valley between her breasts, promising to uproot her tenacious grip on the gown, while his other hand moved behind her back to clasp hold of her buttock. All too soon she would be swept up into his arms and taken to her bed. Except that she didn't want that. If she was going to surrender herself to this marriage, then it had to be in *his* bed, the bed wherein she would likely bear their offspring.

Raelynn found it very odd indeed, but somewhere in

the last few moments she had lost her nervousness, as if the small nudge he had given her over the steep ridge of her impasse had been enough to settle her mind on the course she would take. She was definitely not retreating like some shy, young maid now. She had thrown aside her inhibitions as if they were nothing more than filthy rags. She knew what she wanted, and she would not be satisfied until she and he were one. And if it came to be that he was playing deceitfully with her, then heaven help her.

The corners of her mouth curved slowly upward in a poignant smile as she threaded slender fingers through her husband's thick hair. Leaning down, she brushed her lips against his temple and then, with her fine white teeth, nipped at the uppermost part of his ear, causing him to start and clap a hand to the side of his face as he straightened.

A handsome brow angled upward sharply as Jeff stared down at his young wife in widening curiosity. If this was some new way she had contrived to tease and torment him, he would have no part of it. She could stay a virgin in her damned room until all hell froze over!

His eyebrow jutted upward to an even loftier level as Raelynn smiled up at him provocatively, making no effort to repair her dishabille. Turning, she strode away from him with hips swaying with a slow, wanton movement, giving Jeff cause to wonder if he had married an unmitigated tease. A brief moment later he became convinced of it when she glanced over her shoulder with an invitation in her eyes that promptly reversed the dwindling of the manly bulge. Deliberately she rolled a shoulder, sending the nightgown slithering down her arm, allowing him a glimpse of a pale orb, albeit from a rearward angle. Upon facing away again, she gathered the gown across her buttocks, yielding him every detail the clinging cloth could afford.

A brightening gleam lit Jeff's eyes as he idly

scratched his chest. There came a time in each man's life when he had to put all finesse aside and do what came naturally though he might well be hell bent for his own destruction. At the present moment making love to his wife seemed the most natural thing in the world.

Raelynn's fine nose lifted to emulate a haughty noblewoman as she coyly played a game of pretense. "You're drooling in your beard, knave," she pompously complained, looking at him loftily. "Now depart from my room and give me peace from your presence. I wish to summon water for my morning bath and cleanse myself at my leisure. Only when I'm dressed and properly attired will I consider your invitation to visit the couturier."

"Minx," Jeff muttered and, with a low, playful growl, sprinted after her, causing her to squeal like a child in a game of chase as she skittered behind a chair.

Briefly Raelynn faced him over its winged back, but she soon discovered the piece provided no safe haven from the grinning swain who pursued her. He leapt around the back of it just as she skirted a nearby table. The door to his bedroom was before her, and she raced toward it, barely managing to thrust it open and escape around another chair and table. In her haste, she released the nightgown, inadvertently giving Jeff something tangible to grasp. His hand caught its flying hem, and in the next instant a shocked gasp was wrenched from Raelynn as he gave the cloth a downward yank, splitting the gown completely open down the front. The remnant was promptly whisked free of her arms and banished to the floor.

"Oh, you lewd, knavish cad!" Raelynn cried through her laughter as she scurried around another chair. She tossed a glance over her shoulder, but her long hair flew across her face, blinding her to his whereabouts. "You'd tear a lady's clothes off her back with little regard for propriety. . . ."

She came to an abrupt halt, meeting something very

hard and masculine, to be exact her tall, firmly muscled husband. Her mouth flew open in surprise, and hardly a pause of a heartbeat later she found long arms encircling her naked form. A large hand slipped down her back until it reached her buttock. Encompassing its fullness, he lifted her up snugly against him, making her vividly aware of his unyielding passion.

"Oh . . . oh!" Hardly aware that she had issued the muted gasps, Raelynn stared up at him, awed by the waves of sensual warmth radiating upward from the cloth-bound firmness upon which her womanly softness was now nestled. Suddenly, it was as if she had been caught in a vortex of whirling flames, for her whole body became warm and flushed with excitement. Her soft nipples throbbed against his furred chest, and behind her back she could feel his hand bridging the crevice between her buttocks, pressing her womanly loins against his. Her breath quickened, and she banished her second alternative completely from mind as she slid her arms behind his neck and locked them in a fierce embrace. How could she think of withholding herself any longer from a man who set her whole being ablaze?

"The French doors are open," she breathed shakily, casting a glance toward them. It didn't bolster any admirable impression of an unfaltering will when Raelynn realized that her concern centered primarily on a fear that they could be interrupted again, this time by unwary servants. As for her paltry resolutions, she had ceased to care, at least for the moment. Jeffrey was her husband, after all, and she desired his attention perhaps as much as he yearned to bestow them upon her. "Anyone who passes on the porch will see us."

"Our privacy is secure, madam," Jeff murmured huskily, lowering his head until his lips hovered above hers. "None of the servants would dare venture past our rooms when there's a possibility that we might be occupying them, especially mine. That rule has long been established, so rest at ease. We're quite alone, madam. Trust me."

Claiming her mouth, he ravaged its honeyed depths with rapacious greed, searching, demanding, devouring all that was within reach of his tongue. His hand came up to encompass the back of her head as his face slanted across hers, and it became an intoxicating exchange of lips and tongues as he found himself drinking in the sweet nectar of her passionate response.

By the time Jeff lifted his head and set her to her feet again, most of the strength had drained from Raelynn's knees. His sturdy chest provided support until her world settled back into place. Finally she leaned back within his encompassing arms and found his smoldering gaze devouring her breasts. Appeasing an earlier desire, she swept her hands across the width of his tautly muscled shoulders and, in a languid caress, brushed slender fingers across male nipples all but hidden by the dark hair covering his chest. The knotted sinews of his waist were steely hard, and for a moment her fingertips traced across them admiringly before venturing to the top of his trousers. Her voice was a warm, husky whisper as she began plucking open a side placket. "It's not fair that I should be the only one naked, Jeffrey."

"Banish the thought, madam," he murmured huskily and grinned as he stepped back slightly, allowing her freedom to continue. His own hands moved over her pale body, eliciting a quickening excitement that left her eagerly anticipating his provocative advancements. When the last closures of his trousers came free, his waistband sagged away from his taut waist, causing her to cast a hesitant glance upward. Her timidity was obvious as her teeth tugged nervously at a bottom lip.

"Help me," Jeff urged huskily, banishing her doubts.

With a growing involvement in this titillating game they were playing, Raelynn lent him assistance in sweeping the trousers downward, at least until she glimpsed his manly nakedness, and then, in some awe, she re-treated with cheeks burning. Indeed, the vibrant heat he now displayed infused her whole being with warmth.

Jeff peered askance at his young wife as he stripped off his trousers and tossed them aside. The sudden uncertainty in her eyes alerted him to her mounting fear. "It's all right, Raelynn," he cajoled in a hushed tone. Reaching out, he threaded his long fingers through hers. "I'm only flesh and blood. You've seen me before." He brought her up close against him, allowing her to feel *the enemy* against her. "Don't be afraid. We were made for each other."

She trembled, fully conscious of the manly blade that would rend her virgin's flesh, but Jeff gave her trepidations little time to solidify into a full-fledged fear. His opening mouth seized hers again with impassioned fervor, snatching her thoughts away as he demanded her response. Tentatively she yielded her lips and tongue to the flaming heat of his kiss until the fires began to rage out of control, leaving her feeling as if she would be devoured in his consuming greed.

When Jeff finally straightened, he had settled it in his mind that he would not allow time for interruptions. He needed her as much as the air that he breathed.

Sweeping Raelynn up in his arms, he carried her to his bed where he pressed her back into the rumpled sheets. His tongue flicked slowly over a pliant peak, sending liquid fire spiraling downward into her loins where it seemed to burn with a strange kind of hunger that yearned to be fed.

Rolling, they lay alongside each other, kissing, caressing, exploring. His mouth blazed a fiery trail over her breasts, licking, suckling, devouring as his thigh encroached between the sleekness of hers. Drawing a pale limb up over his hip, he slowly teased her with the heat of his desires, stroking his maleness against the dark veils shrouding the secret places of her womanhood until Raelynn began to shudder. Yet the tremors had nothing to do with fear or aversion, rather a rushing excitement that left her nearly breathless for want of something beyond her ken.

His smoldering eyes roamed her as he continued his pleasurable assault, but now with more dedication. Staking his claim upon her, he swept his hand down over her breasts, the slender waist and skimmed downward along the outside of her legs before moving upward again, this time along the inside of her creamy thighs. She started slightly at his intrusion, and then her breath caught at the sensations he created within her as his fingers began to ply her flesh. It was as if she were being jolted by liquid fire, waves of it pouring upward through her senses, setting her whole being aflame. She began to writhe and pant and in some embarrassment over what she was experiencing, she tried to turn aside, but Jeff pressed her down, unwilling to desist until she was truly his. His invasion proved a heady forage indeed, driving her into a kind of frenzy as he delved upward with strengthening dedication. Stroking her own breasts, she arched her back and offered them to him with a kind of wanton boldness that she had never experienced before. Greedily he devoured them, heightening her excitement until she thought she couldn't bear it.

"Please, Jeffrey." She was incognizant of what she wanted; she only knew that his manly heat seemed to feed the fires burning in her loins. Slipping a hand behind his neck, she pulled his head near and kissed him with all the passion he had awakened within her. Locked together in a fierce embrace, they rolled upon the bed, their thighs entwined, their tongues playing in the sultry heat of each others' mouths, their hands boldly searching out the private places.

Caught up in the headiness of their passion, Raelynn slid a trembling hand over her husband's firmly muscled chest, moving it past his waist and along the thin line of hair that traced downward over his taut belly. Beneath her wandering inspection, Jeff held his breath as he awaited that moment wherein she would touch him. Her fingers traced the manly flesh timidly, seeming almost fearful of hurting him, until he covered her hand and began to instruct her. Hardly a moment passed before he felt his restraint begin to crumble.

"Oh, love, love . . . there's no turning back now," he breathed. His eyes melded with hers as he rose above her and searched her face for any evidence of fear or reluctance. Caught up in the growing hunger of her own desires, Raelynn lifted her hips to his in an unmistakable invitation.

Jeff's breath wafted from him in a sigh of overwhelming relief and awe before he lowered his mouth upon hers and kissed her with tender ardor. Suddenly a burning pain pierced Raelynn's loins, wrenching a gasp from her as the steely shaft drove home. She squeezed her eyes tightly closed against the throbbing discomfort of the rent flesh and pressed her face against the base of her husband's neck as she dug her fingers into his shoulders. His lips sought hers again and played provocatively until she began to answer his devouring mouth and cavorting tongue.

In a moment all thoughts of pain were swept behind her and banished to the far reaches of her mind. Raelynn never knew the precise moment when he began to caress her loins with his. The slow, smooth, rhythmic thrusts seemed so effortless on his part; a long, leisured stroking that massaged the hurt away; a burgeoning excitement; exhilarating, scintillating pleasure washing through their merged bodies; senses skimming over billowing currents; quickening movements that drew her up with breathless gasps to meet his thudding hardness; waves of pulsing rapture sweeping over and through their entwined bodies; a swelling tide that lifted them up upon foaming crests; crashing breakers that seemed blindingly brilliant; and then shimmering, thrilling, unending ecstasy.

Washed up on the white beach of tousled sheets, they lay in the rosy aftermath of their passion, her head upon his shoulder, a brown hand encompassing her hip, a slender arm flung across his chest, and a sleek limb resting across his thighs. Though neither of them complained, the threat of dissolving seemed imminent.

Smiling dreamily, Raelynn traced a fingertip through the mat of hair covering her husband's chest and sketched a male nipple as she marveled at what she had just experienced. "I think I could sleep for a whole week now," she sighed softly. "But only if you'd consent to stay with me."

"We'll have to move your clothes back in here again," Jeff breathed, pressing a kiss upon her brow. "We could even share a bath."

Raelynn rose up upon his chest and smiled down into his shining eyes. "But I thought you already had a bath this morning."

A slow grin stretched across his handsome lips, displaying the taut depressions in his cheeks as his hand swept down her naked back. "Aye, but I find the idea of playing with you in my bathtub quite intriguing, madam. Would you be willing to indulge me?"

Her smile was warm and inviting. "Most eagerly, sir, if you, in return, would be amenable to allowing me a few privileges."

"As many as you want, my dear, as long as you stay within the confines of my arms."

2

*E*legant little shops abounded in Charleston, proclaiming its wealth as one of the most important ports along the eastern seaboard. It was a gracious city, well maintained by its residents, and rightly known for its charming atmosphere. Its streets bustled with activity, its docks the same.

Jeff's shipping company was located near the wharf. It, too, was a busy place with ships either being loaded or unloaded nearby and six-in-hands in the process of returning or pulling large wagons brimming with cargo to other vessels docked in different areas of the port. It was in the shipping yard where the Birmingham carriage made its first stop, allowing Jeff to drop off the recently reviewed ledgers to his bookkeeper.

"I won't be but a moment, my sweet," he assured his wife, squeezing her hand affectionately before stepping down from the black landau and striding toward the three-story brick building.

Raelynn watched from the window of the conveyance as her tall, nattily garbed husband made his way past workmen who called out a cheery greeting or waved to him from afar. His affable responses and ready repartees to humorous comments or teasing banter, which met him along the way, affirmed that Jeffrey Birmingham was well-liked among his employees. He even paused to speak with a man of middling years from whom he parted a moment later with a handshake and a mutual chortle as well as an enthusiastic pat on the back bestowed upon him by the brawny fellow.

Smiling in secret pleasure, Raelynn settled back against the landau's cushioned seat to await his return, hardly begrudging the time she had been given to relish the memories they had made together earlier that morning. In the hours that had since elapsed, one truth had become strikingly clear; she was immensely satisfied, even delighted with the choice she had finally made in yielding herself to Jeffrey's husbandly initiation into marital intimacy. What had followed their union had further solidified her belief that she had chosen wisely. Even the simple acts of bathing and dressing had proven infinitely more pleasurable with a bold, handsome participant, who was not above indulging in some frisky horseplay. Indeed, until this day in history she had remained ignorant of the attention-getting results of a linen towel being popped against a naked backside, but when she had returned the favor, she had suffered some surprise, learning very quickly that Jeff's attack had been much more gentle and playful, for in slapping him she had left a red welt upon his buttock that had, in the making, drawn a genuine "Ouch!" from him. Her worried apologies and soothing strokes had soon led them into more kissing and fondling, which they had later deemed well worth the initial pain. In every respect Raelynn was feeling as happy and content as any young bride who was thoroughly entranced with her amorous husband.

Jeffrey Birmingham's manly appeal was like a strong magnet, to which heretofore she had found herself being drawn closer with each passing day. In the last few hours, however, that progression had advanced by mind-staggering degrees until she was led to think that she was even more susceptible to his physical appeal and winning ways than Nell or any of the other hopefuls who had once yearned to have Jeffrey Birmingham for a husband. She had never deluded herself into believing she was the only female in Charleston or the surrounding area who had become thoroughly infatuated with the man. He was too handsome for any woman to entertain such a notion. The only difference between all the other maidens and herself was Jeff's own preference in choosing her, and she was infinitely glad he had.

A shadow passing alongside the landau made Raelynn glance around in time to see a roughly garbed man strolling past the last window. She barely caught a glimpse of the back of his hat-covered head before he moved beyond the opening, but she had no real reason to lend the fellow further heed. Considering the fact that she was a complete stranger to most of the city's populace, she felt no curiosity as to his identity or appearance. In the next moment she wished she had been more inquisitive. At least, if she had, she might have had time to flee the carriage and find her husband. As it was, she was without benefit of Jeffrey's comforting presence when Olney Hyde stepped back to the window and tilted his head aslant to peer in.

"Why, if'n it ain't Mrs. Birmin'am, all decked out like some gent's birthday present," the curly-haired scamp drawled, displaying a poorly contrived surprise as he dragged off his cap. No less cocky than he had been in Gustav's presence, he swept his gaze from her pert bonnet down to the pale peach floral muslin gown covering her soft bosom, where it lingered overlong.

Raelynn was grateful her square, lace-edged neckline

was demure or she might have found herself blushing even more than she was. Whereas Jeff's perusals evoked a sensuality within her that was hard to ignore, she was highly insulted by the brazenness of this rascal's scrutiny. Though probably as much as five years her senior, Olney seemed much younger, especially in comparison to her husband, but she hardly considered that fact a compliment. To her, he seemed the epitome of a naughty young tough, whom she really didn't care to confront on any terms, let alone now when she had no one but an aged driver to serve as her protector. Still, she managed to gather a fair measure of bravado and gave snide retort to the scamp. "Well, Olney, I'm rather surprised to see you walking about so blatantly on the streets of Charleston. I thought you'd be skulking around in some dark, dank alleyway somewhere. Sheriff Townsend will certainly be interested in hearing that you're still in the city. As you probably know, he has been searching high and low for you. I'll be sure to tell him I saw you just as soon as I can."

"Aye, ye do that, Mrs. Birmin'am, an' whilst ye're doin' it, I'll be tellin' Mr. Fridrich how fetchin' ye're lookin' nowadays, a damned sight fancier than when he last saw ye. Ye know, he really regrets my not makin' ye a widow that night I accidenta'ly shot yer husband. He ain't ne'er had nothin' taken from him afore, leastwise a wench. O' course, most o' the ones what he's had o'er the years ain't been nearly as high-falutin' or, for that matter, half as enticin'. Ye might say that losin' ye has set his temper awry, 'specially since he gots only one arm what's o' any use now."

Raelynn scoffed at the rogue's claim. "Accidentally, ha! From what I've heard from Kingston, you took deliberate aim, fully intending to kill my husband, no doubt for the purpose of appeasing your employer."

Olney shrugged his brawny shoulders indolently. "Well, now, a bloke's got ta peer down the sights o' his pistol real careful-like when he only means ta crease a fella's scalp. I'm a fair shot, that I be, but 'ere are some things what just takes time an' attention. I bet yer Mr. Birmin'am couldna've done any better if'n he'da've taken aim. He might've missed Mr. Fridrich completely if'n he'da've really meant ta shoot him."

"My husband would never consider doing such a thing unless forced to defend his home or his family! He doesn't go around shooting people simply because he takes a notion, as you seem capable of doing at the slightest provocation, Olney. As to that, I remember quite distinctly when you held a pistol to my head and threatened to do away with me if I didn't conform to Gustav's dictates."

"That was only ta make ye awares o' who was boss. Mr. Fridrich was in some kind o' awful misery wit' his arm an' all, an' 'ere was Doc Clarence needin' yer assistance. But no! Ye were a-jeerin' at Mr. Fridrich like the cold-hearted bitch ye are." He shook his head in exaggerated bemusement. "I swear, I don't know what Mr. Fridrich sees in ye. I'll grant ye, ye're a winsome li'l thing wit' a shape ta match, but as for meself, I likes women wit' some heart . . ." his pale gray eyes danced with prurient amusement as he dropped his gaze to her soft bosom again and held his cupped hands out away from his own male breasts, "an' melons as big an' ripe as . . ."

"Don't be vulgar, Olney," Raelynn snapped, highly miffed. "It shows your lack of breeding."

His lips twisted in a derisive smirk. "Oh, I suppose a fancy liedy like yerself would be more interested in a bloke's breedin' instead o' what's in his breeches."

Raelynn's eyes flashed indignantly. His lewd talk was getting to be a bit more than she could handle. It was one thing to converse with Jeff about body parts, but quite another thing entirely to endure obscene references to those same areas when they came from a wily rapscallion. "You'd better be on your way, Olney, before my husband returns and finds you here. Or you're going to wish you had."

"I ain't worried none 'bout that 'ere rich gent ye married. Why, I could best an ol' buck like him any day o' the week. 'Sides, I knows how ta keeps meself safe an' out o' the reach o' his sort. Me folks packed up ta sail here after leavin' 'ose filthy tenements o' Southwark. Indentured themselves ta do it, they did. Now that I thinks o' it, maybe we didn't live so far away from that highfalutin London mansion where Cooper Frye said ye were born. M'liedy High An' Haughty, that's what ye be. But I've been in this here area since I was knee-high ta a duck an' can tromp through Carolina swamps wit' as much ease as some folk stroll along Church Street. Thoughs ta tell ye the truth, I ain't afraid ta prance meself along any boardwalk in Charl'ton an' thumb me nose at yer Mr. Fancy Breeches *or* that 'ere ploddin' sheriff friend o' his."

Raelynn caught a glimpse of a familiar figure emerging from the upper office of the warehouse and turned a confident smile upon her antagonist. "You'll have a chance to do just that in another moment, Olney. That old buck, as you call him, is coming back this very moment."

In spite of his boastful claims, Olney took his leave with undue haste, but in fleeing the landau, he captured the attention of the one who was presently descending the back stairs of the warehouse. Jeff had no trouble recognizing the curly-headed blond and immediately gave chase, wrenching a frightened gasp from Raelynn, who scrambled down on trembling limbs from the conveyance.

"Jeffrey, come back!" she cried in spiraling apprehension. Her husband made no effort to comply, but with coattails flying out behind him, raced after the stockier, shorter-legged man, by swift degrees closing the distance between them. Raelynn clasped a hand to her swiftly beating heart and tried once more to persuade him to give up the chase. "He may have a pistol, Jeffrey! Please! Come back!"

A briskly approaching six-in-hand of stout drays hauling a heavily weighted wagon brought Jeff up short in the middle of the street. By the time he skirted around it, he faced a hired livery passing in the opposite direction. As for Olney, he was nowhere in sight.

Determined to find the young tough, Jeff ran along the thoroughfare for several blocks, hurriedly glancing down alleyways and into open doorways of shops. He found no evidence of the young miscreant. What was worse, he had no idea in which direction Olney had gone. Frustrated and angry with himself for having let the brigand escape, Jeff gave up his pursuit and strode back toward the carriage, pausing briefly at the entrance of his shipping yard where he picked up his top hat from the dust. Brushing it off, he approached the landau and gave his wife a rakish grin as he settled the topper jauntily upon his head.

"Good as new."

"That may be all well and good for your hat, Jeffrey Birmingham, but I've aged considerably in the last few moments," Raelynn quipped in exasperation. "I wish you wouldn't scare me like that. Olney has already proven himself capable of shooting you for his own gain. You have a crease in your scalp to confirm that fact. Running after the rascal is an open invitation for him to make another attempt on your life. And just think how delighted Gustav would be if Olney managed to kill you."

Jeff was keenly aware of the German's desire to claim his wife in any manner he could, which did much to nettle his temper whenever he thought about it. "I can imagine the height of that oaf's elation should such a fate befall me, my pet, but I have no intention of letting Olney kill me, at least not while I'm facing him." His eyebrows shrugged upward briefly. "My back is a different matter entirely." Slipping a hand beneath Raelynn's arm, he assisted her into his carriage as he muttered, "I just can't abide the idea of that toad roaming free after he nearly killed me and threatened to do the same to you while you were in his clutches."

Pausing to glance toward the driver's seat, Jeff gave directions to the smartly liveried black man sitting there. "If you please, Thaddeus, kindly take us around to Ives's Couture."

"Yassuh, Mistah Jeffrey. Ah'll be doin' that very thin' just as soon as yo' get lit, suh."

The conveyance swayed slightly as Jeff climbed in and settled into the seat beside his young wife, who eagerly scooted closer. Grinning down at her, he threaded lean fingers through hers and diminished the space between them until their hips were nigh joined and his shoulder overlapped hers. "Now tell me, my sweet, what did that rapscallion say to you?"

Raelynn complied, sparing none of the details of Olney's callousness, though by the time she had finished informing Jeffrey, her cheeks were hotly flushed. "In spite of that oaf's pompous boasts, the sight of you completely shattered his bravado. He lit out like a singed rabbit in his haste to get away. Perhaps next time he'll think twice before calling you an old buck. 'Tis evident you can easily outdistance him."

" 'Twould seem that Olney isn't the bashful sort in spite of Rhys's attempts to find him. I imagine the scamp has been enlisted to carry out his employer's mischief, at least until Gustav fully recovers from his shoulder wound. There's no predicting where Olney may be in weeks to come, but I'd like to be prepared the next time we meet up with him. I should've been more wary this time and not left you alone in the carriage. I shan't be so foolish again, madam."

Raelynn stroked the arm that rested casually against her breast. "I wasn't alone, Jeffrey. Thaddeus was here."

Jeff gently scoffed. "My dear, Thaddeus is nearly twice as old as I am, which makes that scamp a mere pup to him. Olney could have carried you off and left the old man scrambling vainly in his wake."

A pensive sigh escaped Raelynn. "I'd certainly feel a lot safer if Sheriff Townsend could lock Gustav and Olney behind bars for the next ten years." Her fingers traced the tendons and veins etching the lean hand that clasped her own in her lap as she remembered the grief that had nearly overwhelmed her when she had thought that Olney had killed Jeff. Lifting her eyes to admire her husband's handsome profile, she murmured softly, "I lost both my parents within the past seven months, Jeffrey, and not too many weeks ago, I thought I had lost you, too. I couldn't bear it if you were slain. I *beg* you, *please, please* spare me such anguish. Leave the arrest of Olney to your sheriff friend."

Relenting with a chuckle, Jeff brushed the back of his arm teasingly across her soft bosom before his hand left hers and clasped the side of her far thigh. "All right, madam, stop your fretting. I'll try to refrain from frightening you overmuch. From now on, I'll just have to ignore those two culprits while you're with me."

"And what will you do when I'm not?" Raelynn asked and then gently scoffed. "In the short time I've known you, Jeffrey Birmingham, I've come to the conclusion that you're a force to be reckoned with. I just can't believe you could blandly ignore the presence of those two men even when I'm with you. I sense that you can be quite tenacious when you get your dander up. Indeed, the Corsair pirates would be hard-pressed to deal with you should they ever capture one of your ships and ransom it for booty as they've recently been doing to other American ships. No doubt, you'd sail off to confront them with cannons blazing and cutlass at the ready in much the same fighting spirit as you exhibited during my rescue."

Jeff laughed in amusement at such a farfetched notion and shook his head. "That sounds like something my brother would do, my pet, not me."

"I perceive that you and Brandon are more alike than either of you realize, Jeffrey."

"How can you say that, madam?" her husband challenged, tossing a grin over his shoulder. "You've known us hardly more than a fortnight."

"Nevertheless, when Dr. Clarence drew me out of Gustav's warehouse that night and I realized what you were planning to do with the aid of Brandon and your friends, I came to the conclusion that you and your brother were much in accord. At the time, you both seemed eager to launch the attack against those river rats in spite of the odds against you and the others who were with you. Even considering all the men Gustav has in his employ and his well-stocked arsenal, he really didn't have a chance against the lot of you."

"Gustav deserved everything we managed to do to him, Raelynn," Jeff stated with conviction. "In my estimation it wasn't nearly enough."

"I agree, sir, but it's not very heartening for a wife to realize that her husband enjoys a battle as much as a well-versed cavalier."

Jeff's eyebrows flicked upward briefly as he offered a different opinion of himself. "I've always considered myself a rather peaceable sort."

When he turned his head to look at her, Raelynn had a chance to search his face and the sparkling green eyes. Lifting a hand, she lovingly stroked her fingers along his cheek, tracing one of the handsome grooves that always appeared whenever he smiled. "Aye, you truly seem to be that, Jeffrey Birmingham . . . at least until you're riled."

"I can't deny that I was enraged by your abduction, my sweet. It was my most earnest desire to negate the possibility of another such occurrence. You can hardly blame me for making an attempt."

"You mistake me, Jeffrey. I'm not reproaching you for leading an attack on Gustav's warehouse, only saying that it's a little frightening for a wife to discover that underneath her husband's debonair charm there beats a heart of a warrior."

Jeff was intrigued by the tempting softness of his wife's lips and lowered his head to hers, prompting Raelynn to clasp his arm tightly against her bosom. Completely engrossed in consuming the honeyed sweetness of her mouth, he probed its depths with the fiery brand of his tongue, at first gently and then with quickening fervor.

Raelynn all but groaned in disappointment as he drew away. "You shouldn't kiss me like that when there's no privacy to be had nor a bed conveniently near. You must be aware by now what your kisses do to me."

Jeff leered at her. "I know of a nice hostelry where we might linger for an hour or two."

"You're only teasing me," she fussed, dimpling prettily.

His broad shoulders lifted briefly. "Even if I were, the notion is tempting enough for us to consider. Don't you agree, madam?"

Raelynn rolled her eyes, thinking of the outlandish rumors they'd likely garner from such an interlude. "Just imagine the stares we'd receive if we checked out an hour or so after registering. The whole town would be abuzz."

"Aye, but think how well we'd enliven the gossips' rumors for a day or two, my sweet. They'd be ever so grateful."

"No doubt, but I prefer to be a bit more discreet."

Jeff heaved an exaggerated sigh of disappointment. "As you will, madam."

Raelynn perched her chin upon his shoulder, admiring his aristocratic profile. "Would you be at all averse if I were to touch you now?"

His brows gathered in bemusement as he scanned her fine visage. "In what manner?"

Her eyes dipped to his lap, marking the area she was most interested in exploring. "In a wifely manner, sir."

Jeff almost gasped at the sudden thrill her request elicited. After enduring a lengthy celibacy, he had begun to fear that his wife wasn't nearly as appreciative of the delights to be found in a marriage bed as he had first hoped. Since their morning activities, however, he had been greatly heartened. Her latest petition brightened his expectations even more. Sweeping off his top hat, he held it protectively over his lap as he captured her hand within his and molded it around the manly protrusion. "Does this attest to my eagerness, madam?"

Cooing softly in admiration, she inspected him through the closely fitting garment. "Your trousers leave much to the imagination."

Lifting his brow, he eyed her askance. "You can unfasten them as well as I, my pet. I give you leave to do so."

She peered up at him, but could read nothing in his handsome profile from the angle at which she sat and finally tilted her head inquisitively. "Would it unsettle you if I were to be so bold when the carriage is passing through the middle of town?"

"You'd disappoint me if you weren't."

Raelynn grinned like a child who had just been given a new toy. The fact that he welcomed her overtures assured her that she hadn't shattered any rigid marital standard. What they did between them was suitable as long as they were both in accord. "I'll see what I can do about working you free, sir." As she sought to pry the side placket open, she was led to tease, "You know, Jeffrey, you're not making this any easier."

Tilting the topper upward, Jeff considered the telltale

bulge beneath the costly trousers. "Such are the hazards of being a wife, my dear. You can hardly expect me to sit here unaffected when you're trying to get into my underwear. As you can see, I'm eagerly anticipating your attention."

She finally plucked free a packet, and soon her small hand was slipping inside to make her claim upon the warm flesh, snatching Jeff's breath inwardly for a blissful moment. During the ensuing inspection, he strove hard to remember to breathe.

It gave Raelynn a strange sense of wifely satisfaction to be able to elicit the molding of his male flesh. When she could affect a man of his maturity and experience in such a way, she didn't feel nearly so self-conscious about her naiveté or her youth. Indeed, she found it immensely pleasing to see just how completely absorbed her husband became while relishing her caresses, for he sat as one completely enthralled, basking in the titillation as if it had been years instead of hours since he had had the like. It came as something of a surprise, but she realized that she found it just as thrilling to please him as it was for her to be on the receiving end of his rousing stimulations. Having been keenly attentive to his instructions earlier that morning, she tested her newly learned knowledge with an enthusiasm that marked her own growing interest in their mutual familiarity.

Caught up in the sensual headiness of his wife's caresses, it was a long moment before it dawned on Jeff that they were approaching their destination. Clearing the thickness from his throat, he leaned forward and opened the tiny door behind the driver's seat.

"Thaddeus, forget about the couturier's shop for the moment. Take us on a short tour of the city instead. I'll tell you when we want to come back to Mr. Farrell's."

3

$\mathcal{A}$ half hour later, Jeff stepped down from the landau with all the smiling aplomb of a monk and faced his wife with glowing eyes as she moved near the door. They exchanged secret smiles as his fingers squeezed hers meaningfully. Handing her down, he drew her arm through his and escorted her into the three-storied building, which, he explained as they entered, his friend had purchased five years earlier.

According to him, Farrell Ives had reserved the upper two floors of the structure as his own private living quarters, leaving the ground level to be utilized solely for his *haute couture*. As Jeff further expounded, Farrell normally employed eight people, the most important being a young widow, Elizabeth Dalton, who was solely responsible for making the patterns for the new designs and supervising the seamstresses. She assisted her employer in managing the shop and had many other duties that verified her importance.

As a rule, *Ives's Couture* staffed six other seamstresses and a strapping youth who took care of the cleaning chores when he wasn't fetching and toting. In spite of the limited personnel, the shop supplied most of the *haut monde* and style-conscious ladies in the Charleston area with stunning wardrobes for the changing seasons as well as modish frocks and lavish gowns any time of the year. Dainty accouterments were also readily available on the premises and didn't need to be ordered unless a customer had something specific or extravagant in mind.

Jeff ushered Raelynn to a cozily furnished sitting area located near the entrance of a pair of spacious hallways. Long tables, laden with beautiful fabrics in different textures, colors, patterns, and weight, were angled against the walls of both. The smaller corridor provided offices near the front for the employer and his assistant. Behind these were cubicles for fittings. Private sewing rooms for the seamstresses divided the larger hall, at the end of which was a large window of small-paned glass that framed a carefully tended garden. A nearby passageway led to the back door and, off to the side, a stairway supplied access to the upper stories.

Through the doors of the nearest two seamstresses' rooms, Raelynn espied two dummy forms bedecked in fashionable gowns of breathtaking beauty, readily evidencing the talent of the couturier. At the entrance of the last cubicle, a tall, dark-haired woman, of about a score and five, stood talking with its occupant who remained hidden from view. Upon espying the new arrivals, the brunette quickly made her excuses and, with an ebullient smile, hastened forward to greet them.

"Mr. Birmingham, how good it is to see you again," she averred in mellifluous tones. Her dark eyes fairly glowed with a brilliance that matched her smile. But then, with an openly gracious manner and a beauty charmingly enhanced by a pale yellow empire gown, she truly seemed imbued with a radiance of her own.

"Elizabeth, you're looking as enchanting as always," Jeff declared, with debonair flair sweeping his hat before his chest and clicking his heels in a concise bow. His own broad grin evidenced his unquenchable pride as he slipped a hand behind his wife's back and made the introductions. "May I present my bride, Raelynn. My dear, this is Mrs. Elizabeth Dalton. She manages the shop for Farrell with the greatest of ease."

At such praise, Elizabeth softly hooted and banished his claims with a graceful wave of a slender hand before facing Raelynn. "I'm thrilled to finally meet you, Mrs. Birmingham. Mr. Ives has literally been singing your praises ever since the happening outside our shop."

Raelynn's pained smile evidenced her chagrin. "Oh, dear, I was in hopes that no one would remember that, but I suppose my expectations were a bit farfetched, considering the number of people who collected around us that day."

Elizabeth tossed her head in amusement and laughed. "When there's a member of the Birmingham clan involved, my dear, you can be fairly certain that he'll reap a goodly share of attention from Charlestonians. Still, when a lady has been bequeathed with your fine looks, Mrs. Birmingham, you needn't bear the name of a prominent family to gain everyone's notice. 'Twill surely be yours wherever you go."

"Thank you, Mrs. Dalton," Raelynn replied with a gracious smile. "You're very kind indeed. And may I say how pleased I am to finally be visiting Mr. Ives's shop." The blue-green eyes sparkled with enthusiasm as she admired the elegant interior and, with a womanly appreciation for beautiful things, the bolts of costly materials displayed on the nearby tables. "This definitely looks like a woman's paradise."

Warm laughter spilled melodiously from the dressmaker's lips. "Oh, it is, absolutely, but please, Mrs. Birmingham, do call me Elizabeth. I'd feel especially honored."

"The pleasure is mine, Elizabeth," Raelynn warbled. "And I'd be equally gratified if you'd favor me by addressing me by my given name."

Elizabeth grimaced ever so slightly. "You have a beautiful name, to be sure, but if you wouldn't mind, while we're here in the shop, I should use the more formal address for the sake of the other employees. Mr. Ives insists that his seamstresses show proper respect to his customers, and it makes it easier for them if I abide by that standard as well, at least while I'm here." She chuckled as she added, "He even has them calling me Mrs. Dalton, a formality he considers needful for maintaining discipline in the ranks. If I didn't know better, I'd be inclined to think he was once a seafaring captain. He certainly runs a tight ship here."

Jeff chortled at such a farfetched notion. "I'm afraid your employer would be hopelessly lost with a compass and a sextant, Elizabeth. He's too much of a landlubber."

The three joined in a moment of mirth before the older woman swept sparkling eyes down the length of Raelynn's gown. It had been among the prettiest day dresses that *Ives's Couture* had recently sold, and she was delighted to see it being worn by such a fetching lady. "Mr. Ives's business will surely reap a wealth of benefits once the city's populace catch a glimpse of you bedecked in his fashions, Mrs. Birmingham. In praising you, Mr. Ives went so far as to claim that you were just as beautiful as your sister-in-law. I was sure his assertions were exaggerated until today."

Raelynn's radiant cheeks evidenced her delight over the woman's compliment. "Heather is so gorgeous that I must accept it as a tremendous honor to be compared to her."

"As well you should, Mrs. Birmingham," Elizabeth

readily rejoined. "I can't imagine another lady in the area as attractive as the pair of you."

Raelynn tilted her head thoughtfully as she considered the brunette. Obviously the woman had reservations about her own beauty, but Raelynn was more than willing to enlighten her. "Have you taken a look at yourself in a mirror lately, Elizabeth?"

The other clasped a hand to her cheek in sudden dismay. "Oh, dear, do I have a smudge or something on my face?"

"No, of course not," Raelynn reassured her with brimming amusement, totally taken with the woman's lack of vanity. Elizabeth Dalton was a slender, dark-eyed beauty who could definitely hold her own in the realm of feminine pulchritude. "My question was meant merely as a tribute to your own exceptional comeliness, nothing more."

Realizing her blunder, Elizabeth flushed a deep shade of crimson, but promptly shook her head, denying the possibility that she could compare with such a winsome pair as the Birmingham women. "Thank you for your kindness, Mrs. Birmingham, but you just don't know how beautiful you are. I could never hold a candle to either you or your sister-in-law."

Raelynn reached out and gently laid a hand upon the other woman's arm. "If I were you, Elizabeth, I wouldn't place any valuable tokens wagering on that assumption. There's no question you'd lose."

Jeff offered his wife support in that premise. "Raelynn isn't just being kind, Elizabeth," he assured the woman. "She's being truthful. In fact, my advice to you would be to place your bets on the opposite end of that spectrum if it comes down to such a wager. You'd clearly come out a winner."

Elizabeth waved a slender hand before her face, making much of her attempt to cool her burning cheeks.

"Take pity on me, both of you," she pleaded with an effervescent laugh. "You're making me blush."

Raelynn came readily to the woman's defense by turning the subject elsewhere. "Since being bestowed a fair sampling of what your seamstresses make here in the shop, I haven't ceased to admire what was purchased for me. As recently as a year ago, I enjoyed designing many of my own clothes. Of course, that was while my father was still alive and we were able to afford far better clothes than the gown I was wearing the day Jeff rescued me from my uncle. My couturier in London was gracious enough to translate my sketches into very fine examples of what I had created. When my family fell on hard times, he paid me for my designs and boldly claimed them as his own to his customers. I really didn't mind since he kept raising my fee to keep me placated, but I'm afraid I'd be hard-pressed to fashion clothes as sumptuous as the ones I've recently been wearing. I understand that Mr. Ives actually made the selections when Jeffrey sent Mrs. Brewster over here to buy me clothes. The milliner was simply gushing over Mr. Ives's talents when she came back to her shop. She said she had never realized before that day that such a talented entrepreneur was residing right across the street from her."

Amusement tugged at the corners of Elizabeth's lips. "Yes, Mrs. Brewster did seem in a rare dither here that day. I don't think she had ever actually taken a close look at Mr. Ives before she came. He definitely has a way of awing some women when they see him face to face. But in regards to your clothing, Mrs. Birmingham, Mr. Ives would never have left another to choose your gowns and other accouterments considering that your husband and he are such close friends. Yet I must be honest. There weren't that many garments on hand at the time, so it was a fairly simple task to make the selections."

The woman continued with a casual shrug. "Usually we make only what our customers order, but an unusual

situation developed after the garments were finished. I
shan't mention any names lest I embarrass the fine people involved, but the young lady for whom the gowns
were originally made was left bereft of the funds to pay
for them by an unfortunate incident. It seems that her
brother had laid out the total sum of their recent inheritance on a race in which a stallion he had raised from a
colt would run against one other horse. The stallion was
indeed very fast. I saw the black race once myself. The
brother had high hopes of doubling their combined fortune when he was lured on by the challenges of another
who seemed a novice on the subject of fine steeds. Unfor-
tunately the brother's stallion was found dead in the stall
the morning of the race, allowing Mr. Fridrich, the owner
of the second horse, to win the purse without his entry
even running. Mr. Ives saw no need to burden the girl
any more than she was already over the loss of her
wealth by demanding payment. If there was a culprit in
this tale, then both Mr. Ives and I share the belief that
Mr. Fridrich's hired henchmen poisoned her brother's
horse. Frankly, I think the man should be horsewhipped
for what he did."

"I assume that's none other than *Gustav* Fridrich,"
Jeff queried. When he received an affirmative nod from
the woman, he voiced his opinion with acid distaste. "I
agree about the horsewhipping, Elizabeth, but then, I personally think the man should have been locked away as
soon as he stepped off the boat from Germany. Many
Charlestonians have suffered because of him, and I have
a feeling that many more will fall prey to his schemes."

"I understand from Mr. Ives that Mr. Fridrich was the
one responsible for kidnapping your wife," the brunette
replied. "After hearing such rumors about him, I've become convinced the man is no less than a scoundrel."

"A devious reprobate if ever I saw one," Raelynn
agreed and then heaved a sigh, feeling immensely sorry
for the pair who had lost their livelihood. "I sympathize

with the young lady and feel a measure of remorse for having benefited from her ill fortune, but I've been enjoying the clothes so much, Elizabeth, that it's hard for me to feel too regretful. Not only are the garments beautiful beyond description, but I was greatly impressed by the great care and attention that went into making them. I've never seen finer needlework anywhere, even in England."

Jeff laid an arm about his wife's shoulders and grinned down at her. "Farrell's talent for designing ladies' finery cannot be denied, my dear, but Elizabeth is primarily the one responsible for the care that goes into every stitch. She was once a respected seamstress in her own right before she lost her husband. Now she imparts much of her talent and expertise to the other women who work here."

Laughter spilled from Elizabeth's soft, pink lips. "Oh, dear, I'm afraid all this flattery is going to go to my head, and Mr. Ives won't like that at all. I'd better go upstairs and inform him that you're here." She swept a hand to indicate the chairs and settee that provided a cozy sitting area in the hall. "Please, make yourselves comfortable while I'm gone. I'll be back shortly."

Raelynn hastened to plead, "If you wouldn't mind, Elizabeth, I'd really enjoy taking a closer look at all the lovely fabrics I've been eyeing since I came in. Is it permissible?"

"Oh, absolutely, Mrs. Birmingham," the woman eagerly encouraged. "You may find something you can't do without." She cast a mischievous glance toward Jeff before advising his wife, "Keep in mind that it's an appropriate time for ladies to plan their wardrobes for the fall season. We have some wonderful velvets in deep, rich hues that would be positively stunning with your auburn hair. We also have a dark turquoise that would be especially gorgeous on you, and though most women shun black until they become widows, with your fair skin and hair, it would be divine."

Jeff rolled his eyes heavenward and moaned in feigned distress. "I can see it now, stricken by poverty in the prime of my life."

Elizabeth's eyes danced impishly. "Oh, but, Mr. Birmingham, just think how grateful Mr. Ives would be if you made him a wealthy man."

Jeff scoffed lightheartedly. "As if he weren't already."

In the woman's absence, Raelynn strolled to the far side of the hall to examine several silk brocades that had drawn her attention. Everywhere she looked, she found herself in awe of the materials on hand. There were fabrics of such exquisite texture, beauty and quality that she could only imagine the cost of having just one gown made from any of the bolts of cloth.

Displayed on top of an ornate bookcase was a collection of small mannequin dolls garbed in miniature versions of fashionable costumes that could be ordered. Residing behind the lead-partitioned glass doors of the cabinet were countless leather-bound volumes of fashion plates, drawings and detailed sketches of patterns. If a patron couldn't find anything pleasing in these books, as outlandish as the notion seemed to her, Raelynn had no doubt that the gifted couturier would prove amenable to designing something especially elegant, no doubt at a more extravagant cost.

Smiling up at her husband as he drew near, Raelynn swept a hand about to indicate the many tables laden with velvets, silks, woolens and heavy satins. "I must say, Jeffrey, I never expected such an abundance of imported fabrics here in Charleston. Your friend must have invested a fortune in the materials he has available here."

"Farrell prides himself in offering his clientele not only the latest fashion but the finest cloth from which to make them. He's quite a dapper fellow himself."

Raelynn remembered Farrell Ives as the man who

had magnanimously supplied her husband with the coins to buy her from her uncle after the latter had tried to sell her to Gustav Fridrich. Jeffrey had offered an exorbitant sum for her, one which Cooper Frye had found too tempting to refuse. By extending a temporary loan to Jeffrey, Farrell had saved his friend the trouble of fetching the money from his shipping company several blocks away. His help had speedily concluded the matter.

Raelynn could recall very little detail about the people who had formed an ever widening circle around them that day, but she had no difficulty conjuring a mental image of the couturier. He had literally stood head and shoulders above most of the onlookers, equally matching the height of the Birmingham men. A flawlessly trimmed Vandyke beard had accentuated his handsomely chiseled features, and she was of a mind to think that with his closely cropped, sun-streaked brown hair and vivid blue eyes, he was every bit as admirable looking as her husband or his brother, Brandon. Only Jeff could tell her more about the clothier.

"You said that you and Mr. Ives are very close friends, did you not?"

"Aye, love. I've known him since our youth. His talent for designing clothes and choosing the right fabric to complement them came mainly from his own desire to dress well. His parents were much poorer than those of his rich, snobbish cousins, and he was often made the laughingstock of his kin because he had to wear their hand-me-downs. He repaid them by learning to use his fists and gained a reputation as a fighter ere he reached a full score of years. He proved successful in that sport and, after a few years, saved enough from his boxing matches to hire a seamstress to make his designs. That was perhaps seven or more years ago. Even from the beginning, it was evident Farrell was no simple clothier. He was too talented to settle for ordinary fashions. Eventually he became known as *Mr.* Farrell Ives by those who had once laughed at him. He was certainly a good man to have on our side when we stormed Gustav's warehouse. He helped us win the fray."

"What lies are you telling your pretty wife now, Jeffrey me dearie?" a deep male voice queried in laughing amusement, momentarily startling Raelynn. She turned just as Farrell Ives ducked his head beneath the low lintel of the doorway leading from the narrow passageway into which Elizabeth Dalton had disappeared moments earlier.

"That you're proficient with your fists and a pair of pistols," Jeff replied with a chortle as he strode forward with a hand outstretched in friendship. "Haven't you learned by now, Fancy Man, that you can't hide out from all these women you've hired? They're bound to find you sooner or later."

The two men clasped hands in a hearty handshake before Farrell grinned. "It's not the seamstresses that worry me, Jeffrey dearie," he murmured, "but a widow who has obviously set her heart on finding herself another husband."

Had they been alone, Jeff might have probed for an explanation, but he was anxious to make the introductions. "My dear," he said, drawing his wife forward with a welcoming arm outstretched, "it's time you formally made the acquaintance of a very good friend of mine, Mr. Farrell Ives. Farrell, this is my wife, Raelynn."

"Enchanted, Mrs. Birmingham," Farrell murmured, his lips widening into a white-toothed grin. His neatly clipped mustache turned up subtly at the ends, accentuating the thin lines of whiskers that trailed downward into his pointed beard. Sweeping into a lissome bow, he bestowed a light kiss upon her fingertips. "Rarely do I have the pleasure of seeing my designs worn by one so fair."

"I'm honored to meet you at last, Mr. Ives. . . ." Raelynn assured him, bestowing a charming smile upon him.

The couturier silenced her with an uplifted hand. "Farrell, please. None of that formality stuff."

"Farrell," she conceded with a soft laugh, "but only if you'll consent to call me Raelynn."

"Raelynn it is, then, and may I say that your husband and I made an exceptional purchase when we bought you from your uncle."

She dipped her head pertly in acknowledgment of his praise. "I must thank you for your timely assistance, Farrell, but if you wouldn't think me uncouth, I'd rather not claim Cooper Frye as my uncle. Whether he is or not has yet to be proven in my mind. In short, I hope I come from better stock."

The clothier's smile broadened. "I had trouble envisioning the oaf being close kin to an angel. I'm relieved to know there's a possibility that he isn't."

"If you can stop drooling over my wife long enough to lend me your attention, *Mr.* Ives," Jeff prodded good-naturedly, "we'd like to enlist your services in designing a gown for Raelynn to wear at a ball that I'm giving to celebrate our nuptials the middle of October."

"I'll lend whatever talents I have to the matter, my friend, but only if I'm invited."

Jeff heaved an exaggerated sigh as he slid a fleeting glance upward. "What I must go through to get this fellow to conform to my wishes."

Farrell winked askance at Raelynn. "For your wife, I'd do it for nothing, but since you've been so filthy rich all your life, Jeffrey, you need someone to remind you that your every wish isn't going to be granted with a snap of your well-manicured fingers. You'll have to pay through the teeth in this instance."

A gentle clatter of dishes brought the couturier's attention promptly around to bear upon one emerging with a tray heavily laden with cups, saucers and a silver coffee and tea service from the passageway. His employee's look of consternation warned Farrell that his assistance was required posthaste.

"Good heavens, Elizabeth, let me take that before you

drop it," he urged, with long strides rapidly crossing the room. "It looks too heavy for you to even consider carrying all that distance."

The woman sighed in relief as she gave the service over into his capable hands. "I'm sorry, Mr. Ives. I didn't realize it was so cumbersome until I was halfway here, and then there was no place to set it down. I thought Mrs. Birmingham would prefer tea, and I know how you men enjoy your coffee, so I brought both."

"You're as thoughtful as always, Elizabeth." Her employer flashed her a smile, brightening the rosy hue of her cheeks before he faced his guests. After deftly whisking the tray to a table residing in the midst of the settee and chairs, he straightened and rubbed his hands together in anticipation. "I could stand some coffee. What about you, Jeffrey? Raelynn and Elizabeth, will you both be having tea?"

"I should finish instructing the new girl if you have no further need of me, Mr. Ives," Elizabeth said, retreating several steps.

"Nonsense, Elizabeth. Have someone else explain to her what she'll be required to do here. I'd like for you to stay and share in the refreshments while we discuss some ideas for a new ball gown that we'll be making for Mrs. Birmingham."

"Yes, of course, Mr. Ives. If that is your wish."

"It is, most assuredly."

She seemed a bit flustered beneath the grin he swept toward her. "Then let me go ask Mrs. Murphy to take over for me. I'll need to fetch another cup anyway."

"Don't be long."

"Only a moment, sir."

As she hurried from the parlor, Jeff swept a glance around in time to catch his friend casually observing the subtle sway of his employee's hips. The stylishly narrow skirt of the Empire gown was most obliging to inspection, for it not only evidenced the graceful slenderness of the woman who wore it, but it also defined her nicely turned backside. At the moment the couturier seemed especially appreciative of the view. Whether he realized it or not, his close scrutiny was typical of perusals common among bachelors seriously on the prowl for a mate, if not one long-termed, then surely for the night, but as far as Jeff knew, there had never been anything either now or in the past between Farrell and the women he employed. Throughout his years as a clothier, he had always drawn a line between his business affairs and his personal life. Over time he had courted nearly every young, winsome maiden in the area, much as Jeff had done, without making any lasting commitments.

Elizabeth Dalton was from the business side of his life and undoubtedly, for that reason, hadn't fallen into the same category as his light o' loves. It certainly wasn't because men found her unappealing. On the contrary, since the death of her husband, Emory Dalton, she had purportedly turned down as many marriage proposals as Farrell had employees, but then, such rumors could not be confirmed since Elizabeth was as mum about herself as she had been about her late spouse.

In the very early stages of Elizabeth's marriage, Emory Dalton had taken to gambling and, by the time their second anniversary rolled around, had managed to lose what little he had earned farming and breeding horses as well as everything that his wife had made sewing and had later received from the sizable inheritance her parents had left her upon their death. Emory started drinking along about the time he realized he was squandering their possessions. The more he indulged in strong drink, the meaner he became, eventually working into a habit of slapping his wife around when he became vexed with her or at his ill-fortune at cards.

On several occasions during this period Jeff had shared a brandy or two with his clothier friend and had lent a sympathetic ear when Farrell had voiced his suspi-

cions about Emory's treatment of his wife. It was only
after actually witnessing such an occurrence that Farrell
had severed his friendship with the gambler, which had
begun during his early boxing days. That division had
come about shortly after the couturier had been summoned to a local tavern where Emory had been creating
havoc. The gambler had lost heavily at cards and been
so enraged by his circumstances that nothing had been
safe within his reach. The barkeep had begged Farrell to
take his friend home, and upon their arrival Emory had
given the very pregnant Elizabeth the back of his hand
with enough force to send her reeling halfway across the
room. Enraged by the man's brutality, Farrell had
slammed a fist into Emory's jaw, all but breaking it and,
in the process, rendering him unconscious. The couturier
had then carried Elizabeth upstairs to the bedroom she
had shared with her husband. He had gently soothed her
weeping and nursed her bruised jaw until she finally
quieted beneath his tender care. Upon returning to the
couple's parlor, he had found Emory trying to shake off
the fog in his head, but the man had become vulgar,
accusing Farrell of coveting his wife. A whole string of
slurs had followed until Farrell, highly incensed by the
man's insults, had warned his glowering friend that if he
ever laid a hand to Elizabeth again in violence, it would
be his last day on earth. Hardly a week later, a keen-
eyed gambler accused Emory of cheating at cards and
when Emory drew a small pistol from his coat, the man
shot him through the head, killing him instantly.

Jeff's own gaze followed Raelynn as she wandered
off to search the other tables for noteworthy fabrics, and
he wondered if his own expression revealed the pleasure
he derived from watching her. Lest he be caught ogling
his own wife, he reminded the clothier, "You said it's not
your seamstresses who worry you, but a widow out to
find herself a husband. Is it Elizabeth who vexes you?"

"Good heavens no, man!" Farrell laughed at such an

absurd notion. "She provides the only sanity in my life. I was speaking of a certain widowed milliner whose shop is right across the street. Ever since you sent her over here to buy clothes for Raelynn, she has taken to popping into my shop with special little desserts or dishes she has cooked for me, but then, she's just as likely to come when she isn't bearing any offering. I tell you, Jeffrey, that woman has driven me to seek refuge in my apartment more times in the last two weeks than I ever did before in a three-month period."

Jeff hooted in glee. "Blow me away if Thelma Brewster hasn't taken a shine to you, Fancy Man."

Farrell's brows shrugged upward briefly. "Never mind that she's more than twenty years my senior and as fluttery as a silly virgin on a carriage ride with a horny roué. The way she has been acting, a body would think I've been trying to get underneath her petticoats." He snorted. "As if I'd even care to."

"I take it that she goads you a mite."

"More'n a mite, Jeffrey. She has the strangest way of bustling into my shop soon after some sweet young thing comes sashaying in to order a new gown. I've enlisted Elizabeth's aid in warning me of Mrs. Brewster's approach, but the seamstresses usually keep her so busy that she can't always keep watch. And I don't trust another to be as discreet. Mrs. Brewster was here not even an hour ago with these little pastries she baked for me." Casually he indicated a plate of flaky breads that resided on the silver tray beside the coffee service. "I saw her coming and took refuge upstairs. I tell you, Jeffrey me dearie, if I ate everything that woman has brought over here since she started visiting, I'd be rolling through these halls."

Jeff made an earnest attempt to bridle his amusement, but it invaded his tone nevertheless. "I'd offer my services, Fancy Man, but I have no idea how I can help.

I certainly don't want to invite that sort of attention upon myself."

"Since you're now a married man, I would assume Mrs. Brewster considers you well beyond her reach. The way she chases after me, though, I've become leery of even leaving my shop by way of the front door. You know I've never given too much consideration to the idea of taking myself a wife, but lately, I've found myself pondering the notion more and more, just to keep that milliner out of my hair, which is a damned poor reason for a bachelor to resign himself to marriage. It goes to show how desperate I'm beginning to feel, but I'll try not to jump out of the frying pan into the fire just yet. As many women as I've courted, I've yet to find a sweet little miss who doesn't bore me to tears."

"Does Elizabeth bore you to tears?"

Farrell rolled his wide shoulders uneasily. "No, of course not, but she works for me."

"Oh, yes, that makes a difference," Jeff gently needled.

Farrell settled a suspicious squint upon his friend. "Precisely what do you mean by that remark, Jeffrey me dearie?"

"Only that you've apparently turned a blind eye to Elizabeth. Haven't you ever noticed how beautiful she is?"

"Oh, I've noticed all right, but I haven't let it go beyond that point. She overheard me threaten Emory the night I laid him out flat. When I brought his body home several nights later, Elizabeth stared at me as if I had suddenly become a two-headed monster. I think for a few moments there she actually believed I had killed him. While I was digging his grave, she sat in a chair on the front porch just watching me. She was very solemn, very distant. She never cried or carried on. Then, after a time, she went into the house, and when I followed a short time later, I found her down on her knees, mopping up the floor. It took me a few moments before I realized that her water had broken and that she had gone into labor. She refused to let me carry her upstairs or, for that matter, to even come near her. I rode back into town to fetch a midwife and paced Elizabeth's front porch like any expectant father until Jake was born. The midwife even brought the boy out for me to see, as if she had some wild idea that I was the father. I knew damn well she was acquainted with the family and must have known that Emory was the sire, unless of course he had gotten into one of his ranting moods and shot off his mouth about my coveting his wife. Anyway, after paying the midwife to stay the night with Elizabeth, I returned home.

"Elizabeth's circumstances became desperate after word got out that Emory was dead. People began hounding her to pay his debts, threatening to take what they could find at the farm as trade when she didn't even have enough money to provide a decent meal for herself. I offered her a job here, but she said that people would talk about us more than they were. After refusing to become my assistant, she learned what she'd be making cooking and scrubbing floors for Charlie at the inn. A pittance, at best. That's when she decided she couldn't raise Jake on what she'd be getting there. Once she accepted my offer, I paid a nursemaid to care for her son here at the shop while Elizabeth made up my designs. After she sold the farm, she moved within walking distance of the shop. I tell you, Jeffrey, until she began sewing for me, my designs never looked so marvelous. Since then, it has been strictly business. She now supervises the other seamstresses and makes the patterns for my designs. Why, just the other day she hired a young, unmarried chit of a girl in a motherly way who, Elizabeth tells me, is extremely talented with a needle. . . ."

Jeff stiffened apprehensively. "Would that chit's name be Nell?"

"Why, yes, I believe it is. Are you acquainted with her?"

"Well enough to know that she shouldn't work on my wife's gown."

Farrell's lips twitched behind his Vandyke. "Caught on you, is she?"

"You don't know the half of it. She accused me of being the father of her babe while Raelynn was there to witness our argument."

Farrell swept his friend with a lengthy perusal before lifting a skeptical brow. "To tell you the truth, Jeffrey, I thought your tastes were more refined than Nell. She doesn't appear to be your type at all."

"She isn't."

"So what would you like me to do about her?"

"Nothing more than what you've already done. I refused to be blackmailed into giving her any money, but Nell will need whatever she earns here to provide for her baby and herself. I can't imagine that she's that far away from giving birth. You're her best hope for getting the kind of money she'll be needing."

Farrell straightened uneasily as he noticed Raelynn approaching a cloth-laden table near the room in which Elizabeth had ensconced Nell. He exchanged a worried glance with his friend, who rose to his feet in a sudden quandary, but it was obvious that if Jeff bade Raelynn to return, Nell would likely recognize his voice and make an appearance.

"Elizabeth," Farrell called, settling Jeff back into his chair with a patting motion of his hand, "bring our lovely guest back with you so we can have our refreshments. I'd like my coffee now."

Elizabeth reappeared and, with a smile, escorted Raelynn to her anxious husband. The dark-haired woman graciously served as hostess and poured their separate brews before settling back in a chair with a cup of tea for herself. The plate of pastries was passed around, and while they were being relished, Elizabeth offered suggestions as to the type of gown she thought should be made for Raelynn.

"Mrs. Birmingham's skin is so fair, the cloth must be of a soft, pale hue to do credit to her flawless complexion."

Farrell nodded thoughtfully as he studied Raelynn over his own cup of coffee. "Aye, a pink as dainty as the blush on her cheeks."

"Soft layers of silk, the top one bejeweled with tiny, lustrous beads," Elizabeth murmured, gazing at their subject.

Once again the couturier inclined his head in agreement. "I can see it now, Elizabeth . . . a gown as slender as the lady herself, with small capped sleeves and a short, beaded train. Satin slippers should be made for her, and of course, she'll be needing a lace fan sewn with shimmering beads. She should be no less than dazzling."

Much in awe of the imagination of the couturier and his assistant, Raelynn glanced from one to the other in amazement. Finally, with a smile, she turned to her grinning husband. "I've never known a ball gown to be conjured from one's imagination with such ease and compatibility. I used to spend hours and hours sketching clothes, but I usually tossed aside far more than I thought worth keeping."

"You used to design clothes?" Farrell queried, his interest growing by swift degrees.

Raelynn inclined her head in a slow nod, not wishing to give the impression that she was well versed in the field. "For a brief time, once merely for the pleasure of it and then, later, to put food on our table while my mother and I were still residing in England. Before that, when we could afford better clothes, it was entirely done for my mother and myself."

Winking at her, Farrell gave her a grin before slanting

a puckish glance toward Jeffrey. "Is it too late to steal you away from your husband?"

Realizing that his bantering was mainly aimed at his friend, Raelynn curbed any evidence of her threatening amusement and lifted slender shoulders in a casual shrug, feigning disinterest. "I fear so. You see, I've become quite attached to Oakley and would be loathed to leave it. . . ."

"Oakley? Oakley?" Jeff repeated as if sorely chafed by his wife's expressed preference.

Raelynn dimpled prettily as she settled gleaming eyes upon him. "Well, of course, I'd miss you, too, Jeffrey."

"Humph!" Her husband folded his arms across his chest, giving every indication that he had been insulted, but at the hilarity of the three, he relented enough to grin. "I suppose I shall have to make a more lasting impression on my bride ere she finds a plantation more grand than mine."

Raelynn reached across and consolingly stroked her husband's hand. "I don't think that will happen, dearest. Oakley is quite beyond any lady's expectations."

"Thank heavens for small favors," Jeff grumbled, evoking their laughter.

Sitting back in her chair, Raelynn raised her cup to take a sip of tea as her eyes swept casually down the hall. When a young, pregnant woman of no more than ten and six stepped into the corridor, it was enough to start her hands to shaking. The girl was petite and very pretty with bright golden hair, but her pale blue eyes narrowed menacingly as they ranged over Raelynn, who managed with some dignity to return her cup to her saucer without spilling the contents over herself. The girl's gaze moved on and grew noticeably softer when they came to rest upon Jeff.

"Nell," he greeted stoically, giving her a brief nod of recognition.

She lifted a quivering chin as if wounded to the quick

by his distant tone, and for a lengthy moment, she seemed to struggle with some inner turmoil as her blue eyes brimmed with tears. Through the gathering moisture, she turned to glower at Raelynn who sat frozen in her chair. The girl caressed her own distended belly, deliberately reminding the other woman of her condition, and managed a smug smile, which at best was badly contrived.

Following Raelynn's stare, Elizabeth turned in growing curiosity. "Is anything wrong, Nell?"

The girl looked at the woman as if awakening from a dream. "No, Mrs. Dalton," she croaked in a voice choked with emotion. "I just thought I heard familiar voices, but I guess I was mistaken."

Bestowing a last glare upon Raelynn, Nell returned to her cubicle and gently closed the door behind her.

Jeff realized that he had been holding his breath ever since Nell had come out of her room. Gradually he released it, thankful there hadn't been another argument or angry confrontation with which he'd have been forced to contend. But then, he wasn't at all certain that this would be the end of it. Nell was definitely *not* the predictable sort; he had learned that the night she had crawled into his bed.

"I hate to rush off and leave such worthy company, Farrell, but my wife and I have other shopping to do," he announced, setting aside his coffee cup and squeezing Raelynn's hand. She sat as if stunned, her cheeks unusually pale. It was not hard to imagine what anguish she was now feeling, wondering if he had sired Nell's child. After what they had experienced together that morning, the sight of the girl had no doubt brought the brumes of gloom back upon her. "Perhaps we should get about it."

"If you wouldn't mind sparing a moment more of your time, Mr. Birmingham," Elizabeth begged as she returned her own cup and saucer to the silver tray, "I'd really like to take your wife's measurements before you leave."

In view of the necessity of her request, Jeff graciously yielded her the time. "Of course, Elizabeth. Raelynn's ball gown takes precedence over everything else. Nothing we'll be doing today will be of greater importance. I just thought my wife would enjoy venturing into some of the nicer shops in Charleston."

Farrell grinned behind his neatly clipped whiskers. "Should I consider it a compliment that you came here to mine first? Or do you love me so much, Jeffrey me dearie, that you can't stay away?"

Jeff made a great show of being unduly shocked. "What? Love a conceited, dandified *nouveau riche*? Are your wits addled, man?"

Raelynn's smile indicated an easing of her anxiety as she glanced between the two men. Elizabeth pressed slender fingers to her own mouth to squelch the mirth that bubbled up within her as she looked at Farrell, who, with an expression of exaggerated distress, had fallen back into his chair, but the man proved himself just as adept at a rejoinder as his friend.

"Egads, Jeffrey, are you so jealous of my good looks and manly physique that you must voice your callous affront within your gentle wife's hearing? What must she think of you? A cad, no less!" Rising with overstated grace, he faced Raelynn and executed a flamboyant bow. "Madam, if you're ready to cast this oafish knave aside, I'd be honored to give him twice the sum he gave your uncle just for a sweet smile from your lips."

"You already have the best I can offer, sir," she warbled, her heart dragging free of that dark morass of uncertainty as she yielded to the clothier's humor. "Even if my life were threatened this very moment, I don't think I could make a better attempt or smile any broader."

In a calmer moment the two women rose to leave the room, but Farrell begged momentary leave of the Birminghams before drawing Elizabeth aside. He spoke to her in a hushed tone before she nodded and murmured a response. Then, upon facing Raelynn with a smile, Elizabeth escorted her to a private fitting room in the adjoining hallway.

Farrell returned to Jeff who had been indulging himself in a husbandly propensity by admiring his bride. When the door closed behind her, the couturier gained his full attention. "You needn't worry that Nell will damage Raelynn's gown while it's here in the shop. Elizabeth will talk to her. She has a great empathy for the younger women who work here and goes out of her way to reason with them when they're in the wrong. Usually they come around to a more sensible way of thinking and eventually can see where they may be at fault. I've asked Elizabeth to counsel Nell and help her come to terms with the fact that you're married now. Personally, I believe the girl is fortunate to be working under Elizabeth. Yet, for all of my assistant's concern for them, she expects them to conform to the rules we've established here. Don't annoy the customer is the first principle to which they must adhere. They all know that if they overstep the boundaries we've established here, it will likely mean losing a position that pays them good wages. That threat serves to quell their animosities to a goodly extent. Nell will surely take that into consideration once the rules are explained to her and, at least while you're here in the shop, will avoid you and Raelynn. Beyond this place, I can make no guarantees."

"You're fortunate, my friend, to have Elizabeth working for *you*," Jeff assured the man, a slow grin making its way across his lips. "You ought to consider what disaster would befall you if Elizabeth ever decided to accept some gentleman's proposal of marriage."

Farrell looked aghast at such a notion. "Don't even mention such a thing, Jeffrey! I'd be ruined."

"Then I'd advise you to consider what you'd be willing to do to keep your talented assistant beneath your wing, my friend. Who knows when a handsome gallant might sweep her off her feet and steal her from you?"

Farrell's brow quirked above a menacing glare. "You need your mouth cauterized with lime, Jeffrey me dearie, and I'm just the one to do it."

Tossing back his head, Jeff laughed in hearty amusement. It seemed that he had gotten his point across very effectively.

$\mathscr{4}$

$\mathscr{J}$eff was a generous man by nature and even more inclined to indulge his young bride. In an earnest endeavor to mark with something especially stunning the occasion of the actual consummation of their marital union, he drew Raelynn to a small shop specializing in fine jewelry, but upon reaching its entrance, she laughingly demurred and tugged at his arm.

"Oh, please, Jeffrey. You've given me so much as it is. I don't need costly gems when I have you for a husband. Let's just walk for a while and look into the shop windows. I haven't done that since well before my father was arrested."

Gallantly Jeff swept a hand toward the boardwalk stretching out ahead of them. "Your wish is my command, my lady."

They strolled along the street, pausing often to accept greetings and good wishes from neighbors and friends who had been acquainted with Jeff for a considerable length of time. In the midst of these strangers, Raelynn was relieved to find at least one familiar face. Upon espying them, Thelma Brewster had hurried out of her millinery shop with a vivacious smile.

"Oh, don't you two look as delicious as icing on a cake," the woman trilled. "I haven't seen hide nor hair of either of you for nigh these two weeks past. Indeed, when I saw you going into Mr. Ives's shop, I almost marched myself over there to visit with you, just to find out what has happened since we last parted, but alas, I had customers at the time. Through the grapevine, I heard that you had gotten married. Nearly fainted away in shock, I did, but of course, it was the wisest thing to do, considering all the gossips in town, and the two of you being such a good-looking couple and all."

"In view of your prudent advice, Mrs. Brewster, I deemed it favorable to take Raelynn as my wife," Jeff informed her lightheartedly. "You were right, of course. Oakley has ceased to be the lonely place that it once was. I've never been happier."

Chortling, the woman clapped a hand to a plump cheek. "When I urged you to find a mistress for Oakley, Mr. Jeffrey, I never dreamt you'd do so that very selfsame day, but I was absolutely delighted when I heard the news."

"We're grateful that you saw fit to loan us the use of your private quarters after our confrontation with Cooper Frye," he replied. "You might be interested in knowing, Mrs. Brewster, that I proposed while drinking tea at your table."

"Oh, how romantic!" Thelma Brewster sighed dreamily. "And to think it happened in *my* kitchen."

Raelynn took hold of the older woman's fingers and pressed them with gentle warmth. "I'll never forget your kindness to me, Mrs. Brewster. Thank you for being so considerate."

"Oh, tish!" Blushing with pleasure, the milliner shook her head at the younger woman's attempts to thank her. "I did nothing more than offer you some tea and the use of my kitchen. Mr. Jeffrey did all the rest, first by saving you from being trodden underneath that passing coach and then, only moments later, from your uncle's mercenary schemes. I'm sure you know by now that here in Charleston our gentlemen are most gallant."

"Nevertheless, Mrs. Brewster, you offered your gracious hospitality when we most needed it," Raelynn assured her. "We shall always be indebted to you."

The milliner smiled, pleased by their show of gratitude. Jeff extended his appreciation a bit further by suggesting that his young wife had need of another bonnet or two to go with her new gowns. In this instance, Raelynn was willing to accept his largess, for in passing the millinery, she had seen several that were at the very least exceptional. She had little difficulty choosing a half dozen to try on and posed prettily in each for her husband. By the warming glow in his eyes, Raelynn was wont to think that he was enjoying his newly acquired status as husband. When she asked which of the hats he liked best, he showed no hesitancy in selecting the prettiest two of the lot, leaving her little else to do but smile and eagerly nod.

Upon leaving the milliner's shop, Jeff deposited their purchases in the carriage and then, with Raelynn on his arm, continued wending his way down the boardwalk. Thaddeus followed with the landau at a snail's pace, now and then pulling over to let other conveyances pass on the street. Even so, he was always near at hand just in case the couple wanted to ride or go to some other area of the city.

When Raelynn and Jeff paused at a quaint inn to share a light lunch, other couples crowded around their table to extend hearty congratulations and good wishes for what seemed a marvelous match. When the couple returned once more to the boardwalk, Thaddeus waved a chortling farewell to another driver and climbed to his seat on the landau. More introductions were made here and there along the way, making Raelynn's head spin with all the names and faces she'd later have to recall. As the afternoon progressed, she became increasingly cognizant of the fact that her husband knew a surprising number of people and had more friends than seemed possible for only one person.

Old women seemed to adore him, and with good cause, his young wife smilingly determined, for he was especially generous in lending his attention to them, as if they were the very joy of his life. He called them fondly by pet names and squeezed their fingers affectionately as he bestowed brief kisses on wrinkled cheeks or blue-veined hands, evoking giggles or secret smiles, at times all but hidden behind dignified miens.

The easy camaraderie Jeff readily exhibited with other men left her much in awe of the one she had married. Whether hunting companions, scholars, or associates in some business venture or another, these male acquaintances of his gave every indication that they thoroughly enjoyed her husband's ready wit and felt totally at ease to reciprocate with humorous quips or hearty banter.

Jeff conveyed an unmistakable respect for ancients, some of whom had tutored him. They had amusing stories to tell of the youth who had been ever wont to try and soothe the temper of his older brother whenever that one got into a fray or to stand valiantly beside him and fight until they were both nigh bloody when the opposition outnumbered them and demanded physical confrontation. When the younger men congratulated him upon his recent marriage, they did so with great gusto, clapping him heartily on the back and ragging him unmercifully about his haste to see the deed done, as if he had been afraid some other swain would snatch his winsome bride out of his grasp. Still, they seemed genuinely pleased to both see and converse with him.

Comely, well-bred young ladies displayed more reserve when greeting Jeff. Some eyed him surreptitiously with a measure of longing, while others, ignorant of his recent marriage, tossed fetching smiles his way and, with well practiced coyness, flicked long lashes as they peered at him askance. It seemed part of the rote of enlightenment that, after being so completely taken with the man's presence and engrossed in guilefully flirting with him, these maidens would then glance at Raelynn in curious wonder. After Jeff's introductions, some seemed genuinely astounded, a few even stricken by the news that he was now wed, affirming Raelynn's growing suspicion that Nell was but one of many comely young maidens who had held aspirations of first gaining Jeffrey's regard and then, some time later, of becoming his wife.

Jeffrey had no pressing engagements or any particular destination in mind and was simply content to enjoy the balmy day and the presence of his young wife. With Raelynn's arm tucked within his, he paused often to look at numerous displays in the shop windows they passed and to solicitously inquire if his bride was at all interested in taking a closer look at anything. At an import house, Raelynn momentarily scanned the bric-a-brac neatly exhibited behind the small, square panes of the window stretching across the front of the shop. Seeing nothing of real interest, she was about to turn aside when she caught sight of a brass-bound wooden coffer sitting atop a table inside the store. Unable to believe her possible good fortune, she leaned forward in rapt attention, oblivious to the fact that she pressed the brim of her flower and beribboned bonnet to the glass in her attempt to view the chest better. Similar pieces surrounded the piece, but the one upon which she had fixed her gaze was definitely the most notable of the lot. Even if she hadn't recognized it as the coffer in which her father had once hidden a small cache of gold coins, Raelynn would have desired it for herself.

"Do you see that box over there on the table, Jeffrey?" she asked, pointing toward the item.

He leaned near to peer through the glass. "Aye, love. A handsome piece, it is. Would you like to have it?"

"At one time, that coffer belonged to my father. Shortly before his arrest, he bade my mother to guard it carefully until he had need of its contents, but he died before any of the gold coins it contained could be of benefit to him. During the sea voyage, my mother began to fear that the box would be stolen by some of the other passengers and asked Cooper Frye to safeguard it for us. She assumed she could trust her brother, but sad to say, that was the last we saw of it. When my mother asked him to return the coffer, he gave the excuse that someone had stolen it. Even so, he continued to live like some high and mighty lordling aboard ship while we did without. We had hoped the coins would see us through our first year here, but they were obviously used by that greedy crook to fill his own belly and appease his thirst for strong drink. Seeing the box here in a shop so close to the waterfront causes me to renew my suspicions about Cooper Frye. I think he had it within his possession all the time and, as soon as he left the ship, sold it at the first shop he came to. If *he* didn't, then certainly someone else did."

"There's no reason why it can't be yours again, my sweet," Jeff assured her. "It may well be the only tangible memory you'll have left of your father."

She squeezed his arm affectionately. "I would be pleased to have it, Jeffrey, truly I would."

"Then it shall be yours, my love."

Barely had they stepped into the cool, pleasant interior than a portly gentleman with thick, silver hair hurried from the back. "A fair good morning to you both," he greeted with a pleasantly reserved smile. "Can I be of service? Or would you perhaps prefer to browse for a while?"

"Actually we're interested in that richly grained coffer you have on the table over there," Jeff answered, indicating the box.

"Lovely piece, isn't it? Not overly ornate as some tend to be. English, of course. Probably made in the last century, the sort a nobleman might keep on hand for important papers and the like."

"When you purchased it, was there anything inside the coffer?" Raelynn asked softly.

"Why, no, it was quite empty." He looked at her quizzically. "Are you perhaps familiar with this particular piece, madam?"

Slowly she reached out a hand and caressed the lid. "Very familiar. Once upon a time it belonged to my father."

"The coffer is so unique, I can't imagine there being a duplicate here in Charleston," Jeff offered in a museful tone.

Raelynn swallowed with some difficulty and indicated an indentation in the brass covering a corner. "You see this? I was just five years old when this particular dent occurred. My father was holding me on his lap when my mother called me. I started to get down, but I slipped and nearly cracked my head against the raised hearth. My father caught me in the nick of time, but in doing so, he accidentally knocked the chest from the table with his elbow. I was so proud that he had saved me from getting hurt that I boasted of his deed to my friends and showed them the ding that had resulted. They thought he might have gotten angry about it, but he overheard their comments and reassured them that what had really mattered most to him was the fact that his little darling hadn't gotten hurt." Hurriedly blinking against threatening tears, Raelynn sought to collect her poise, but her throat tightened to the degree that she was forced to fall silent.

The proprietor of the shop discreetly busied himself rearranging small china figurines on a sideboard as Jeff laid an arm about his wife's shoulders. She glanced up, her eyes shadowed by her painful loss, and found the emerald orbs tender with sympathy. She swallowed hard against the lump in her throat, accepted a clean handkerchief from him, and hurriedly dabbed at the moisture welling over her lashes. Regaining some measure of composure, she managed a faint smile.

"I'm all right," she reassured him softly. "Truly I am. Indeed, I have much to be thankful for." Smiling into his eyes, she left no doubt that as her husband, she had every hope that he would prove her greatest blessing.

Jeff lifted her hand to his lips and gently kissed her fingertips in silent tribute. Tucking her hand within his arm, he faced the shopkeeper, who, upon turning, offered a kindly smile to Raelynn before meeting her husband's gaze.

"Sir, I'd like to buy the coffer for my wife," Jeffrey announced, "but I'd also be interested in hearing how you came by it. Do you have any memory of the one who sold it to you?"

The man stroked a finger musefully across his chin as he tried to think back. "I believe that particular piece was brought in here by a man who had just arrived from England. He kept referring to himself as Ol' Coop. He said the coffer belonged to his sister before her death and that he needed as much as I could spare to care for his niece. Am I to assume, young lady, that you're his niece?"

Raelynn had no wish to claim kinship to a man who had allowed her mother to die while he had selfishly indulged his own propensities to drink and gamble. "He said he was my uncle, sir, but I have reservations about the truth of that possibility. If anything, he was a despicable swindler who preyed on us for profit."

"Had I any notion the box was not rightly his at the time, madam, I would never have purchased it. I don't normally barter with thieves, but when he said he had a niece to care for, I was in hopes he was a benevolent sort. Now I must believe that I was mistaken. I humbly beg your pardon."

"It has been my conviction, sir, that in his lifetime, Cooper Frye has managed to dupe a lot of people," Raelynn stated softly. "You weren't the first, nor do I think that you'll be the last. My own mother was taken in by his claims of kinship and died as a result."

"I'm terribly sorry," the proprietor murmured in solemn empathy.

"My sorrow is fading with each passing day, sir. The recovery of my father's coffer means a great deal to me. I'm thankful you bought it and that I saw it here in your shop. I'm even more grateful that my husband is willing to buy it for me. The box will become a treasured keepsake which we can hopefully hand down to our offspring in years to come. If you hadn't purchased it, I'd still be wondering what happened to it."

"You're as gracious as you are beautiful, madam," the shopkeeper averred with a kindly smile. "And it is my wish that in the months and years to come the coffer will become an even greater asset as you store away memories of your father."

കൈ"THEY'RE COMIN' OUT NOW," OLNEY HYDE announced, leaning near the window of the hired livery in which he was now safely ensconced. Chortling softly, he gestured toward the couple who were just emerging from the shop across the street. "Look at that! Mr. Birmin'am's done gone an' bought yer liedy somethin' else."

"*Dummkopf!* Get back before somevone sees yu!" Gustav Fridrich snapped irately. "Or haf yu forgotzen zo zoon zhat yu're still vanted by zhe sheriff?"

The curly headed blond grinned cockily as he consid-

ered the older man whose stocky frame dominated the
opposite seat of the well-worn carriage. The German was
nearing two score, stubborn to a fault, and lame now in
one arm, which seemed forever destined to be kept
bound up in a sling. He had thick, blunt features, a shining bald head, wiry brows, and pale-blue eyes, the coldness of which could almost freeze a man. At the moment,
they were hot, angry, and glaring a hole through his
younger companion.

Shrugging off the harsh reminder with a casual twitch
of his brawny shoulders, Olney relaxed back into his own
seat. "Ain't no use in frettin' yerself 'cause o' that lame-
witted sheriff, Mr. Fridrich. He ain't gonna find me. I
knows this here town an' all the areas 'round 'bout it like
I do the back o' me hand. I can come an' go just as
much as I please wit'out Sheriff Townsend bein' none
the wiser."

"It vill be zhe back of my hand zhat yu'll be getting
if yu cause me any more trouble," Gustav barked. "I
haven't forgotzen zhat it vas yu who shot Herr Birmingham and made his pistol go off and shatter *mien*
shoulder! Nor do I zhink zhe sheriff iz as stupid as yu
make him out to be. Yu, however, may be lacking vhat
he iz not. If not for zhat freight wagon and my timely
intervention earlier today, Herr Birmingham vould haf
caught yu and no doubt haf relished beating yu to a
bloody pulp before personally escorting yu to zhe sheriff's office."

Olney scoffed. "Maybe he would've, maybe not. Just
'cause Birmin'am's close ta a head taller'n me don't mean
he can best me. I'da've hit him in the gut afore he
could've even swung a punch. Anyways, I forgot ta tell
ye thanks for askin' the driver ta halt for me on the street
like ye did." Olney's shoulders shook as he recalled his
adversary's frantic search after the livery had passed.
"Yes, sir, we sure fooled that fancy man, we did, but ye
know, Mr. Fridrich, ye ought not ta get inta such a tem-

per o'er what's already been done. It ain't good for yer liver."

Yu imbecile! Vhat do yu know about livers?"

"Only what I've heard Doc Clarence tellin' ye, but enough ta figure out yers is a-gonna turn green wit' all that bile a-workin' in it."

"Yu prattle inanely about matters beyond yur ken," the German sneered, "and yu annoy me in zhe process."

"More'n Mr. Birmin'am?"

Gustav's lips curled in disdain as he swept his gaze out the window and fixed it glaringly upon the tall, well-garbed man presently strolling with his ravishingly beautiful bride on the boardwalk across the street. Noting the wooden box his handsome adversary was toting, Gustav grumbled ill-temperedly. "No telling vhat zhat fool has bought for his *frau* now. He's too stupid to realize zhat he vill only spoil zhe girl buying her everyzhing she asks for. Vhen she iz mine again, she vill learn better."

Olney canted his head curiously. "Just how ye plannin' on snatchin' Mrs. Birmin'am back now that Frye's plan ta sic Nell on Mr. Birmin'am ain't panned out? Mrs. Birmin'am was supposed ta hate her husband after Nell accused him o' bein' the cause o' her fat belly, 'ceptin' the redhead don't look like she's a-bearin' any hard grudge against him, not the way she's a-hangin' onta his arm an' a-smilin' up at the bloke. Looks ta me like they're gettin' on real fine."

"Yu find Cooper Frye for me and tell him zhat he vill haf to come up vith a much better plan if he expects to live past zhe summer," Gustav snarled. "Tell him zhat I vill even make it worth his vhile if zhis time he can actually be successful in making Frau Birmingham hate her husband."

Unable to comprehend the wisdom of such a plan, Olney waggled his head much like a child begrudging a parent's dictates. "Why do ye need Frye's help when ye've got me? I'm far better able ta do what that stinkin' sot can do. From what I hears lately, he gots his head too much in the puke-can ta be o' any use ta himself, much less ta ye. All that rot-gut whisky he guzzles sure ain't helpin' *his* liver none, that's for damned sure. He'll be dead afore the year is out the way he's been swillin' down that stuff lately."

"Livers again! As if yu knew anyzhing about zhem."

"I'm askin' ye, Mr. Fridrich, why do ye need that souse?" Olney insisted.

"I vould hear vhat new ideas zhe Englishman has to offer me. If he believes he vill die if he disappoints me, he vill prove very resourceful, I zhink."

"A sizable reward would be incentive for anybody." Olney met the pale blue eyes with a calculating glint in his own. "How much extra are ye willin' ta pay ta see the deed done, anyway?"

Gustav briefly pondered the younger man's question. "A zhousand Yankee dollars."

Olney arched a sun-bleached brow in rampant surprise. "Ye really want the li'l wench that much? Even after the way she jeered at ye when ye were in pain?" At the uncomplimentary reminder, his employer raised his chin in growing vexation, prompting Olney to shake his curly head in bemusement. "Ye sure gots a forgivin' heart, Mr. Fridrich, or ye're after somethin' more'n dumpin' that li'l redhair on her arse an' climbin' on top."

"I vill not let *anyvone* take vhat iz mine and zhen enjoy zhe rest of zhe year unscathed! If I let Herr Birmingham or even Cooper Frye continue to live after thwarting me, zhen others vill get zhe idea zhey can turn a deaf ear to Gustav. My business affairs vould be in shambles once vord of my clemency got around."

"Ye'd actually give Cooper Frye as much as that for carryin' out yer orders when he was the one what got ye in this mess in the first place? Did ye forget the man sold ye the girl after he'd already taken seven hundred fifty dollars from Birmin'am for her? Frye deliberately bilked ye. How can ye be so forgivin'?"

"If he brings me zhe girl, zhen it vill be vorth it to me." Gustav pursed his lips briefly in a facial shrug. "If he doesn't, zhen zhe fish vill be feedin' on his carcass ere the end of zhis year. Eventually I vill deal vith him over zhe matter of his cheating me, but it vill be in my own good time, vhen he ceases to be of any use to me . . . after I have zhe vench. If he kills Birmingham in his attempt to placate me . . . " Gustav lifted his thick shoulders in a gesture of casual indifference, "all zhe better. He vill hang for it; I vill not."

Olney was still a bit awed over the man's willingness to expend such a large sum for only one wench when the man wasn't normally satisfied unless he had a half dozen harlots catering to his prurient bent. "Yer pardon, Mr. Fridrich, but are ye sure ye wants ta deal wit' a man ye can't trust? Ol' Coop may rook ye again if'n ye give him any more slack."

"It vill be his last chance tu make everyzhing right, at least for a time. If he cannot do it, he vill die. If he can, I vill give him zhe zhousand minus vhat he stole from me." The German waved his good hand imperiously. "Summon Frye to mien quarters zhis afternoon. I vill discuss zhis matter vith him."

Olney touched his brow with two fingers and proceeded to bestow his own version of an old Arab salute upon his less than honorable benefactor. "Yer every wish is me command, O' great one."

THE BIRMINGHAMS' SHOPPING EXCURSION CAME TO an end later that afternoon when Jeff noticed his wife's fatigue. He hailed the landau and bade Thaddeus to take them on another tour of the city. This time the couple lent their complete attention to the areas through which they passed, Raelynn out of curiosity, Jeff by way of a qualified guide. Later he suggested dinner. "If you're not too tired, my pet, I think you'd enjoy dining at an inn of which I'm especially fond. It's just around the corner if you'd care to walk the rest of the way."

Raelynn felt greatly refreshed after a leisurely ride in the landau, and although she doubted that anything could surpass the fare normally served at Oakley, she was quite willing to go anywhere with her handsome husband. Being on his arm wasn't quite as delightful as being in his bed, but it was nevertheless enjoyable. Thus she had no objection to his suggestion.

"The evening is absolutely delightful, Jeffrey," she said, clasping his arm against her breast as they meandered toward the inn. "If not for the fact that I'm simply ravenous, I'd be content to just walk around again."

"What precisely are you hungry for, madam?" Jeff queried with a meaningful twinkle in his eyes, brushing the encompassed limb provocatively against the swelling ripeness.

Coyly Raelynn smiled up at him in the waning light and felt a tingling excitement sweep through her as his caress awakened her senses. "Everything!"

He groaned in mock frustration. "Now you've done it, madam. I'll now have my heart set on taking a private room here in the city and easing my hunger for you ere the hour is out."

Raelynn caressed his lapel with wifely familiarity. As the time approached for them to return home, she became increasingly mindful of the fact that for the first time since their wedding vows had been spoken, they would be sharing the same bed for the entire night. If the past morning could be counted as a fair indication of the ecstasy derived from the joining of two beings, she could believe they would be too busy playing together and making love to even think of sleeping. "Oh, but I'd rather go home and ensconce myself in yours. We could lock all the doors and stay in bed until we're ready to find other diversions." She glanced up coquettishly. "I have a nightgown you haven't seen yet. I was saving it for our first night together."

The green eyes glowed above her own. "You tempt me beyond my ability to resist, madam."

"Well now, wha' do we 'ave here?" a voice slurred from nearby. As the couple looked around in surprise, Cooper Frye grinned drunkenly and tottered forward. "If'n I can believe me poor ol' eyes, I'd be a-thinkin' it's me own bloomin' ken, the Birmin'ams."

"I see you're not above breaking your word, Frye," Jeff rejoined testily. "According to our agreement, you were supposed to leave us alone."

The bewhiskered, slovenly garbed man veered sideways in an attempt to approach his niece, but her husband promptly whisked her to the far side of him, safely out of reach of the man. Only then did Jeff meet the drunkard's dumbfounded stare. He did so with a noticeable lack of warmth.

Oblivious to the reeking stench of whiskey that clung to him, Cooper blinked blearily as he contemplated the switch. "Wha'sa matter? Ye thinks ye're too high an' lordly ta be associatin' wit' the likes o' me?"

"You're drunk, Frye," Jeff chided jeeringly. "Go find some pigsty and sleep it off."

Of their own volition the older man's eyes seemed to roll about in their sockets until he squeezed the lids tightly shut. Upon opening them again, he waggled his head sorrowfully and heaved a wavering sigh. "They'd only ferrets me out again an' makes me pays up what I owes 'em." Bowing his head, he mulled over his tragic situation in deep dejection. Then, upon issuing a loud belch, he rubbed his nose on a filthy sleeve and squinted up at Jeff. "Ye wouldn't be averse ta lendin' me a couple o' hundred o' yer Yankee coins, would ye, ol' nephew o' mine?"

"I'm not your nephew," Jeff corrected tersely. "And yes, I *would* be averse to lending you money. I've already given you more than you rightly deserved, but at the time, I could see no other way of getting Raelynn out of your clutches. In your eagerness to sell her, you made it evident that you don't care a rip about anyone but yourself."

"Oh, but look wha' I did for ye by givin' ye me niece," Frye argued and leered drunkenly at Jeff as if hoping such logic would motivate the younger man to be compassionate.

"You didn't *give* me Raelynn," Jeff corrected pithily. "I bought her."

Turning to his niece, Frye tried with some difficulty to focus his gaze upon her. "Didn't ol' Coop do well by ye, girlie? There ye be, all decked out in yer finery. But are ye grateful enough ta come ta me aid?" He snorted, emitting more of the foul fumes. "Not e'en a wee bit, are ye."

"Move along, Frye," Jeff urged caustically. "My wife wants nothing more to do with you."

"What's this now? Me own sister's chit, thinkin' herself too good for ol' Coop?" His glaring red eyes came back to Jeff, but keeping them there seemed to pose a problem for the man. "An' ye're no better. I give ye this waif ta do wit' as ye please, but do ye offer me any thanks? Why, given a chance, ye'd likely give me the back o' yer hand! 'Tain't right the way ye're snubbin' yer nose at me. Treatin' me like filthy scum, ye are! An' here I be, down on me luck."

"Perhaps in your present muddled state, Frye, you've forgotten the terms of our contract," Jeff retorted crisply. "If so, I shall endeavor to refresh your memory. At least thirty witnesses can attest to the fact that you signed a contract in full knowledge of what you'd be giving up if you didn't conform to the restrictions laid out in that agreement. Bother us again, and you'll forfeit the seven hundred fifty dollars I gave you for my wife. And believe me, if you can't repay me in full, you'll find yourself working as a hired hand on my plantation, under the personal direction of my overseer, Frank Fergus. And you won't be seeing a jug of whiskey until you've repaid me to the last dollar. Now, Frye, don't you think you'd better leave us in peace before you have to work for a living?"

The sot opened his mouth several times, emitting more of the foul fumes, but the ability to speak seemed to momentarily elude him. Finally he muttered, "Can't hold on ta a bloomin' farthin', I can't. Slips like water through me fingers. 'Tis a bloody curse, livin' from hand ta mouth as I do." Woefully he clasped a shaking hand to his forehead as if totally ignorant of any blame he might have had in creating his predicament. "An' here I be, a-fearin' for me very life. That'll slip away, too, just like water, if'n I don't jumps when they say hop."

Unable to make any sense of the man's mumbling, Jeff tucked his wife's arm within his and guided her around the inebriated sponge. According to Raelynn, almost five months ago the man had appeared at the humble stoop of the cottage wherein she and her mother had taken refuge from the derisive scorn evoked by the treasonous charges laid against her father in London. Much to the astonishment of Evalina Barrett, Frye had made claims of being her brother, who had been lost at sea at a fairly young age. He had maintained that he had been rescued by pirates who had forced him to serve them until a thrice of years ago when he had been sold to a Spaniard who had later lost both his purse and him in a wager against an Englishman who had finally sailed back to London. From the beginning, Raelynn had suffered doubts about the authenticity of the man's tales. Like his wife, Jeff couldn't imagine the relationship having much merit, for the two were as different as the east from the west.

The couple progressed around the next corner and,

from there, approached an inn situated in a private area and surrounded by well maintained gardens and live oaks. Its carefully clipped lawns conveyed an atmosphere of a private residence, but the delectable aromas wafting from the kitchens tempted many residents and passersby to make inquiries into the fare. Having often dined in the inn's garden amid the delicate scents of roses, jasmine and an abundance of other flowers, Jeff was of a mind to think that Raelynn would enjoy the private areas as well as the delectable repast.

The proprietor, a genial, round-faced man, hurried forward with a buoyant smile and greeted them enthusiastically as they stepped through the open doors of the entrance. "Oh, come in, come in, Mr. Birmingham. I was told you had brought your lovely wife to our fair city today, and on the chance you might be bringing her here, I took the liberty of saving your usual table on the veranda."

Jeff was hardly surprised by how swiftly rumors of their shopping excursion had made their way to this particular area of the city. Nor was he unappreciative of the results. "Nothing happens here in Charleston that you don't hear about it within the hour, Bertrand. Your customers keep you well informed."

"There's some truth to that," their host jovially agreed as he led them through the elegantly furnished interior and out to a gracious portico veiled from the street by an artfully draped tangle of English ivy and wisteria vines. A table had been prepared for them behind a lattice trellis, affording as much concealment as the couple desired.

"This is lovely," Raelynn murmured in relief as she settled into the chair Bertrand had drawn out for her. Although she had enjoyed meeting Jeff's friends and acquaintances, she had every hope of relishing the rest of the evening in his private company well secluded from prying eyes and those eager to gain an introduction.

"Would you like to begin with a glass of your favorite

wine, Mr. Birmingham?" the proprietor queried. "And perhaps a shore-crab bisque my chef boasts is his very best yet?"

"In that case, we'd better sample some," Jeff replied with a chuckle and turned to Raelynn as the man left. "Take my word for it, my dear. You've never had bisque as tasty as what you're about to receive."

"I can hardly wait," she assured him, smiling eagerly. She hadn't realized just how hungry she had become. At the merest thought of food, her mouth began to water in anticipation.

Cooling zephyrs freshened the air with the scent of the sea as it gently ruffled the edges of the white linen tablecloth. An ornate hurricane lamp sat atop the table, encompassing them in a softly glowing aura of light. Along the vine-bedecked porch, other secluded islands of radiance could be seen, all of them set in the midst of an almost magical evening filled with fireflies and the melodic plucking of a harp that drifted soothingly throughout the garden.

Raelynn sighed contentedly as she glanced around. "What a wonderful place this is, Jeffrey. And what a delightful way to end our first shopping excursion to Charleston together. Thank you for bringing me here."

Jeff smiled, grateful their encounter with Cooper Frye hadn't left his wife feeling distraught or shaken. She had definite cause to hate the man for what he had done to her mother, and yet, for the moment at least, it seemed as if she had been able to thrust Frye from her thoughts.

As his eyes delved into those liquid pools of aqua blue, he was reminded of that moment wherein they had floated back to reality after making love. It had been apparent that she had never dreamt such ecstasy could be experienced by mere mortals. She had searched his face as if he had been some kind of god, yet he, too, had been amazed at the dazzling heights of rapturous joy to which he had soared while joined to her in the intimate rites of love. He could only lay the cause of such bliss to his good fortune in finding a woman who was the very essence of the one who had haunted his dreams for nearly half his life.

In the past Jeff had never lent much consideration to the possibility that he might be lonely. After all, he had his brother, his sister-in-law, close friends whom he held in high esteem and more casual acquaintances who were wont to invite him out hunting and to a variety of other functions. Yet he was just beginning to suspect that for at least a decade his heart had been pining for a gentle, loving mate that romantics in poems and verses were wont to claim would eventually come along, the other half of him, so to speak, the one who was truly meant to complete the entity that they would become. During the day of shopping he had taken immeasurable delight in being with Raelynn and especially in being the recipient of her adoring smiles and softly cooing admiration. What he had experienced had been a far cry from the stilted reserve he had maintained while escorting her to social events during the past couple of weeks. Today her tender-eyed gazes and melodious voice had been enough to convince him that all was very, very right with his world.

Raelynn watched the subtle play of emotion in the emerald orbs and tried in vain to read her husband's thoughts. Finally she gave up her futile attempt and tilted her head wonderingly as she smiled at him. "What are you thinking about, Jeffrey?"

"Just considering my recent blessings, my sweet," he murmured, reaching across the table to take her hand. "I never thought I'd find the woman who haunted my dreams until you came into my life." His thumb stroked the soft, inner curve of her palm as his eyes delved into hers. "Sometimes, when I let myself muse on the secrets of life, I begin to think that from the dawning of time we were meant for each other. Not too long ago I had foolishly made a mental list of all the requirements a wife would need to please me although I despaired of ever being content once I married. It wasn't until you came into my life that I began to perceive some change of heart. Now I find myself thinking that you fulfill every facet of those wifely conditions I once mentally conjured, as well as some I didn't even consider at the time."

Touched by his words and the subtle, intimate caress of his thumb, Raelynn could only admit her own reflections. "Some mornings, before the rising of the sun, I wake and think back on the direction my life has taken. At times, I wonder if the situation in which my mother and I found ourselves might have improved if we had stayed in England, if my father might have been absolved of any wrongdoing after his passing, or if we'd have continued to experience hardship. I was terribly grieved by the loss of my parents. For a time, I resented the sea voyage which had taken my mother's life, yet, for all I know, she might have died from a broken heart had we stayed in England. If we had, I wouldn't have met you, and I'd never have known what I was missing. Strange, but I now feel as if I'm where I belong . . . with you."

A hypnotic grin slowly traced across his handsome lips, bringing into play the enticingly handsome concavities in his cheeks. "I'm infinitely grateful you came into my life, madam, even if you nearly flattened me in the process."

Raelynn giggled at his teasing humor. "You don't know how close you came to getting your face slapped when you swooped me up into your arms, sir. I was highly offended by your audacity to even touch me until I tasted the dust from the passing coach and realized you had very likely saved me from being trampled."

Jeff dipped his dark head forward. "My pleasure to be of service, Mrs. Birmingham."

"Mrs. Birmingham . . ." she repeated blissfully. "It

sounds very nice coming from your lips . . . very possessive, in fact." Her eyes glowed suggestively as she readjusted the white linen napkin in her lap. "Perhaps we should consider taking a room here in Charleston after all."

The green eyes twinkled with amusement as he shook his head in a slow, negative motion. "Not a chance, madam. You've aroused my curiosity about your nightgown, and I'd fight a whole army of foes rather than deny myself an opportunity to see you garbed in it or, more explicitly, the pleasure of removing it from your soft, luscious breasts and sweeping it down past your pale, sleek thighs. . . ."

"Shhh." Raelynn glanced around nervously. "Someone may hear you and think the worst of us."

His shining eyes melded with her. "We're newly wedded, my sweet. Only a prig would consider us depraved."

A slight inclination of her head drew Jeff's attention to the fact that their waiter was approaching with a tray bearing goblets of wine. Jeff winked at her above a tantalizing grin before he leaned back in his chair to await the man. Even so, his fingers remained entwined with hers.

For the main course, they enjoyed breasts of duck in port sauce, wild rice dressing and a selection of vegetables. Although Raelynn found each dish a sumptuous delight, the bread pudding with rum sauce clearly won her vote for being the most delicious. Afterwards, demitasse cups of coffee were brought to the table before Jeff thought of ordering tea for his wife.

"I'll try the coffee," she volunteered before he could summon their waiter back.

Jeff arched a dark brow dubiously. "Are you sure? The coffee may keep you awake all night."

The corners of her mouth curved upward coquettishly. "Were you planning on letting me sleep?"

"Drink your coffee, madam," her husband urged. The taut depressions in his cheeks lent his grin a devilish charm that was irresistible, especially to a young wife who was already well on her way toward being totally captivated. Lifting his own cup, Jeff silently toasted her. "We have a long night ahead of us."

5 ❧

Rain-freshened breezes wafted in through the open French doors and windows of the master's bed-chambers, billowing lace panels out beyond the deep, green velvet draperies elegantly drawn aside by braided silk cords. Through the wavering divisions of ornate cloth, sunlight filtered in, seeming almost fickle after penetrating the swaying boughs of the live oak growing near the end of the house. At times, bright shafts came through the foliage unrestricted and, like a gleaming sword of light, pierced the windowpanes, dazzling the eye of the beholder. Other moments, fluttering leaves scattered the rays before they could escape, sending them flying in every direction, like fireflies frolicking in care-free abandon.

Whatever the shape of the capricious brilliance, it seemed intent upon searching out some sublime nectar as it swept over the one lying amid the rumpled sheets.

The blazing beams highlighted auburn tresses curling in glorious disarray upon a downy pillow and impishly chased across darkly lashed eyelids serenely closed in slumber, but whenever the radiance masqueraded as a scintillating array of tiny specks, it seemed to take special delight in dancing across swelling mounds partially concealed by a snowy white sheet edged with embroidered lace.

Lean, brown fingers reached out and, with careful diligence, lifted away the covering, exposing the pale, lustrous body to the dappled light. From the edge of the bed where he stood tall and naked, Jeff slowly perused the curving form now illumined by the whimsical radiance of the solar orb. It was much like considering a lavish feast; he didn't know exactly where to begin.

Bending a knee upon the edge of the mattress, Jeff leaned across the bed until he lay braced on an elbow beside his sleeping wife. For a long moment, he made no effort to touch her, only admired her dainty features and softly parted lips, but the temptation to do more than just look proved stronger than his power to resist. As lightly as the brush of a butterfly's wings, his mouth caressed hers with fleeting kisses, parting her gently curving lips until they began to respond. Her creamy throat provided a pathway to more tantalizing ground, and soon he was savoring the sweetness of a delicately hued crest. Smiling sleepily, Raelynn threaded slender fingers through the short, raven strands at his nape and arched her back to receive the best of his attention. He gave it eagerly and continued on with fervent dedication until she was all but writhing beneath his delicious assault.

"Please, no more, Jeffrey," she pleaded. Against her will she had found herself swiftly advancing toward that same rapture he had taken her to time and time again during the night gone past. "I'm nigh faint."

Pressing her down flat upon the bed, Jeff leaned above her and smiled down into eyes that had grown luminous with desire. "Why would you have me stop now, madam?"

Admiringly Raelynn traced a forefinger over the male visage as the scent of his cologne drifted with the strength of a well-aged brew through her senses. The morning light bathed the chiseled planes and angles of a warmly bronzed cheek and the muscular contour of a shoulder and arm, making her keenly aware of his fine, manly appearance. Had he been some Greek god who had awakened from stone to vibrant life, he could not have aroused her awe more readily.

Her fingers continued their inspection, touring the fascinating grooves that marked his handsomely chiseled cheeks. From a distance, a stranger might have supposed them small scars that had puckered his cheeks, albeit captivatingly, except that when he grew solemn, they disappeared entirely. Just as quickly they deepened with the degree of humor he displayed.

During the brevity of their marriage, Raelynn had come to the realization that she had difficulty believing in her own good fortune. Being the wife of such a man seemed a position reserved for loftier, more dignified ladies, not one barely past the difficult years of puberty. Just as frequently she had wondered when reality would awaken her and she would realize that all of it was nothing more than an enchanted dream. "Because I want to wait for you."

"Do you now?" Grinning, Jeff cocked his head curiously as his hand paused. "And have you no liking for my caresses?"

Beneath his glowing eyes, a blush crept into her cheeks. "So much so, Jeffrey, that you make me forget everything else, and I am swept away by the bliss you create within me, yet I enjoy such pleasure far more when we're joined as one and can share the experience as husband and wife."

He searched her face, amazed by her wifely commitment to their unity. Not more than a day or two ago, he had suspected something entirely different about the woman he had married. "You're not overly tender after our night of love?"

Though Raelynn lowered her gaze from his probing stare, her mouth curved upward winsomely at the corners. "I forget about all of that when you assuage the hurt."

His lips twitched as he teased, "No longer afraid of my base parts, madam?"

Color suffused her cheeks even as she shook her head with a definite denial. She sent a fleeting glance chasing upward. "You've made me crave *everything* about you."

Willing to accommodate his beauteous wife, Jeff rolled upon her, but surprise soon lit Raelynn's face when she realized that he had other things in mind. His eyes gleamed into hers, much like those of a puckish little boy pestering a girl with pigtails. Except that this was no child's play, but a married couple bent on extracting exotic delights from every moment of their foreplay. Raelynn became a willing spectator to his teasing as he used his maleness to awaken that part of her that was most sensitive to stimulation. She experienced the same quickening excitement, the same catches in her breath as he had done in the carriage the day before, yet, whereas his passions had gone unappeased until they had gained the comfort of their bed, she had every hope that both of them would reach that lofty height well before they ever left its soft confines.

Lifting her head from the pillow, she kissed his brows, his cheeks, his nose and his subtly cleft chin with a womanly appreciation for all that she saw. In claiming his lips, she soon gained his ardent response, and their mouths and tongues joined in an avaricious search. Still, he tantalized her, stroking himself against her dewy softness, boldly skimming beneath the outer fringes, until strengthening tremors began to assail her. Unable to sub-

due a muted moan, Raelynn rose up against him in an
anxious quest to ensnare the fiery blade. Chuckling softly
at her mounting impatience, Jeff yielded to her urgings
and pressed fully home, causing her breath to catch at
the onrushing waves of pleasure that washed over her.
Scrubbing her hands over his tautly fleshed ribs, she
cooed near his ear as she whispered assurances that she
did indeed feel as if she had been made for him. In the
next moments she was meeting his quickening thrusts
with a growing eagerness to please and be appeased.

RAELYNN CLASPED THE SHEET HIGHER OVER HER
bosom and, in spite of the restrictions of the confining
shroud, shuffled across the room to an east window, from
whence she could view the world outside. Jeff had informed her that they would have to wait until their bath
cooled before they could make use of it. During the inter-
val, she had sought to familiarize herself with her new
wifely domain and to see all the sights available from the
master's chambers. She could hear Jeffrey stropping his
razor in the bathing chamber as he hummed softly to
himself, evidencing his cheery mood after a night of sensual delights and, more recently, a return to their own
private nirvana. Though hardly a qualified judge of
voices, she was led to believe that he could sing fairly
well as a baritone; he certainly could hum on the proper
key, but as far as making any final judgment, she would
just have to wait until he actually burst out in a song. A
bride normally had many things to learn about her
spouse, but in her case, there was much more than the
usual, considering the fact that they had been complete
strangers mere hours before they had spoken their vows.

Pulling aside a silken panel, Raelynn scanned the sce-
nery beyond the window and smiled as she took note of
the early weanlings frolicking in a lush meadow beyond

the stable. Apparently they were feeling rather frisky in the cooler weather presently gracing the countryside. Seeing them chase each other about, she made a mental note to ask her husband to take her out for a ride one day soon and to show her some of the land that comprised the plantation. It was doubtful with the thousands of acres he owned that she could view it all during one afternoon's excursion, but she had to start somewhere. Then, of course, there was the fact that she hadn't been riding for almost a year, and though like the older foals, she was anxious to test her skills, she wasn't all that confident about her stamina.

In turning aside from the window, Raelynn became mindful of the desk that was angled in such a way that the front of it faced three corners of the room, allowing whatever light that streamed through the French doors and window to be of immediate benefit to anyone working there. Residing on top of the finely tooled leather were a pair of glass inkwells in a brass holder that bore a small statue of a bronze horse and a slender brass sheath for a quill. Nearby lay a curved knife with a handle carved in the shape of a ram's head. Although rather large for such a service, she could imagine that it functioned fairly nicely as a letter opener. The hazard would be if it slipped across a hand or finger, for the blade looked positively wicked.

Her gaze fell on a leather-bound volume lying open on the desk top. In growing curiosity she picked up the book, turned it over to see the title, and discovered that she held within her grasp a copy of *"Minstrelsy of the Scottish Border"* by Sir Walter Scott, a collection of poetry published in Britain to great acclaim the previous year. It had sold so well that many of Sir Walter's readers had gone in want of a copy. To see the book here in the Carolinas left her totally amazed by the resourcefulness of the man she had married.

Raelynn leafed through the pages, noting as she did

so that the edges had been neatly cut to the very last page, no doubt by the knife she had just seen. Jeff had obviously readied the book for a reading and, from the presence of a bookmark tucked near the center, she guessed that he was in the process of indulging himself in that particular pastime.

Raelynn smiled at the idea of her quintessentially masculine husband having a desire to read such a book. Jeff conveyed such a strong manliness in nearly everything he did that it was difficult to imagine him enjoying poetry. More pronounced than the pleasure he took in reading was his love of horses, his skill with firearms, his dedication to his work, his plantation, shipping company, and the lumber mill he owned with his brother. Then, of course, there were his very manly attributes, some of which made her blush with secret delight to recall.

"Our bath is now tolerable, madam," Jeff announced, stepping from the bathing chamber with a scant linen towel wrapped about his narrow hips. "Coming?"

"Your obedient servant," she said, playfully bobbing a curtsey before him.

Jeff braced his fists against his lean waist and, feigning the scowl of some dreaded pharaoh, peered down his noble nose at her as he arched a dark brow to a lofty height. "A servant, you say?"

"Yes, my lord," Raelynn replied in a guise of humble obedience. "Your every wish is my command."

"Is it now?"

She peered at him suspiciously and decided she didn't trust the devilish gleam in his eyes. Her responding grin was reminiscent of an elfish sprite. "Then again, sir, a lady must have some reservations."

"I see." He thrust out his chin reflectively as he pondered her reply. "What about scrubbing my back?"

Raelynn dipped her head in a consenting nod. "I believe I can manage that well enough, sir, but only if you'll scrub mine first."

"Agreed." Jeff pivoted about-face and strode back into the bathing chamber as she struggled to follow along behind in spite of the sheet that seemed dedicated to coming loose and tripping her. Pausing to readjust her makeshift clothing, she scooped up the bottom of the linen and quickly joined him.

The large, elongated copper bathtub all but dominated the room and, as she had discovered the day before, was spacious enough to comfortably accommodate both of them. Jeff halted beside it and, freeing the towel, tossed it aside, leaving his wife fully cognizant of his growing assets, those same which she had blushingly recalled hardly a moment ago. The heat now infusing her cheeks had naught to do with shame, but a warming admiration of all that she saw.

"You seem distracted, madam," he challenged, glancing at her askance with a smile that resembled a leer.

"So do you, sir," she rejoined meaningfully.

"Aye," he admitted. " 'Tis a weakness I suffer when you're around."

"I see no weakness, sir." Deliberately Raelynn dragged the end flap of the sheet from her substitute bodice and, with a wiggle, hastened the shroud's descent to the floor, capturing her husband's undivided attention. Biting a grinning lip, she sauntered forward provocatively and reached out to claim the object of her interest, snatching his breath forthwith. "I hope you don't parade yourself before other women as casually as you do with me, sir," she said with more than a grain of sincerity. "I wouldn't be at all averse to staking my claims on you with claws bared now that we have truly become man and wife."

"What you have in your greedy little hand, madam, is yours alone to have and to hold," he assured her, carefully avoiding any mention of past involvements. "As for Nell, you'll never have anything to worry about, please believe me."

Raelynn grinned up at him as he slid an arm behind her. "As long as you understand what will set my temper awry."

"I understand completely, madam, for I, too, would be greatly offended if you were to bestow your attentions upon another man." He extended a hand to assist her into the bath. "The water will be getting cold if we stand here much longer."

Suffering some reservations Raelynn considered first the tub and then his long legs. "Don't you think you should get in first this time, Jeffrey? We sat at opposite ends yesterday, but it wasn't as cozy as it could be if we were sitting together."

Grinning, Jeff inclined his head, readily acknowledging the truth of her statement. "I didn't want to seem a cad by going first or dictating the way I thought it should be, madam, but you're right, of course. It would be a lot cozier if we're both at the same end."

Some moments later Raelynn lounged back contentedly against her husband's chest as he lathered soap over the hills and valleys of her bosom and all the other tempting terrain within reach.

"I've a mind to let our neighbors take a gander at you, Mrs. Birmingham."

"Gander?" She was all but purring from his ministrations, but grew curious nevertheless. "Whatever do you mean, Jeffrey?"

"Gander . . . you know, look."

She cast a coquettish glance at him over a glistening shoulder. "Surely not quite like this, Jeffrey? I think I should get dressed first . . . unless, of course, you don't mind your friends seeing me completely naked."

"I do indeed, madam," he whispered, nuzzling her ear. Bending low, he nipped playfully at the dainty lobe as his hand slid around to encompass a round breast. He eyed the delicate pink protrusion thrusting outward through his fingers and marveled at how pale and lustrous her skin looked in comparison to his. "When I spoke with Reverend Parsons in Charleston several days ago, he all but made me promise that we'd attend the Sunday social coming up this weekend at church. 'Twill be a chance for you to meet some more of our neighbors before our ball."

"And will Nell be there perchance?"

"Wench," he growled playfully and batted the water in front of her face, drawing a protesting squeal from her. She returned the favor, which soon evolved them in a contest of dampening proportions. Some time later they stood adorned in nothing more than towels as they considered the floor, where a large ring of water wreathed the outer limits of the tub. Like children, they entered into a race to see who could clean up more of the puddles before the task was complete. The game definitely entailed some scurrying on the part of Raelynn, who was not above treading upon her husband's bony feet in an effort to get to a wet area first or pinching his backside to move him swiftly out of the way.

It was just as much fun for the imp to run up behind him while he was wiping up the floor and to reach underneath the towel, well forward of his buttocks, bringing him upright like a stiffly coiled spring. When the tables were turned, however, that was an entirely different story, or at least it was from Raelynn's point of view, for she was not above screeching, stamping her foot to show her irritation, and threatening dire consequences over his outrageous audacity to accost her in such a lewd fashion, which of course only enticed her husband to do it all the more.

&GARBED IN NOTHING MORE THAN A LOOSELY FLOWING *peignoir*, Raelynn left the master's suite moments later and entered her former bedroom from which she immediately rang for Cora. After selecting a soft, white muslin

day dress adorned with a blue satin sash and striped vertically with narrow, embroidered bands of the same hue
upon which had been appliquéd tiny pale blue flowers,
she set about garbing herself in stockings and chemise.
She was just slipping the gown over her head when the
housekeeper arrived with a young, black woman whom
she immediately introduced as her cousin, Tizzy.

"Mistah Jeffrey said yo'd be needin' a lady's maid,
Miz Raelynn. Tizzy used ta work for some folks in Vir-
ginnie 'til her pa went ta fetch her last week wit' a letter
from Mistah Jeffrey an' a bag o' coins ta buy her papers."

"You mean she's a slave?" Raelynn asked, noticing
an ugly laceration on Tizzy's cheek.

"Well, she'll have ta works for de mastah 'til she pays
off de debt he laid out fo' her. O' course, dat won't be so
hard what wit' Mistah Jeffrey bein' such a fine gentl'man
an' all."

Raelynn lifted the girl's chin to inspect the raw gash.
"Whatever happened to your face, Tizzy?"

"My ol' massah, he comed home drunk as an ol' robin
eatin' ferment'd berries an' started whippin' ever'one in
sight, includin' his missus. Ah tried ta help Miz Clare
'cause she always been like an angel ta me. Dat's when
Mistah Horace snatched up a knife an' swung 'round on
me in a rage. Afore ah could skedaddle, he whisked it
across my cheek. If'n Miz Clare hadn't laid a vase o'er
de back o' his head an' knocked him out cold, ah'da've
been a gonna fo' sho'. Aftahwards, Miz Clare sent a rider
ta my folks, beggin' fo' dem ta finds a way ta fetch me
home. Straightways my pa comed here ta Oakley an'
asked Mistah Jeffrey if'n he could help." Grinning, Tizzy
spread her arms and declared, "An' here ah is."

Raelynn laughed at the young woman's exuberance.
"My husband is indeed most gallant, Tizzy, of that I have
no doubt. In my case, I was saved from a conniving uncle
who wanted to sell me to a horrible man, but Mr. Jeffrey
came to my defense when I most needed a champion."

"Yo' means yo' was sold . . . jes' like me, Miz Rae-lynn?" the servant asked in amazement.

Raelynn nodded. "Yes, Tizzy, just like you. As I understand it, almost as many white people have been sold in this country as blacks, except that most of them have become indentured servants rather than slaves. Many were transported here as prisoners on English ships, mainly from Ireland and Scotland. Sad to say, a few of those wretched souls have been condemned to a life of intolerable hardship here by their masters. You and I both are fortunate to have found a safe haven here in Mr. Jeffrey's house."

Tizzy shook her head, hardly able to absorb the wonder of it. "Ah heared o' white folks bein' sold inta bondage afore, Miz Raelynn, but ah nevah figgered ah'd be a-workin' for one whad was almost a slave."

Soft laughter spilled from Raelynn's lips. "I have my husband to thank because I'm not. He not only saved me from my uncle's devious plans, but he brought you here to help me. I've been at wit's end trying to do something with my hair."

"Yo' needn't worry no more 'bout dat, Miz Raelynn. I'll be takin' care of it from now on, thanks ta Mistah Jeffrey. No doubt 'bout it, he sho' is a fine gen'leman, Miz Raelynn. My pa bein' sayin' dat for years. Ah doan knows whad ah'da've done if'n Mistah Jeffrey hadn't bought me."

"I'm immensely glad that Mr. Jeffrey saw fit to buy us both, Tizzy."

Tizzy cackled in full agreement. "Yas'm, so am I!"

Once they returned to the matter of grooming, it didn't take long for Tizzy to arrange the rich auburn hair into an enchanting coiffure. For an added charming touch, she attached narrow ribbons of blue satin that flowed over a cluster of ringlets she had bunched together near the top of her new mistress's head.

Prettily coifed and gowned, Raelynn danced around on pale blue slippers before the standing mirror.

"How do I look, Tizzy?"

"Jes' downright beaut-ti-ful, Miz Raelynn."

⟡THE WALLS OF THE DINING ROOM HAD BEEN RICHLY decorated in a *trompe d'oeil* fashion, creating the illusion that a garden surrounded a merrily splashing fountain on the far side of the long, mahogany dining table, around which Chippendale chairs were neatly nestled. The butler, always nattily garbed in a crisply starched white coat and black knee breeches, stockings, and buckled shoes, was already setting out serving dishes and a large silver compote filled with fresh fruit on the sideboard.

"Good morning, Kingston," Raelynn greeted cheerily, sweeping inward with a vivacious smile.

The black man's face lit up with a wide, white-toothed grin as his dark eyes settled on her. Word had already filtered down through Cora that the new mistress had as late as yesterday morning been ensconced in the master's chambers, which in Kingston's estimation made everything at Oakley just about as close to being perfect as possible until offspring began arriving. Only then would it be ideal. "An' a right fine good mornin' ta yo', too, Miz Raelynn. Yas'm, it sho has the makings for a mighty nice day."

"The weather seems very refreshing for a change," Raelynn observed as she sank into a chair near the head of the table. "A bit cooler, don't you think?"

"Yas'm, it sho' is." Taking up a silver teapot, Kingston poured the brew into her cup. "Ah heared tell from Mistah Jeffrey dat where yo' comes from, Miz Raelynn, de weather is cooler'n it is here most any time. He was hardly more'n boy de first time he went o'er dere, but he say dat aftah de family comed back home, dey had ta get used ta de weather all o'er again." The butler chortled and shook his graying head. "I 'spect yo've been sufferin' somethin' mighty awful yerself from de heat hereabouts. Yo're probably wonderin' why in tarnation yo' sail so far 'cross de ocean jes' ta get here."

"There have definitely been times when I thought the heat here intolerable," Raelynn acknowledged with a chuckle. "Mainly, I suppose, because an unusually warm day in England is still much cooler than even the weather we're experiencing today."

Pursing his lips, Kingston mulled over her answer. "Whad would de English call days like whad we was havin' afore today, Miz Raelynn?"

"Hades," Raelynn answered with bubbling amusement, drawing a deep chortle from the black. "I've heard it said that one of the reasons the colonists won their freedom from England was simply because British soldiers went into battle wearing stiff stocks, woolen breeches and those dreadfully hot, red jackets buttoned all the way up to their chins while the Yankees dressed quite sensibly." She accepted a hot roll from the breadbasket the servant offered and rolled her eyes to emphasize her lamentation. "After personally being subjected to a Carolina July, Kingston, I'm inclined to venture a guess and say that just as many English soldiers succumbed to the heat as those who fell from gunfire. There have actually been a couple of days when I was sure I would do the same."

The butler threw back his head and haw-hawed in amusement. "Yo' ain't seen nothin' yet, Miz Raelynn," he warned jovially after calming. "Jes' wait. August's a-comin', so's ye'd best get yo'self set. But yas'm, I heared dat afore 'bout de soldiers, an' den dere are folks whad say we won de war 'cause dem Lobsterbacks marched shoulder ta shoulder inta battle whilst our soldiers hid behind bushes an' trees an' picked dem off like a glutton eatin' peas from a pod. De Indians learnt de Yankees ta be real sly-like 'cause dat's de way dey was a-killin' us. A ways back, more'n a score o' years now, I seen me plenty o' dem Lobsterbacks, but I al'ays skedaddled afore any o' 'em took it in dere heads ta use me for target practice."

A moment earlier, Jeff had paused in the doorway to admire his wife in the gardenlike atmosphere of the room. The sight made him reconsider his long-held disdain of its décor, which had been left much as it had been before his purchase of the plantation. He had once deemed the murals a bit flamboyant for his more subdued tastes in spite of the wont of many Charlestonians to embellish foyers and other rooms with similar motifs, but the serene beauty of his wife seemed right in keeping with the tranquil garden scene. He felt immeasurably blessed when her shining eyes came upon him, for her welcoming smile glowed back at him with all the brightness of his own private daystar.

Raelynn basked in a moment of pride as she swept her gaze over her husband. Unquestionably his tall, manly physique and handsome features were deserving of all the attention women were wont to bestow upon him. Not only had she seen proper young ladies eyeing him with surreptitious reserve along some of Charleston's fashionable streets the day before, but later in the afternoon, when he had stepped briefly from the carriage to talk with several of his teamsters near the docks, several harlots had stopped their hawking long enough to scrutinize him in unabashed boldness. Even during a short stroll in a more influential area of the city, Raelynn had glanced casually around and found a winsome miss trying to disguise her sudden confusion after being caught gaping. Mere moments later, a parasol was hurriedly lowered to hide the blushing cheeks of its bearer, a dignified woman of an age perhaps as much as a score and ten.

Although more slender than his brother, Jeff was just as athletic and handsomely proportioned. Recently Raelynn had taken time to study the portraits of his parents and had determined that although Jeff, like Brandon, favored his physically stalwart father in both face and coloring, her husband had apparently inherited his own finer boned frame from his mother, who, Jeff had said, had been as slender as a reed to the day she died.

Presently Jeff was casually dressed in a white, full-sleeved shirt, taupe riding breeches, and black boots, all of which were complemented by his trim form. As he approached, a lazy, hypnotic smile curved his lips, warming her as surely as any caress.

When Jeff halted beside his wife's chair, he clasped her thin fingers within his and, leaning down, placed a doting peck upon her brow. A more thorough kiss had been his desire from the first moment he had seen her in the dining room, but he had no doubt that a demonstration of that nature would have shocked their butler.

"You're looking no less than radiant this morning, my sweet," he averred. "I trust you've met your new lady's maid, and are pleased with her?"

"Very."

The green eyes glowed warmly in approval as they slowly swept the length of her, from her charmingly coifed auburn hair to her slender blue slippers. "From what I can now ascertain by looking at you, Tizzy has been able to make perfection the epitome of empyreal loveliness. Quite simply, madam, you look like an angel."

Raelynn dipped her head in laughing acknowledgment of his flattery. "Thank you, kind sir, not only for your praise, but also for your thoughtfulness in bringing Tizzy here to serve as my lady's maid. I'm sure I shall never again have to worry about my hair, my clothes, or anything else while I'm in her care."

"In view of the fact that Cora has so much to do as housekeeper, I was forced to consider other alternatives for your lady's maid. Then, too, I had to think of my pride." His lips twitched briefly with a threatening grin as he struck a lofty pose to emulate a pompous lord. "To stroll down a boulevard with a beautiful, exquisitely groomed lady and to watch everyone turn and stare in admiration nurtures my conceit no small degree."

With a gay laugh Raelynn flung up a hand and shooed away such foolish logic. "You have no need to feed your pride on my appearance, sir. All you have to do is cast a glance about you the next time you visit Charleston. If you didn't notice all those pretty young maids who twittered and chirped when they espied you sauntering down the street yesterday, Mr. Birmingham, then I certainly did. Truthfully, they did little for my self-esteem."

"What of the men who drool after you, Mrs. Birmingham?"

She scoffed and feigned amusement over a subject that at times troubled her unmercifully. If women adored him so, then a wife had to expect that he was forever receiving invitations into their beds. "I saw far more of the former than the latter, sir. Indeed, it makes me wonder how many maids you've led about on a string."

"Reassure yourself, madam," he murmured, bending toward her again with a captivating smile and glowing green orbs. "My eyes are only for you." He settled the matter with a soft kiss upon her lips, and when he straightened, they found themselves alone, which seemed convenient for a more thorough, warmly titillating kiss.

Raelynn laughed shakily as he finally drew away and, with some surprise, realized that she had threaded her fingers through the short, curling hair at his nape. Leaning back in her chair, she gazed up at him with eyes that had grown dark and luminous. "Your kisses make me swoon," she breathed. "Even from the first, they were like a strong wine sapping my will and the strength from my limbs."

Jeff lifted her slender fingers to his lips. "Your smile does that to me, madam."

He stepped away from her with that same magical wink and hypnotic grin that made her heart flutter and settled into his chair at the head of the table. His preference for having her close at hand while dining had been established on the night of their wedding. From where he now sat, he had only to stretch a hand out to touch her.

"Did you manage to get any sleep last night, my dear?" he asked as he spread a linen napkin over his lap.

Reminded of the recent hours in which they had made love, Raelynn blushed with warm pleasure as she lifted a teacup to her smiling lips. "Enough, thank you. And you?"

His green eyes gleamed as they caressed her. "Actually, I can't remember sleeping . . . or, for that matter, letting you sleep. Still, I must have, for I feel marvelously relaxed and invigorated. But then, perhaps I'm giving credit where it isn't due."

Jeff took note of her vibrantly hued cheeks and guessed that he had caught her thinking back on the intimate moments they had shared. Beneath his quizzically elevated brow and smilingly perceptive gaze, Raelynn could do naught but smile and shrug in helpless admission. He reached across and, taking her hand once more, raised it to his mouth as their eyes merged in warm accord. His softly caressing kisses were as light as thistledown on her fingers, effective in evoking warm shivers along her spine.

"Heavenly day, sir," she managed breathlessly, amazed by the potency of his knee-weakening persuasion, "*you're* extremely dangerous to a lady's peace of mind. Just a few moments ago, I was thinking of merely enjoying a cup of tea and the morning banquet. Now you have me all aflutter wondering if I'll shock the servants if I lead you back to our bedroom."

The emerald eyes grazed her in a way that left no doubt that breaking the morning fast was far from his mind. "I suppose we should eat first." A soft chuckle escaped his lips. "You'll need your strength to endure my attentions."

"I'm really famished," she admitted, leaning forward with a tantalizing little grin. "In fact, I can't remember ever being so ravenous . . . except, of course, on the voyage over here. 'Twould seem, Mr. Birmingham, that our recent activities do strange things to me."

"Eat hearty, madam," he encouraged. "There is much more to come. As for this morning, I thought you might enjoy riding out and looking over the plantation. Would you consider accompanying me on such a tour?"

"Oh, yes, Jeffrey. In fact, I was going to ask if you would grant me such a favor. You must have read my mind."

Reveling in their new-found contentment, they lingered longer than usual over breakfast. Though Kingston hovered near and encouraged them to eat heartily of the tempting dishes the cook had prepared for them, it was as if they were entirely alone in the huge house. Their eyes, never straying far from the other, communicated things that were lovingly intimate and best left unsaid in a houseful of servants. Their hands touched often in private little ways that might have brought a blush to the cheeks of beholder had that one perceived exactly what those secret strokes imparted. But then, when such gestures were conveyed in the private language of love, that strange mystical prose which softened eyes, moistened lips, and left hearts soaring with joy, how could another have discerned their meaning?

⊱A RIDING HABIT HAD NOT BEEN AMONG THE CLOTHES that Mrs. Brewster had brought back from Ives's Couture for Raelynn before the wedding. Thus, when Jeff escorted his young wife outside, she was still wearing the same blue and white gown she had donned earlier that morning. To shade her face from the sun she had donned a large-brimmed straw bonnet, the blue ribbons of which she had tied in a charming bow aside the delicate lines of her jaw.

"I suppose we'll have to find you a nice, gentle mount," Jeff teased as he cast a glance toward her. "Now be sure and tell me when you've had enough of riding and want to return home. I wouldn't want to tire you overmuch when I have every intention of involving you in some further activity tonight."

Raelynn caressed the arm through which she had looped her own and released a worried sigh. "I haven't been riding in so long a time, Jeffrey, I fear my tiring will come sooner than later. You just may have to call for the carriage to fetch me home."

"Never fear, madam. I shall attend you perfectly well *without* a carriage."

Raelynn glanced up at him with a brow arched inquisitively, but Jeff was quite willing to let her remain in the dark. Offering no explanations, he swept her along the path toward the stables.

The white, clapboard structure was reminiscent of an enormous dog-trot cabin replete with a high-pitched roof and a wide passageway that ran down the middle of it and opened to the outside when the doors at both ends were folded back. Behind and to the sides of the barn lay more than a hundred acres of gently rolling meadow upon which the horses were pastured behind white board fencing.

Individual paddocks had been set aside for the stallions. Even from a distance, these fine steeds gave every appearance of being extraordinary animals of remarkable energy and flashy strides. Raelynn soon learned that her husband had culled most of them within the last three years from the best breeding farms in Ireland and England.

"When I began to restore Oakley," Jeff murmured

thoughtfully, idly slapping a crop against the top of his boot as they wandered past the paddocks, "most of my attention was devoted to laying out the areas best suited for the different crops, yet even then, I nurtured an unquenchable desire to have the plantation known one day as much for its fine horses as its productive fields."

"You'll succeed," Raelynn assured him with unrestrained confidence. She was certain her husband could achieve any goal to which he set his heart and mind, for she sensed within him a strength and determination that she had rarely glimpsed. Her father had been of similar resolve. Even after his imprisonment, he had been confident that right would prevail. Perhaps it would one day, for she had no doubt that he had been innocent of all the treasonous deeds he had been accused, but exoneration would do him little good now that he was moldering in the grave. It would only be his offspring who would revel in his name being restored to the honor it once held when he had been known unquestionably as a faithful servant of the king.

Glancing about, she realized that Jeff's vision of an outstanding collection of horses could already be glimpsed in the fine, arched necks and prancing gait of the foals trotting alongside their mothers. It was also evident that his ambition was contagious, for the grooms and handlers labored at their tasks as if they owned a sizable stake in the breeding farm. They clearly took pride in their accomplishments.

Upon entering the stables, Raelynn became immediately impressed with its neatness. Except for the equipment presently in use, everything was in its place and had either been oiled, cleaned or brushed. The huge outer doors had been folded back at each end earlier that morning, allowing breezes to sweep through the entire length of the stable. Even on a warm day, the circulation of air and the large, fenced trees shading the barn would keep the interior reasonably cool, not only for the animals in their stalls, but for the men at their work.

The floors throughout were of hard-packed clay covered with a thick layer of shavings from the Birminghams' lumber mill. A clean, fresh scent pervaded the place, due in part to the mulch and the breezes, but also to the small amounts of lime that had been mixed in with the bedding to control the odors.

Here again, trainers and grooms were hard at work, either readying two- and three-year-olds for their morning workout or cleaning stalls and bathing horses. Some of the men tipped their hats politely to her while others grinned either broadly or sheepishly, whatever the particular disposition of the man. Again Raelynn's mind spun beneath the avalanche of names that descended upon her. Still, she recalled the anxious employee who had met her husband upon his return to the stable after the latter had raced his black stallion, Brutus, across the countryside at a breakneck pace in an effort to ease his frustration with her. That incident had happened almost a fortnight ago, shortly after she had announced that she needed some time to consider Nell's accusations before she could willingly yield to his husbandly right to consummate their marriage vows.

"Sparky, here, is one of my trainers," Jeff announced, identifying the one she had heard that particular night. The young man had snatched off a scruffy hat in polite deference to her gender and proceeded to crush it between large, calloused hands as he cast shy glances toward her. "Sparky keeps the horses in line for me, including Brutus who is without question the orneriest beast I've yet ridden. I've sworn at times that Sparky's mother must have whelped him on the back of a steed. He has a natural way of handling horses that makes it look a lot easier than it really is."

The trainer waggled his bright red head as a ruddy hue infused his freckled cheeks, but his wide grin clearly evidenced his pleasure over his employer's praise. "There you go again, Mr. Jeffrey, raisin' everybody's expectations o' me. You're gonna get me into an awful heap o' trouble one o' these days, talkin' the way you do. Soon folks'll be expectin' me ta do miracles or somethin'."

"Never fear, Sparky," Raelynn consoled him cheerily. "I shall expect nothing more from you than what I see you do with my own eyes. Is that fair enough?"

"Yas'm, Miz Raelynn, that's real fair," he agreed with an eager nod.

"It's nice to make your acquaintance, Sparky," she assured him warmly. "Now tell me, if a lady were to ask you to find her a very noble horse among the steeds my husband owns, which one would you choose?"

A small, wiry individual with bowed legs and a broad grin scurried in from outside before Sparky could answer. Inclining his head in greeting first to Raelynn and then to Jeff, the older man spoke with the lilt of his native Ireland. "Ah, sir, I see ye've brought yer pretty missus ta have a look at yer fine collection of steeds, eh? An' there's yerself, sir, lookin' for all the world like the mouse what chewed a hole ta the grain." He cackled gleefully as the others laughed, and then, squinting an eye toward Jeff, queried, "Would ye be a-thinkin' o' takin' yer missus out for a ride on Kelton this fine day, sir? Ta be sure, the mare would give yer lady a nice, smooth ride, that she would."

"Gerald O'Malley is in charge of the breeding program," Jeff explained. "Several years ago he came over with the studs and brood mares I had purchased in Ireland. Under his care, the horses endured the voyage without suffering any harm. He has been proving his worth ever since. I couldn't do without him."

The elder's face compressed into a multitude of wrinkles as he grinned at her. "O'Malley be what folks call me, missus. If'n ye're o' a mind, I'd be honored if ye'd be doing the same."

"Of course, O'Malley." Smiling, Raelynn tipped her head to indicate her compliance, and then cast a glance down the long row of stalls. "But tell me, O'Malley, where is this mare, Kelton, you mentioned? Is she here in the stable?"

Jeff gestured behind her. "Kelton is a nice, gentle mount. Very level-headed and sure-footed. If you think you need a horse to take care of you, then she'll certainly do that for you."

" 'At will be Kelton, all right," the Irishman agreed with a chortle. "Takes her time, she does, but she'll be gettin' there in the end wit' no undue fuss along the way. Aye, that she will."

Raelynn wasn't overly thrilled with all the reassurances she was receiving. There was such a thing as being too well-broke, which usually meant *boring*. A quick glance into the stall where the mare stood lazily scratching her neck against one of the supporting timbers left visions of the two of them plodding lazily along far behind Jeff and his steed. Peering askance at her grinning husband, who she was beginning to suspect was finding some humor in her apparent aversion, Raelynn smiled gingerly. "A small measure of excitement wouldn't go unappreciated, Jeffrey. I've ridden before and don't need to be babied."

Curbing his grin, Jeff faced his young trainer. "The lady asked your opinion, Sparky. Which steed would you choose for her?"

Jeff's amusement had already proven contagious, and Sparky was eager to contribute some of his own wit. "Well, suh, there's always Ariadne. Your lady would see some *real* spunk with that orn . . ."

"Where is she?" Raelynn asked without waiting for him to finish.

Sparky gulped at her readiness to chance such a ride and, now more than a bit apprehensive, glanced toward Jeff, whose change of countenance lent visual evidence of his sudden concern. Warily the trainer pointed toward the third stall down the aisle, and before Jeff could object, Raelynn hurried toward it. As she stepped near, a fine, high-headed, liver-chestnut mare of perhaps three years snorted and shied away from the bars of her domain.

"Is this the one?"

"None other than Ariadne," her husband acknowledged reluctantly.

Raelynn tilted her head aslant as she looked back at him. "As in Greek lore?"

"Aye, the daughter who was turned to gold by her father, King Midas."

"Is the mare truly a treasure?"

"She has the bloodlines to make an excellent brood mare," Jeff acknowledged. "But she's spirited and not easily ridden, definitely not by novices."

"She's beautiful," Raelynn replied with a measure of awe as she reached a hand through the bars of the stall. The mare snorted and danced back instantly, but as Raelynn's slow, coaxing voice encouraged her, the animal tossed her fine head and paced forward cautiously, obviously curious. Murmuring softly, Raelynn stroked the velvety nose as Ariadne stood very still and blinked her large eyes, relishing the attention and the soothing tones. "I wish I had an apple to give you, Ariadne, but if you'd let me ride you today, I promise to bring you one after we return. Would you like that?"

Blowing into the extended palm, the mare arched her elegant neck and nickered softly, drawing laughter from Raelynn. Pleased that she was making progress, she continued stroking the steed even as she became mindful of her husband's approach.

"I don't think you should ride Ariadne," he announced with measured care. "She's high-strung and can't be trusted. Quite simply, madam, I don't want you to get hurt."

"Riding was one of my greatest pleasures before my

family's fortunes changed so drastically, Jeffrey. We not only lost our home and all our possessions, we had to stand and watch our horses being led away by the king's stable hands. We were told that they would be given to the men who had brought evidence of treason against my father once their claims were verified. Regrettably he died before his trial, and the accusations against him were allowed to stand."

Jeff understood only too well how a magnificent animal like Ariadne could placate a distressed soul and heal it of past hurts. Consolingly he laid an arm around his wife's shoulders and drew her near. "Perhaps Ariadne will be a better mount for you once she has been worked for several more months. She needs to learn some manners before she can be trusted."

Raelynn gazed up at him pleadingly. "But couldn't I exercise her today while we're out riding?"

"She'll get all the exercise she needs, madam, but with the trainers, at least until she starts behaving herself. We can decide later if she's fit for you."

"But she seems perfectly suited for me now," Raelynn cajoled. "She came to me readily enough and seems quite gentle."

"Nevertheless, madam, I must stand by my decision. I'll not chance your getting thrown, perhaps even seriously injured. You're too precious to me."

Raelynn doubted that any amount of pleading would make her husband change his mind. He knew the mare far better than she, and she had to respect him for doing what he considered right under the circumstances, no matter how disappointed she might be. After all, this was no weak-willed individual she had married. He was considerate and kind, far more than the men whom she had casually known in her lifetime, yet he wasn't at all reluctant to deny her request when he thought it prudent.

Realizing that she hadn't yet asked his opinion, Raelynn peered up at him from underneath the brim of her bonnet as her lips curved upward flirtatiously at the corners. "So which steed would you suggest I ride, Jeffrey?"

He smiled, relieved that she hadn't become miffed by his refusal to yield to her pleas. "I have in mind a nice-tempered gelding that I'm sure you'll enjoy taking out for your first tour of the area."

Lifting his head, Jeff gestured to O'Malley. "Saddle Stargazer with the sidesaddle Miss Heather uses when she comes."

" 'At I'll be doin' right away, sir," the Irishman answered and scurried off to do his employer's bidding.

Several moments later, Raelynn gasped in pure delight as O'Malley led a tall, handsome bay from the last stall on the right. Raelynn couldn't remember ever seeing a gelding so striking. His neck was wonderfully arched, his ears small and pointed inward, his head and large eyes seemingly without flaw. But that was hardly the best of it, for the animal seemed to literally dance sideways down the aisle, elevating his hocks in a flashy, high-stepping gait.

"Oh, Jeffrey, he's gorgeous!"

"I thought you might like him. He's got a lot of action in his gait, but he minds well and is very gentle with Heather."

"Would ye be wantin' Brutus saddled, sir?" the elder queried.

"I'd like to enjoy the ride with my wife today, O'Malley, instead of cursing that beast from here to hell and back again. Saddle Majestic for me, if you please."

The wiry man grinned and touched his brow in a brisk salute. "Right away, sir."

A short time later, Jeff lifted Raelynn to the back of Stargazer and then swung up onto the handsome stallion that had been readied for him. They rode away from the stables but, upon espying Cora waiting near the house with a basket and an old cotton quilt slung over her arms, they reined their steeds to a halt near the housekeeper.

The black woman grinned up at her master. "Ah thought yo'd be agreeable ta havin' a picnic somewhere, Mistah Jeffery, so's ah packed this here satchel wit' lemon cake, fried chicken, corn fritters, an' de lak. Dere's even some chilled lemonade in a corked jug if'n yo' gets thirsty. Maybe today it'll even stay cool for a change." Cora glanced about and drew in a deep breath, as if savoring the fragrance of the day. "Yo' sho' picked a fine day ta take off from work, Mistah Jeffrey. Ain't many days yo've given yo'self ta relax lately, so's I figgered yo' is well deservin' o' some time off ta enjoy a picnic."

"Cora, you're a dream," Jeff declared with a chuckle as he dismounted. Taking the items from her, he secured them behind Raelynn's sidesaddle before swinging up on the stallion again.

Reining Majestic alongside the prancing gelding, Jeff took his wife past the crops closest to the grounds of the main house, letting her see the plants from which cotton was harvested. The bolls were still green, but Jeff dismounted, cut one open, and allowed her to view what was inside. In the weeks to come the cotton would be maturing, the pods would be opening, and the field hands would be sent out to pluck the white fluff from its sharp nest, no easy task when the bolls pricked nearly every finger bloody and the broiling sun beat down upon their backs.

The couple progressed to the rice fields, and there Raelynn saw acres of land flooded over with water, creating the essential conditions and nutrients to produce a bountiful crop. From there, they traversed along a winding lane, looking over fields, one where a small herd of cattle grazed and, nearby, another where cornstalks had grown taller than a man. They rode leisurely on for another pair of hours and, upon passing through a wooded copse, finally halted near a live oak which dominated a knoll beside a sunlit stream. The tree's widely spreading, gracefully draping limbs not only furnished abundant shade for the area but also provided a protective screen around the tree.

Jeff swung down and came around the back of the gelding to sweep Raelynn off its back. Holding his wife clasped within his arms, he let her slide down the length of his body until his parting lips snared hers. For a long moment he kissed her without reserve, and when he finally relented and tried to set Raelynn to her feet, she refused to stand alone. Sighing dreamily, she leaned against him, seeming as weak as a rag doll. Jeff did the only sensible thing and laid her over his shoulder, drawing giggles as he fondled her very fetching backside through the cloth of her gown. When he freed the ties securing the quilt and basket, he slipped his free arm beneath them and gathered them up within the crook of his elbow.

Taking his burdens to a spot beneath the wide canopy of moss-draped limbs, Jeff lowered the leather pouches to the ground before whipping the quilt around and spreading it out, at least as much as he was able while still holding Raelynn. He kicked the curled and rumpled corners flat with a booted toe, and then leaned forward to lower his giggling wife to the quilt. Smiling at her with eyes glinting puckishly, he bent near with a suggestion. " 'Tis a perfect spot for sporting on a quilt, don't you agree, my sweet?"

" 'Twould truly seem that way," Raelynn agreed, smiling coyly. His opening mouth lowered, almost covering hers until she added, "The food smells wonderful though. Shall we eat now? I'm starving."

Jeff growled in mock anger. "You, madam, are definitely an imp."

When he sat back upon his heels, she immediately followed and, bracing up on her knees, gave him a kiss that fairly fanned his imagination, encouraging him to reach out to take her to him again, but, with a mischievous little laugh, Raelynn wiggled away. Catching her bottom lip between her teeth, she peered at him with eyes sparkling with delight as she doffed her bonnet and tossed it aside. Then she promptly presented her back and began unpacking the basket.

"You little tease," Jeff accused, reaching out to pinch her buttock.

"Ouch!" she cried and tossed back an exaggerated pout. "You bruised me."

"Let me see," he urged and sought to lift her skirts. A swat on his knuckles drew nothing more than a deep chuckle from him. It hardly discouraged him. Reaching out, he drew his wife back upon his lap and cupped a round breast possessively. "Now I have you, vixen, and this time you won't get away."

Raelynn tilted her head aside accommodatingly and closed her eyes in sublime pleasure as he nibbled at her neck and brushed his fingers across a nipple until it grew taut beneath her gown. Deftly he plucked open the fasteners at the back of the garment and began pulling it over her head.

"What about the food?" she breathed in a trembling sigh as his hands slid upward from her waist to encompass the swelling mounds.

"We'll eat later," he whispered near her ear, unfastening the tiny buttons running down the front of her chemise. Her undergarments followed the way of her gown, allowing his hands to roam unhindered. In the bright, scintillating flashes of light reflecting off the water, her naked breasts looked unusually pale beneath his darkly bronzed fingers, much as they had done earlier that morning, yet they warmed readily to his attention. He grew bolder still as his hands wandered downward, snatching her breath in pleasurable gasps as she yielded herself in rapturous awe to his whim.

They finally went on to savor other things, the food that Cora had packed and, some time later, the nearby stream into which Jeff led Raelynn. They approached it as naked as the day they had been born, but he was a lot more comfortable about that fact than Raelynn was. She had never ventured past the doors of a bedroom in a state of nudity before and was timid about going into the open areas surrounding the stream. Yet when Jeff swam away from her, leaving her safely near shore, she waded farther out into the deeper water.

"Come, love," he bade from the middle of the stream. "The water is nice out here."

"I can't swim," she confessed, never having imagined herself being devoid of clothes outdoors, much less being naked in a pool of water.

Jeff's lips curved in a devilish grin. "Well, I guess I'll just have to throw you out into the deep and see how quickly you can tread water."

"You wouldn't dare!" she gasped and, seeing the knavish glint in his eyes, quickly turned toward shore, not at all willing to trust him. She squealed in sudden distress as she heard him swimming rapidly toward her and glanced back to confirm her fears. He was definitely approaching a lot faster than she could trudge through the water. In growing anxiety, she renewed her efforts to reach dry land, which to her horror now seemed an ocean's length away.

Suddenly Jeff's arm swept around her waist, and she was dragged back against a long, muscular body where she was snugly imprisoned by an encompassing arm. His hips and thighs formed a chair for her buttocks as his free hand moved over the tempting curves of her body. "Now I have you, wench."

Raelynn was nearly frantic. "Please, Jeffrey, don't throw me out into the deep water. I'll go under for sure, and what will all the servants think when they see me with my hair dangling wet around my ears? They'll be suspicious, for sure."

"Never fear, my love," he breathed, nibbling at her ear. "I just want to hold you again for a while. It isn't often that I get to see you stripped bare in the full light of the sun."

Laughing in relief, Raelynn jabbed him in the ribs with an elbow. "Beast! What you really wanted was to see me panic."

"Aye, I like the way your breasts bounce when you're trying to run through water," he teased with a chuckle. "But I really would like to teach you how to swim. . . ."

She stiffened apprehensively. "Jeffrey Birmingham, if you throw me in, I'll never forgive you."

"I don't intend to, madam. Just lean back and relax in the safety of my arms," he coaxed. "I won't let you go until you know how to float on your back. Then I'll see about teaching you how to swim."

"My hair will get wet," she fretted aloud.

"We'll sneak into the house when no one is looking."

Relenting, she leaned her head back against his shoulder. "You can be very sly when you want your way, sir."

"When I want you, my love, I can be downright devious," he breathed, nibbling at her ear.

Cautiously she gave herself over into his supporting arms and allowed him to hold her as she floated on the surface of the water. Jeff's grin became increasingly lecherous as he perused the sights. Never before had he seen such a delectable view, two ripe melons and an island of reddish brush floating in a calm sea beneath a bright sun. Until now, the like of such scenes had been strictly evoked in dreams, not right beneath his very nose. It was not to say, however, that he hadn't indulged in a few fantasies of his own creation in his lifetime.

It wasn't long before Raelynn actually began stroking through water without aid. Jeff hovered near for the sake of safety, at least until he realized the fair skin was taking on a pinkish cast. Then he began scrambling toward her in anxious haste.

"We'd better get you dressed, madam, or you'll be

howling your head off in pain. I only hope it's not too late."

"Call a carriage," Raelynn groaned, feeling weighted down by iron bands as she waded out of the water. "I don't think I can get back into the saddle again for a whole month. My backside definitely feels as if it has turned to stone."

Jeff swept her up into his arms. "No need for a carriage, madam. I'll drape the quilt across in front of me to provide some cushioning for you and take you home on the back of Stargazer."

Raelynn smiled contentedly as she pressed her brow against his cheek. "You can attend me, sir, anytime you wish to."

"Promise?"

"Promise."

Raelynn was already wincing by the time they arrived home, but not necessarily from the aftermath of the sun, rather from the hours she had spent in the side-saddle. She refused to call Tizzy to help her bathe, envisioning the shame she'd suffer once the girl became aware of her problem. Without a doubt, every part of her was tinged beyond her normal fair coloring. Thus she relied upon Jeff to assist her. He did so tenderly, first bathing her in tepid water, rubbing a soothing balm over her skin, and then, afterwards, massaging her aching muscles and the bruised posterior.

"I suppose this means I won't be taking you to the Sunday social," he mused aloud in droll humor as he plied her backside with a cooling ointment. He fought a battle to subdue his laughter. "By then, you should be able to pass as a brown-skinned Mohican or perhaps even a toad with all the freckles that are bound to appear. You know, you should probably resign yourself to the fact that your once flawless skin won't ever be the same."

Jeff could restrain himself no longer, and his laughter burst forth as if with a will of its own, prompting Raelynn to toss a glare over her shoulder. "Jeffrey Birmingham, you're making light of all this, despite the fact that I'm simply mortified by my present predicament. I can neither stand, sit, nor lie down with any reasonable comfort, and yet you're guffawing like you've never seen anything funnier. Believe me, sir, if I had my wits entirely together, I'd find some way to leave your chambers and seek seclusion in mine."

"Preen your feathers, my pretty dove," he cajoled, leaning near to nuzzle her cheek. "I'll still love you no matter what color you are or how spotted you may get."

At that, Raelynn seized a pillow and swung it with all her might into the grinning face of her husband who stumbled back in uproarious mirth. Diligently she tried to curb her own amusement, but it slipped out until she was laughing as hard as he. Never had the house rang with such merriment before, but Jeff had every hope and expectation that in the months and years to come, there would be much more of it to nurture their hearts and minds.

6&

𝒥t was a very proud Jeffrey Birmingham who escorted his fetchingly garbed wife through the doors of the church and into the pew where Heather, Brandon, and their three-year-old son, Beau, were already seated. The young tike broke out into a wide grin when he espied his uncle and quickly scooted around his mother and Raelynn in his haste to climb onto the elder's lap.

"Unc' Jeff, yo' wanta see my frog?" the youngster whispered confidentially, his blue eyes searching the face above his own as he thrust a small hand into the pocket of his linen jacket. "I gots it hidden where Mama can't see."

Clasping a hand to the boy's back, Jeff leaned forward and grinned at his sister-in-law, whose expression grew increasingly perplexed as she tried to determine just what was going on. She recognized that particular gleam in her brother-in-law's eyes only too well; she had seen it numerous times. Mischief was brewing, she had no doubt.

In the next instant, her sapphire-blue eyes widened in horror as her son thrust a frog beneath his uncle's nose. To make matters worse, it croaked rather loudly, drawing the attention of the whole congregation. Twittering laughter quickly erupted from the onlookers who, in amused curiosity, craned their necks to see what would follow. Seeing the need to intervene, Heather promptly readjusted her lace shawl in an effort to conceal her child-bearing state and sought to push herself to her feet.

By now, Brandon had become apprised of the situation and, laying a large hand upon his wife's arm, gently urged her back into the pew. "Never mind, love," he soothed with a soft chortle. "I'll take care of the frog *and* our son."

After making his way around the front pews, Brandon approached the end of the bench where his brother sat with the boy. He leaned near Jeff's ear to whisper, "I should let you handle this matter since you'll probably be needing practice in the not-too-distant future."

"Shouldn't I be instructed by example first?" Jeff inquired mutedly through a grin as the other lifted Beau from his lap. "I'll grant you, there's a lot to learn, but you should be an expert by now."

Brandon offered him a grin. "If this next one is a girl, I'll have to start learning all over again. Hatti swears boys and girls are as different as day and night."

Reflectively Jeff pursed his lips until he nodded. "That's good to know. Just think of the confusion it would create if we weren't able to tell male from female at birth. Life would certainly prove boring after that."

"Dear brother, I wasn't referring to the differences in our anatomy," Brandon corrected with a pained grin. "I was talking about dispositions."

The younger flicked a forefinger back and forth between the two of them. "You mean the difference between our personalities?"

Brandon heaved an exaggerated sigh. "Has anyone ever told you how exasperating you can be?"

"Well, as a matter of fact, you have, on a regular basis."

"Obviously my complaints have never settled down into that hard head of yours," the elder quipped.

Jeff grinned puckishly. "Are you talking about mine?"

"Who else's, Wart?"

Held in the child's tenacious grasp, the frog croaked all the way down the aisle, drawing applause and hilarious laughter from nearly everyone who was aware of the happenings. Raelynn giggled behind a handkerchief and glanced aside at Heather who could only smile and shake her head.

Once order had been restored, the service began with Reverend Parsons making an effort to appear unaffected. He cleared his throat and glanced around until silence prevailed. "We'll be singing a hymn now," he announced with a measure of calm, "but before we do, I would suggest that the one who was making an effort to sing, kindly restrain himself so the rest of us can find some enjoyment in the song. I'm afraid he sounded like an ol' bullfrog."

Uproarious laughter filled the church as Brandon muttered jovially, "Amen!"

Once the sermon had been concluded and the congregation was dismissed, folks began gathering outdoors. The elderly Mrs. Abegail Clark made her way across the yard with the help of her long parasol, which she used primarily as a walking cane.

"Jeffrey Birmingham," she called, commanding his attention, "I'm dreadfully put out with you for not bringing your lovely bride over to my house and making us acquainted. And here I thought you loved me."

"Oh, I do, love, I do!" He swept off his top hat and

placed it over his heart as if to swear an undying truth. "You're the light of my eyes, the nurturing warmth of my heart. . . ."

"Fiddledeedee, you young whippersnapper!" she retorted with a chuckle and lifted the tip end of her cane to indicate Raelynn. "Now introduce us before I grow even more vexed with you."

Gallantly Jeff swept her a courtly bow and performed the honors. "My lady, may I present my lovely wife, Raelynn, to you and all others within hearing distance." He faced the beauty at his side and smiled into her eyes as he took her slender hand. "My love, this feisty dowager is Abegail Clark, an old friend of the family. She all but adopted my mother, Catherine, while she was still alive."

Raelynn sank into a gracious curtsey before the elder. "A pleasure, madam."

"Nay, girl, the pleasure is all mine," the elder assured her kindly. "I've been waiting some years to see who this young gallant would choose for a wife, and though I've heard rumors of the difficulties you've had to face since your arrival, it's obvious you've weathered them amazingly well and have come through no worse for them. May I extend a fond welcome to the Carolinas, my dear, and a blessing that God may watch over you and keep you safe and happy through a long and fruitful life."

Taking the initiative, Raelynn stepped forward and gently pressed her cheek against the one that had grown wrinkled through the years. "Thank you, Mrs. Clark. I shall hope that I prove worthy of your expectations."

Mrs. Clark hurriedly blinked at the tears that gathered in her eyes and, upon clearing her throat, glanced around to find herself in the midst of the Birminghams, one and all. Eagerly she stretched out a hand to Heather, drawing the younger woman quickly forward. "So good to see you, child. It has been a couple of weeks since you were last here. I was afraid you might be suffering some difficulties with the child you're now carrying. Have you been well?"

"Oh, yes, of course, Mrs. Clark," Heather reassured her, smiling radiantly. "Beau had a slight fever last week, that's all, and of course, you heard about the commotion the week before.

"Mr. Fridrich, you mean." The older woman clucked her tongue in distaste. "He's a brute, that one."

"Thanks to him, none of us got any sleep until everyone was at home safe and sound. Once the ordeal was over, we could hardly hold our eyes open." Heather cast a mischievous glance toward her handsome husband. "Reverend Parsons would surely have thought bullfrogs had invaded the church if Brandon had started snoring during the service."

Her husband's jaw descended forthwith in a fair imitation of one who had been shocked out of his senses, evoking the laughter of his family and friends. "Madam, I protest. You accuse me unjustly. I don't snore."

Heather rolled her eyes in feigned disbelief and, lifting her hand before Mrs. Clark, measured off a degree by bringing her thumb and forefinger slowly together. She cringed in mock fear as Brandon stalked near, but she quickly burst into giggles as he caught an arm about her shoulders and, with a growl, threatened to take a bite out of her slender nape, much to the hilarity of those who watched.

"Unc' Jeff," Beau said, leaning his head far back and squinting up at the tall man. "Will yo' help me catch 'nother frog? Pa made me turn the other one loose so's I could go back inta church."

Jeff passed his hat to Raelynn and, bending down, swooped the youngster into his arms. "Maybe your pa will bring you over and let you look for one in the pond near my house. You can catch plenty of them over there, but you must promise me that you won't bring them into church again. They like ponds and the outdoors, and that's the best place to keep them."

"But they'll get 'way from me out there."

"It wouldn't be hard to catch another . . . anytime you want to. Promise?"

The boy lifted doleful, black-lashed blue eyes to his uncle. "Guess so, Unc' Jeff."

A sudden realization struck Jeff, and in some astonishment, he looked past the boy's head, claiming his brother's attention. "Beau has blue eyes! But I thought they were . . ."

"Green?" Heather queried, stealing the word from his mouth. She laughed and, turning her head slightly, peered at Jeff saucily from around the brim of her bonnet. "They've been blue for more than three years now. I thought you'd have noticed by now."

"But they *were* green, weren't they?"

Grinning, Brandon thrust out his chin, indicating his fetching wife. "I swear she talked to the fairies and coaxed them into changing the color of Beau's eyes. If you're satisfied with the way you look, you'd better watch her tricks. Next thing you know she'll be turning yours blue."

Heather grinned contentedly as she faced Jeff. "I wouldn't dare tell your brother that he was mistaken about the color." She wrinkled her nose and playfully winced as Brandon snorted like a cantankerous bull. "Truth is, babies' eyes have a way of changing in the first year. What we thought were green eyes were just blue ones in the making."

The Birminghams and Abegail Clark laughed in hearty amusement at Heather's simple logic. As she glanced around at the cheerful faces that surrounded her, she shrugged girlishly. It was the tantalizing little grin she wore that prompted Brandon to dismiss the fact that they were standing within full view of nearly the whole congregation. Drawing her near, he bestowed a kiss upon her suddenly gaping mouth.

Hurriedly pulling away, Heather glanced around in some embarrassment to find several, normally beady-eyed spinsters now gawking in astonishment. "Brandon, people are watching. Behave yourself."

Nevertheless when Brandon cast a smile toward the trio of old maids and drew her back with an arm about her shoulders, she leaned against him with a grin that was nearly dazzling. Her compliance certainly caused the three onlookers to raise their brows and glance knowingly at each other.

As for Raelynn, she had found the show of affection between her in-laws quite refreshing and felt led to slip her hand within Jeff's as she lifted a loving smile to him. No words were exchanged as his eyes searched hers, but had he asked, she would have found explanations beyond her ability. She was just simply glad that she was part of the Birmingham clan.

≈IT WAS TOWARD THE END OF SEPTEMBER WHEN THE final fitting for Raelynn's ball gown was scheduled to take place. Knowing that Nell would be working at Farrell's shop, no doubt with her new son in close proximity, Jeff utilized every precaution within his capability to prevent a confrontation between the young seamstress and his wife. Thus, he did the only sensible thing a gentleman could do under the circumstances and that was to set aside some time to escort Raelynn to the shop himself rather than merely having Thaddeus drive her in. Upon their arrival, he was greatly relieved when he learned that Nell had asked for the day off to run errands. He could only hope that she would decide to leave the area for good. As much as the idea might have distressed her, he never wanted to see her again.

Men were not allowed in the fitting rooms, a fact which left Jeff nearly champing at the bit as he waited for Raelynn to reappear. A whole wardrobe of clothes and other accouterments had been ordered for the fall season for her, and he began to chafe at the prospect of having to bide his time through many tedious fittings, especially since he seemed to be the only male customer on the premises. He was definitely surprised and relieved when Raelynn came out garbed in the shimmering ball gown. As he watched with a feeling of awe, she seemed to float across the room toward the mirror to which Elizabeth had directed her.

"Close your mouth," Farrell advised with a grin as he came to stand beside Jeff. "And for heaven's sakes, man, pick up your jaw."

"Beautiful!" Jeff breathed, seemingly in a daze as his eyes swept down the length of her.

"Of course," the couturier replied and proudly polished his nails on his lapel. "I designed it."

Jeff pointedly arched a brow as he gave his friend a sidelong stare. "I meant my wife, Fancy Man."

Farrell shrugged nonchalantly, never losing his affected aplomb. "Well, that's true of her, too, of course. In fact, it's hard to say which is lovelier. Nevertheless, your wife's beauty has definitely been magnified by my creation. She has the kind of form that would complement a shroud. She's tall, slender and moves like a dream. . . ."

"Stop drooling," Jeff cautioned, bestowing upon the man an outrageously indignant glare that should have belied the twinkle in his eye. "She's spoken for."

"Yes, well, I've been trying to remind myself of that fact for the last few weeks and have decided I should take your advice. . . ."

"What advice is that, pray tell?"

"I shall be escorting Elizabeth to your ball." He looked askance at Jeff in time to see a grin break across his face. "Do you mind?"

"Well, I'll be damned!"

"In that case, perhaps I shouldn't," Farrell replied, stretching his neck above his collar as he straightened his handsomely tailored frockcoat. "I wouldn't want you to be cast into hell or anything like that, Jeffrey."

The green eyes danced with puckish humor. "It's long overdue, my friend, but I'm relieved to hear that you're finally making use of that ol' noggin of yours. I thought it was good for something. I just didn't know exactly what until now."

The couturier cleared his throat, uneasy about making certain confessions. "Actually, I've taken Elizabeth out a time or two for dinner since you were last here, Jeffrey. On business, of course. What with our past difficulties, that excuse seemed the best way to get her to accept my invitations." The clothier flicked his brows upward as he revealed a past astonishment. "What I hadn't expected to confront was the audacity of some men to openly ogle her while she was with me. Believe me, Jeffrey, I saw more than the usual froth running down their jowls, which, by the way, I grew increasingly desirous of punching."

"Meaning you saw a threat of your talented assistant being stolen away and led to the altar by an infatuated swain?" Jeff prodded, amusement shining in his eyes.

Taking offense, Farrell ran a finger beneath the band of his collar at his nape, as if he now found it too tight. "Dammit, Jeffrey, you make it sound as if I'd court Elizabeth or even marry her merely to save my business from certain disaster."

"You mean you wouldn't?"

A cantankerous snort evidenced Farrell's irritation. "You make me out to be a conniving scoundrel, Jeffrey, and that's not the way of it at all. Elizabeth is a damn good-looking woman whom I've admired for some years now. Of all the young fillies I've ever courted, there isn't one among them who can compare. It just finally dawned on me that I've been letting hurtful memories of past years dictate my actions even as late as last month. As yet, I'm not sure that she would appreciate any attempt on my part to ease our relationship into something less formal than employer and employee, but I think it would be much more relaxing and enjoyable to set my sights on the dove in my own back yard rather than trying to pluck the feathers off the neighbors' chickens."

"Smooth your ruffled nape, my friend. I'm just delighted to hear of your change of heart. Two months ago you were still gazing past her, or at least you seemed to be. It's a relief to know you've become more short-sighted."

"Short-sighted, hell. I'm nigh cross-eyed. I didn't realize she was so much underfoot before. It's somewhat like looking at the end of my nose."

"And you don't appreciate that," Jeff vocally deduced.

"Hell and damnation, Jeffrey, you can be as vexing as a ten-foot alligator. I didn't say that."

Jeff was growing more perplexed by the moment. "Then what *are* you saying, Fancy Man?"

The couturier sighed in exasperation, not at all sure he could explain it all well enough. "Elizabeth has been so close at hand all this time, it never really dawned on me what I was doing until recently."

Jeff searched for enlightenment. "Meaning that you've mainly been ignoring her?"

"Nooo," Farrell fussed. "You should know better than that, having been the bachelor for so long. I know well enough that you were no different than I am now. I saw the way you'd size up a woman when she wasn't even aware of you looking at her. Bachelors can't seem to help themselves. Maybe it's something instinctive, or the fact that appeasement doesn't come that often unless a man gets desperate enough to seek out harlots, but I've never been led that way. Nor do I think you were. When a good-looking woman comes within view, we can mentally strip 'em, dissect 'em, and bed 'em all in a matter of a moment, at times without being completely aware of what we're doing. I didn't have to search for a better looking female to use as a standard by which I could judge all the other women. Elizabeth was here all this time, which made it easy for me to compare others to her, but, by the same token, I was so used to having her around, I never realized I was going through the same mental scenario many more times with her than all the others put together. Strip her, dissect her, and bed her . . . all in my mind. Emory put a name to it." Farrell shook his head as if aghast at himself. "Coveting. That's what I was doing long before she ever became a widow, and I wanted to hit the man for telling me that."

"What are you going to do about it now?"

Farrell blew out his breath in frustration. "That, Jeffrey me dearie, is what pickled the pig on the poker. It's damned frustrating, but I don't know if I *can* do anything about it."

Jeff cocked a wondering brow as he considered the couturier. His friend hadn't been blind after all, just wary of old grudges, and what would follow, no one could predict.

☞LATE THAT AFTERNOON THE LANDAU PULLED UP IN FRONT of Oakley house to allow the master and mistress of the manse to alight. Shortly after Jeff handed Raelynn down and the conveyance pulled away, their attention was promptly snared by an angry voice that seemed to be coming from the back of the house.

"An' ah says, yo' ain't gots no business bein' here, Missy. All yo' wants ta do is make mo' trouble for Mistah Jeffrey. Ah knows dat for a fact, jes' like ah knows what yo' did nigh ta a year ago. Now yo' takes yo'self off afore de mastah comes home an' finds yo' skulkin' 'round dis place like some no-account white trash."

Recognizing the butler's voice, Raelynn looked up at Jeff in acute surprise, thoroughly astonished by the servant's harsh tones. Kingston was usually the very soul of propriety and unswerving patience, yet at present, his gruff voice was filled with outrage. "Who in the world can Kingston be talking to like that, Jeffrey?"

Her husband's lean cheeks had darkened perceptively, and his eyes had taken on a cold glitter that chilled her to the bone. Facing her, he clasped her arms and, meeting her gaze directly, bade firmly, "Wait here, Raelynn. I'll tend to this."

She nodded hesitantly, reluctantly committing herself to staying behind while he faced another confrontation, which had similar qualities of that night wherein Gustav and his ruffians had forced their way into Oakley. Except that this time, it was obviously a woman . . . or, perhaps more accurately, a girl by the name of Nell, making trouble.

Worriedly Raelynn chewed at a bottom lip as her eyes followed Jeff around the end of the house. She could only wonder how he would handle the situation. If he were the debaucher as Nell had claimed, would he reveal that fact? Or would he skillfully hide his involvement in the form of outrage?

A moment later, Raelynn started abruptly as she heard him bark in irate tones.

"Just why in the devil have you come out here?"

"Oh, Jeffrey, I've been waiting for you for nearly an hour now," a feminine voice complained sweetly. "I was beginning to think I'd have to leave, what with Kingston talkin' to me so mean-like. I knew you'd be wonderin' about our son, and I just wanted to show him to you. I named him Daniel after me pa. I hope you don't mind."

Raelynn clutched a trembling hand to her throat. She had felt a great measure of relief when Farrell had told them that Nell had asked for the day off to tend to some pressing business. Now she understood Nell's reasoning. The girl had obviously planned her offensive well in advance and had chosen to launch her cannonball in a place where there wouldn't be any threat to her job.

"Well, as a matter of fact, I do mind, Nell," Jeff answered caustically. "The babe may well be your son, but he sure as hell isn't mine. Now stop this chicanery or I'll have you carted back to Charleston again, this time in the back of a wagon, and you can bet I won't be instructing *anyone* to find you a room. I can only wonder what rake you invited into the last room I paid for. 'Tis obvious you didn't waste any time getting with child after leaving here."

Nell's cajoling tones were pleasantly subdued. "Look at him, Jeffrey. He's a right beautiful little boy. Why, he's the most adorable baby I've e'er seen, and with all that fine, black hair and his li'l eyebrows anglin' up just like yours, he's bound to be the very image of you. Why, I wouldn't be at all surprised if his eyes turn green. I just have to wonder at times if'n he's gonna favor me atall, what with him already favorin' his pa so. Look at our son, Jeffrey. Can't you see the resemblance?"

"Stop harping on a lost cause, Nell!" Jeff barked. "I have no idea who the father is, but this much I know . . . it isn't me!"

"He's got black hair and . . ."

"Thousands of babies have black hair! That doesn't mean I've sired them all!" Jeff bellowed.

Raelynn struggled to subdue the sickening feeling roiling in the pit of her stomach. The scene was hardly much different than what had evolved the first time Nell had come out. The girl was just as insistent and Jeff no less incensed. If anything, he was even more irate over her audacity to accost him a second time at his home. Although Raelynn couldn't imagine that he'd be unaffected by the situation, his rage frightened her. When Jeff normally seemed so even-tempered, this display of temper caused her to wonder what really lay beneath that carefully maintained facade of levelheaded aplomb.

Raelynn glanced around in hopes of finding something that would draw her attention away from the argument presently going on behind the house, but even as she searched, she knew it was ridiculous to expect her thoughts to be diverted for even a second. The odds of that happening were about as great as the earth pausing on its axis.

Nell grew noticeably petulant. "You don't have to shout, Jeffrey. I'm standing right here."

"Well, truthfully, young lady," he retorted snidely, "I'd be overwhelmed with delight if you were to do me a special favor and take yourself and your son back to Charleston or, for that matter, off the face of the earth, as long as it's well out of my sight."

"You're just afraid of what your wife's gonna think when she gets a peek at our son," Nell challenged in a hurt tone.

Jeff lost any aplomb he once might have had. "Get out! Right now! I'm not going to waste my breath talking to you about this matter another moment. And don't *ever* come back here again! If you do, I swear you'll be taking your life in your hands, because right now, young lady, I'd like to throttle you! So I would advise you to get the bloody hell out of here before I do!"

Jeff's voice softened as he questioned his butler. "Kingston, does she have a carriage waiting somewhere?"

"Yassuh, Mistah Jeffrey, she sho do. Right in front o' de house."

"Then would you kindly . . . or by force, if need be, escort Miss Nell to it and inform the driver that he's not to stop until he's entirely off my property."

"Yassuh, Mistah Jeffrey. Ah sho will."

Raelynn waited in a poorly contrived semblance of calm as Nell came stomping angrily around the end of the manse. Kingston scrambled to catch up with the girl, but to no avail. Aqua eyes met briefly with blue, and in that moment Raelynn was brought face to face with the indisputable meaning of visual daggers. It was rather like being pierced to the bone.

Nell's upper lip curled upward in a disdaining sneer as she stalked toward her rival. "You think you have Jeffrey all to yourself now with all his money in the palm of your hand, don't you? Well, Miss Rich Bitch, I'm not finished with him yet. I'll see you both shamed 'til you can't bear to be seen in public. Then perhaps Mr. Tightfisted High an' Noble Lord Birmingham will relent and give me what I'm askin' for. 'Tain't as if he don't have enough ta spare." She snorted contemptuously. "Bet if'n you whelped a dozen, his purse wouldn't suffer none."

Nell dismissed Raelynn with an arrogant toss of her head and stalked down the drive to where the hired livery had stopped within the curve of the lane. Kingston hustled in her wake and was there to offer a helping hand when Nell paused beside the carriage step to readjust the bundle she carried within her arms. After a final glare toward Jeff, who now stood stoically beside his wife, she accepted the butler's assistance into the conveyance and never looked back.

The carriage rattled off down the lane, allowing Raelynn to release her breath in a long, quavering sigh. Still trembling, she peered up at her husband who had swept his frockcoat back from his chest and jammed both hands finger-deep into the pockets of his finely tailored trousers. His expression of concern clearly conveyed the fact that he was expecting some contrary reaction or comment from her, for his eyes watched her carefully and a dark eyebrow was sharply notched at a discomfited angle. Perhaps under the circumstances, she should have had something profound or serious to say, but at present, Raelynn just couldn't think of anything notable. Distractedly she glanced around and mutedly observed, "One should never count on the sky not falling around here. It seems to do that on a regular basis."

*T*he melodic strains of a waltz drifted on airy wings throughout the halls of Oakley Plantation house as the tall master of the manse swept his young wife in ever-widening circles around the candlelit, flower-bedecked ballroom. The bejeweled hem of the lady's gently flaring skirts swirled caressingly against her husband's black-stockinged calves in much the same manner as her slender fingers idly stroked the fabric of his finely tailored coat. His dapper evening attire of blackest silk, accentuated by a white, nattily tied stock and crisp, high-collared shirt, contrasted handsomely with the pale rosy blush of her beaded gown. In like degrees, his raven hair and burnished good looks emphasized the fairness of her ivory skin and the shining luster of her auburn tresses.

The two had eyes only for each other and were blissfully unaware of their guests drifting to the outer limits of the dance floor from whence they watched in admiration, many enthralled with the easy flowing grace of the pair. Others were not so graciously inclined. For at least a decade now, neighbors and friends had been cognizant of the attention the Birmingham brothers had garnered from a company of smitten females in the area. Now that the elder of the two had become firmly ensconced in a marriage to a beautiful wife and had a second child on the way, much of that infatuation had fallen to the younger who, on his own, had unwittingly acquired a vast following of lovesick devotees. Many of these same bedazzled maidens were present at this evening's festivities as members of families who had been acquainted with the Birminghams for a goodly number of years. Some were pampered darlings of avaricious parents who had seen the wealth of the Birminghams as something they could hopefully gain access to through marriage. Mothers and offspring were wont to hiss and sneer as they cast haughty glowers toward the object of their envy and the cause of their frustration. Recent hearsay had it that the newest Mrs. Birmingham had become the recipient of the zealous attention of one Gustav Fridrich, a brutish German who had been so intent upon having the girl for his own that he had broken into Oakley House and taken her captive. The rejected maids and their doting parents enlivened many a rumor about the event, suggesting that the lady had actually been sullied by her abductor and that her handsome husband, always a gentleman, had merely done the honorable thing by refusing to cast her aside.

More flattering compliments flowed from a different sector, not only liberally extolling the praises of the attractive couple, but also expressing admiration for the lady's gown. All were wont to surmise that the garment had cost her husband a sizable sum. But then, many shrugged away any thought of censure, reasoning that when a man was as rich as Jeffrey Birmingham, it was understandable that he would be of a mind to bestow lavish gifts upon his wife, for she was indeed exquisite.

Farrell Ives and Elizabeth Dalton exchanged smiling glances as they overheard comments praising the lady's gown. In silent tribute to the couturier's talent, his loyal assistant squeezed his arm. The gentle pressure in no wise went unnoticed by the stalwart man. Indeed, it did much to provoke his surprise, for the lady had never displayed any willingness to touch him either casually or deliberately unless she had been required by some definite reason to do so.

Farrell lowered a questioning gaze upon the dark-haired beauty, and when Elizabeth looked up, their eyes met with startling results. In the cerulean orbs, a warmth began to glow, more than hinting of a manly desire as he plumbed far below the depth of the darkly hued iris. It was the first time he had ever captured her gaze long enough to lend him some hope that her heart was susceptible to an intimate search of her hidden emotions. For an instant he glimpsed fertile ground, and his lean fingers brushed across the delicate bones of her hand, trying to communicate all the feelings he had held in check for years. Her breath halted, and for barely an instant she seemed to waver between a smile and some unknown fear. Then her soft lips began to tremble, and a fluttering sigh wafted from them.

A poignant longing seemed to fill the very essence of Elizabeth's being. As much as she yearned to respond with a womanly warmth to Farrell's questioning stare, she knew only too well the danger of yielding to those hypnotic, powerfully masculine smiles. Too often she had witnessed his effect on unsuspecting young maidens who had ventured much too close and, without warning, suddenly found their hearts hopelessly ensnared. Those mesmerizing blue-eyed stares had the strength to weaken the knees as well as the wits and wills of not only tender virgins but older widows as well, as Mrs. Brewster had recently demonstrated. Being merely his employee, Elizabeth understood the folly of lowering her guard, for she would be loath to see him scurrying to find a place to hide were she ever to forget her self-imposed restrictions. Still, it had been an arduous task to ignore the sinking feeling that had affirmed itself in the pit of her stomach each and every time she had been required by proper etiquette to stand calmly by while she watched the man practice his irresistible cajolery on some sweet young thing in his shop. The gloom that had followed such occurrences had left no question in her mind that, perhaps more than anyone, she yearned for some small bit of his attention for herself.

In a hard-won guise of unaffected insouciance Elizabeth withdrew her hand, hoping her employer wouldn't notice how it was shaking, and forced herself to look elsewhere in an effort to calm herself. The refreshment tables drew her attention and offered her an honest excuse to put some distance between the clothier and herself. "If you wouldn't mind, Mr. Ives, I'd like to see what I can find to eat at the refreshment table. I'm afraid in my haste to be ready on time, I failed to eat." She indicated a general direction. "Besides, several of our younger customers are eyeing you, no doubt hoping for a dance. I'm sure you'll want to oblige them."

Farrell slipped a hand beneath her elbow, hardly encouraged by her efforts to send him chasing after other maids. "Actually, I'm of a mind to join you, but I must say, Elizabeth, you don't have to be so formal while we're away from the shop. You know my name better than anyone. I give you leave to use it."

Elizabeth sought to speak, but found that her voice had lost its strength. Clearing her throat, she made another attempt. "Do you think I should be so casual when there are so many listening ears about? Thus far, we've managed to avoid the damage of gossips' slurs by not associating with each other in public. Should the rumormongers hear me addressing you by your given name, they may be wont to make much of the familiarity."

Farrell was seriously tempted to curse all the nosey biddies to a life of unending boredom. Reluctantly he accepted Elizabeth's excuse, not that he agreed with her, but he knew of the difficulty it would entail getting his assistant to change her mind. She could be damnably iron-willed at times, especially when it came to personal matters and, he suspected, affairs of the heart.

In another area of the room, a tall, handsome woman of middling years peered through her lorgnette as the younger Birmingham couple waltzed past. Loftily raising a brow, she leaned aside to the shorter lady who stood near her elbow. "Surely I misunderstood you, Mrs. Brewster. Did you say that Mr. Birmingham found his bride under a coach? That sounds rather like he found her under a cabbage leaf in his neighbor's garden. Eligible bachelors here in the Carolinas don't go hunting for brides in such an odd fashion, do they?"

The plump, round-faced woman started in surprise at her companion's deductions and, in a highly agitated state, fluttered her lace fan, making the peacock feathers on her elaborate headdress flutter as well. "My dear Mrs. Winthrop, I said nothing of the sort! Miss Raelynn certainly wasn't *underneath* a coach, although she might have been if Mr. Jeffrey hadn't leapt into the road after her."

The tall gentleman standing beside them lent his attention to the plump milliner. "Do tell, Mrs. Brewster. You've stirred my imagination to the point that it must now be satisfied."

"Most eagerly will I do so, my lord," Mrs. Brewster rejoined with a nervous little twitter. She flicked her thin lashes coyly as she began to relate the details of the younger couple's meeting.

Unaware that they were being discussed in nearly every circle of guests, Jeff continued to sweep his bride about the ballroom as he basked in the adoration shining in her darkly lashed, aqua eyes, much as a man might revel in the warm rays of the sun in the midst of a frigid land. "Have I told you this evening, my pet, how utterly enchanting you look? But then, I've yet to see you when you've been anything less than ravishing. Indeed, I'm most aware of that fact when you're wearing nothing at all. Are you enjoying yourself?"

"Immensely," Raelynn assured him, her soft lips curving upward enticingly. Dancing with her handsome husband made her feel as if she were a young girl again, being swept around a garden in the arms of *her* Prince Charming. Her fingers slid inward across the broad expanse of his shoulder and, in the guise of smoothing a satin lapel, caressed his hardened chest beneath the fine cloth of his frockcoat. "You make me feel very much like a princess, Jeffrey."

"Your appearance attests to your right to feel that way, my dear. I'm nigh besotted indulging myself in the sights. Your new gown is certainly no less than resplendent. Even so, it fails to equal your radiance. If not for the vivid recollection I have of watching your toilette, I'd be of a mind to think that Farrell had talked you into wearing it without all those frilly undergarments women are wont to pile on underneath their clothing. It clings to you divinely."

Smiling, Raelynn allowed her thoughts to drift back to before the ball. He had looked for all the world like some dark-skinned sultan admiring his favorite concubine as he lounged back upon her chaise and watched her dress. Tizzy had been more than a little anxious arranging her hair under his close attention and had dropped the comb countless times until Jeffrey had taken pity on the girl. Retiring from their chambers, he had closed the hall door behind him, allowing the maid to breathe a sigh of relief. "The satin they used to make my shift is so sublime, it makes me feel utterly delicious."

Jeff pressed a hand behind the small of her back, bringing his young wife imperceptibly closer. "You *look* utterly delicious, madam, so much so that I've been wanting to devour you since you left me alone in the tub."

Raelynn peered up at him flirtatiously through silken lashes. It was just like her handsome husband to turn her words around to his advantage. "I meant inwardly, Jeffrey."

"I'd really like to take another look at your chemise," he teased with a grin as his gaze dipped briefly to her bosom.

"We have guests, Jeffrey."

"That doesn't keep me from recalling how beautiful you are underneath all that fine apparel or how enticing you look when you're lying warm and sated with desire in my arms."

Raelynn's cheeks deepened to a rosy hue as she thought of the many times he had made her forget herself in the passionate fervor of their union. Though her only experience in the art of lovemaking was what she had learned in his arms, he seemed a very bold and accomplished lover. She had never dared ask how he had come by such knowledge. Nevertheless she was wont to wonder at times, but that usually caused her to suffer recurring doubts about Nell and others he might have pleasured. Still, whenever those glowing emerald eyes settled on her and silently communicated his cravings, he could make her dismiss everything from mind but her growing involvement with the man. It was a simple fact that, whether clothed or as naked as the day he had been born, Jeffrey Birmingham could command her complete attention. "I have visions just as titillating, sir."

A roguish grin slanted across his lips. "It seems we're of one mind, madam. Nearly every hour of the day my thoughts hearken back to what we do together in the privacy of our bedroom. It's nice to know you're affected in much the same way."

She tilted her elegantly coifed head curiously. "I've been wondering about something, sir."

"Yes, madam?"

"Our bed would sleep a whole family comfortably. Did you have some particular penchant in mind when you specified its dimensions?"

"I suppose upon espying it, one might have cause to wonder if it had been ordered especially for the purpose of accommodating a couple's activities in bed."

"You mean it wasn't?" she challenged sweetly.

His eyebrows flicked upward briefly above smoldering green orbs. "Very likely, madam. You see, for some years past I've carried in my mind a vision of a naked, pale-skinned goddess who could lure me into rapturous dreams. Her breasts were delicately hued, soft and round, her belly of the creamiest hue, her thighs so temptingly joined together, I became fairly besotted with a desire to mount them. My yearnings became deeply seeded, and I began to aspire to the belief that someday I would be able to claim the lady of my dreams and bring her to life with a kiss."

"Your kisses would bestir the heart of the most reluctant maid, sir."

"You were reluctant yourself once upon a time."

"Only because I was ignorant of all delights that awaited me in your arms."

Jeff threw back his head and laughed in hearty amusement, causing his wife to glance around in sudden chagrin. She couldn't predict how their guests would respond to her husband's unrestrained hilarity, but as one might expect, the two of them now claimed the attention of nearly every person in the room. Still, that didn't bother her nearly as much as the fact that they had also fallen prey to the glum stares of the dejected. Young as she was, she had obviously shattered the hopeful prospects of women several years older than herself, some of whom were young widows with far more experience with men.

"Jeffrey Birmingham, what will our guests think?" she whispered, striving hard to sound stern. The difficulty for such a task seemed mainly centered on the gratification she felt being the wife of such a man. "Just look, Jeffrey. There's no one else dancing. We've become the attraction for this evening. People will presume the worst."

"Aye, such fantasies bestir their imagination," he assured her, swirling her about. He gave her a grin closely reminiscent of a leer. "If they could read my mind, madam, they'd be doubly shocked."

A dimple showed at the corner of her mouth as she fingered the lapel of his frockcoat again. " 'Tis evident your thoughts don't need stimulating, sir."

"Not as long as I have you for a wife, my love. All I need do is look at you, and my aspirations and *other* things raise to lofty heights."

Lifting her gaze coyly to his, she emulated a museful vein. "*Other* things being?"

A dark eyebrow angled roguishly upward as the green eyes gleamed back at her. "You're teasing me, madam, and I'm wondering for what purpose. If you wish a private demonstration, I'm sure we can find someplace where I can exhibit my ardor without causing you undue embarrassment."

Raelynn's fingers tracked a trail up to the high collar of his stiffly starched shirt. "It's fairly easy to ascertain by the questionable fit of other men's clothing that you've either been gifted with an exceptional tailor or a superb physique, sir. I would never mind a private exhibition."

Jeff peered at her obliquely, growing more intrigued by the moment. "Any specific area you'd like to view, madam?"

"You know, Jeffrey, you really should lift your sights above your loins," she teased sweetly. "You might discover that there are other parts of a man's body just as worthy of admiration."

"You haven't answered me," he pressed, reluctant to move away from such a titillating subject. "As a bride of three months going on four, do you ogle other men to make a comparison to me? Or do you do so merely out of curiosity?"

His question drew an honest gasp from her. "I don't ogle other men, Jeffrey."

"You ogle me."

Her fine nose lifted loftily. "That's different."

Jeff leaned above her ear to whisper, "I like it when you do."

A captivating grin curved Raelynn's lips as she cut her eyes aslant at him. "The pleasure is mutual, sir."

"Oh, oh. Now you've done it."

His wife glanced up in bemusement. "What's wrong?"

"We'd better change the subject before I embarrass myself," he cautioned. "These breeches can be damned revealing at times."

The aqua eyes slipped downward briefly, drawing an amused chuckle from him.

"Got you!"

Raelynn tossed her head, like a child who had been thoroughly miffed by the prankish trick of a hopeless tease, but the corners of her lips seemed to have a will of their own as they curved in amusement. "I wouldn't have been at all surprised, knowing what a lecher I have for a husband."

"I became a lecher the day you entered my life, madam."

Satisfied, Raelynn smiled and resumed toying with his carefully wrapped stock. "And I became a wanton the day you took me into your bed, sir. I can hardly think of anything else."

Servants moving about with trays laden with libations, musicians extracting melodious notes from instruments, elegantly arrayed ladies and gentlemen talking in muted tones seemed somehow detached from the private world in which the couple had entered. Yet it wasn't until Jeff had relinquished Raelynn for a dance with an elderly gentleman of impeccable character that he realized how time seemed to slow to a snail's pace when they weren't together. Even as he talked with some of his hunting companions, his eyes seemed inclined to watch her dutifully smiling and dancing with the elder. When, after bestowing another such glance upon her, he encountered the blatantly amused stare of his brother, Jeff felt his own cheeks grow ruddy in chagrin.

"Pleases you a mite, does she?" Brandon gently prodded, stepping near.

"More'n a mite," Jeff readily acknowledged as he gave his brother a crisp nod of affirmation. He allowed himself a final glance at Raelynn before he turned and followed along behind his older sibling, much as he had oftentimes done as a child.

Heather was seated in a large, wing-backed chair with her dainty, slippered feet residing on a low footstool and a lace shawl carefully draped around her shoulders in such a way as to mask her ponderous belly. Earlier that day, Jeff had instructed servants to place the chair in a spot where the expectant mother could view the entire room without having to move about, the only possible hindrance to her visual range being the guests who might overlook her presence.

"Little chance of that," Jeff had replied when Kingston had posed such a question. "Even well along with child, she'll have her own circle of admirers and friends who'll make sure that doesn't happen."

As expected, Heather was surrounded by a small collection of guests who had paused to pay their respects. Farrell Ives had led Elizabeth Dalton upon his arm to that very spot where they were now engaged in conversation with the charming Mrs. Brandon Birmingham. In much the same manner, Thelma Brewster had hastened across the room, but only after noting the couturier among those presently talking to the pregnant beauty. Thelma brought her companions with her, the widowered English lord and Lydia Winthrop, both of middling years. Although Mrs. Winthrop had grown up near the Charleston area, in the last score of years she had taken up residence in London after marrying a wealthy Englishman. Recently she had made the voyage to visit friends in the Carolinas. As for the nobleman, he had lived most of his life near that great metropolis in England and had every intention of returning once he concluded his business in the area.

"My dears, have you met Lord Marsden?" Lydia Winthrop queried, with an elegant sweep of her hand drawing the tall, lank gentleman forward. "We became acquainted while sailing here from London. Nasty weather, we had, too. Tossed our ship about more than I could abide, but that is neither here nor there. Lord Marsden came here on a quest to find a suitable track of land to buy as a wedding gift for his daughter and her fiancé. Mrs. Brewster assured us that it would be perfectly acceptable with our host if his lordship came along with us, seeing as how the Birmingham men could likely advise him on the best acreages to be had in the area."

Lord Marsden cleared his throat as if he were about to launch himself into a long speech. "Yes, of course, I didn't wish to intrude, you see, but these kindly ladies insisted. I sincerely hope our host isn't averse to strangers imposing upon his hospitality."

Heather smiled up at the man. From where she sat, he seemed to loom over the pair of ladies who flanked him, especially the portly Mrs. Brewster, who was nearly a half head shorter than the more elegant Lydia Winthrop. As for his lordship, he was definitely a bland sort, tall, lean, long of limb, with lank, brown hair and a dour face typical of some pompous aristocrats. Although his dark blue frockcoat and breeches were finely tailored, they were as sober as the man's face.

"Rest easy, my lord," she urged graciously. "I'm sure my brother-in-law will be honored by your attendance. But as to your purpose here, Jeffrey and Brandon are both capable of assisting you in your search for land, but if you're not overly pressed for time tonight, please enjoy the festivities and help yourself to the refreshments. Jeffrey has an exceptional cook, so the cuisine promises to be simply delectable."

"Thank you for making a foreigner feel at home, madam," Lord Marsden replied graciously. "You're very kind indeed."

"My pleasure to be of service, my lord. Now, please," Heather bade, "enjoy yourself and feel free to have a look around if you'd like. Since so many guests have made requests to view the improvements that have been done here at Oakley, most of the rooms will be open for inspection. The house is a fine example of the plantation homes in this area and has become a real gem since my brother-in-law refurbished it. Only Jeffrey's personal chambers will be reserved for his private needs and those of his immediate family during the festivities."

Lord Marsden responded with an abbreviated bow. "Your family is most courteous, madam."

Turning aside, he followed the two older women who were strolling across the room. When Lydia Winthrop paused to indicate the ceilings and walls of the ballroom that were elegantly embellished with flower festoons of delicately hued pargetry adorned with elaborate gilding, his lordship dutifully followed her gaze upward.

"I remember this place when Louisa's parents lived here," Lydia mused aloud. "It was a fine house then, but nothing at all to what it is today. Never once did I imagine it could look this grand."

"Albeit, madam," his lordship replied, "in comparison to the great homes of London, you must agree that it seems a bit wane. Yet I suppose in contrast to the humble dwellings I've seen here in the Carolinas, it would be equivalent to a modest English estate, although nothing too grand, you understand."

Mrs. Brewster's buoyant smile faded forthwith. The fact that her own tiny apartment and millinery shop took up less space than the room they were occupying made her wonder if, after a visit to her establishment, Lord Marsden would be inclined to look down his long, thin nose at her. She thought it wise to lead the subject elsewhere. "Miss Heather is a very fine lady, perhaps the most enchanting in the area . . . besides Miss Raelynn, of course."

His lordship withdrew a snuffbox and sprinkled a little powder on the back of his hand. Inhaling a few small particles into each nostril, he raised his head and pompously elevated his brows as he pressed a handkerchief aside his nose. "She bears the coloring of those dastardly Irish. Is she?"

Momentarily struck speechless, Thelma Brewster searched her memory. "I-I think so. I mean, I seem to recall hearing someone say her mother came to England from Ireland after her marriage to Heather's father."

Lord Marsden bounced on his toes as he lifted his angular chin almost level with his long nose. "Too bad."

The milliner felt the back of her neck prickle uncomfortably. If the man thought Heather Birmingham beneath his lofty peerage, then how much farther down the scale would he rank most of the Charlestonians, herself included?

Lydia Winthrop smiled blandly at the man. "You'll find the citizenry of this area are little concerned with titles and nobility, my lord. You must remember that although this territory was once under English rule, it's no longer subject to the authority of the monarchy. People here desired their freedom from autocracy enough to fight for it."

"Rebels . . . Yankees . . . all the same," Marsden replied imperiously.

The plump cheeks of the milliner drew sharply inward in a shocked gasp. The awe she had formerly felt for the nobleman was quickly turning into vexing ire. Indeed, if she had to listen to any more of this Englishman's long-nosed arrogance, she'd be liable to lower a punchbowl over his dark head. In an effort to turn the subject once again to something less confrontational, she indicated the bountiful fare laid out on the tables. "You'll not likely find food as tasty as this in all of the Carolinas, my lord. Wouldn't you care to take a plate and sample some?"

Lord Marsden touched his lace handkerchief almost daintily to the side of his nose again and sniffed. "I dare not ask what has gone into the making of these dishes. Such rich victuals may well prove the death of me."

"Well, 'tis doubtful you'll be finding any kidney pie around these here parts, your lordship," Mrs. Brewster retorted, casting a jaundiced eye toward the man. English lord or not, he definitely needed to be taught some manners. "As for me, I can hardly wait to begin."

Lydia passed the milliner a plate as she smilingly invited, "Shall we?"

Heather caught sight of Jeff making his way toward her through the crowd of guests. As he drew near, she stretched forth a welcoming hand and laughed like an eager schoolgirl. "I was wondering what I would have to do to get your attention. As much as you've been dancing with Raelynn, I was sure I'd have to break in and ask you for a dance myself just to get a chance to talk with you. Your ball is quite lovely, sir. Thank you for inviting us."

Winking at her fondly, Jeff brought her thin fingers to his lips before he stepped back and swept her with a teasing perusal. "Madam, may I say that you look very much like a hen upon her nest, waiting expectantly for her egg to hatch."

Heather laid a small hand upon her belly and contentedly drummed her fingers against it. "Any week now."

"Feeling all right, princess?"

"Perfectly," she assured him, her smile deepening. Then she cast a loving glance toward her husband and heaved a small sigh as that one leaned against her chair. "Or at least I would be if your brother would relax just the tiniest bit. I swear, he watches over me as tenaciously as a dog with a juicy bone."

Her happy tone dismissed any hint of reproach and drew a grin from her husband. That worthy proceeded to caress his wife's shoulder. "You must forgive me, my sweet, but as you appear on the threshold of ushering our new offspring into the world, I believe I may be allowed a small degree of anxiety."

Heather gave him a saucy pout. "Oh, posh, you know perfectly well that it may be another two weeks or so yet before our daughter hatches. At least, that's what Hatti said. You must have forgotten what I looked like a few weeks before Beau arrived. Something closely reminiscent of a frigate with its weighty prow plowing through water, I would imagine."

Laughter made the rounds among those who stood near her chair, yet in spite of Brandon's amusement, Jeff glimpsed some evidence of strain in his countenance, similar to that which his brother had experienced a thrice of years ago when he had faced Beau's birth. More than anyone, Jeff knew how firmly Heather held her husband's heart ensnared and that the merest thought of her enduring the pain of childbirth or, worse yet, of her dying during her labor stole away Brandon's peace of mind. In spite of her fairly easy delivery the first time, there always loomed a threat of complications, and until it was over, Brandon could not settle down and live at peace with himself.

"Believe me, my sweet," her husband replied huskily, taking his wife's delicately boned hand within his and squeezing it affectionately, "I've forgotten nothing of my ordeal, and that's why I fret now."

When Heather lifted a dewy-eyed look of tender regard to her spouse, Jeff felt as if he had inadvertently trespassed into their intimacy. In turning aside, he faced Farrell, who had also witnessed the exchange of loving devotion between the pair. Rarely had that one glimpsed the like of such closeness between a married couple. It was a loving unity that a bachelor could well envy.

"Jeffrey, me dearie, you're looking quite dapper for a change," the clothier remarked with more than a hint of mischief and struck a lofty pose as his host turned a grin upon him.

"Egads, Fancy Man, you almost rival my wife's appearance," Jeff teased as he swept his gaze down the length of the other's tall, broad-shouldered frame. Not a stitch was out of place in the long, narrow-fitting trousers of charcoal gray pinstripe, waistcoat of silver-scrolled brocade, white shirt and cravat, and black, claw-tailed frockcoat. He couldn't help but admire the fashionable clothes.

Farrell preened in exaggerated conceit as he ran his thumbs beneath the lapels of his finely tailored coat. "You think so?"

"Aye, I do."

"Come to my shop when you have time to spare, Jeffrey me dearie, and I'll teach you some of the finer points of style. You could certainly benefit from my advice."

A dubious grin accompanied Jeff's quip. "I'll consider your offer if I ever want to masquerade as a dandy."

The bearded face fell forthwith as Farrell made much of his distress, in the process drawing laughter from everyone who witnessed his visual deflation. "I swear, Jeffrey, you can be downright offensive when your jealousy is tweaked."

"Now don't pout," Jeff urged drolly. "I didn't intend to offend you. Truth is, you're looking as pretty as a Carolina peach."

Elizabeth cast a glance awry at her handsome escort and, upon espying his toothy grin, seemed suddenly distressed as if sorely lamenting the damage their host had done. "You'd better not feed the man's vanity more than you have, sir. His head is getting top-heavy, as it is. Please remember. I have to work with him."

"Stuck on himself, is he?"

Elizabeth rolled her eyes, magnifying her inhibitions. "You'd never hear such a comment from me, sir . . . as much as I may think it."

Capturing her hand within his, Farrell chortled goodnaturedly. "I think it's time we showed this oaf of a host that he's not the only one who can dance a waltz. Besides, my dear, I'd like everyone to see your new gown."

"Another one of your creations, Fancy Man?" Jeff queried with a lopsided grin.

"Actually, my assistant, here, designed and made the frock herself. Quite lovely, don't you think?"

The deep magenta gown truly did justice to the beauty of the fair-skinned brunette, and in gallant appreciation of all that he saw, Jeff executed a flamboyant bow. "You're looking exceptionally beautiful tonight, Miss Elizabeth. Quite exquisite, in fact. You put your employer to shame."

A soft chuckle escaped Elizabeth as she sank into a charming curtsey. "Thank you, Mr. Birmingham."

"Jeff," their host corrected. "Or if you're so inclined, Jeffrey. While you're away from your employer's shop, Elizabeth, I must insist on a more casual address than Mr. Birmingham." His dancing eyes flicked briefly to the couturier before he added, "And you can tell him I said so."

Laughing, Elizabeth dipped her head in a fleeting nod of consent. "As you wish, Jeffrey."

"Enjoy yourselves, my friends," their host bade, with a flamboyant wave of his hand urging them onto the dance floor. "I'll join you there as soon as I can find my wife."

Jeff's gaze was drawn to Raelynn as if by a will of its own, and for a moment he stood marveling at her regal beauty as she was swirled about the floor by another friend, Sheriff Rhys Townsend. The huge man was amazingly light on his feet, and although Raelynn seemed dwarfed by his size, she had no difficulty following his lead. In truth, she was taller than Heather by several degrees and seemed almost willowy in the long, narrow-skirted gown that flowed with subtly clinging grace from her shoulders to the floor. Jeff thought the gown a bit deceptive, for he was fully cognizant and, as her husband, most appreciative of the ripe curves that lay hidden beneath the shimmering sheath. Their weeks of intimacy had taught him to see beyond the outer shell of the lovely, vibrant woman and to read the true depth of the lady hidden within. He realized with some surprise that for all the pleasure he derived from their passion and marital familiarity, some deeper, richer emotion was taking root in his heart. It had a quality that was outside his realm of experience. As yet, he could put no name to it. Still, it was very pleasant knowing that she was his alone.

As he indulged himself admiring his wife from afar, Jeff was struck by a sudden mental image of her with her belly swollen with child, much as Heather's was now. He had once teased Raelynn about having several dozen offspring. Now the thought of even one rounding out her belly provoked such profound longing that it almost robbed him of breath. On the cusp of it, and hardly aware of what he did, he began weaving his way through the labyrinth of dancing couples. When he clasped Rhys's shoulder, he evoked a surprise that was at the very least farfetched.

"Well, Jeffrey, what're you doing out here by your lonesome?" the sheriff asked, as if the idea that a man might want to dance with his own wife had never occurred to him. In his own concocted vernacular Rhys chided, "You oughta get yourself a girlie if'n you want ta dance."

"I know that, my friend. That's why I've come for my wife. Go find your own before she sends her brothers out to drag you off the floor."

"Well, it wouldn't be the first time." Rhys chortled as his eyes lit on the petite blonde who was eyeing him from the sidelines. "I guess I'm gonna have to teach my li'l darlin' how to dance or one o' these days she's gonna be nailin' my hide to a barn door. Mary can get a mite resentful sometimes when I yield my feet to the music and seek out a dancing partner."

Raelynn glanced toward the winsome, young woman. At the moment Mary clutched an embroidered shawl self-consciously over her midriff, lending much to the supposition that she was in the earlier stages of a pregnancy. "I think I'm feeling some of that resentment even now, Rhys," she ventured, her eyes sparkling with unquenchable humor. "You'd better make haste to make amends, or Mary will be dragging you off the floor by the ear."

"Sure thing," he rumbled through his laughter and touched two fingers to his brow in a casual salute before flapping his arms and making much of his alacrity to join his wife.

Raelynn and Jeff relented to their amusement over the sheriff's propensity to play the comedian and continued to laugh as Rhys made a great show of explaining himself to his spouse. At present, Mary had her pert nose tilted upward, feigning a highly offended manner.

After a courtly bow, Jeff invited his wife to join him

in a waltz and immediately received a welcoming answer in the form of opening arms. For several moments he swept her around the perimeter of the floor in ever widening circles as they relished the music and the presence of each other in silence. Then Raelynn peered up at him with a wondering smile.

"That was rather bold of you, Jeffrey, coming out into the midst of our guests to stake your claim on me. Did you want me for something in particular?"

Arching a brow, he grinned down at her. "Only to dance with you whenever I feel like it. I'd hardly call that bold, merely . . ." He lifted his head thoughtfully, seeking the appropriate word, and then nodded decisively, ". . . sensible."

From beneath a lengthy fringe of silky black lashes, Raelynn shot him a glance that was somewhere between dubious and amused. Such a look made Jeff smile in secret contentment. The idea of keeping his wife a bit uncertain as to how *sensible* he intended to be regarding his husbandly prerogatives was certainly not objectionable to him. After all, there was such a thing as taking a spouse too much for granted.

All the same, Jeff felt a niggling uncertainty when he saw her small, white teeth chewing at a bottom lip. Whatever unquenchable male inclinations had rallied in an effort to keep her just a bit off balance in regards to her womanly assessment of his character was now encumbered by a desire to have her always feel safe and secure as his wife.

"Raelynn, my love, I'm not overly jealous, certainly not of my friends when they lend you some . . ." His assurances were abruptly silenced by her tantalizing smile.

"Very sensible, of course," she murmured as her fingers worked their way to the short strands of hair at his nape. "I much prefer dancing with you, Jeffrey."

Of a sudden, the music seemed to soar in joyful rhapsody, and Jeff ceased to think of anything beyond his simple appreciation of the woman in his arms . . . and in his heart. Of late, she seemed the very reason that it beat the way it did.

Moments later, Jeff and Raelynn meandered hand in hand to the refreshment tables, and it was there that the milliner introduced them to Lord Marsden and Lydia Winthrop.

"Such a lovely affair," Lydia assured the couple graciously.

"Yes, absolutely," Lord Marsden agreed in a more cordial vein, winning the smiling approval of Mrs. Brewster.

Lydia quickly explained his lordship's mission to Jeff. "We thought you or Mr. Brandon might be able to direct his lordship in this matter."

"We'd be delighted to assist him," Jeff assured them and faced the man directly. "You're welcome to return here to my home anytime while I'm in residence, my lord, or to even stop by my shipping company. You can be reasonably assured that I'm there on Wednesdays, but as for the other days of the week, I cannot say. I have other business interests that demand my time, but I'm also just as prone to stay at home and take account of my crops, stables and other things that are of utmost importance to me." Surreptitiously Jeff reached back a hand and, threading his lean fingers through those of his wife, squeezed them gently, silently affirming that she was the one who really claimed the best of his attention. "I'll be happy to lend you whatever assistance you may require, my lord."

"Thank you most kindly for your generous offer, sir. I would certainly be indebted to you if you could help me conclude my business here speedily so I can return to England well before the nuptials are announced. Truly, if I must endure another sea voyage the like of which Mrs. Winthrop and I have already suffered, then I may never get up enough nerve to board another ship as long as I live."

His comment evoked their laughter, allowing Mrs. Brewster to renew her admiration for the man. After all, he was a lord of the realm and had even seen fit to invite her for a turn about the dance floor.

&Being at an elegant ball with a wife rather than merely a female companion was a new experience for Jeff, and he was not above taking marital license whenever the opportunity presented itself. Raelynn seemed more than willing to foster his husbandly advances with a few wifely ones of her own. Indeed, such moments were limited only by the amount of secrecy or concealment they were able to garner throughout the evening. Her hand settling possessively upon his backside while they were wedged in a corner talking to friends or the back of his arm brushing her breast were teasing little sweetmeats that made them smile at each other in warm communication.

It was equally satisfying for Jeff to return to their bedchamber after Mrs. Brewster had accidentally splashed punch over the starched whiteness of his shirt and to find his wife perched on the end of the overstuffed chaise with her skirts drawn up nigh to her hips. She was just dragging off a badly snagged stocking when he arrived and began smoothing on new hosiery as he doffed his coat and shirt. He was ever wont to admire her long, sleek limbs and, with a husbandly appreciation, hovered near with all the dedication of a lusting roué. Nibbling at her earlobe, he whispered lewd suggestions in her ear until Raelynn was giggling like a new bride. His proposals proved provocative, especially to Jeff who became increasingly dedicated to the idea of enjoying some marital intimacy. Kneeling before her, he covered her throat and bosom with languid kisses as his hand wandered with bold familiarity beneath the hem of her gown. Raelynn's breath caught at his advance. A moment later it escaped in a fluttering sigh of pleasure as she relaxed against him. When his lips traveled upward to ensnare hers, commanding a fervent answer, she yielded her mouth completely, meeting his probing tongue with slow, sultry flicks of her own.

A moment later Jeff lifted his head and searched his wife's face for the depth of her commitment to this moment. Soft, dewy eyes merged with his, and a warm shiver gently shook her slender frame as she recognized the passion blazing in those green orbs. A long, muscular arm moved around behind her hips and swept her forward to the end of the chaise, opening her up to him as he freed the fastenings of his breeches and slowly sheathed himself in her womanly warmth.

Things became increasingly focused, at least until several twittering ladies approached from down the hall and entered the bedroom next door, where they eagerly praised the changes that had been made to the house in recent years. Frozen on the threshold of erotic rapture, the couple clung to each other as they listened in waiting apprehension. Before the ball, the draperies had been drawn closed over the French doors of the master's chambers, but the glass portals had been left standing open to catch the wafting breezes. As a result, no one could predict what curious soul might decide to venture out onto the veranda or even dare to enter the private quarters.

Discomfited by their guests' proximity, Raelynn pressed a trembling hand against her husband's chest and looked up at him pleadingly. "Later," she whispered as her palm stroked the furred expanse. "When we have more privacy."

Jeff pressed his lips near her ear. "Then come downstairs and let me hold you in a waltz until my blood cools."

"As if it would," she replied and started to laugh, then hurriedly buried her face in his shoulder until she could subdue her amusement. She glanced back at the mantel clock as it began to chime. "Ten o'clock. Not much longer now. Then we can be alone together."

"You'd better leave first," Jeff murmured huskily, withdrawing from her. "If I go down now, I'll shock our guests."

Rising with him, Raelynn snatched a kiss from his lips and, with an admiring glance downward, stepped away from him with a grin.

8 ❧

*I*n gracious compliance with the duties of a hostess, Raelynn smilingly accepted every invitation to dance and, in the lulls between, conversed with many of the ladies. She quickly discovered that Heather was a radiant, vivacious beacon to which she and others were irresistibly drawn. Thus, when she was unsure of herself, it seemed only natural to seek out the fortifying presence of her sister-in-law. Aware that she had aroused a fair amount of curiosity by marrying one of the choicest bachelors in the area, Raelynn tried to answer all the probing questions as pleasantly and as accurately as possible. Yet, through it all, she began to sense that a small collection of ladies were resentful of her. Never mind that they hid their malice behind brittle smiles and subtle innuendoes, they made her feel very much like an outsider, as they no doubt hoped to do. She was, after all, a foreigner who had usurped a highly coveted commodity in the form of one, Jeffrey Lawrence Birmingham.

Yet, even as she struggled to dismiss their cattiness, Raelynn became increasingly aware of her own rising euphoria. After despairing of even surviving the sea voyage across the Atlantic, she had not only been rescued from the enslavement that Gustav had intended for her, but she had been whisked into a marriage with an extraordinary gentleman who was every bit the man she had once aspired to have in a long-dormant fantasy. Yet *Jeff* was no dreamy illusion, but flesh and blood. And he was hers, not theirs. He was immensely charming, delightful to be with, and much more of a courtly gentleman than she had realistically imagined she would ever find in the *wilds* of the Carolinas. Not only that, he seemed a perfect match for her. Where she was weak, he was strong; where she was gentle and submissive, he was firm and aggressive; where she was clever at managing the house, the servants and a host of other things, he was astute at his many business affairs, his horse operation, and running the plantation. In a variety of different ways they complemented each other. Yet above all, they were lovers thoroughly enthralled with each other. The only nagging fear came from the fact that everything seemed *too* perfect. There just had to be a flaw somewhere.

If she were living in the midst of some fairy tale, her existence could not have been more captivating. The spacious ballroom, now aglow with twinkling crystal candelabra and costly chandeliers and aswirl with gracious people, seemed a place of enchantment. Even the rain pattering down upon the roof and the walks twining through the gardens provided a fresh, sweet essence that enlivened her spirit and made her feel a bit giddy, as if she were actually soaring on gossamer wings, like a tiny fairy in an unseen world. It was all too magical and beautiful, yet very, very real, she kept telling herself. She was here! Alive! And this was no fantasy, no child's illusion.

Once again, Raelynn made an effort to devote her attention to the elderly gentleman with whom she was presently dancing. She smiled at his muttered statement, hardly cognizant of what he had said, and hoped fervently that it didn't require an answer. Her mind wandered irresistibly to that fervently anticipated moment wherein she and Jeffrey would be free to return to the privacy of their bedroom. A warm blush swept upward from her breasts as she thought of Jeff's long, muscular form moving with slow, rhythmic passion upon her own, but in allowing herself such delectable fantasies, she missed a sweeping turn and trod upon her partner's toe. His wrinkled face briefly registered a painful grimace before he recovered a somewhat strained aplomb.

Patting her hand soothingly, he shushed her worried apologies. "No need to fret yourself, girl. No harm has been done."

Raelynn chided herself for allowing herself to get so caught up in unrestrained musings about her husband that she'd act like a mindless chit. She just hoped the elderly gentleman hadn't somehow connected her preoccupation with her flushed cheeks and bated breath, or, if he had, would merely lay it to some other cause rather than her lustful reflections.

"My dear girl, you must rest yourself," the elder urged solicitously, finally taking note of her distress. His concern deepened as he considered her flushed face. "Surely you'll be fainting from fatigue if you continue dancing as you have been."

Seizing upon the excuse, Raelynn graciously accepted his assistance from the dance floor. "You're very kind, sir."

Her relief was immeasurable when Jeff met her with a glass of fruited wine. "Here, love, you look as if you need this more than I do. Besides, I don't think I can take another sip until I find some relief."

"Relief from what?"

Jeff grinned at her, bringing into play the handsome grooves in his cheeks before he leaned near to whisper.

"Your naiveté comes into play most fetchingly, madam, but right now, I'm sorely pressed, for the privy beckons, you see."

"It's raining outside," she warned, her lips curving enticingly. She was hardly aware of her warmly glowing eyes caressing the face above her own. Admiring her husband had become almost second nature to her, and she had ceased to take account of all the times her gaze was inclined to shift in his direction and then linger for lengthy moments.

"Actually, my love, it stopped some moments ago. In any case, I have to go. It has become a dire necessity."

"Don't be long." She felt her heart trip as he winked at her in his all-too-magical way. As he hastened off, she sought to turn aside, but grimaced suddenly as a sharp pain shot through her heel. No doubt it had become blistered from all the dancing she had done. She cast a glance toward the clock and decided she had just enough time to go upstairs and slip into a more comfortable pair of shoes before she could expect Jeffrey to return.

"May I have this dance, madam?" a deep voice inquired from behind her.

Raelynn turned to find Farrell Ives grinning down at her.

"Elizabeth has deserted me to dance with your brother-in-law," the couturier explained, escorting her back onto the dance floor. "She's trying to soothe his qualms about Heather's upcoming ordeal, but I don't think it's doing much good. I experienced that same sort of trauma only once in my life, but it left a lasting impression upon me. The memory certainly allows me to feel a great empathy for Brandon."

Raelynn canted her head curiously. "I didn't realize you were married, Farrell."

"I'm not. Never have been."

"Oh, then you must have sisters . . ."

"Nary a one. I was born the last of seven brothers."

"Goodness, your father must have been very proud to have so many sons."

His bearded mouth twitched with amusement. "Aye, that he was, but as handsome as we all were, we went through some hard times just the same."

She laughed at his wit. "You know, Farrell, if I thought you were really as conceited as you make yourself out to be, I'd make an earnest effort to warn women away from you, for surely none would be able to hold a candle to you."

His eyes gleamed puckishly. "I knew my looks were impressive, but I never realized before that they also put the women to shame, too."

"You're hopeless," she warbled through her laughter.

He feigned a sigh of lament. "That's what everybody tells me."

"You should be careful," she warned, making no attempt to curb her grin. "One of these days someone is going to take you seriously and think you're really caught on yourself."

He chortled. "Only a fool would be so foolish."

After another lengthy sweep around the ballroom, Raelynn peered up at him again, her brows gathered in a baffled frown. "You've made me curious, Farrell."

"How so, madam?"

If you haven't ever been married and don't have any sisters, would you kindly explain what you meant when you said you've experienced the kind of tension that Brandon is presently going through? Are you saying you were present when a baby was born? Or are you talking about something else entirely?"

"I was there when Elizabeth gave birth to Jake. At one time, her husband was my closest friend, and after he was killed, I took his body home to bury. That same night Elizabeth's labor started. I was as worked up as a fish on a hook until the midwife came out to the porch and showed me the baby. Elizabeth never once cried out through the whole of it, but I could hear other little noises that affirmed the fact that she was in pain. By the time it was all over, my knees were as weak as water."

"Then you've known Elizabeth for some time," Rae-lynn concluded.

"I met her late husband, Emory, in my earlier boxing days. We became friends. He went to Georgia to work for a while, and when he came back, he introduced me to his fiancée, who had come with her parents to visit him. I thought Elizabeth was the most beautiful woman I had ever seen in my life, but, of course, she was already spoken for. I provided the ring as best man at their wedding. The rest is a long story. Before her husband was killed, he gambled away all their money, leaving Elizabeth in dire straits. After his death, she came to work for me and has helped my business to become what it is today. Even with what she now earns, Elizabeth still scrimps and saves for the boy's future. She says she wants him to have a better start in life than his father had."

"I'm sure Elizabeth was grateful that you were there when she needed you. Since then you've probably proven yourself a friend in many other ways."

Farrell made no comment. What could he say when he was not at all sure where he stood with the raven-haired beauty?

THE GUESTS STAYED MUCH LATER THAN RAELYNN had ever expected, and when finally they began to make their departures, it was past midnight. She stood beside her husband at the front door of the plantation house and graciously extended her appreciation of their attendance. More often than not she took advantage of her husband's supporting arm and leaned against his sturdy frame. It had been a long and exhausting day, and though she had entertained recurring fantasies about the night ahead, she wasn't at all sure that she would stay awake long enough to even get undressed.

In the night sky, a slender shaft of moonlight seemed to struggle for survival amid the gathering clouds. The beam of light finally disappeared altogether behind a turbulently roiling mass as strengthening breezes, bearing the scent of an approaching rain, set tree limbs to swaying overhead and open French doors crashing against their jambs. Servants rushed to close them as guests hurriedly waved and scurried to their carriages. The mischievous wind seemed bent on sending top hats cartwheeling down the drive and cloaks flapping almost vertically out behind their owners.

Brandon and Heather were among the last to leave, and as the elder Birmingham escorted his wife to the door, Raelynn smilingly observed his tender solicitations. Since becoming Jeffrey's wife, so much had happened that she had had little time to consider how truly fortunate she was to be a member of the Birmingham clan. The realization had first dawned on her at the church social when Brandon's delightful family had captured her heart. Brandon, himself, had accepted her with gentle courtesy, for which she would always be grateful. As for Heather, that lovely lady was already becoming as near and dear to her as a sister.

"You were enchanting, my dear," Heather whispered as they embraced fondly.

"Thank you for being here when I most needed you," Raelynn murmured with a gentle smile. "It seems there are still a few maidens who simply loathe the idea that I'm now Jeffrey's wife."

"Oh, yes, indeed!" Heather waved a graceful hand after the line of carriages vanishing off into the darkness. "I can practically see frustration blazing a trail behind at least a half dozen of them as they try to accept the fact that my brother-in-law is forever lost to them."

Jeff tightened his arm about Raelynn's slender shoulders, bringing her closer against him. "Our hasty marriage has given Charleston society something to chew on 'til well past Christmas."

"Take my word for it, Brother," Brandon observed with a muted chuckle. "It won't stop nearly that soon."

"I know," Jeff acknowledged, heaving an exaggerated sigh, "not until we're old and gray."

"Now that's more the truth of it," Brandon affirmed and clapped a hand upon his brother's shoulder. "Sorry as I am to tell you this, Jeffrey, but the gossips will flay us with their tongues until we're laid low in our graves, and just maybe, they won't even relent then."

"Thanks for your heartening words of encouragement, Bran," Jeff replied tongue in cheek, making much of his dejection. "I could've gone a score of years without hearing that."

"You're welcome," the elder rejoined with a chipper grin.

"Don't look so proud of yourself," Heather chided her husband with her laughter as she slipped an arm through his. "We're just as susceptible."

"How well I know," Brandon conceded and settled a large hand upon her distended belly. "At least with this baby there hasn't been as many tongues wagging as there was with Beau."

Heather giggled. "That's because Jeff and Raelynn have recently garnered most of the attention."

Accepting his wife's cloak from a servant, Brandon spread it about her shoulders and fastened the silken frogs beneath her chin. Heather looked up into his glowing eyes with a winsomely mutinous pout, drawing a chuckle from him as he gently chucked her beneath the chin. "Indulge me, my sweet. I feel a pressing need to take care of you."

Casting a wry glance down at her own belly, his wife sighed forlornly. "By the time this baby is born, you're not going to even allow me to walk."

Scarcely had the words crossed her lips than her husband swept her up into his arms. Ignoring her startled squeal, he queried, "Why should I wait till then, madam? You scarcely weigh more than a mite even now. Besides, I find you much easier to control when you're safely within my arms."

Whatever reply Heather might have made was lost as Brandon laughingly bade his own farewells and bore her swiftly down the steps to their waiting carriage. Raelynn's last glimpse of her sister-in-law was when Heather leaned out the carriage window and waved farewell amid a flurry of giggles spurred on by Brandon's attempts to drag her back into his arms.

As a chuckling servant closed the front door, Jeff followed his brother's lead by swooping Raelynn up into his arms and whisking her to their bedroom, leaving Cora and Kingston grinning and shaking their heads.

"Yassuh, somebody's always puttin' somethin' fermented in de punch," Kingston observed, his shoulders shaking with his erupting chuckles.

The master's suite offered a sweet respite for the couple after the tumult of the party, but tonight it was even more refreshing as the scent of rain still lingered in the rooms. The bedchamber was a private retreat that no servant, unless summoned, would dare enter while the master or mistress was there. Now, after the last of the guests had gone, the couple's seclusion was deemed secure.

As much as Raelynn had fantasized about how the evening would end, she now felt completely drained. When her husband laid her upon the bed, she sighed contentedly as she kicked off her slippers and smiled up at him. Earlier in the evening, the bed linens had been folded down by a servant, and she stretched luxuriously upon the freshly scented sheets, content to be able just to relax.

"You'll have to undress me," she cajoled charmingly,

walking a pair of fingers up her husband's sleeve. "Otherwise, I shall have to call for Tizzy."

"No need to do that, madam, when I'm here and eager to be of service." Jeff's leering grin bested anything that Gustav could have ever managed. Unceremoniously he flipped her onto her stomach, drawing an exaggerated "oomph" from her, and proceeded to unfasten the placket that trailed downward from the top of her gown to well below her waist.

Once Jeff had loosened her gown enough to allow her to free herself from the bodice and the top of the satin chemise, Raelynn slid both garments off her shoulders and pushed them down to her waist. Gathering a pillow within her arms, she snuggled her chin contentedly upon it. "You know, sir, if you please me well enough, I just might keep you on as my lady's maid."

For that, Jeff gave her a lusty slap on the posterior.

"Beast!" she cried in feigned outrage.

"Beast, is it?" He slid the shimmering sheath down her body in one fell swoop, this time eliciting a genuine gasp of surprise from his wife.

"On second thought, I'll keep Tizzy," she concluded with a giggle.

Since Elizabeth had complained during a fitting session that his wife's pantalettes created unsightly bulges beneath the ball gown, Raelynn had elected not to wear anything other than stockings and the lace-trimmed satin chemise under the dress. As a result Jeff was wont to admire with more than just his eyes the way the undergarment cleaved to her buttocks, and for a lengthy moment he caressed her fetching derriere through the soft satin. Lending himself totally to the task of stripping the shift from her, he took advantage of every curve and vale within immediate range, sliding his right hand beneath a soft breast as his left followed the gentle curve of her back down to her buttocks and thighs, in the process pushing the chemise lower. Once he dragged the garment free, he turned her over again and proceeded to strip away her stockings.

After laying aside the garments, Jeff braced his arms beside her and smilingly searched her face as he leaned over her. Her eyes were soft and liquid, melding with his, and as if awed by something beyond his ken, she lifted a hand and caressed his cheek with a sort of reverent wonder. Touched by her tenderness, he pressed a lingering kiss into her palm. Strange words rose unbidden to Raelynn's lips, words that she had never before spoken to anyone other than her parents. The ease with which she had almost blurted them startled her, for she had never thoroughly considered them ere this moment in time.

Though Jeff realized his wife was physically spent, he couldn't resist a long, grazing caress over her naked body. Even bone-tired, Raelynn caught her breath at the sensations he awakened within her. Then his hand stroked into more private areas, and willingly she opened herself to him as her eyes darkened with desire. She watched him undress, and when he stood beside the bed totally devoid of clothes and bold as any man could be, she welcomed him with uplifted arms.

Much later, Raelynn drifted off to sleep with her head upon her husband's shoulder, her leg bent and resting across his sturdy thighs. As she sank into the depths of slumber, she whispered something that Jeff couldn't quite catch at first. He canted his head to hear her better, but nothing more than a softly wafting sigh came from her lips.

Stuffing the pillow more firmly beneath his head, he smiled at the ceiling. He knew what her low murmur had sounded like, but at this point in their marriage, he couldn't be sure if he was letting his imagination sweep him away.

9 ✑

Stirring from the pleasurable arms of Morpheus, Raelynn lay for some moments trying to determine what had
awakened her. The draperies which had earlier been drawn
across the French doors had since been pulled aside. Beyond the upper panes of glass in the last portal, a bright
October moon hovered in the night sky while vaporish
clouds, driven by a westerly wind, drifted across its luminous face. The zephyrs rustled the tops of the huge trees.
Now and then she could hear the boughs of the live oak at
the end of the house scraping the brick facade, but beyond
that meager sound, the room was deathly silent.

Her hand reached out to the far side of the bed in
search of the man in whose presence she had learned to
trust and take comfort. Alas, no one was there. Her eyes
probed the darkly shrouded areas of their chambers, but
alas, she found no smallest evidence of the man within
the confines of the room.

"Jeffrey?" she called in a muffled tone, and her brows gathered in deepening confusion as the silence continued. Clearing her throat, she made another effort in a somewhat louder tone. "Jeffrey? Where are you?"

Once again a hushed stillness answered her.

Sweeping back the covers, Raelynn swung her legs over the side of the bed and hurriedly donned the nightgown and robe Jeff had left on a chair beside her commode. She searched the bedside table, found the tinderbox and managed to light the oil lamp residing there. By its meager light, she peered obliquely at the clock on the mantel.

Half past one!

At best, she had slept for no more than forty minutes. But where had Jeffrey gone? Why had he left their bed?

Rubbing her arms against the chill sweeping inward on the wings of the night breezes, Raelynn wove an unsteady path across the room. The currents flowing through the open French doors were fairly bracing, but she gave hardly a second thought to the insufficiency of her garments as she stepped out onto the veranda. Certainly Jeffrey was out here, she assured herself, but after a glance in each direction, she grew even more mystified, for she realized she was quite alone.

To her knowledge, Jeffrey had never once wandered from their bed in the middle of the night, and she was greatly troubled by his absence, for she had no idea what had prompted him to leave. Had he heard a noise that he had found troubling? Instantly Gustav came to mind, and at the possibility that that boorish lout might have decided to come back with his men to do more mischief, perhaps to revenge himself upon Jeff, a violent shudder shivered through her.

"Jeffrey, where are you?" she called forlornly.

Suddenly she fell victim to a chest-constricting emotion comparable to the grief she had suffered after each of her parents' deaths. No longer confident of her husband's safety, she felt lost and forlorn. It seemed as if in an instant of time her whole life had become barren and destitute.

Raelynn clutched a trembling hand to her throat in some astonishment and stared into the shadows surrounding her as a slowly awakening awareness began to dawn. "Oh, Jeffrey," she whispered. "What work have you done in my heart?"

No answer came; nor did she have a need for one. Her emotions had transcended everything she had ever known before. The feeling likened itself to a burgeoning warmth that ran like a winding river through her, infusing her very being with essences of joy, serenity, benevolence, devotion and . . . Raelynn canted her head as she strove to bring the eluding thought into focus. No longer merely infatuation, she thought, but was it really love?

Out of the corner of her eye, Raelynn caught a glimpse of a flickering light off in the distance and glanced around expectantly, only to be met with a darkness faintly mottled by the moonlight shining through the foliage at the tops of the lofty oaks. Wondering if she had imagined the tiny radiance, she squinted in the direction from whence it had seemingly come, hoping to find a viable source for the ephemeral twinkle. At first, she saw nothing, only heard the wind rustling through the leaves and a few droplets of rain falling belatedly to the ground, but as she swept her gaze slowly about, the lower branches of the live oak dipped downward with the impetus of the freshening breezes, allowing her to verify that there was indeed a wane light, and that it appeared to be coming from the stables.

Normally at such an hour, the trainers and grooms would be asleep, but if there was perhaps a problem with one of the horses, then, with a certainty, they'd be up and moving about. Quite possibly Jeff had noticed the light from the house or had heard something and gone out to investigate.

Raelynn ran back into the bedroom and hurriedly donned slippers before making her descent of the stairs at the end of the porch. She raced across the lawn, shivering as she went. Upon reaching the stables, she quickly discovered that the meager illumination was streaming from a single lantern hanging from a buttressing beam in Ariadne's stall. Though the door stood open, she could see no sign of the mare and felt a sudden stabbing concern that the beautiful animal had colicked and was perhaps down in her stall.

Worry quickened Raelynn's strides, but barely an instant later, she was brought up short by a sudden squalling.

A baby? Her mind had trouble accepting such a feasibility. *Here in the stables?*

Raelynn no longer walked. She ran. Toward the stall. Upon reaching the door, she clasped the corner timber and was about to swing inward when she was brought to a stumbling halt. Ariadne was nowhere to be seen. In her stead was a hideous nightmare. Raelynn had a sudden, sweeping vision of blood. Everywhere! On the fresh wood shavings covering the clay floor! On the bodice and skirt of a yellow dress! On slender fingers curled limply in death! On a small bundled form from whence came the outraged wailing of an infant!

Raelynn clasped a trembling hand over her mouth to smother a threatening scream as her eyes swept along the small, trim form sprawled grotesquely across the thickly mulched floor. Though the skirt was splotched with dark stains, the source of the bleeding seemed to have come from the area of the midriff. A deep pool of the gore had soaked the yellow gown above the slender waist. From there, Raelynn's gaze rose upward to the golden hair and the youthful face.

"Nell!"

It was hardly much more than a strangled whisper that escaped Raelynn's throat, but at the sound, a tall, manly form rose from the dark shadows obscuring the corner of the stall. A startled gasp was wrenched from her and, in sudden trepidation, she stumbled back, fully expecting to be attacked by this culprit who had killed the girl. Then the lantern's glow lit upon the man's face, and she could only stare in confusion at his chiseled profile and bloody shirt.

"Jeffrey? What are you doin . . ."

Her eyes swept downward to the knife that hung limply from his grasp, a gleaming blade with a handle carved in the shape of a ram's head.

"Raelynn . . ." His voice sounded strange, as if it came from a distant vale. He stepped toward her, reaching out his free hand. His face looked strained, his mouth drawn in a grim line, his eyes strangely shadowed by an emotion she had never seen in them before. She stared at him as if he were a stranger. Yet, less than a pair of hours ago they had made love as man and wife, and only a moment ago she had come to a heartfelt realization . . .

Her eyes dropped again to the blade that he still held and, from there, swept to the dead girl. In an instant, her awakening awareness that this man was as dear to her as her own lifeblood, her recent awareness that a change was taking place in her own body, the joy she had come to know in her husband's arms and in his house were cruelly trodden beneath the heart-wrenching emotions of past doubts and fears, the heartache of parents who had been cruelly betrayed, and a deeply buried sense that her fairy tale existence was too good to be true . . . Whatever joy she had recently been savoring as the wife of Jeffrey Birmingham was marred by the sweeping stain of blood. A sobbing cry surged upward from the pit of her being, and this time she could not contain it.

"Noooo!"

No longer able to suppress her horror and the hideous suspicion that now assailed her, Raelynn retreated. For a moment, Jeff seemed frozen. Then, with a muttered curse, he hurled the bloody knife into the bedding near the corner of the stall and stepped toward her.

"Hear me out, Rae . . ."

A slash of her hand negated any possibility of that happening. Blinded by tears, she whirled and fled his presence, forcing every measure of strength she possessed into her legs as she broke into an all-out, desperate run toward the house. She should've known! It had all been too perfect! Jeffrey, their marriage, her growing involvement with the man! But it had all been a sham, a deceitful lie!

Her heart hammering wildly, her choked sobs smothering her, Raelynn threw a teary glance over her shoulder and found her husband striding swiftly after her. By the time she bolted up the porch stairs, she was gasping for breath between harsh, anguishing sobs. Swiping an arm across her face to wipe away the flooding rivers spilling forth in gushing torrents, she raced into their bedroom and glanced around desperately for a place to hide. Jeffrey knew his chambers far too well for her to feel safe in any shadowed corner here. The best she could do was to delay him in his search while she sought a way to escape.

Gasping from fear, torment and the exertion reaped from her fierce effort to escape, Raelynn slammed the French doors closed along the veranda and then dashed across the room, brushing away tears as she ran. Once she slipped into the hallway, she closed the portal quietly behind her. Barely had she gained the security of her former bedchamber and turned the key in the lock than she heard footfalls in the hall. It had taken Jeffrey less than a thrice of moments to discover her deception.

Jeff tested the door briefly before he rapped his knuckles against the plank. Knowing well that his wife was terrified after what she had seen, he made an effort to keep his voice gentle and softly subdued, "Raelynn, my love, don't be frightened of me, please. I didn't kill Nell. You've got to believe me."

Crouched on the bed, shivering with fear and heart-rending emotions, Raelynn pressed violently shaking fingers to her lips to smother her sobs. In the dark gloom that surrounded her, she stared fixedly through blurring tears at the wooden barrier that stood between herself and the man she had come to know as husband and lover. She heard him mutter a curse and then, in some relief, his footsteps retreating to his bedroom. In the distance, a door opened and closed. She listened warily in trembling trepidation as silence reined unimpeded for what seemed like a century or more. Then a soft thump on the porch and an advancing light sent her flying off the bed as she realized what she had forgotten. One of the pair of French doors was always kept unlocked for the servants!

An instant before her husband reached the double doors, she slammed the bolt home, securing her safety, at least temporarily. Bathed in the glow of the oil lamp, the two of them stood facing each other, scant inches apart, separated not only by the glass-paned, rectangular-shaped muntins of the French doors, but by the horrible suspicions that had suddenly erupted between them.

A booted foot could have easily dispensed with the barrier, but Jeff knew that breaking down the door would likely send his wife fleeing like a woman possessed and, no doubt, solidify the awful suspicions in her mind. Somehow he had to soothe her fears.

Meeting her gaze through the wealth of tears brimming her eyes, Jeff made every attempt to speak calmly. "Raelynn, my love, I realize you've had a terrible shock, but there's no reason for you to be afraid of me. Don't you understand? When I reached the stables, Nell was already dead. I was just falling asleep when I heard her scream, and I went down to investigate. Now, please, Raelynn, my love, just open the door and let me talk with you. I'm not going to hurt you. I would never do such a thing."

Over and over, the hideous reminder of Nell lying bloody and lifeless in the horse stall jolted Raelynn with waves of shocking horror. She had no idea why the girl had come out to Oakley again after Jeff had warned her not to, but with all the guests arriving and then later departing, Nell's presence would hardly have been noticed, certainly not by any of the staff. The stable hands had been assigned the task of fetching water for the teams of visiting carriages soon after their arrival. It was a courtesy extended in consideration of the lengthy jaunt from Charleston and neighboring plantations and the possibility of the festivities lasting until the wee hours of the morning. After performing the service, the grooms had likely gone to their respective quarters and then, later, to their beds.

Perhaps once again, Nell had come to the plantation to plead for support for a child she had insisted was Jeff's, conceivably having reasoned that if he could give such a lavish ball in honor of his wife, then surely he could afford a monthly stipend for the babe. Nell's most recent accusations had attested to her inability to comprehend Jeff's reluctance to share any portion of his wealth with her and her offspring in spite of his vast riches. Quite simply she had failed to understand his refusal to be blackmailed. Though he could expend a generous sum saving a black girl from the abuse of her former master, there was a hard-core stubbornness within Jeff that would not allow him to be coerced by threats. Raelynn had seen it in her father, and she had glimpsed it in her husband. That hadn't bothered her in the least. What now plagued her was the possibility that Nell might have driven Jeff beyond the limits of his patience. He had told the girl during her last visit that he wanted to strangle her. If he had become truly vexed with her, there was the possibility that he had lost his temper and put a permanent end to her harassment.

Much as Raelynn shrank from the idea of her gallant, handsome husband harming *any* woman in *any* fashion, she could not dismiss what she had seen with her own eyes. He had been holding a bloody knife that had obviously killed Nell, a knife that he himself owned and normally kept on his desk in the bedroom. How could she thrust those facts from her mind?

Raelynn's face contorted with wrenching emotions as cascading tears continued to flow unheeded. Jeff was her beautiful husband. He had saved her from the dire fate of becoming Gustav's possession, had transported her into a world of luxury, and had taught her the joy of marital bliss and fulfillment as a woman. Yet, at the moment, she felt as if she really didn't know him at all. The experience of the past year had taught her how easily one could trust the wrong people and be betrayed by them. Hadn't her own father been accused of traitorous deeds by other noblemen, albeit strangers to her? Her mother's acceptance of Cooper Frye as her long lost brother had eventually led to her tragic death aboard ship. Lately *trusting* seemed a very risky business indeed.

"Please go away, Jeff," she choked tearfully, fearing now to meet his gaze through the glass panes. Those darkly translucent eyes silently pleading for her to listen and to believe in him had the strength to rend her very soul. "I need time to sort this matter out in my mind and for the shock to ease. Perhaps I can think more clearly after I'm allowed some time to myself."

Jeff lifted a hand to make another appeal, but when his wife's gaze became riveted on the extremity, he glanced toward it and realized his fingers were covered with sticky gore. Slowly he lowered his arm to his side and heaved a despondent sigh. Talking to his wife at this point seemed futile; she was clearly terrified of him.

Slowly he walked away, retreating to his bedchamber and leaving her to consider his innocence or guilt.

Exhausted and trembling so violently she could hardly stand, Raelynn turned on wobbly limbs and stumbled back to the bed. Flinging herself across it, she buried her face into the pillows and allowed her sobs to flow unrestrained. The cold, dark, murky feeling in the pit of her stomach refused to yield to reason and trust. It was as if Jeff had already been convicted, and there was only the hanging to be witnessed.

Dark, impenetrable gloom settled in with a vengeance, and at length, mental exhaustion dragged her down into a dazed stupor. Merciful darkness flickered at the edge of her awareness, drawing her down into a dark, deep vale.

◦≫"GRACIOUS ME ALIVE, MISTAH JEFFREY! IS YO' WOUNDED, suh?"

Having scrambled out of bed and dragged on a dressing robe on his way downstairs, Kingston was still blinking sleep from his eyes when he caught sight of his approaching master. The shock of so much blood had widened the dark orbs precipitously. Almost as swiftly his jaw had dropped.

The slamming of several doors had awakened Kingston even in his quarters on the top floor of the manse. Before hastening from his room, he had seized a stout stick, which after Gustav Fridrich's visit, he had been keeping underneath his bed on the chance that the German and his unruly rabble would come back and launch another forceful invasion. Yet, upon espying his master, Kingston had cause to wonder if he should have collected the medical supplies instead.

Jeff could imagine the morbid spectacle he presented in bloodstained garments and with his hands and arms smeared with sticky red. Though he had been on his way to awaken the butler and issue instructions, in view of his own appearance, it now seemed necessary to allay the man's qualms. "The blood isn't mine, Kingston. I'm afraid it came from Nell. Someone stabbed the girl to death in the stable. Her baby is out there, too, squalling his head off, but, as far as I know, he's unharmed. What I need you to do is to fetch the boy and find him a wet nurse, but you'd better be prepared for a ghastly sight. Whoever murdered Nell was rather vicious about it."

Jeff paused to force the scene from the forefront of his own thoughts. After a moment he heaved a troubled sigh and continued. "Send one of the grooms to Charleston to fetch the sheriff. While we're waiting for him, ask Sparky and Thaddeus to search the stall for some clue to the murderer's identity."

Kingston finally closed his mouth and gulped. "Yassuh, Mistah Jeffrey. Ah'll be seein' ta those things right away, suh. But in de meantime, be there anythin' yo'll be needin'? Yo' sho' is lookin' mighty upset."

Jeff could think of several things right off, beginning with the reasons behind Nell's death and the name of her murderer. "I am, Kingston, but there's nothing you can do about that. It will probably take some time for me to get over the brutality of this foul deed. Considering my last confrontation with Nell, I suppose people will be thinking I had something to do with her murder."

"Naw, suh!" Kingston shook his head, affirming the fact that such an idea had never crossed his mind. "At least, not any o' us whad's been knowin' an' workin' for yo' for a while. If'n yo' had it in yo' ta do somethin' like dat ta Miz Nell, then yo'da've been o' a mind ta beat one o' us or maybe dat ornery mule, Brutus, but yo' ne'er even been so much as cross wit' us, Mistah Jeffrey."

"I was certainly *cross* with Nell," Jeff pointed out.

"Yassuh, an' so was ah, but yo' had good reason ta be aftah whad she done tried ta do, sneakin' inta your bed when yo' was asleep an' den tryin' ta say yo' made a baby wit' her. Why, ah was so vexed wit' her ah wanted ta take a switch ta her myself."

"There's a baby in the stables crying to be fed, Kingston," Jeff reminded the man. "We shouldn't stand here talking about this matter while the boy is in need."

"Yassuh, I'ma goin' now."

Upon his return to his bedchambers, Jeff made quick work of removing his bloodstained clothing. The water in the washbowl was tepid, but he hardly noticed. He scrubbed his hands, face and chest with soap and water, wishing he could scour with the same cleansing results the bloody scene from his mind.

Once more garbed in fresh clothes, Jeff picked up a lamp and made his way back along the veranda to the French doors behind which his wife had taken shelter. The room was dark, and only by the soft light streaming from his lamp could he see her huddled in a knot on the far side of the bed. The meager radiance failed to draw a reaction, leaving him no other option but to conclude that his wife had fallen asleep in the midst of the horrible trauma she had suffered.

It was just as well, Jeff mused dismally. Her mind needed the soothing succor of sleep after what she had seen. If he had been able to block the morbid scene from his own mind in such a way, he'd have gone right then and there to his bed, but he had heard Nell's pitiful requests for some show of affection and was now plagued by a deep remorse for not having helped the girl in a way that, in the simplest sense, could not have been construed as kowtowing to her blackmailing demands.

A pensive sigh slipped from Jeff's lips before he realized that he was as tense as a twisted cord. He had a clear idea what the scene in Ariadne's stall must have looked like to Raelynn. After all, he had been holding the murder weapon, a knife that had obviously gone missing from his desk sometime during the ball. Anyone attending the affair could have entered his chambers and taken it, for that's exactly what the murderer had done, stolen his knife to kill a young girl.

Growing curious as to the child's welfare, Jeff went downstairs to make inquiries and intercepted Kingston just as the butler was returning with the wailing infant.

"Lawsy, Mistah Jeffrey," the man drawled above the squalling. "Ah ain't ne'er seen de likes o' a woman stabbed afore. For a li'l thing, Miss Nell sho' lost a lot o' blood. Ah was sure dis li'l fella was hurt, too, what wit' him all covered wit' blood an' squallin' enuff ta raise de roof, but he's jes' mad, Mistah Jeffrey, jes' like yo' said."

Jeff glanced down at the baby who was making every effort to let his distress be known. Considering the fact that the tiny face was compressed in a small, outraged ball, it was impossible to make any firm judgments as to the infant's looks. Other than black hair, any resemblance between the two of them seemed farfetched in spite of Nell's assertions, but then, coincidences had a way of happening.

"Have you found a wet nurse yet?"

"Yassuh, de overseer's wife say she can nurse Mistah Daniel right along wit' her own. Ain't gonna be no trouble atall, Miz Fergus said ta tell yo'." Kingston glanced aside as he heard the patter of brisk footfalls and inclined his head toward the housekeeper who was hurrying toward them from the back of the house. "Here's Cora now, suh. She's come ta fetch de babe for Miz Fergus."

Cora gathered the bawling baby into her arms and checked him over quickly to verify for herself that the gore on his blanket wasn't from him. "We'll look aftah de po' li'l fella, Mistah Jeffrey. Doan yo' go worryin' yo'self none atall 'bout him."

Having been reassured in that area, Jeff returned to the stables and felt some relief when he noticed that a sheet had been draped over Nell's body. Sparky and Thaddeus had been given the task of sorting through the wood shavings and, when Jeff appeared at the stall door, the younger man stepped near.

"We ain't found nothin' yet, Mistah Jeffrey." The trainer cast a nervous glance toward the covered body. "We've searched everywhere but underneath Miz Nell."

"The sheriff can do that after he gets here," Jeff said, taking pity on the two men.

Visibly relieved, Sparky nodded jerkily.

Thaddeus shuffled from the stall, solemnly shaking his head. "Mistah Jeffrey, ah've asked all de stables hands, but I can't find nobody whad heared or seen whad went on here last night."

Jeff glanced down the aisle toward the other stalls before he returned a bemused frown to Sparky. "But where is Ariadne?"

"We put her in the paddock next to the stables last night, suh, but since then, we ain't seen hide nor hair o' her."

"Why in heaven's name did you put her out, Sparky? You know that if she takes it into her head, she can jump any fence on my land."

"Well, suh, she was a-kickin' the boards o' the stall next ta hers an' makin' such a racket, we was afraid she was gonna knock down de barn. I tell yo', Mistah Jeffrey, she was madder'n ol' wet hen. The minute I opened the stall door, she came a-chargin' out like her tail was on fire. Nearly trampled me in her haste ta be gone."

"Did you perhaps notice if anyone was in the stall next to hers?"

"Like I said, Mistah Jeffrey, she come a-stampedin' outa there like a flyin' demon. After I got holdt o' her, I didn't bother takin' a lantern an' havin' a look-see in the stall. There didn't seem ta be any need at the time. I was more concerned about gettin' her settled down."

"Can you remember about what time that was, Sparky?" Jeff probed.

The trainer scratched his chin thoughtfully. "Maybe

'round eleven or even a li'l later. Can't remember for sure, suh."

"Search the next stall to see what you can find, Sparky. If a stranger was hiding there at the time, it could explain why Ariadne was raising up a ruckus."

"That fool mare would've kicked the fella's head off if'n he'da've tried goin' inta her stall, but I guess that didn't happen, 'cause I ain't seen another body laid out around here."

"The murderer might have taken such a chance in order to hide out from one of you. Maybe that's what set Ariadne off in the first place."

"Well, if'n the fella still has his head, he's probably nigh senseless. That mare's too ornery for just any fool ta get cozy with."

Thaddeus cast a doleful glance at the sheet-draped body and shook his head mournfully, overwhelmed by the grotesque horror of it all. "Whad kind o' man could do such a thin', Mistah Jeffrey? Killin' a li'l gal what's done had herself a baby jes' seems like somethin' de devil'd do."

To kill a young mother with a nursing infant definitely seemed a violation of nature, Jeff mentally agreed. People in the area would be aghast at the foulness of the deed. What was worse, Nell had been killed in his stables. Realistically he could imagine that Raelynn would only be the first of many who'd be suspicious of his involvement in the girl's murder.

The tears and fear Jeff had glimpsed in his wife's eyes when she had stared at him in the stables pierced him anew. Somehow he had to persuade her of his innocence.

He faced Sparky again. "Are any of the other horses missing?"

"No, suh, not that I'm aware."

Jeff grew more determined. "Send someone out to

find Elijah, Son of Wolf. I'd like to find out what he can make of all of this."

"Yes, suh, Mistah Jeffrey."

Upon his return to the plantation house, Jeff ensconced himself at his desk in the study and tried to concentrate on his account books for the plantation as he awaited the arrival of Sheriff Townsend. More than an hour later a knock sounded on the door.

Kingston entered at his summons. "Elijah's here, Mistah Jeffrey."

"Show him in."

A tall, thin man of an age about two score five entered the room with hat in hand. He had obviously been awakened from a sound sleep by the summons. Nevertheless he was garbed in the clothes of his preference, buckskins and moccasins. His nose was lean and bore an aquiline curve, his features sharply chiseled, his black hair straight and cut bluntly just below his ears. His cocoa brown skin bore a reddish tinge, indicating his mixed blood. Rumor had it that Elijah's mother, once a beautiful mulatto slave, had been taken captive at the age of five and ten by an Indian warrior, who had later made her his wife. A pair of years later another warring tribe raided the warrior's camp, and after finding her husband dead, the mulatto had slipped away with her son. Thereafter they had lived in a hut on the outskirts of Charleston and fended for themselves until Elijah's twelfth winter, when she had succumbed to pneumonia.

"Yo' sent for me, suh?" Elijah asked in a deep voice that resonated in the room.

"Yes, I did, Elijah, and I thank you for coming so promptly." Jeff peered at him questioningly. "Did anyone tell you what happened here?"

"Sparky let me know details on way ta house, suh," the pathfinder acknowledged.

"The murder of the girl occurred in one of the horse stalls. At present, her body is still there. See what you can find in and around the stables. For a beginning reference, you can check the footprints of everyone working out there. If you come upon any prints that aren't familiar, see where they lead. If they disappear near a set of carriage or wagon wheel tracks, we may be reasonably assured that the fellow either arrived or left by that mode of travel. If you should find a double pair of prints, one belonging to the girl, we can be fairly certain that Nell came out here with her murderer, but I leave you to be the judge of that."

Any remaining traces of slumber had vanished from Elijah's eyes. They were now keen, alert and imbued with a brighter light. "Sparky say it rain here last night. If water not wash prints away, I can do that, suh."

Jeff managed a bland smile. Elijah's tracking skills were nearly legendary throughout the Carolinas. Several years ago, the man had been sent out to search for a young child who had wandered off over rough terrain and bare rock ledges. Elijah never once lost the trail and eventually brought the youngster home safe and sound. Similar stories of his abilities assured Jeff that the man could find what others might overlook.

"Do your best, Elijah," he urged. "Sheriff Townsend should be here shortly. If you find anything significant, you'll be helping him solve this dastardly crime."

Elijah left the study, and in his absence, Jeff began to pace about the confines of the room. Permanently etched in his memory was a haunting impression of Raelynn's face stricken with horror. A strengthening desire to put things right between his wife and himself became almost overwhelming, and he struggled against the impetus that nearly drove him to leap up the stairs and to confront her about her readiness to believe the worst of him. There was that part of him that was highly offended by her refusal to hear him out. Once before she had taken Nell's accusations seriously and had cast him from her bed, but he knew what Raelynn had recently seen would have shocked any woman. He also recognized the possible folly in stampeding her. If he faced her again and saw her quailing before him in mortal fear, it would nearly tear his heart out. No, he told himself, it was far better to let her have some time to put things into perspective. Perhaps then she could extend to him some marital courtesy by trusting in him through thick and thin.

Sipping from the cup of hot coffee that Kingston had brought to him, Jeff turned his gaze toward the windows. Little had he imagined after the grand affair which they had enjoyed the previous night that today would be comparable to hell. Sadly he watched the first dawning rays stretch out over Oakley and heaved a sigh of lament.

10 ⊱

*T*he sun had just risen above the tree-lined horizon when Sheriff Rhys Townsend and the rider who had been sent out after him arrived on horseback. The tall, brawny man swung down from his saddle and, with his usual easy rolling gait, strode across the front drive. When he climbed the front steps, Jeff was already crossing the porch to meet him.

"Good of you to come so quickly, Rhys."

The sheriff doffed his hat as he followed his friend into the main hall. "Your man said you had a murdered woman here, Jeff. What the hell happened?"

Jeff gestured toward the study. "We'll talk in there if you don't mind."

Rhys nodded and, entering the room, plunked himself down into his favorite leather chair. A moment later Kingston entered, bearing a silver coffee service, and poured the sheriff a cup from the ornate pot. Gratefully

Rhys nodded his thanks as he accepted the brew and then motioned for the servant to leave the service.

"If I'm going to remain standing on my feet, Kingston, I'll be needing lots more of this stuff. Some people don't have any compunction about keeping a fella up till the wee morning hours and then rousting him out of his bed barely an hour after he reaches home."

Kingston managed a weak smile in spite of the trauma that still held the household in its grip. "Yassuh, Mistah Rhys, and dat's de gospel."

As the butler left, the sheriff downed the strong, black contents without lowering his cup. Jeff came around to the front of his desk and leaned back against the top edge, prompting Rhys to set aside his cup and glance up at his host. Meeting his friend's gaze, Jeff quietly explained what had happened, at least as much as he knew.

"I was just falling asleep when I heard a woman scream. That was about one in the morning. After realizing that it had come from the general direction of the stables, I lit a lantern and went down to have a look around. I found Nell in one of the stalls with her baby. The girl was still alive, but only barely. She begged me to remove the knife. I did so, hoping I could stem the flow of blood, but she was fading fast. She asked me to hold her close just for a moment as if I really, truly cared for her. I did so, and she died in my arms." He shook his head at the grim memory. "I can't imagine the kind of monster who would do such a thing. The girl couldn't have been more than six and ten years old at the most."

"Did Nell say anything else to you, perhaps some indication of the killer's identity?" Rhys Townsend asked. Noticeably absent was the rough dialect he was inclined to fake.

"No, she just seemed concerned about her child's welfare. She asked me to find a woman to care for him."

"Then she realized she was dying?"

"I would imagine so. She had lost a lot of blood and had grown very weak."

"Yet she made no effort to name the one who had stabbed her."

"None whatsoever. She just seemed to be grateful that I was there." Jeff's face was grim as he recalled her pitiful attempts. "She ran her hand over my sleeve and tried to smile at me."

"After she succumbed, what did you do?"

Jeff hesitated. He was reluctant to expose Raelynn's suspicions of him, but he could hardly avoid answering the question. "I sat back in the shadows for a while, just staring at Nell's body, stunned by the savagery of her murder. A few moments later, my wife arrived. She had also been awakened. I'm not entirely sure by what. I think she came out to see where I was. Naturally, she became distraught when she saw Nell."

"Where is she now?"

"Upstairs sleeping. At least, she was a few moments ago. Right now, I'd rather not see her disturbed any more than she has been, if it's at all possible, Rhys."

"I can talk with her later." The sheriff reached across to the silver service and helped himself by pouring another cup of coffee. "Do you suppose Nell came out last night to have a look-see at you and your guests?"

Jeff lent his attention to the liquid in his own cup as he silently debated his options. Though it might well incriminate him in the girl's murder, he saw the need for further explanations. "Nell came out here to the plantation the middle of July, shortly after Brandon and I had left you and your men to search Gustav's warehouse for stolen goods. On the porch of this very house, she accused me rather loudly of being the father of her unborn child. When my wife came out, Nell had the audacity to suggest that Raelynn and I get an annulment. At the end of July, I saw her briefly at Farrell's where she had started working. Then, about a week ago, she came out here again, I suppose to show me that the infant bore some resemblance to me."

Rhys lifted his brows to a lofty height, but Jeff waved away the man's unspoken question with a slash of his hand. Long ago he had come to the realization that his friend was very adept at coaxing people to talk. Largely by facial expressions and silently biding his time, Rhys managed to encourage confidences. Yet Jeff saw no point in withholding information about Nell's accusations. If Rhys didn't already know about them, then Jeff suffered no uncertainty that the man would find out the truth quickly enough. All he had to do was ask the servants working in the house. In spite of some peoples' suppositions, no doubt arrived at because of the sheriff's affected speech, Rhys was neither a fool nor a dimwit.

"If the boy favors me some small whit, Rhys, then it's because he was sired by a man who may bear some resemblance to me. I'm not the child's father, not by any stretch of the imagination." Jeff sighed and decided to start over from the beginning. "More than a year ago, I hired Nell on for a time to make monogrammed linens for the house. I had heard that she was talented with a needle, and as it turned out, I was very pleased with her work and paid her a good wage. One night, while I was asleep in my room, she slipped into my bed and began fondling me. When I woke up and realized what she had been doing, I sent her packing."

"I take it that nothing of an intimate nature happened between you."

"Definitely not! If Nell was a virgin when she slipped into my bed, then that's how she left it. But as close as I came to climbing on top of her in my sleep, I didn't dare take any chances with her being in the house. I certainly didn't want to have to do the *honorable* thing by her. As soon as she had packed her belongings, Thaddeus took her into Charleston and got her a room there. Obviously it didn't take her long to find herself a man who wouldn't kick her out of his bed, because she had her son almost nine months to the day I let her go."

"Do you think she deliberately tried to get pregnant to implicate you?"

"I really don't know what she did. I never made any effort to understand her reasoning behind it all. She was nothing more than a child to me. Believe me, when I realized who was in bed with me, it was like taking a plunge into an icy pond."

"Apparently she considered herself in love with you."

"A brief infatuation, possibly. She would have grown out of it in time . . . if she had lived."

"Did you and your wife wake up at the same time this morning?"

"No, I left her sleeping in our bed."

"Did she follow you down immediately after you left her?"

"Sadly enough, no. She came later, and the way things looked at that time, I'm afraid her first impression was rather faulty."

"Meaning she came to the conclusion that you had killed Nell?"

"Exactly."

"Have you explained to her what happened?"

"I tried to, but she ran away and locked herself in another room."

"And she's there now, asleep?"

"Yes."

"What about the servants?" Townsend asked. "Were they all in their beds?"

"All but a dozen hired men I had charged to keep watch over the roads east of us and to warn us against a possible attack from Gustav, but they were stationed too far away from the stables to see or hear anything."

"Do you think Gustav is somehow involved in this?"

"It's my earnest belief he's in it somehow. I don't know that he would actually pay one of his men to kill

Nell just to cast the blame on me, nor do I believe that he would do such a deed himself, especially now that he has only one arm that's of any use. With all the men who work for him, who knows what any one of them is capable of doing, given a strong enough incentive. Though it's difficult for me to believe any of them would actually kill a girl just to get me involved, I suppose anything is possible."

"Didn't Olney Hyde threaten to kill Raelynn while she was their captive?"

"He did."

"I seem to recall that Gustav was pretty insistent about keeping your wife, and now it seems that Nell's murder has driven a wedge between you two. It could be Gustav's aim to see that division lengthened into a legal separation or possibly even your hanging."

"I'm sure Gustav would enjoy that, considering what we did to him that night."

"Olney Hyde is definitely living up to his name," Rhys reflected ruefully. "That rascal is hiding out just like a wily fox. Although I've heard enough rumors to know that he's still around, I haven't yet been able to catch him."

"As I told you in late July, my wife spoke to him outside my shipping company. That's when he told her that Gustav was sorry that I was still alive. Olney also said that his parents came here from England when he was but a boy. He boasted about being able to hide out in the swamps. Perhaps that ability comes with the name." He offered a terse smile at his poor attempt at humor. To be certain, his heart just wasn't in it. Every time he said his wife's name, he was inundated by memories of her flight from the stables. "From what I've learned since then, Olney knows the lay of the land around here as well as anyone, if not better. In view of that fact, I'm not at all surprised he can stay hidden. The only one I know who'd be able to find him is Elijah, and

I've already sent him out to have a look around the stables."

Rhys set his cup and saucer down on the tray beside him and, bracing his hands upon the arms of the leather chair, hefted himself to his feet. "It's about time I did the same."

"I'll walk out with you."

Upon nearing the barn, they were joined by Elijah who offered some possible theories. "Earlier rain wash some tracks away, leave ground soft for two different pair that come later," the scout informed them. "Fancy, hand-made boots make one. Other not so fancy make second pair. Both men go out back o' stables and into paddock alongside where horse was taken. Maybe fancy boots chase other."

"Fancy boots certainly doesn't sound like Olney Hyde," Rhys muttered, glancing aside at Jeff.

"No, more like something I would wear," Jeff admitted. "But I haven't been inside the paddock in several days."

"Let's have a look-see at what you've found, Elijah," the sheriff suggested, "and then, I'd like to hear what you make of all of this."

It was just as the scout had said. One pair of footprints not only resembled those that Jeff made with his own boots, but they were as close in size as identical twins. The other set of tracks had been made by a man with much larger feet and who overran his shoes along the outer edges.

Rhys peered at Jeff. "Did you get a good look at Olney's feet when we raided Gustav's warehouse?"

"I wasn't interested in *his* feet," Jeff quipped sardonically. He faced Elijah with a query. "What can you tell us from these tracks?"

"Fancy boots came afterwards, scuffed shoddy ones. Fancy boots return to stable. Other ones end where hooves dig deep in mud, like when horse carries rider."

The sheriff glanced beyond the area in which they were standing. "Did you find any other tracks around the house or in the drive?"

"Passage of many feet an' horses' hooves leave no hint of girl's arrival. Thick, short grass on lawn around house conceal too well. Elijah could find nothing."

"So which pair of tracks do you think belong to the murderer?" Jeff queried, going back to their earlier topic.

Elijah lifted his lean shoulders in a noncommittal shrug. "Maybe after man murder Miss Nell, he stole horse ta escape. Someone see him in barn, give chase. Maybe true, maybe not. It could be other way just as easy."

"Follow the mare's tracks," Jeff instructed. "See where they lead. In the meantime, I'll show the sheriff the stall where Nell was killed."

Rhys waved the scout off and then faced Jeff. "Let's get this nasty business over with."

Jeff accompanied Rhys into the stable and stayed in the aisle outside of Ariadne's stall as his friend examined the body and the wound. After several minutes, Rhys sat back on his haunches and glanced around at Jeff.

"Looks like the girl was stabbed as many as three times at very close range. One gash actually looks like it stopped bleeding; at least one or both of the other two killed her." Rhys casually scanned the area around Nell. "She hasn't been moved or touched since you left her?"

"No, I told Sparky to leave her be." Jeff gestured briefly to the bloody weapon lying in the mulch. "The knife is over there. That's where I dropped it after Rae-lynn became frightened."

Rhys lifted the weapon gingerly. The stains on the gleaming blade revealed its cruel use all too clearly. "Haven't I seen this before?"

"I take it with me when I go hunting," Jeff informed him with measured care. "You probably saw it during one of our trips together. When I'm at home, I usually keep the knife on top of my desk in my bedroom to slice apart pages of new books, which, before Raelynn came along, was my habit to read at night in bed. Since I used the knife before the ball to cut a loose thread, I would assume it was taken sometime during the festivities."

Rhys tested the keen edge. "Pretty sharp, isn't it, Jeff?"

"Like I said, I take it with me when I go hunting. I keep it that way on purpose. I never know when I might venture out to get some wild game. But then, when it's sharp, it makes a cleaner cut when I slice apart pages."

"It's a handsome knife. How did you come by it?"

"My father gave it to me on my twelfth birthday. It serves as a memento of times gone by. It always came in handy when Brandon and I used to go fishing and hunting as boys. We camped out a lot, and since I had the sharpest knife, I always got the chore of whittling down green branches to roast our food over a fire."

Glancing back at the dead girl, Rhys shook his head sadly. "Such a damned, beastly waste." After a lengthy pause, he blew out his breath as if he had found this particular task especially grievous. "Once in a while I used to see Nell going into a church near my office. If I can borrow a wagon and have your men wrap her body up in a blanket, I can take her remains into Charleston and ask the pastor there if he'd perform the burial. I'm sure that would be a relief off your mind."

Jeff's own breath eased outward slowly. "An immense relief, Rhys."

"Why don't we go up to the house now and have a look in your bedroom while Thaddeus and Sparky take care of loading the body?"

They were just leaving the stairs at the end of the second-story veranda when Cora came out of the French doors of the master bedroom carrying a pair of muddy boots.

"Ah'll have dese here boots clean fo' yo' in jes' a jiffy, Mistah Jeffrey," she announced, about to hasten away.

"Wait a minute," Jeff bade, delaying her with a hand upon her arm. "Where did you find those?"

"In your bathin' room, Mistah Jeffrey, behind de door. Ah seen 'em in dere when I was a-cleanin'. Sho surprised me ta see 'em so muddy, yo' bein' so particular an' all 'bout your clothes an' things. Don't yo' wants de boots cleaned, Mistah Jeffrey?"

Jeff cast a worried glance toward Rhys. "I didn't get them muddy."

"Calm yourself, my friend." The sheriff clapped a hand upon his shoulder. "You're not going to be convicted of a crime because of a pair of muddy boots. Now tell me, are they yours?"

"Yes, of course, they're mine, but I haven't worn them in nigh to a week. And as we both can see, this mud is fairly fresh."

"So, in the last week someone could have taken them from your room without your being cognizant of that fact," Rhys mused aloud. "Then, too, perhaps they did so last night, along about the time they took your knife from the desk. Were the doors of your bedchamber open all that time?"

"Yes, of course. They're generally left standing ajar as long as the weather permits. Last night was pleasant enough. I saw no need to close them."

Rhys faced the housekeeper. "Did you find anything unusual while cleaning Mr. Jeffrey's rooms this morning, Cora?"

The black woman nodded eagerly. "Well, suh, dere was somethin' mighty peculiar 'bout dat snuffbox I found on de floor near Mistah Jeffrey's desk. As far as ah know, he ain't ne'er sniffed de stuff."

Arching a brow at a dubious angle, Rhys considered the tiny receptacle that she had given him. When he glanced up at the other man, a small measure of his unquenchable humor rose to the surface. "Do you sniff the snuff on occasion, my friend?"

"Good heavens, man, no," Jeff rejoined with an abortive laugh.

"Does your wife?"

Jeff rolled his eyes in exasperation. "No, dammit, at least not that I'm aware."

"Olney Hyde really doesn't appear the type either," the sheriff pondered aloud.

"Dere was somethin' else dat ah figgered was kinda peculiar, too," the housekeeper volunteered.

Jeff settled a curious stare upon his housekeeper. "What was that, Cora?"

"Yo' know dat wood box yo' bought Miz Raelynn back in July?"

"Her father's coffer?"

" 'Tweren't no coffin, Mistah Jeffrey. Ah mean dat small, li'l box about so big," briefly she indicated the size by spreading her hands, "what was a-settin' on top o' Miz Raelynn's chest o' drawers."

"I know the one, Cora," Jeff assured her with an amused smile, his first for the day. "What about it?"

"Well, suh, ah found it on your desk, an' it looked ta me like somebody done took a knife an' tried to pry open de seams in de bottom."

"But it was unlocked."

"Ah knows dat, Mistah Jeffrey, but jes' de same, dey chiseled holes in de wood linin' de very bottom."

Jeff glanced toward his desk in search of the chest but found it gone. "Where is the coffer now?"

"If'n yo' means de box, ah took it downstairs ta see if'n Kingston could smooth out de gouges."

"I'd like to see it," the sheriff informed her. "Can you fetch it for me, Cora?"

"Sho thing, Mistah Rhys. Ah'll go be back directly."

Rhys faced Jeff. "You said this box belonged to Raelynn's father?"

"Yes, we found it in an import shop. Cooper Frye

obviously sold it to the shopkeeper shortly after their ship docked."

"Cooper Frye is her uncle, is he not?"

"Raelynn doesn't want to admit that, but the man claims to be. Supposedly he was lost at sea at an early age and came back to England a few months before Raelynn's father died. From there, Raelynn, her mother and Cooper Frye sailed here to the Carolinas."

Cora returned with the coffer in short order and gave it over to the sheriff. Just as she had said, the wood in the bottom of the interior had been seriously pitted.

Rhys examined the box for a moment and then shook it near his ear. "I don't know why anyone would mar the inside. There doesn't seem to be a secret compartment. If there is, it certainly doesn't sound as if there's anything in it."

Jeff looked the coffer over briefly and came to the same conclusion.

"I'd really like to talk with Raelynn now, Jeffrey," his friend said. "Perhaps she'd know why someone tampered with the box."

᠃RAELYNN LET THE SILKEN DRAPERY FLUTTER FROM her hand as she stepped away from the French doors. She had heard the sheriff's arrival and, through the glass paned portals, had seen him accompany her husband to the stables. Upon their return, she had hoped that the lawman would be leaving. She desperately wanted, nay needed, more time to reclaim her composure before confronting Jeff about what had happened in the stables, but it seemed that that reprieve was not to be granted. Already she heard hurrying footsteps approaching her room. A moment later Cora scratched on the door.

"Miz Raelynn, Mistah Jeffrey say de sheriff wants ta

speak wit' yo'. Dey'd like for yo' ta come down directly ta de study."

"Send Tizzy upstairs to help me dress," Raelynn instructed through the portal. "I'm still in my nightgown."

"Yas'm, ah'll tell de sheriff he gonna have ta wait awhile afore yo're able ta come down."

Half an hour later, Raelynn paused at the foot of the stairs to listen to the low timbre of male voices drifting from the study. To stand before Jeff now, remembering how he had looked in the stall, would be extremely difficult for her. Her emotions were fraught with her own terrible fears and suspicions. As Jeff's wife, she knew she should have been more loyal and believed him incapable of murder, yet the fact remained, the image of him standing above Nell with a bloody knife in his hand had been forged into her memory as solidly as an iron spike driven into a timber.

When Raelynn entered, Jeff promptly left his seat and, in a gentlemanly manner, came around to hold a chair for her. Rhys had also risen from the edge of the desk where he had been leaning. His eyes followed her until she had settled herself stiltedly into the proffered chair.

"Mrs. Birmingham," he said formally, resuming his perch. "I appreciate the fact that you were able to come down. I fully understand how trying this ordeal has been for you."

"Thank you for your consideration, Sheriff Townsend," she murmured in a hushed tone, feeling the need to reciprocate with the same kind of stilted decorum. The fact that she avoided meeting Jeff's stare widened the chasm between them. She clasped her hands in her lap, the better to conceal their violent trembling, and spared a quick glance up at the lawman. "Shall we proceed?"

"Yes, ma'am, of course." Rhys cleared his throat and shot a glance toward his friend. "I understand from Jeff that you arrived at the stable some time after he discovered Nell's body. Could you tell me how you came to be there and what you saw?"

"I awoke when I realized Jeff was no longer in our room. When I noticed a light burning in the stable, I thought there was some kind of trouble with one of the horses and that my husband had gone out to see about the matter. When I entered the stable, I heard a baby crying. I ran to the stall where the lantern was burning, and saw Nell." Raelynn clenched her hands and squeezed her eyes tightly shut as she tried to banish that gruesome scene from her memory. When she continued, her tone was barely audible, but at least she was no longer crying. "Blood was everywhere."

"Jeff said that Nell begged him to pull out the knife," Rhys confided with measured care. He was aware that the couple had wed shortly after meeting and that they really hadn't had much time to become acquainted before that event. If he could somehow help Raelynn to trust Jeff, then he had every expectation that she wouldn't regret it in the end. He had known Jeff since their early youth, and it went against his grain to entertain the premise that his friend could do such a foul, murderous deed. If Jeff could befriend cats, then there was no doubt the man had a most tolerant nature. But then, considering his own aversion to felines, Rhys wondered if he was being at all realistic in making such a comparison. "Your husband did so, hoping to help Nell, but by that time, she only had a few moments to live. Can you verify any of this?"

Raelynn gulped, trying to subdue a shudder. "As far as I know, Nell was already dead when I arrived." She chanced a glance toward Jeff, who had taken a chair beside her. His manner seemed strangely calm, and he gave every appearance of being keenly attentive to her answers. With some difficulty, she continued. "My husband was kneeling in the shadows. I didn't see him immediately. When he rose to his feet and stepped toward Nell,

I thought at first that he was someone else. When I caught sight of the knife in his hands, I guess I must have panicked. I ran back to the house. I've been upstairs ever since."

Rhys reached around and, sweeping the brass-edged coffer from Jeff's desk, brought it forth and braced it upon his thigh. Having gained the young woman's complete attention, he opened it and allowed her to view the damage that had been done within the interior. "Cora said that this was probably done sometime during the ball. Were you apprised of the gouges that were made before this present moment?"

Raelynn was shocked. Though she searched her memory, she couldn't recall having noticed the chest at all after Jeff had carried her to their room. But then, they had been so involved with each other, she wouldn't have noticed anything else. "I knew nothing about the damage. Why would anyone have done that?"

"That's what we were hoping you could explain," Rhys replied, setting the coffer behind him again. He fished into his coat pocket and, upon withdrawing the snuff box, set it on the table beside her chair. "Have you ever seen this before?"

"To the best of my knowledge, I haven't."

"Cora found it on the floor beside the desk in the bedroom you share with your husband. Someone had also left your father's coffer on top of the desk, where I understand from Jeff that his hunting knife is normally kept. Now, we know that the knife was used to kill Nell. Jeff has verified the fact that it was the one he withdrew from Nell in an effort to stop the bleeding. Since it was taken from the desk, I can only assume that it may have also been used to mar the interior of the coffer."

Raelynn realized her mouth had fallen slack and hurriedly snapped it shut. She peered at the sheriff, trying to sort the logic of what he had said. "You mean to say that someone came into our bedroom, riddled the interior of my father's coffer, possibly with Jeff's knife, during which time he might have dropped the snuffbox, and then some time after that, took the knife out to murder Nell. It just doesn't make any sense."

"That's exactly what I've been thinking ever since I started trying to solve this puzzle. It just doesn't make any sense," Rhys agreed. "Why would anyone steal into your room, whittle on a box and then go down and murder a girl with the same knife?" He pursed his lips thoughtfully and gazed about at the ceiling molding, as if seriously considering it for the first time. "Unless, of course, Nell came up by way of the porch stairs and entered your husband's bedroom, hoping to find Jeff there, and discovered instead a man who had an interest in your father's coffer. If that was the case, then the man might have killed her to keep her quiet. But unless we can ascertain exactly why anyone would be interested in an empty coffer, that leaves me without a clue as to what really happened. Of course, there's always the possibility that the murderer is completely deranged and just wanted to test the blade, first on wood and then on something softer?"

Seeing Raelynn shudder squeamishly, Jeff rose with his usual lithe grace from his chair and faced his friend, having heard enough. "Really, Rhys. Is this necessary?"

Rhys waved him silent as he leaned forward and gazed intently at Raelynn. "Tell me what you can about the coffer."

"I don't know why anyone would have wanted to damage my father's box." Raelynn's whisper was strained and barely audible, but in careful detail she went on to explain how her sire had given the coffer filled with gold coins to her mother, that he had died in prison after being accused of treason against the crown, how she and her mother had arrived at the decision to sail to the Carolinas after Cooper Frye came into their lives, and that it was that one who had sold the chest to an import dealer.

"You said your father instructed your mother to keep the box until he had need of its contents. Was he talking about the gold coins inside or something else entirely?"

"To my knowledge there was never anything else but the coins inside."

"It didn't have a secret compartment?"

Raelynn sank back in her chair in surprise. "There might have been, but I was never made aware of the presence of one. Nor do I think my mother was cognizant of a hidden compartment. My father never made any reference to it when he urged my mother to keep the coffer safe. When he told her to safeguard the contents, we assumed he was talking about the gold and that he would have need of that bit of wealth later on when he came to trial."

"Do you suppose he meant for you and your mother to use the gold for your needs and to bring the box back to him when the time was right?"

Raelynn was completely astounded by his supposition and yet thoroughly able to accept that it had merit. Still, why would anyone in the Carolinas be interested in what the box might have contained?

"If there's not a secret compartment," Rhys offered, "why would anyone pry at the bottom of an empty box?"

"I don't know! I don't know! I just can't believe anyone here in this country would have reason to search for a hidden partition in my father's coffer." Raelynn clasped a trembling hand to her brow, striving for control. She was very close to bursting into tears. She knew that Rhys Townsend was a close friend of her husband, and that he would likely make every effort to direct suspicion away from Jeff. It might have been the reason he was harping on her father's box. As for the knife, the idea of it being taken off by a man was feasible, too, but Jeff could have also been the culprit if he had become riled by Nell's demands that he acknowledge her bastard child as his own.

Raelynn didn't have an explanation for any of it and could only guess at the many possibilities. All she knew was that she had seen her husband in the stall near Nell's bloody body. He had been holding the murder weapon, and his clothes and hands had been stained by glistening red. Those particular details had been enough to send her fleeing in fear, and yet the sheriff seemed wont to dismiss them in an effort to cast the blame on some imagined culprit.

Raelynn squeezed her eyes tightly shut against a wave of threatening nausea brought on by a sudden, mind-numbing throbbing in her head. "I need to return to my room," she whispered. "I'm feeling sick."

"I've bothered you long enough," Rhys acknowledged in empathy and got to his feet. "I'll be going now, but if you should happen to remember anything pertinent about this matter, Mrs. Birmingham, please be sure and let me know as soon as you can."

Raelynn nodded numbly and remained seated as the two men left the parlor. Only then did she find the strength to push herself to her feet and make her way to the door. In the entrance hall, her legs nearly buckled beneath her, and she stretched out a hand to the wall to steady herself. Behind her, the front door stood open. Through it, she heard the sheriff's deeply resonant voice drifting into the hall.

"Thanks for having the wagon brought around, Jeff. If you can spare a driver, he can bring it back. Otherwise, it may take me a few days before I can return it."

"Stop by the stables on your way out and pick up a groom. It will save you a trip out."

"With so many guests here last night, Jeff, it will be difficult for me to question them all to see if they might have heard or seen anything before they left. You can bet there'll be plenty of talk about this incident in Charleston. Since Nell was killed on your property, people will no doubt wonder what connection you had with her murder. You'd better keep your wife out here for a while so she won't hear the gossip. You know how nasty some people can be. They'll likely think I didn't arrest you because you're my friend."

"Thanks for coming out, Rhys," Jeff murmured. "I appreciate all you've done."

"What are friends for?"

Jeff's friend! Raelynn mentally groaned, nearly crumpling against the wall. *Would he, for the sake of their friendship, allow a murderer to go unpunished?*

Trembling, she crossed the hall, mounted the stairs, and sought the privacy of her former bedchamber. Once there, she locked the door and sat on the edge of the bed. Staring listlessly across the room, she could only view the sheriff's remarks as a fair indication that he believed Jeff innocent of Nell's murder, but he hadn't seen what she had seen, Jeff standing over the girl's lifeless body, and all that blood on his shirt! On the knife he held! On his fingers! In her mind!

11 ❧

*T*here was something totally distracting about racing a stallion across the countryside without regard for how fast the animal was moving or how uneven the terrain stretching out ahead of them. Jeff certainly wasn't in a mood to care, not when he was in sore need of an activity that would take his mind off the cold, dark emptiness that had settled into his vitals. Years ago, he had come to the realization that the best way to put his thoughts into proper perspective was to get on the back of a horse and ride across the countryside for an hour or so. Brutus's temperament always challenged him, and at present, Jeff welcomed the diversion. It was this or morosely mulling over his wife's willingness to believe the worst of him.

Jeff rode past the spot where he had made love to Raelynn, but the memory of that blissful afternoon darkened his mood progressively, for it brought to mind the difference a night's passing could make in a man's life. Now that his wife suspected him of murder, he had no doubt that their marriage would be reduced to a mere travesty. Indeed, if he could deduce anything from her refusal to talk with him, then he could imagine that she wouldn't be satisfied until there was a space of a whole continent between them.

Jeff muttered a savage curse, and forcibly banished those disturbing conjectures from his mind. He touched his heels to the stallion's gleaming flanks, and soon they were racing around a bend, beyond which Jeff espied a stout tree recently uprooted by strong winds. It was just large enough to offer him a definite dare. Reining the animal about to face the goal, he patted the silken neck and spoke soothingly. Brutus seemed to sense the task required of him, for his small, pointed ears pricked forward in alert attention. Prancing in heightening excitement, the horse waited for the command. It took no more than a light touch of a booted heel to send him racing toward the fallen tree. As they reached the obstacle, Brutus soared upward, tucking his forelegs beneath him, and propelled himself in a wide, graceful arc that carried him with plenty of space to spare over the barrier.

Jeff felt his own heart lift at their success, recognized it for the stolen pleasure that it was, and decided to indulge himself further. Turning the animal, he caught sight of something in the distance that offered more of a challenge, a three-tiered split rail fence enclosing a fallow field.

"Let's see what you're really capable of, boy," he urged, once again using his booted heels to propel the animal forward.

Upon nearing the fence, Brutus pushed himself off the ground with an impetus that sent him flying over the obstacle. Like a swan lighting on water, he descended, first on his forehooves and then on his hind two, and continued the graceful stride until his master pulled back lightly upon the reins.

Chuckling in pleasure, Jeff patted the stallion's neck affectionately and murmured lavish praises. Brutus flicked his tail and nickered softly in response, with unusual forbearance accepting his master's approval.

For several miles, Jeff walked the magnificent animal, allowing him to cool before urging him again into an easy canter. Brutus readily obeyed, thoroughly amazing Jeff. At times, the steed had proven ornery enough to require a second prodding, on some occasions even a third. It gave Jeff serious cause to wonder if his imagination wasn't running away with him. Rare though such an idea was, Brutus almost seemed to be demonstrating some measure of compassion toward him, as if the animal could actually sense his gloomy mood.

Other jumps were taken with a shared willingness to seize whatever excitement could be found. Twice the stallion almost stumbled, and were it not for Jeff's skill at keeping his seat in the fine English saddle, he would have gone sailing. One of these near mishaps came after an especially daring jump, high enough to take both man and beast far beyond the realm of prudence. Jeff finally drew rein, realizing he was treading very near the sharp precipice that bordered on reckless disregard. He stroked the arched neck of the steed and once again praised him as a worthy steed. Still, Jeff felt infinitely better after working off most of his tension and frustration. Seemingly, of their own accord, his thoughts settled down with crystal clarity.

Whatever Raelynn's suspicions, he knew he had to extend every privilege a man could bestow upon his wife during this time of uncertainty. In view of the apprehensions presently roiling within her, it would be sheer madness for him to try and force her into some kind of acceptance of his innocence, no matter how false it might prove to be underneath the surface, or to bring her to heel by husbandly dominance. Coercion of that nature definitely ran contrary to his principles. Yet, in giving her time to reaffirm her trust in him, he could foresee himself having to endure another lengthy abstinence, and this time he seriously doubted that a fortnight would suffice in bringing an end to their present rift. He had gotten comfortable with their intimacy and everything else involved in their marriage, and he was loath to see all of that end.

Some years ago, he had become cognizant of his brother wrenching his gut out for want of Heather. At the time, Jeff had made up his mind that he would never yield to that kind of torment. Yet here he was again, foreseeing the difficulty in being around his wife, seeing her, feeling her presence, smelling her fragrance, without his insides being twisted inside out in his desire for her. Given enough time, Raelynn *might* return to his bed. A few days of husbandly restraint he could bear, but not months and years on end. In the latter case, he'd feel like a man whose entrails were being drawn out before a scheduled quartering.

There was also the matter of his good standing with neighbors and acquaintances. It would certainly not be outside the realm of reality for them to suspect him in the murder of Nell. Neither could he go around broadcasting his innocence to all who would lend an ear. Unless accused outrightly, it would be more judicious by far to hold his tongue and remain distantly detached from the snide whispers and narrowed, suspicious stares.

Jeff couldn't actually say that he had made peace with his difficulties by the time he neared the stables; the thought of separate bedrooms certainly brought the brumes of gloom sweeping back upon him. Nevertheless he had come to the realization that there would be trouble up ahead, not only in his marriage to Raelynn, but possibly in his good standing with the citizens of the area. When it came time, he'd just have to deal with both circumstances in his own way, and hopefully right would prevail.

By the time Sparky finally espied horse and rider approaching the stable, he had been thrown into an anxious dither. Considering how long the pair had been gone, the trainer had fully expected the stallion to come home with nothing more than an empty saddle and could hardly contain his relief when he realized his fears had been for naught, at least in this instance.

"Lawdy mercy, Mistah Jeffrey," he panted after racing out to meet his employer, "ye had us all wonderin' if'n ye were a-dyin' someplace from a broken neck. Thank goodness ye're safe."

Jeff swung down from the saddle. "As farfetched as it may seem, Sparky, Brutus was a perfect gentleman today. So treat him well tonight. He has earned it."

"Yes, suh, I'll do that. Maybe if'n I give him a few extra oats, he might take the hint that it pays ta be nice."

"Just don't feed him too many or he'll be friskier than ever."

"Feelin' his oats, ye mean," Sparky concluded with a chortle.

A corner of Jeff's lips twitched, the best smile he could manage. "Something like that."

Kingston was just coming out of the front door of the house when Jeff arrived at the porch. Immediately the butler echoed the young trainer's concerns. "Praise be, Mistah Jeffrey. Sparky said yo'd gone off on Brutus, an' we was all a-worryin' somethin' fierce, wonderin' if'n yo'd be comin' back alive."

"Any word from Elijah?" Jeff asked, striding across the porch without pausing. He entered the main hall and finally glanced back for an answer as the butler scrambled after him.

"Naw, suh, nothin'. Mistah Brandon, he heard de news, an' he come a-lookin' fo' yo'. We tol' him yo'd gone out on Brutus, an' he ask me ta send someone o'er aftah yo' comed back so dey'd know yo' was safe. He say Miz Heather'd be worryin' herself sick till yo' did, but ah'm a-thinkin' Mistah Brandon was doin' some mighty tall worryin' 'bout yo' hisself. He sho did a lot o' pacin' de floors an' lookin' out de windows whilst he was here."

Loosening the stock at his throat, Jeff strode to the cabinet in his study and poured himself a short measure of brandy. "I'll send someone over to Harthaven with a note to let my brother know that I'm back and will probably be retiring early. In the meantime, double the guards around this place. I don't want any more strangers intruding without having adequate warning of their approach."

"Yassuh, ah'll do dat very thin', but, suh, ah gots ta tell yo' . . . ?"

Jeff downed the brandy in a single toss of a hand and looked at the butler who, he realized, seemed greatly troubled. "What is it, Kingston?"

"Cora . . . she say she knocked on Miz Raelynn's door maybe four or five different times ta ask if'n she'd be a-wantin' somethin' ta eat, but Miz Raelynn still ain't answered."

"My wife is likely asleep. Right now, that's the best thing for her after what has happened."

"Yassuh, dat's de truth." The butler hesitated, reluctant to broach his other concern, but there was no help for it. "We'uns was also a-wonderin' 'bout Miz Nell's baby. Cora says he's doin' real fine at Miz Fergus's, but we was a-thinkin' yo' might be wantin' ta see de li'l fella befo' yo' retire dis evenin'."

Jeff paused in pouring himself another draught. He had a great affection for his young nephew, but apart from that, children in general held no interest for him. He had simply never thought much about them. No doubt, when he had his own, his views would change . . . *if* that day ever came. Considering the present schism between Raelynn and himself, he could make no guarantees that that event would ever come to fruition.

Setting down his glass, he faced the butler squarely. "Kingston, I'd like to make myself very clear about this matter. Nell's child is an orphan, to my knowledge without kith or kin, and because of that, I will allow him to remain in my home until such a time that he's either claimed by Nell's kin or another couple adopts him. Until then, I expect him to be cared for with both kindness and compassion, either in my house or at Mrs. Fergus's. But know this, Kingston, Daniel is *not* my son, and no one should labor under any misconception that he is."

Kingston nodded vigorously. "Ah knows dat now, Mistah Jeffrey. I ne'er thought fo' an instant dat yo' was his pappy."

"I appreciate your trust in me, Kingston, but it wouldn't be totally out of the question for you to have some doubts about that fact after Nell said the child bears a passing resemblance to me. *If* he does, it's purely a fluke of nature. He also probably resembles Mister Brandon, our late father, and some of our kin in England, not to mention a whole host of strangers. We can only hope that his father may decide to do the honorable thing and claim his bastard child. It will be difficult enough for the boy as it is, what with the little tike growing up without a mother. To have the condemning stain of bastardy besmirching his life would see him defeated ere he has a chance to begin."

"Yassuh. Be a hard thing fo' Mistah Daniel ta survive in dis world widout his mammy, but when he gots no name an' no pappy either, den fo' sho he's a-gonna have a hard time growin' up."

"For the time being, Daniel has a home here, and if I hear of anyone on the premises mistreating him because his mother had him out of wedlock, I will deal harshly with that person. Let it be understood now, I'll tolerate no malicious condemnation of the child from those who either work for me or come into this house."

A smile played at the corners of Kingston's mouth.

"Yo' sho gots a strong, tough side, Mistah Jeffrey, but yo' also gots yo'self a stout heart, no doubt 'bout dat. No doubt 'bout dat at all."

Jeff cocked a brow at the man. "A stout heart, eh? Well, right now, I have a stout hunger for food, and I'd appreciate it most kindly if you'd fetch me a tray and bring it here to my study before I start bellowing my head off."

"Yassuh, yassuh!" Kingston's chuckles flowed out behind him as he scampered down the entrance hall. His voice drifted back, assuring Jeff in overstated humbleness, "I'm a-shufflin' along as fast as ah can, massuh. Yassuh, massuh, ah's a-doin' dat very thing."

A meager smile plucked at Jeff's lips before he tossed down the second brandy. Though he was tempted to pour himself another, he went to the front windows and, for a long time, gazed out over the tree-studded grounds encompassing the plantation house. A few stars began twinkling through the leafy shroud as his thoughts wandered back over the day's tumultuous events and Raelynn's pain and fear of him. He yearned to comfort her; his own heart needed to be assuaged by her willingness to give him a fair hearing, but he had grave doubts that she would accept any kind of solace or explanation from him until his innocence had been established. For the time being, he was inclined to let things stand as they were between them. If by some miracle she would have a change of heart, then he had to trust that she'd let him know in short order.

He ate the supper that Kingston brought him, and after setting aside the tray, he sought distraction in the volumes of bookkeeping generated by his many business activities. When he caught himself making the same mathematical error for the third time, he snorted in disgust and tossed aside the books, quickly deciding that his accounts would have to wait until he could give them his full attention.

He found himself rubbing the back of his neck and realized a deeply seeded ache had established itself there, no doubt derived partly from the jumps he had taken with Brutus and partly from his own tension. As he rolled his head to ease the discomfort, his eyes fell on the brass-trimmed coffer that Rhys had left on his desk. Out of a growing curiosity, he picked up the box and held it near the lamp where he could examine it more closely. He perused the interior, but found naught of noteworthy interest. Though he turned it upside down, he again saw nothing to give him reason to suspect that there was any kind of hidden space located within the chest. He was about to return the piece to his desk when he noticed, on the right-hand bottom side, a seam that was wider by hardly a hairbreadth's difference than on the opposite side. Taking up a thin letter opener, he pressed the tip of it into the space and carefully probed along the tiny division. Near the end, the point sank into a slight indentation. Nothing happened until he pushed the tip into it. He heard a "click," and much to his surprise, a strip of wood, no thicker than his index finger, flipped open along the bottom edge. Slanting the coffer toward the lamp, he peered inside the slender opening, fervently hoping that he would find something that would provide a viable reason for a man to kill a young mother. The compartment was almost as wide and as long as the coffer itself, but alas, it was empty.

Jeff muttered a curse in roweling frustration. No amount of wishing on his part could change the outcome of what he had discovered or provide enough proof to verify the fact that the hole had once held secret documents of great importance or at least *something* that would have given Raelynn reason to believe that Rhys had been right. As much as Jeff hated to admit it, he was right back at the apex of his dilemma.

Rising from his desk, he glanced at the clock on the mantel and realized that it was much later than he had imagined. Beyond the windows, the sky was a midnight blue sprinkled with a myriad of stars. The moon had risen and was so bright he could actually see shadows beneath the huge live oaks sprawling across the front lawn.

A strange yearning swept over Jeff as he stared out into the night. Although he couldn't determine exactly what he craved, the feeling was nevertheless intense. Part of it, he determined, was a desire to recapture the happiness that had been his before his discovery of Nell. Yet whatever plagued him was infinitely more complicated than that. He could only guess at what it was in truth. Perhaps, after believing that he had discovered within Raelynn some missing part of himself or that loving entity that they were meant to be, the pain of seeing his dreams cruelly snatched away a second time had left him struggling against an insidious melancholy, an emotion that had, for the most part, been a stranger to him throughout his life.

Under the circumstances, he couldn't blame Raelynn for being confused and afraid. Hadn't he, several years ago, seen his own brother leaving Oakley during which time Louisa Wells had owned the property and hadn't he arrived at the same conclusion as Raelynn when he had found Louisa murdered? Brandon had been innocent of the deed, but the evidence had pointed to his guilt. Yet, for all of his past susceptibility to doubt his brother, Jeff knew he couldn't allow Raelynn to nurture her fears and suspicions indefinitely. She was his wife; he *needed* her loyalty and trust. In plain reality he *needed* to be with her; he couldn't bear the anguish of being apart from her. He had gotten too comfortable in his role of a nurturing, caring husband. Now he needed some of that same nurturing care from his wife.

Wearily Jeff rubbed his hands over his face as he sought some practical solution to his mounting problems. The only way he could bring a swift end to the estrangement between Raelynn and himself was to make every effort to discover the murderer and to see the culprit brought in with enough evidence to convict him. As for the present moment, fatigued as he was, it was far better for him to postpone any attempt to see Raelynn until the morrow. By then, they would have both had time to rest and think things through.

Jeff had settled on that bit of wisdom and was about to leave the study when Cora came skittering down the front hall. Kingston was right behind her, making every effort to halt her before she could intrude upon the master of the manse, but the woman was much younger and more adept at outmaneuvering the aging servant. Before the butler had time to reach the portal, she had already flung herself through it.

"Yo' jes hold your horses," Kingston exclaimed a bit irately as he followed her. "Dere ain't no cause fo' yo' ta be pushin' yo' way in an' botherin' Mistah Jeffrey right now. He's had enuff ta frazzle him for awhile widout yo' vexin' him more'n he is."

"It's all right, Kingston," Jeff interjected, lifting a hand to halt the butler's scolding. Despite their deep and abiding respect for one another, it wasn't the first time he had had to settle differences between the two servants. He sincerely hoped that this latest row didn't have anything to do with Nell's baby. He had been a bachelor too long to have any desire to become an adoptive parent overnight. Facing his housekeeper, he lent her his undivided attention. "What has gotten you into such a stew this time, Cora?"

"It's Miz Raelynn, suh," Cora informed him, wringing her hands fretfully. "Ah been a-knockin' an' a-knockin' on her door for hours now an' she still doan answer my pleas, Mistah Jeffrey. Dat ain't right, suh. Doan matter how upset she is, she gots ta eat fo' de baby."

Jeff was thoroughly bemused. "What in the blazes does Nell's baby have to do with my wife eating?"

" 'Tain't Nell's baby ah'm a-talkin' 'bout, Mistah Jeffrey. It's yours an' Miz Raelynn's. She done got herself wit' child, an' ah'm a-fearin' she's done gone an' packed herself off de premises."

Jeff shot past the servants in a flash, leaving them both gaping in surprise until they recovered enough of their wits to hasten after him. Jeff leapt up the stairs, taking them three at a time. Once he gained the upper landing, his long legs quickly devoured the distance to the room in which his wife had withdrawn herself. The door was locked, as he had expected, and there was no sound of movement from within. Rattling the knob, he barked through the wood, spurred on by a sharp, goading fear that she had indeed left the house. "Raelynn, open the door this instant! If you hear me, please do so, or I'm going to break it down!"

No answer came. He pressed an ear to the portal, hoping fervently to hear a sound, at least some evidence that she was still there, but he had already settled on the foreboding assumption that he wouldn't.

"Yo' wants me ta go 'round ta the balcony door, suh?" Kingston asked, hurrying forward.

Jeff was in no mood for such a practical entrance. If Raelynn had left and she was, indeed, with child, he didn't care if he had to knock the whole house down to find her. His search would begin here. Grimly he bade, "Stand back."

As Kingston and Cora gawked at him in stunned awe, he raised a leg hardened by years of riding and smashed his booted foot against the planks. The heavy door bucked at his assault, but remained intact.

"S-suh," Kingston stammered, shocked by this indication of violence from a man he had always assumed was the very epitome of self-restraint. "It won't take me no more'n a minute ta check . . ."

Jeff's foot struck the door again, and under the pressure of his blow, the wood splintered near the lock. Beneath the strength of another assault, the portal, minus the lock, swung inward. Inside the room a lamp burned on the bedside table. The French doors were standing open and, as he had feared, there was no sign of Raelynn.

Cora peered around Jeff's arm and clasped a trembling hand over her mouth as she realized her qualms had not been for naught. "Oh, sweet merciful heaven, dat chile's done up an' left. Whad could've possessed her, Mistah Jeffrey?"

His visage was grim. The thought of his pregnant wife wandering unprotected beyond the sheltering walls of Oakley while a murderer remained on the loose turned his blood to ice. Facing Kingston abruptly, he bade the man, "Go down to the stables and tell Sparky to put a working saddle and a rifle holster on Majestic and to outfit him for a lengthy jaunt. And hurry!"

Cora didn't need instructions. "Yo'll be needin' food, water, blankets an' all kinds o' other things. Enuff fo' two. No tellin' how long yo'll be away tryin' ta find Miz Raelynn. Ah'll have everythin' packed by de time yo've collected your gear, Mistah Jeffrey."

Jeff didn't bother answering. He was already striding to his own chambers. Once there, he shrugged into a sturdy jacket, clamped on a hat, and dropped a sheathed hunting knife into the pocket of his coat. Returning to his study, he unlocked the gun cabinet and removed a long rifle and a brace of pistols. He thrust the latter through his belt, slung the leather cords of a pair of black powder horns over his shoulder, and stalked outside with rifle in hand.

Sparky was already leading Majestic out of the stables when he arrived. Jeff shoved the rifle into its sheath behind the saddle and hung the powder horns from the pommel.

"Is Stargazer or any of the horses missing from their stalls?" he asked, casting a glance toward the lantern-lit aisle.

"No, suh. I've checked every stall. There ain't even a blanket missing."

"Damn!" The expletive exploded from Jeff's lips as he realized the danger his wife would be in if she *did* meet up with the murderer. At least on horseback, she'd have had a chance to escape.

He was in the process of equipping Majestic with the basic essentials that would allow him to stay out in the woods for several days when Cora came scurrying out of the house. Panting from her haste, she delivered the items she had assembled to him.

"Yo' brings dat sweet chile home, yo' hear?"

"I hear, Cora," Jeff muttered solemnly, checking the blankets, bedroll and oilskin slicker that Sparky had rolled up tightly in a tarp and secured behind the saddlebags. The saddle itself was larger than his fine English saddle and sported a modified horn, which he had discovered long ago could be extremely useful in many difficult situations. There was even a place to hang a coiled rope, which Sparky had been insightful enough to include in the supplies.

"Anythin' else ye'll be needin', suh?" the trainer asked with a measure of concern detectable in his voice.

"Looks like you've taken care of everything, Sparky," Jeff replied, bringing a hint of a smile to the younger man's lips as he swung up into the smooth leather seat.

The stallion seemed to sense his master's urgency, for when Jeff touched his heels to his flanks, Majestic leapt into motion. Soon they were racing down the lane and disappearing into the night.

JEFF DREW REIN ON A RISE NEAR THE STREAM WHERE he and Raelynn had once made love and observed the moon as it slid behind the heavy forest masking the horizon. With its descent went the meager light that had thus

far guided him in his search for clues to his wife's whereabouts. Bereft of even its meager glow, he couldn't hope
to follow her trail with any measure of success. He could
go no further; it was as simple as that.

Dismounting, he set about building a fire just in case
Raelynn was near and wanted to return. Then he unsad-
dled the stallion and led him to the stream. As the horse
bent its head to drink, Jeff's gaze fell upon a scrap of
gauzy, lace-adorned fabric clinging to a nearby bush. He
plucked it loose and examined it carefully by the firelight.
His throat constricted when he recognized it as a frag-
ment of the muslin gown Raelynn had been wearing
when she had come downstairs to answer Rhys's
questions.

Although Jeff realized his tracking skills by no means
matched Elijah's, he had nevertheless learned some simple basics from the scout. Upon leaving Oakley, he had
made a wide circle around the house, looking for some
indication of Raelynn's destination. He had finally espied
signs of a hurried passage wandering off into the under-
brush. Hoping that he had been wrong and that his wife
hadn't really become so disoriented as to go off in a direction that would eventually lead her into the swamp, he
had nevertheless followed the scant trail until he had
reached the stream and, beside it, made the discovery
that confirmed his fears.

Jeff swept his gaze beyond the area, carefully probing
the shadows, all the while hoping against hope that in
some tiny protected niche he would find Raelynn huddled in a small knot, trying to keep warm. Having no
success, he carefully scanned the darkness farther ahead.
As difficult as it was for him to accept, his wife was probably more afraid of him than anybody or anything. Nevertheless, she was out there in the wilds alone, no doubt
shaking to the core of her being. At least he prayed she
was alone rather than in the company of Nell's killer.
The one who had taken Ariadne had lit out in the same

direction, no doubt to discourage anyone from following him. Hopefully the man had progressed far beyond the area where Raelynn was presently roaming, but if for some reason he had decided to double-back and was even partially skilled at tracking, then he would likely come across Raelynn's trail. If he found similar scraps of muslin, the man would hardly be inclined to flee, for it was apparent the cloth had been torn from a woman's garment. Raelynn would be at the man's mercy, and if it ever came to her being taken, Jeff could only pray that the horse thief wasn't also a murderer.

That disconcerting thought proved dreadfully poor company when Jeff tried to snatch a few moments of sleep. It was not to be. Morbid images of Raelynn in serious peril assailed him relentlessly, leaving him staring into the blazing fire. He wavered somewhere between wanting to shake some sense in that beautiful auburn head of hers and an even stronger desire to hold her safely within his arms. As a result, he passed the hours of darkness awake and totally disquieted.

*M*oonlight glistened off the water that Raclynn had cupped within her palms, and though she stared into the shimmering liquid, she saw nothing but a recurring vision of Jeffrey standing over Nell's body with a bloody knife in his hand. She had a vague recollection of having left her bedroom without any particular destination in mind two days earlier, just as the afternoon was aging to a ripe old age. Spurred on by a rising panic and a pressing need to flee before her husband returned to the house, she had fled in anxious haste, taking no provisions for a lengthy flight. She hadn't even brought along a cloak with which to protect herself from the deepening chill of the autumn evenings, one which she had miserably endured underneath the sprawling limbs of a live oak some distance from the manse, the second in a greensward surrounded by tall grass. Of food, she had given little consideration, though she hadn't eaten at all the day she

had left. She had found a few berries and two sweet potatoes which had obviously fallen from a wagon during the
harvesting of a field. The potatoes she had eaten raw,
forced by a lack of a knife to bite through their skins
after rubbing them clean. The poor fare had hardly
equaled the scrumptious meals at Oakley, but now, even
the pair of yams were gone.

Slowly Raelynn glanced about, only vaguely aware of
the water dribbling through her fingers as she peered into
the deep gloom of her surroundings. Cast in the night
shades of black and dark gray, nothing looked familiar.
For all she knew, she could have been a hundred miles
from the plantation by now or in another realm entirely.
It certainly seemed as if she had been stumbling around
for untold ages. Considering the dazed trauma into which
she had sunk after espying her husband in the midst of
the gore in the stables, it was a wonder she wasn't still
sitting in a confused stupor in her bedchamber.

Wearily Raelynn scrubbed a hand across her cheek
and brushed away ratty tendrils that had become hopelessly ensnarled with twigs and dried leaves. The weighty
mass hung down her back and over her shoulders and,
at times, had brought her to a complete halt when some
portion of it had become entangled on a branch or thorny
bush. The inconvenience of having to contend with its
length had given her cause to regret the fact that she had
refrained from severing the tresses when the urge had
first struck, for her fingers were now raw from her numerous efforts to free herself.

Had she been in any frame of mind to prepare for
her departure, she'd have certainly bound her hair up in
braids, but after dismissing Tizzy in an anxious quest to
be alone, Raelynn had brushed out the curling mass herself, fully intending to return to her bed before the sun
set, but her thoughts had stumbled like a wounded hind
over the sequence of events that had occurred after she
had gone in search of Jeff. Her mind had grown weary

of the constant churning, and out of her muddled reasoning, a dread that Jeff, upon his return from his ride, would try to question her about what she had actually seen, began to plague her. Fearing the outcome of such a meeting, she had fled in a panic, giving little heed to how she would survive without food or less regard to the flimsiness of her clothing, wearing the same muslin gown and leather slippers she had donned shortly after receiving Sheriff Townsend's summons.

Raelynn peered up into the night sky, trying to get her bearings. Having lived to a large extent in a London manor surrounded by tall trees and thick foliage, she had had little opportunity to observe the passage of the moon and the stars. The lunar orb appeared lower in the starlit blackness above her head than when she had last viewed it, and she could only guess that the hour was very late. The possibility that she was also far removed from Oakley now filled her with a strange melancholy that left her struggling against an overwhelming urge to pour out her sorrow in another bout of wrenching sobs, but the soft hooting of an owl from a nearby tree reminded her of the need to act prudently in regards to her situation.

Since departing the house, she had gotten herself thoroughly lost, but worse than that, she had no notion what kind of wild animals might view her as their next meal or, for that matter, what murderer might be roaming about in search of another victim. If Jeff was truly innocent of stabbing Nell as he had claimed, then without a doubt the real culprit was still free, perhaps even wandering about in these very woods. What better place to hide from the sheriff than in the midst of a forest? Olney had certainly touted his ability to stay out of the lawman's reach by retreating into the wilds. Others might well be of the same mind and wily adeptness.

If, on the other hand, Jeff was guilty of killing Nell in a fit of rage, then there was yet another falsehood with which she must deal: the very essence of the man himself. The gallant knight whom she had once supposed her husband to be now seemed in these passing hours far less real and more of a figment of some girlish fantasy. The image she had erected of him had been too perfect, too handsome, too noble and far too admirable to have been realistic. Yet, in spite of her doubts, Raelynn's heart cried out in protest, assuring her that she was wrong, that Jeff was all of those things and more, and that she was an utter fool for doubting him.

The bloody scene in the stables flashed once again before her mind's eye, making Raelynn recoil in shuddering aversion. The horror promptly churned up a wave of nausea, which erupted in a series of dry heaves until at last the spasms expended themselves, allowing her to slump back upon her heels. She felt perilously weak and pressed a trembling hand to her sweat-dappled brow, wishing once again that she would have had enough foresight to provide for herself better. The ground upon which she knelt bore a damp chill that penetrated her thin garments and evoked shivers that shook her whole frame. Very likely if she stayed put much longer, she'd catch her death.

By dint of will, Raelynn stumbled to her feet and leaned against a nearby tree as she sought to determine just where she was, but she was totally devoid of any knowledge of the area into which she had wandered. Still, if she wanted to live, then by some method or other she had to make her way out of this dense tangle of growth and return to civilization.

Precisely in which direction presented a dilemma too difficult for her frazzled brain to puzzle through in an orderly fashion. In the gloom she barely discerned a small knoll rising up beside the stream at which she had knelt to drink. Climbing upon it, she slowly turned about in full circle, but every direction appeared identical. She definitely saw no hint of a lane.

Capriciously she set her sights toward the right, but

before she had gone a stone's throw, she became inundated with misgivings. It made no sense to wander aimlessly about in the woods. As far as she could determine, two rational choices were open to her. She could either make an attempt to reach Charleston *or* to strike out for Harthaven. The two lay in opposite directions, with Oakley situated between but within much closer proximity to the neighboring plantation. If she went to Harthaven, then she'd have to depend on the kindness and understanding of her in-laws. She had no doubt that Brandon and Heather possessed both in abundance, but she'd be putting them into a difficult position, basically asking them to shelter her from Brandon's brother.

If Charleston became her destination, then she'd be entirely alone in a city wherein she had no claim on anyone. She'd have to depend on herself, find work and lodging, and somehow survive, as she had fully expected to do upon her arrival from England. She would no longer be able to claim the privilege of being Mrs. Jeffrey Birmingham, wife of one of the richest men in the territory. She might even be censured, condemned as bold, and looked down upon for removing herself from her husband's household even by people who might have a tendency to wonder if Jeff was guilty of Nell's murder. A disloyal or disobedient wife was bound to be held in contempt by all, yet she thought she could bear that particular criticism far better than chancing a rift in the Birmingham family to which she had once been so glad and proud to belong.

Resolved to turn her sights toward Charleston, Raelynn again contemplated the best direction for reaching her chosen destination. For the first time in her life she lamented her lack of attention when her tutors had tried to instruct her in the finer points of where the moon rose and set according to the calendar. Her regret did little to ease her predicament.

She searched her brain, trying to recall anything of

importance that she might have unconsciously noticed during the many trips she had taken to either Charleston or Harthaven. A particularly stirring moonlit interlude in a carriage ride from Harthaven came readily to mind. Jeff had been feeling quite amorous at the time and hadn't wanted to wait until they reached home to engage in a little marital petting. The details seemed forever etched upon her memory, especially the band of light from the lowering moon that had streamed into the windows on the right side of the carriage where she had sat. Very distinctly she recalled that when Jeff had pressed her back upon the velvet pillows padding a cushioned corner and opened her bodice and chemise, her breasts had gleamed with a silvery luster before the shadow of his head had encroached upon the rays.

A small, elated cry escaped Raelynn as she spun about to face what she supposed was an easterly direction. If her calculations were correct, then she was now facing Charleston. But then again, perhaps she wasn't. Either way, if she wanted to find her way out of the woods, she had little choice but to strike out in that particular direction and test how firm or shaky her theory really was.

This she did for an interminable length of time. To some extent the activity helped to dispel the night-born chill, but she was ever reminded of the fact that the shoes in which she had already trudged for many hours were ill suited for rigorous use. They had been fairly new when she had first donned them a pair of days ago, and soon after launching out on her sojourn, she had grown increasingly cognizant of the fact that she had leftover blisters from the ball. At first, her feet had merely started aching, then to throbbing, and lastly to burning after the sacs of pus had opened and become raw. Nevertheless, Raelynn made every effort to ignore the sharp pangs and to plod ever onward.

Her sore feet were hardly her only discomfort.

Shortly after entering the dense forest, thorns had not only pierced her scalp at certain junctures but had also caught at her sleeves and shirts, easily shredding the fabric and, in the process, gouging her arms until they were nigh as scratched and bloody as her fingers. Frequently the thick tangle of vines covering the forest floor had caused her to trip, at times even to fall. It became an effort to pick herself up and to keep going, but no matter how weak and exhausted she might have been, she felt driven by a growing need to find civilization. Indeed, the way things were going now, she could die from starvation in the midst of the forest, and it would take weeks, perhaps months, before anyone would find her moldering body.

An exclamation of dismay escaped Raelynn as she realized of a sudden that she had failed to notice that she had been slowly veering from course. Much too often she had taken the path of least resistance through the thick undergrowth without paying proper heed to her lunar bearing. In short, the direction in which she had thought she had been going for at least half an hour was not the same one toward which she was presently heading, for the moon was now on her left side.

Once more, tears welled up to blur her vision, and with a sinking heart, Raelynn wondered how much ground she would have to retrace. In the midst of contemplating her choices in this unhappy quandary, she became mindful that what had once been a low cacophony of sounds in the forest had risen to an incessant drone. Not only had she lost sight of her direction, but she had inadvertently stumbled from high ground into a lower, marshier area. The air was warmer here, which was hardly reassuring in spite of her complaints about the discomforts of the cooler weather. If anything, she knew herself to be in greater danger than ever before. It wasn't necessarily the mosquitoes and gnats that made her anxious as much as her awareness of reptilian creatures known to move much more quickly in tepid climes and weather.

Mindful of just how susceptible she was presently to being thrown into a panic, Raelynn was reluctant to credit the strange, slithering sensation that seemed to be moving across her slippered toes for what she feared it was. Warily she forced herself to glance down, and immediately a scream bubbled forth from her throat as she saw a fairly large snake sliding over her feet. Kicking the reptile into a nearby pool, she shuddered convulsively and began weeping in hysteria, too tired and disoriented to make any attempt to subdue her racking sobs.

When at last she calmed, Raelynn knew without a doubt that she had come to the end of her resources for yet another day. She was exhausted, confused and thoroughly terrified of the denizens of this dank marsh. Going on under similar circumstances seemed the height of folly, if not downright calamitous. Besides, she had had enough, at least for the time being.

Spurred on by yet another sinuous movement in the nearby bushes, Raelynn scrambled up the nearest trunk without further hesitation. She hadn't dared climb a tree since she was a young girl. Once she had taken great delight in ascending as far as she could go. She was still cognizant of the basic fundamentals and, in spite of her attire, managed to gain an acceptably high branch, which helped her feel a bit more secure. From her perch, she was able to consider the terrain she had just left. The moon was descending rapidly out of sight, taking with it most of the light, yet she could almost swear that where she had recently stood, there were still strange, twining movements upon the damp moss.

Resolved not to budge from the tree before the fullness of dawn, Raelynn leaned back against the rough bark and closed her eyes. She wasn't so foolish as to actually consider sleeping, for that was the surest way to tumble from her perch. She just needed to find a small measure of rest.

No sooner had she settled herself than the faint flicker of something black and ominous flying across her limited range of vision shattered her aspirations. In growing trepidation Raelynn shrank back against the sturdy trunk and watched warily for the approach of more bats. Struggling desperately not to cry, she breathed a silent prayer and waited for another morning to come.

☺JEFF HADN'T GONE VERY FAR AFTER BREAKING CAMP before the faint signs of his wife's passage led him down toward the marsh. Having dreaded that Raelynn would go that way, he continued on until he came to a spot where it looked as if she had turned around. Her change in direction hadn't improved her destination by any stretch of the imagination, for she had only plunged further into the swamp.

The rising of the sun banished the relative coolness of night, and the temperatures began to climb steadily. Mosquitoes swarmed in abundance around them, as did the pesky gnats. Majestic shied uneasily beneath their relentless attacks, but the stallion obeyed Jeff's nudging knees and continued on valiantly.

During his boyhood years, Jeff had frequented the swamps with Brandon and had grown up with a keen knowledge of them, as well as a well-warranted respect. Together he and his brother had learned the best spots for hunting and fishing and, over a period of time, had become acquainted with the human inhabitants of the marsh who, for one reason or another, preferred to remain aloof from ordinary society. An old recluse known as Red Pete had seemed ancient when Jeff had been nothing more than a lad. When Jeff drew rein in front of the wooden shack the man called home, the place looked deserted, but that was to be expected. Like his few neighbors, Red Pete was cautious about company and would hide out until reasonably assured that it was safe to make an appearance. Jeff chewed on a strand of sweet grass as he waited. A slight movement in the trees behind the shack finally affirmed the presence of his host.

An old man with a face like a shriveled apple emerged and looked his visitor over carefully with narrowly squinting eyes. Dressed in what had all the appearances of being rags topped off by an elaborately embroidered waistcoat, the ancient limped forward on a pearl-handled cane. "Thought I'd be seein' ye sooner or later, Jeffrey. How ye been keepin'?"

In spite of his years, Red Pete still looked fit, Jeff thought. As yet, the carrot-hued hair, for which the man had come by his name, showed no signs of dulling.

"Tolerably well," Jeff drawled.

"An' that there brother o' yourn's, he doin' all right?"

"Better than ever. Brandon is going to be a father again in a month or two."

"Good for him." Red Pete chortled and scratched his shirted chest with a hairy hand. "Heard he'd got hisself a right fine li'l gal o'er there in England. Ye settled down, too, kind of?"

Jeff's brows lifted briefly in a noncommittal answer. It was that *"kind of"* which led Jeff to surmise that some word of his present circumstances had reached even out here in the swamps. That was hardly a surprise. In spite of their reclusive lifestyle, Red Pete and his kind had always seemed remarkably well informed about the happenings in Charleston and on the plantations roundabout.

"I expect you know by now that I'm searching for my wife," Jeff replied. "Seen anything of her?"

Red Pete spit a long stream of tobacco juice in the general direction of a tree stump and shook his head. "Not a hair, but I seen Elijah last night. He was trackin' for ye, he said."

Jeff inclined his head in a slow nod. "I sent him out to see what he could find of a horse thief. Is he having any luck?"

"Reckon so. Said a man named Hyde was on horseback ahead o' him for awhile, makin' tracks easily seen, like maybe somethin' had scared him. Then it looked ta Elijah like the man got hisself thrown 'bout two, maybe three miles from here. The horse run off, an' Hyde continued on foot, but he 'peared ta be movin' kinda slow, like he'd been hurt some. Elijah was stayin' on his trail."

"Good man Elijah. Maybe I'll come across the mare somewhere up ahead. In the meantime, if you happen to see my wife, I'd appreciate it if you'd persuade her to stay with you for a spell, at least until I can get back this way."

Red Pete nodded. "I'll do my best, Jeffrey. Ye happen ta know if'n she likes corn fritters?"

Jeff inclined his head in a slow nod. "I believe she has a passing fondness for them."

"I'll make a batch then. She's liable ta be right hungry by the time she gets back around this way."

Jeff sincerely hoped that hunger was the only problem his wife was experiencing after spending two nights on higher ground, the third evening in the swamp, but without elaborating, he thanked Red Pete for his concern and took his leave.

The marsh closed in around Jeff once again, slowing his pace. The drone of insects increased, as did the heat. He pressed on, pausing only to give Majestic a chance to drink, and then resumed his search. The sun had reached its zenith and began its descent before he finally perceived some hope for his success.

RAELYNN HAD DESCENDED FROM THE TREE SHORTLY after dawn. She was stiff, sore, and so completely exhausted that she was unable to differentiate between tensed muscles and utter fatigue. She was also very thirsty, but there was only stagnant water to be had, and she had no desire to start heaving up her stomach again. By the time it occurred to her to sip the morning dew that had collected on the larger leaves during the night, the moisture had all but evaporated. She found enough for a swallow or two, but it hardly sufficed. Of food, she couldn't even bring herself to think. Although there were many plants around her, she lacked the knowledge to discern the difference between those that were edible and others that were poisonous, and she wasn't about to tempt fate. Hunger wouldn't kill her, at least not so quickly, but trying to satisfy it just might.

As the day wore on, Raelynn's weariness, thirst, and appetite steadily increased. The heavy canopy of trees and twisting vines rising up to lofty levels protected her from the worst of the sun, but the stifling heat made her feel as if she were plodding through thick molasses.

Just how far she progressed through the difficult maze was a mystery. The vines covering the ground continued to entangle her feet, and she grew increasingly weary of stumbling and falling. The blisters were excruciating. Only by gathering Spanish moss from the lower branches of the trees and stuffing small portions into her stockings was she able to gain some measure of relief from the stinging discomfort. To protect the bones in her ankles and feet from possible breakage, she tore long strips from her petticoat and wound them first about her slippered feet and then up around her ankles. The bandages lent much-needed support, yet in spite of efforts to ease her plight, Raelynn realized she was feeling positively wretched, to a degree she had never experienced before. Weary, footsore, thirsty and all too vividly aware of the burning emptiness of her stomach, she was greatly tempted to dismiss her resolve and just sit down and cry.

At the moment, however, her spine was too stiff to yield to any degree of bending, sitting or lounging.

Raelynn slogged wearily on through the marshes, knowing that if she stopped, she'd likely give up entirely. A gentle wind sprang up, and even in her predicament, she found it refreshing. It certainly kept the mosquitoes at bay.

In the midst of her despair, the soft nicker of a horse seemed nothing more than a figment of her imagination. Even so, she staggered to a halt and glanced about, desperately praying that someone had come to her rescue, yet fearing her ears had deceived her.

Sweeter by far than the wafting breezes was the sight of Ariadne lazily nibbling on a distant knoll of grass. Immediately Raelynn's heart lifted from the dark morass that had threatened to drag her down. She had no idea what miracle had brought the mare into the swamp, but words could not express the joy she now felt at seeing her.

The mare shook her head briskly to chase away the insects and, for a moment, eyed Raelynn. Unconcerned by the presence of this human, she went back to grazing.

Cautiously Raelynn approached with a trembling hand extended as she cajoled the animal to stand very still and to *please* be especially nice. Amazingly, when she reached out and stroked her along the withers, the mare didn't shy away.

"Oh, Ariadne, I can't believe it is you," Raelynn murmured, her voice choked by grateful tears. "What are you doing so far away from home?" She supposed that if the mare had been able to speak and reason, she might have been inclined to ask her the same question. "I know, Ariadne. We both ran away, and now the pair of us are lost in this infernal bog. I'm beginning to think I was better off where I was. What about you?"

Ariadne continued chomping on the grass, caring little for human deductions or regrets. Raelynn ran a gentle hand over the horse, searching for injuries, but found no evidence of any that were serious. It was obvious, however, that the mosquitoes and gnats had recently feasted on her. Almost a solid layer of tiny welts had been raised beneath the mare's coat.

While Ariadne nibbled contentedly on the grass, Raelynn dragged over a small, broken section of a log to use as a mounting block. Gently patting the mare's neck, she cajoled her in soothing tones, praying all the while the animal would prove tractable and stand submissively still while she hauled herself astride.

Surprisingly Ariadne seemed a good sport about it all, but Raelynn hadn't forgotten Jeff's reluctance to let her ride the headstrong steed and gingerly settled herself upon the mare's back. Being without a saddle was strange enough, but sitting astraddle wasn't very comfortable without some form of cushioning. She twitched, trying to stuff her chemise underneath her to protect the vulnerable areas. Whether her movements disturbed the horse or it was just Ariadne's temperament to be cantankerous, Raelynn soon learned that Jeff's misgivings had been well warranted. Without warning, the mare started bucking and crow-hopping in a circle, sending her rider sailing off into a stagnant pool. The putrid collection of water certainly saved Raelynn a few injuries, but she came up retching from the awful stench of it. The only positive thing about having an empty stomach was the fact that she had nothing to heave up. There she sat in total misery, tears and muddied hair streaming down her face, clothes soaked through with stinking slime, and hips and calves deep in fetid muck. At that precise moment, Raelynn was certain she was the very epitome of everything repulsive.

"Oh, why did I ever leave England?" she moaned dejectedly and began to sob in woeful lament.

If it served as some consolation, Ariadne came over and nuzzled her hair, but Raelynn wasn't willing to accept the steed's apologies without venting a good measure of her wrath upon her. "Get away from me, you ornery nag!" she railed, her voice fraught with tears. "If it's the last thing I do, I'll see you harnessed to a plow!"

Raelynn considered staying where she was, for it would only cost her more pain if she tried moving, but hunger and thirst were very strong incentives indeed. Wincing, she pushed herself to her feet, slipping and sliding until finally she managed to extricate herself from the stink-hole. Bestowing a baleful glare upon the mare, she caught her by the ear and thrust a warning finger before those large, beautiful eyes.

"Now listen very carefully, Ariadne," she ground out through gnashing teeth. "I'm very tired, I'm very lost, I'm very irate with you, so if you have any care for your carcass, you'll allow me to mount you, and then you will take me out of this smelly swamp. Do you understand me?" The mare tried to lift her head, but Raelynn held her firmly by the ear. "If you don't mind your manners, I swear, Ariadne, you *will* become a workhorse, and I assure you, my pretty filly, you won't like that in the least."

Raelynn was sure she was becoming a bit addled, threatening the steed as she was doing, but she really didn't care. What she truly wanted right then and there was a hot bath so she could take a deep breath without smelling herself.

Clasping a handful of the flowing mane, Raelynn drew the mare back to the broken log, stepped atop it, and dragged herself once again onto the horse's back. Clinging to the mane, she waited an interminable length of time for Ariadne to repeat her earlier performance and, after being reassured of the mare's compliance to some extent, turned her in what Raelynn fervently prayed was the right direction. They walked for a lengthy space before Raelynn allowed herself to relax slightly.

Still, she wasn't of a mind to trust the steed overly much and kept a tenacious grip on the mane.

After plodding over torturous terrain for untold hours, the luxury of a smooth ride didn't escape Raelynn's notice. In spite of her unpredictable disposition, Ariadne had an easy flowing stride, for which Raelynn became most appreciative. She was grateful for several other things which the ride afforded, to be off her feet for one thing, and for another, to be sitting above the brambles and thorns that had relentlessly rent her skin and garments.

The breezes that had sprung up earlier had strengthened, bringing with them a refreshing coolness that did much to buoy Raelynn's spirits. For a few moments she even had hopes of surviving her horrendous folly, that is, until she happened to notice that the marsh was becoming progressively gloomier.

Peering up through the lofty trees, Raelynn felt her heart sink and new fears congeal in her chest. The winds she had briefly relished were pushing ominous thunderclouds across the sky. Even as she watched in mingled surprise and dismay, a jagged streak of lightning tore across the sky. A moment later a stinging rain began to pelt her.

A groan of despair slipped from Raelynn's lips as she thumped her heels against the mare's flanks to urge her out of the punishing downpour. Ariadne responded readily, quickening her pace, but the heavy, wet soil of the bog clung to her hooves, impeding her progress. Their passage was further thwarted by the torrent of rain unleashed upon them. They could barely see, much less move any measurable distance. In barely a fraction of a moment Raelynn's clothes became so thoroughly drenched that they were soon plastered like second skins to her body.

There was only one conciliation Raelynn could find

in her present predicament. Now she had all the water she could drink. She just hoped she wouldn't drown in it.

She peered around for the closest haven and tried to guide the mare toward a closely growing stand of trees, but Ariadne was anxious to escape the deluge and surged forward, only to become mired in soft, boggy peat. Though the mare struggled, she couldn't pull herself free.

Unable to believe that she could be so ill-favored by circumstances, Raelynn fought an urge to weep, but the impulse to relent to harsh, anguishing sobs was promptly forgotten as a blinding flash of lightning ripped through the forest, hitting a large cypress a short distance away, the precise area upon which Raelynn had just recently set her sights. The fiery bolt snapped the trunk in half as easily as a dried twig, sending a dazzling spray of sparks flying helter-skelter. Shaken to the core of her being, Raelynn threw up her arms to shield herself from the blinding flares and, in tremulous trepidation, peered over her forearm as the top of the tree plummeted to the ground with a crashing roar, in its rapid descent stripping off many of its own branches and those of nearby trees. Before it reached the ground, a deafening crack of thunder seemed to shake the very ground around them. Ariadne shivered in terror and tried to heave upward out of the bog, but to no avail.

"Easy, girl," Raelynn murmured through fear-stiffened lips, astounded by how closely she had come to being permanently singed black by the lightning. If not for Ariadne becoming entrapped, they would have both been killed. "It's all right, Ariadne. Steady now. We're alive . . . at least for the moment."

The mare calmed a trifle, but stood shivering in the muddy vise. Raelynn hurriedly slid from Ariadne's back, fully intending to help, but immediately gasped in alarm when her own feet began to sink. Frantically she stretched out an arm, barely managing to grasp hold of a low-hanging branch, and scrambled to more solid footing. It proved tenuous at best.

Gingerly testing the footing upon which she stood, Raelynn turned on trembling limbs, but her throat constricted with sudden dread when she saw that the mare had been caught in a marshy hollow that had been softened by the rainstorm. It looked as dangerous as quicksand. The more Ariadne struggled to free herself, the deeper she sank.

Terror swept through Raelynn, as much for herself as for Ariadne. She seriously doubted that she could make it through the thick morass without the mare, and now with the volume of rain coming down, small rivulets were opening up everywhere. Soon they would become life-threatening. Yet, if she sought to help Ariadne, Raelynn knew she could be sucked down into the slough right along with the mare.

In growing panic, Raelynn glanced about, hoping to espy some way of escape for both of them. She certainly couldn't hope to pull the horse free, for she had neither the strength nor the wherewithal to bring about such a rescue. She was virtually helpless.

Suddenly Raelynn recalled the thick vines she had battled. Quite possibly some were sturdy enough to be used to draw the mare out of the bog. Stumbling over the sodden hem of her gown, she searched through the pelting rain for a suitably stout vine and finally stumbled upon a grapevine twining up a nearby tree. She struggled to yank it free, but it was a feat that required every measure of strength she possessed. It didn't help that she was weak from her lengthy fast and being bombarded by rain. Indeed, by the time she tore the climber loose from the branches, she was nearly spent and, in utter exhaustion, collapsed to her knees in the tiny rivulets forming over the ground.

Regaining her resolve, if not a full measure of her strength, she rose to her feet beneath the pelting rain and considered how best to go about harnessing the mare to the vine. The roots were still firmly attached to the ground, serving as an anchor, but she needed some further leverage against the weight of the steed. In that quest she wound her makeshift cord around a pair of young, sturdy trees and kept the vine taut to aid her progress as she approached Ariadne, carefully avoiding the ever-softening sump of bottomless mire as she did so. The horse's fatigue was becoming increasingly evident as her attempts to thrust herself free from the mud declined. Though the realization congealed into a hard lump of fear in her throat, Raelynn had to face the truth of it. If Ariadne's rescue wasn't accomplished within the next half hour, the animal would lose both strength and heart. If she gave up, it wouldn't take long before she would be sucked down into a soggy grave.

Blinking through the sodden tendrils that streamed down her face, Raelynn looped the grapevine around Ariadne's neck and tied it securely in place with strips of cloth torn from her own skirt. Returning to the pair of trees, she hauled on the vine with all of her strength as she coaxed the mare toward her. Obediently Ariadne heaved upward, allowing Raelynn to wrench her makeshift cord a few degrees tighter about the trees, but the headstrong horse shook her head violently, trying to dislodge the now snug lasso. In the process she nearly shredded Raelynn's palms as the rough growth was ripped from her grasp. Tenaciously Raelynn grabbed hold of it again and, with sharp tugs, pleadingly beseeched the mare to cooperate. Again Ariadne lunged ahead in an attempt to dislodge herself from the mud, enabling Raelynn to jerk the vine taut once more. In spite of the continuous bombardment of rain, they made progress, enough to hearten Raelynn when she realized the mare was almost out of the miry pit.

"You're doing it, Ariadne," she cried jubilantly. In the pelting downpour, she couldn't even speak without spitting out rain. "Come on now, girl. Just a few more tugs, and you'll be free."

As if understanding this logic, the mare surged forward again, allowing the grapevine to be wrenched tighter around the trunks, but Raelynn had precious little time to revel in the headway they were making, for, in the next instant, the cord broke against the strain of the horse's weight, sending Raelynn sprawling backward into a puddle and Ariadne sliding back into her muddy prison. Raelynn scrambled to her feet and, with a cry of defeat, clasped clenched fists to her temples in horror as she watched the mare struggling valiantly to lift herself from the ooze into which she was being rapidly sucked. Ariadne shrieked, sensing her impending doom, and thrashed about, but alas, to no good purpose.

∞MAJESTIC'S EARS PRICKED AS HE CAME TO A SUDDEN halt. Jeff shifted the dripping brim of his hat further away from his brow, fully alert to the fact that the steed had heard, sensed, or seen something. Jeff peered through the cascading sheets of rain, scanning the area beyond the trees, but it was heavily shaded by the rainstorm and the dreary grayness of late afternoon. He twisted in the saddle and glanced in every direction, but he saw nothing of any import. Reaching down, he stroked the sodden neck of the stallion. "What's out there, boy? What spooked you?"

Majestic nickered and stared unrelentingly toward the tangled growth far beyond the place where they had stopped. Jeff canted his head, listening intently. He could hear little above the heavy deluge. Most of what he heard, he recognized, the gurgling of streams that had sprung to temporary life, the pelting rain, and the slight shifting of his mount accompanied by almost indecipherable creaks of the leather tack, but there was another sound so far in the distance that he was unable to make it out clearly. Was it a horse's shriek of panic?

Jeff touched his heels to the stallion's flanks, sending him forward in what he sincerely hoped was toward the area from whence the distant, miniscule sounds were emanating. As he drew ever closer, the more certain Jeff became that what he was hearing were the shrill screams of a horse. If that were indeed true, then possibly he would discover the whereabouts of Ariadne, but he could only guess from the indistinct, but hair-raising noises that the mare or some other horse was in grave peril.

Following the anguished shrieks, Jeff reined Majestic through the trees, carefully avoiding the more treacherous open areas of the marsh. When he broke through a tangle of brush into a small clearing from whence the piercing whinnies were coming, he espied the mare immediately, belly-deep in muck. At the moment she was struggling frantically, trying to lunge upward at the end of a makeshift tether. His gaze followed the length of vine stretched taut between the steed and a tree, and his breath left him in a rush as he saw the one responsible for this valiant, if futile, attempt at rescue. His wife was beside the tree, soaked to the very depth of her clothes, straining desperately in the pouring rain to pull the cord tighter around its trunk.

"Raelynn!"

Though the name seemed no more than a whisper in the pelting torrent, Raelynn's head snapped around. Now fully alert to her husband's presence, she lifted a hand to shield her eyes from the downpour. Even so, the moisture dribbling down from her sodden hair forced her repeatedly to blink in an effort to clear her vision. A strange blend of fear, shame, and relief swept her at the sight of Jeff. He sat like some dreadful, darkly armored warrior on the back of the tall steed. She opened her mouth to speak, but words failed her. She had left Oakley, fearing he was a murderer. If true, then he could easily do away with her here in the swamp and no one would ever be the wiser.

Shifting his hat forward over his brow again, Jeff pulled the collar of his slicker up close around his neck and swung down to the ground. Wasting no time on stern rebukes, he worked quickly to free the rope from his saddle and then tied a running noose at one end. This he tossed over the mare's head and dragged it snug before flinging another larger loop around behind her rump. Forming a makeshift harness, he drew the loose end through the front noose and wrapped it about his saddle horn. Remounting, he reined Majestic over solid ground.

Once the stallion felt the tug of the rope, he moved forward with powerful strides, digging his hooves into the sodden turf. Ariadne struggled in protest as the rope tightened around her rump, and for a moment, it seemed as if their efforts would be of no benefit. Then, almost imperceptibly, the mare began to emerge from the quagmire. The instant her front hooves struck firm land, she whinnied in triumph and flagged her heavily muddied tail. Another strong tug from Majestic, and she was completely free.

"Oh, thank heavens!" Raelynn exclaimed in overwhelming relief, erupting in hoarse sobs as she crumpled to her knees upon the sodden ground. Tears spilled forth freely, and she buried her face in her hands as she wept harshly, weeping as much for herself as the mare. As desperate as she had become, she'd have likely died trying to save the animal.

A large hand dropped upon her shoulder, startling a fearful gasp from her. She looked up to find Jeff leaning over her. He was hardly more than an ominous gray shadow in the rain-shrouded gloom, but she thought his eyes glowed with a feral light. Not knowing what to expect, she shrank back and had some difficulty swallowing as she awaited her fate.

"What the bloody hell are you doing out here,

madam?" he growled sharply. "Don't you know what could've happened to you?"

Refusing to yield him an answer, Raelynn turned her face aside and, drawing up into a small, disconcerted knot, hunched her shoulders against the deluge. From every aspect, she looked like a small child waiting to be punished.

Muttering an oath, Jeff scooped his wife up in his arms and carried her back to the stallion. There he stood her to her feet and wrapped a blanket tightly about her. Once he lifted her to the back of the steed, he loosened the rope from around Ariadne's rump and tied the free end to a metal ring behind the cantle of his saddle. Swinging up behind Raelynn, he clamped a protective arm around her and reined the stallion through the dense trees as the mare dutifully followed at the end of her tether.

13 &

*T*he rain had seemingly spent its furor and dwindled to hardly much more than a drizzling mist. Hunched together against its persistent moisture, the couple rode in silence through the swamp. Jeff remained vigilant as he sought to avoid treacherous ground, but Raelynn was thoroughly spent, both physically and mentally. Though she tried to remain alert, her eyelids sagged beneath the weight of her fatigue and her head bobbed forward often until a large hand swept upward and pressed it down gently upon a sturdy shoulder. Her brow found a warm, familiar niche against a corded throat to nestle, and with a sigh, she gave up her futile attempts to stay awake. If Jeff had wanted to kill her, she mused distantly, then surely he would have done so by now.

Darkness encroached with the approach of evening and the thickening forest. Raelynn roused briefly to a vague awareness that the misting rain had ended. A cold, blustery wind had sprung up in its stead and now seemed bent on chasing roiling clouds across the face of the moon. The frigid breezes penetrated to the depths of her wet garments, evoking shivers until her husband opened his slicker and pulled her snugly against his chest. Raelynn found no energy to resist, but leaned inertly against the solid bulwark. As she drifted off to sleep again, she wondered distantly if they would ever find a warm haven.

It was much later when Raelynn struggled up from her dazed trauma and realized that Jeff had halted the stallion. She peered obliquely over her shoulder, having no awareness of how far they had come or, for that matter, just where they were presently. The hovering moon illumined the small clearing they had entered. Near the back of it, a log cabin was nestled underneath the lofty branches of several tall pines. Smoke curled invitingly from the stone chimney, and the soft glow of a lantern shone from the front windows. The ripple of a swiftly running stream drifted to them from somewhere nearby, seeming almost musical as its burbling melded with the harmonious tones of a softly hooting owl perched in a tree some distance away.

"Who lives here?" she murmured thickly through her drowsiness.

"A friend of mine who goes by the name of Red Pete," Jeff replied, sweeping his right leg over the stallion's rump and stepping down. He tied Majestic's reins to a hitching post, dropped the saddlebags over a shoulder, and peered up at her. His lips twitched vaguely with the arduous task of emulating a smile. "Red Pete was once an ordained minister, so you'd better behave yourself, madam. He's not above teaching us both a lesson or two."

"Does he live here alone?"

"He had a wife and a son years ago, but they both

died during an epidemic. After their deaths, he pretty much became a recluse."

Jeff lifted his arms to sweep Raelynn down from the stallion, but she drew back, feeling suddenly wary. She met his gaze hesitantly and saw a handsome brow twist upward to a skeptical height.

"If you mean to sit there all night, madam, you'd better take into consideration the fact that you'll do so entirely alone. As for myself, I mean to get into some dry clothes, have something to eat, and get some much needed sleep."

At the thought of food, Raelynn's demeanor changed to an expression of yearning as her eyes chased toward the cabin. It seemed as if she had gone without eating for at least the last month. Even if her stomach had ceased its growling, her mouth watered readily enough, reminding her that she was starving for something to eat.

"Come along, Raelynn," Jeff commanded, slipping his hands about her narrow waist and whisking her to the ground. Her hollow cheeks evidenced her lengthy fast, and though she might well let pride and fear rule her head, he refused to let her be so foolish. "You must eat for the sake of our child."

Raelynn's head snapped up in surprise, and she gaped up at him, astounded by his knowledge. "How did you know?"

"Cora told me."

"But how could she have known?" Raelynn whispered, no less amazed. "I've never said a word to anyone."

"Aye, you were very private about it, not even telling me," Jeff muttered sourly. "Cora probably figured it out for herself. As for myself, madam, I must apologize. I was too taken with the idea of making love to you on a nightly basis to consider the fluxes you were missing." Tilting his head at a contemplative angle, he swept her with a careful perusal. "How far along are you?"

Folding her arms across her midsection, Raelynn turned aside from his closely probing stare and answered in a muted tone. "A little over two months."

"Obviously you didn't concern yourself about your condition when you lit out like a scared rabbit," Jeff jeered, lending her no pity. "But then, this wasn't the first time you've cast me in the role of villain without giving me a chance to explain or to provide evidence of my innocence."

His caustic tone brought a vivid hue to Raelynn's cheeks, and though she was weak and faint from hunger, she realized she had some small bit of mettle left. "What was I to think when I found you standing over a dead woman with a bloody knife in your hand and your clothes all stained with gore? If you'll remember, you threatened to throttle Nell if she ever came out to Oakley again?"

Jeff snarled with rage and frustration. "If you actually believe I'm capable of such a hideous crime, then, madam, you have little regard for me, but as you've done in the past, you've judged me guilty without giving me a fair hearing. No rightful magistrate would dare convict a felon without a fair trial." He snorted in contempt. "But if you were sitting behind a judge's bench, you'd have had me strung up by now." Jeff saw her lovely face contort with emotion as she struggled to find a sagacious reply, but he had heard enough of her logic. "I'm sure you wouldn't want to be temporarily ensconced with a murderer, my dear, so I'll leave you to find your own bed."

Pivoting about-face, he tied the mare to a hitching post, paused beside Majestic long enough to draw his long rifle from the saddle holster, and then strode to the cabin door where he beat a fist upon the rough-hewn planks. No answer came, and he eased the portal open to peer inside. "Red?" he called out. "Are you here?"

Silence followed his inquiry, prompting Jeff to step

within and glance about. Finding no evidence of the man, he crossed to the door of the small bedroom at the back of the structure, but that, too, was empty. Save for himself, there was no one in the cabin.

Returning to the main room, Jeff scanned the interior. What he saw gave him cause to believe that the place had been vacated as recently as the last hour, perhaps even in the last few moments. He was fully aware that Red Pete was liable to duck out the back when he saw visitors approaching, mostly to be on the safe side, but in this case, the old man had left a welcoming ambience behind to greet his guests.

In the crudely built stone hearth, a fire crackled cheerily beneath a large iron kettle brimming with steaming water. A rough-hewn table, with a pair of primitively made branch chairs tucked beneath its edge, resided in front of the hearthstone. Sitting on the nearest corner of its surface, which constituted a well-worn slab of wood, was a chipped crockery bowl with a large ladle lying alongside it. On the cutting board beside it a knife and a slab of smoked venison had been left seemingly as an invitation. Near the latter, Jeff found a note scrawled in a large hand.

"Might be gone for several days, Jeffrey. Make yourself to home."

Dropping his saddlebags in a chair, Jeff stripped off his slicker and peered into the bowl. Only then did he realize that his wife had come as far as the threshold. He made no effort to face her as he asked, "You like corn fritters, don't you, Raelynn?"

Once again Raelynn found her mouth salivating at the merest mention of food. Her voice seemed tiny even to her as she answered, "Yes." Shrugging off the sodden blanket, she went to stand behind her husband and peered past his arm at the food laid out on the table. "Will your friend be back soon, Jeffrey?"

"No." Jeff's answer was brusque as he continued to

struggle with a husbandly ire. No doubt his wife would have been more comfortable with their host in residence, for it was obvious she was still reluctant to be alone with him. If not for the fact that she was exhausted beyond measure and nearly faint from hunger, she might have lit out on her own again. But then, he was just in a mood to go after her and bring her back.

Flipping his wrist, Jeff shot out a thumb toward the note, making no further effort to explain. She could read the missive as well as he could; she didn't need to be mollycoddled by a suspected murderer.

Raelynn scanned the large script and heaved a forlorn sigh as she flicked a cautious glance about the interior. She had hoped that the one called Red Pete would be at home and could serve as some kind of buffer between them, but that apparently wouldn't be the case. For the first time in their marriage, Jeff and she would be entirely removed from other people while under the same roof. In the past she would have eagerly welcomed such seclusion, but certainly not now, not when she was inundated with grucsomc mcmorics left over from what she had seen in the stables. Now the idea of this degree of marital privacy left her feeling immensely vulnerable.

Her eyes wandered slowly about the room as she sought to thrust aside disturbing reminders. In every corner, she saw evidence of a man who lived in a state of isolation every day of his life. "Why would a minister withdraw into this kind of solitude?"

"I never asked." Jeff only meant to toss a brief glance in his wife's direction, but the green orbs lingered overlong, losing their flinty hardness as they skimmed her bedraggled form. Still, his manly pride refused to yield so easily, not when she continued to cast him in the role of butcher. Her distrust had driven the painful blade in deep, and he was wounded nigh to his very soul.

A Bible lay open near the far end of the table, giving him an excuse to distance himself from her. Lifting it, he shifted the open faces of the pages toward the firelight and took note of where it had been left open. "Proverbs . . ." A short laugh escaped him. "I should have known Red would be inclined to offer a lesson along with his hospitality."

"What kind of lesson?"

The rich timbre of Jeff's voice commanded her full attention in the quiet serenity of the crude shack. *"Who can find a virtuous woman? for her price is far above rubies. The heart of her husband doth safely trust in her, so that he shall have no need of spoil. She will do him good and not evil all the days of her life."*

Raelynn felt her cheeks flaming beneath the chiding verses. She had never even met the vagabond parson, and yet it seemed as if he had spoken directly to her. "How could Red Pete possibly have known?"

Jeff shut the Bible and laid it aside as he peered at her again. "Known about us? Don't let that spook you, my dear." Derision imbued his tone. "I saw Red Pete on my way through here earlier, but, by then, he had already heard about what had happened at Oakley."

"Was he also cognizant of the fact that I had left?" When Jeff responded with a curt nod, she asked in amazement, "But how could a simple parson who lives entirely alone in the woods be aware of what goes on at Oakley? Am I to understand that since we've stopped here for the night that this cabin is still some distance from the plantation?"

" 'Tis a fair jaunt away, but around here, my dear, news travels on the wind. I don't suppose there's much that Red Pete isn't aware of. He certainly knew when to make himself scarce. He probably saw us coming and skedaddled out the back."

Raelynn was astonished at such a notion. "Why would your friend vacate his cottage and leave it for our use?"

Jeff elevated a dark brow as he settled a pointed stare upon her. "Perhaps because he's a nice man. Or maybe he has enough sense not to put himself between a man and his wife when they need to work things out."

Feeling very cold of a sudden, Raelynn wrapped her arms about her damply garbed form. The idea of *working things out* with Jeffrey Birmingham definitely stole away what little grit she had remaining. "No," she murmured, lifting a dainty chin in the guise of a wounded martyr, "he just leaves open Bible verses to make it clear what he thinks of the wife. Apparently it doesn't matter what the husband might have done."

Jeff couldn't resist a caustic barb. "Perhaps Red Pete doesn't like to judge men at the first sign of trouble as you seem able to do, especially acquaintances he has known for some time." Stepping near the hearth, Jeff squatted on his haunches and began poking up the fire. Tossing on more logs, he advised, "But you needn't go presuming about Red or what he's thinking. That message in Proverbs was likely intended for me." Rising to his feet, he dusted off his hands and gestured casually toward the crockery bowl on the table. "He probably meant that message for you."

Raelynn's eyes followed in the direction he had indicated, but for the life of her, she had no idea what he was talking about. Granted, she was thoroughly exhausted, ravenously hungry and greatly in need of sleep, all of which hindered her ability to decipher his meaning, but even if she had been fully alert, she saw nothing that would have come close to solving the riddle.

Noting her bewilderment, Jeff stepped near the table, dipped the ladle into the contents of the bowl and, lifting the spoon, let the batter pour out in a golden stream. "Red Pete asked me if you liked corn fritters. Seems he left the makings and the venison for you to cook. If you don't like the fare he provided, there's always the food Cora packed for us."

"Oh." It was the best reply Raelynn could muster.

Turning aside, Jeff made every effort to smother the

gallantry that seemed eager to escape when he considered the thoroughly exhausted condition of his wife. He lingered overlong at the task of shedding his jacket and shirt and then hung them with unusual care over the backs of the two chairs. By the time he thought he could face his wife again without responding to her plight, she was swaying on her feet in a dazed stupor. He cursed softly under his breath, knowing the battle lost. At the moment she seemed ready to collapse into a crumpled heap where she stood.

He took her gently by the arms and was immediately struck by how slender and delicate she seemed within his grasp. Considering the fact that she had left Oakley directly from her bedroom without venturing down to the kitchen, he could only assume that she had had very little to eat since her departure. Vividly attesting to that supposition were her pale, hollowed-out cheeks. Beneath her eyes, there were dark lavender shadows that made them appear sunken. In all, she was a rather pathetic sight, too pitiful for him to hold tenaciously to his anger.

"Sit down, Raelynn," he bade, pressing her back into a chair and squatting before her. He cupped her chin within his hand as he studied her drawn features and drooping eyelids. "It shouldn't take me but a few moments to put the horses in the barn and give them some hay and grain. When I return, I'll see about taking care of our needs. Until then, don't move. Do you understand?"

Her smooth forehead crinkled slightly as if he had asked a difficult task from her. "Yes."

Jeff's pledge was confirmed by his swift return to the cabin. When he came back, he brought with him a half barrel that he had found hanging beneath the eaves of the roof. Raelynn still sat where he had left her, her head bobbing forward spasmodically as she fought against the strengthening inducement of sleep. When he shoved aside the table and placed the wooden vat on the stone floor in front of the hearth, she started awake and blinked up at him, trying to focus her vision.

"What are you going to do with that?" she asked laboriously, lamely indicating the tub.

"That, my dear, is for your bath." Jeff wrapped a cloth pad around the handle of the large iron kettle, poured the steaming water into the barrel, and added two buckets of cooler water from the well outside before refilling and returning the kettle to the hook above the fire. From his saddlebag he produced a bar of soap and a towel.

"It's always wise to be prepared for occurrences such as these," he crowed, briefly brandishing the items.

His wit went unappreciated as his wife looked at him dully. When he stepped to her, her voice was equally devoid of sparkle. "Please, Jeffrey, I just want to go to sleep."

"After you've bathed and dined, madam, and not a moment before."

He hauled her to her feet, eliciting a weary groan from her, but she stood passively still as his lean fingers worked their way down the back of her torn, soppy, filthy gown. Once the fasteners were free, he slid it down her body, pulling away her shift and pantalettes along with it and letting the garments collect in a heap around her ankles.

Too groggy to feel anything but a desire to sleep, Raelynn made no effort to resist as he turned her around to face him. As he bent and stripped away her stockings, she was forced to brace a hand upon his bare shoulder. His bronzed skin felt warm and full of life beneath her chilled fingers, very much like the man himself.

Raelynn heard his breath catch and glanced down to find him staring at the ugly, broken blisters marring her feet. In some chagrin, she curled her toes inwardly, wishing she could hide the blood-caked moss that had become adhered to her feet.

"It's a wonder you can still walk," her husband muttered sharply.

"The moss helped," she murmured dismally and heaved a sigh, making no effort to cover herself as he straightened. She was so thoroughly exhausted she couldn't even manage a discomfited blush as he considered her taut breasts and the nipples that had darkened to a deep rosy blush since her pregnancy. Even when his gaze swept down to her stomach, she could only watch through a dazed stupor.

The change in his wife's body was subtle, but definitely discernible if one cared to take note, Jeff reflected. He had just been too caught up in the pleasure of fulfilling his husbandly cravings to notice the signs.

"Your bath is ready, Raelynn," he murmured softly, offering her a hand.

Raelynn's knees felt too wobbly for her to even consider ignoring the proffered help. Submissively she slipped thin fingers within his palm and leaned toward him as she lifted a foot to test the water. It was just hot enough to banish the chill, yet it also made her wince in sudden pain as her blisters started stinging. Still, even bone tired, she was not oblivious to the benefits of a bath. She just hoped she wasn't so fatigued that she'd fall asleep trying to bathe herself.

Stepping into the barrel, Raelynn crossed her ankles and sank into the liquid with a long, grateful sigh. For a moment, she sat with eyes closed, luxuriating in the soothing warmth of the water until a splash startled her. The resulting spray of droplets made her blink as the bar of soap sank beneath the surface, bumping lightly against her stomach as it wove a zigzagged path toward the bottom of the oaken tub. Lifting her gaze through the dribbling moisture, she found her husband peering down at her, a dark brow elevated sharply.

"Don't stay in there forever, madam. I'd like to eat

and have a bath myself before we settle down for the night."

"Could you hand me a pitcher of warm water please," she asked, her voice dull with fatigue. She squinted up at him as tiny runnels trickled through her lashes. "I have to wash my hair."

Jeff watched her rub an eye with a fist, much like a child who found it hard to stay awake. "Are you in need of some assistance in shampooing your hair?"

"Yes, I suppose I am, considering I'm having trouble keeping my eyes open," she answered in a tiny voice as violet lids lowered against an encroaching drowsiness.

"Should I bathe you as well?"

Her head dropped forward, and as her wet, snarled hair fell around her face, a weary sigh slipped from her lips. "I'm too exhausted to care what you do."

Jeff watched his young wife for a long moment. She sat slumped in the wooden tub like a limp rag doll. Taking pity on her, he knelt beside the tub and pressed her shoulders within the curve of his arm. She gave herself over entirely to his ministrations, hardly aware of him bathing her face and body, but when he slid the washcloth along the soft cleft between her thighs, she flung her eyes wide and scrambled upright. Staring at him aghast, she met his amused gaze.

"You're very thorough!" she accused in a shocked tone.

"My mother taught me to be at a very young age, madam. Nothing must go unwashed, she said. Besides, I've touched you there countless times already, and you never once chided me about my boldness. If anything," he needled, "you seemed to enjoy it."

"I'll wash that area, thank you," she stated with finality. "You can wash my hair."

Jeff heaved a laborious sigh. "You've gotten prudish, madam. Only a few days ago you let me wash you all over, even there. . . ."

"As you said, that was days ago, and this is now."

"So now it's look but don't touch, eh?"

"Something like that . . . at least until I can sort everything out."

Jeff's own patience had been severely frayed by his young wife's departure from the house and his lengthy search for her through the woods. After realizing she was safe, his relief had turned to a goading resentment over what she had done. Her readiness to believe the worst of him had been tantamount to a slap across the face. In a renewed, mercurial rising of his resentment, he gave her no benefit of a warning, but dumped the whole pitcher of warm water over her head, causing her to gasp in surprise and then fling up her hands to ward off another dousing as he grabbed a second pitcher.

Raelynn sputtered and blinked up at him through wetly streaming hair and trickling water. Spitting both hair and water out of her mouth, she cried, "Do you intend to drown me because I won't let you fondle me?"

"I intend to wash your hair, nothing more," Jeff declared succinctly. He rubbed the bar of soap around the crown of her head and began to work up a lather with lean, hard fingers.

Raelynn squawked in protest. "Don't be so rough!"

"I'm sorry, madam," he apologized without a trace of compassion. "I didn't realize my own strength."

She tossed him a mutinous glare. "I won't have a scalp left if you continue scrubbing it like that!"

"At least your hair will be clean. That's more than I can say for it now. What did you do, fall into a slime pool?" He could guess that that was precisely the case, for she still had flecks of green algae clinging to most of the strands. "You've got enough trash and critters in your hair to feed a bird for a whole year."

"Critters!" Raelynn screeched, scrambling to her knees in a panic. "Get them out!"

"Patience, woman. I'm trying to do just that."

"What kind of critters?"

Jeff sought to curb his laughter, but it kept slipping out just the same. "Slimy things you'd normally find in a swamp. Even a few bugs, too."

Raelynn groaned. Her husband's teasing wit could drive her to distraction at times. "Jeffrey Birmingham, if you're just saying that to frighten me, I'll never speak to you again."

He whisked a strange beetle in front of her nose, sending her surging to her feet with a scream. Like a wild woman, she clawed at her hair, shuddering violently in revulsion as she did so. Jeff fell back guffawing and immediately got a sopping wet washcloth full in the face. His amusement was hardly subdued by the unceremonious christening. Through spits and spurts of erupting laughter, he finally assured her, "Let me finish washing your hair, madam, and then, if any critters are left, I'll comb them out."

"I want them out *now*!"

"Tsk! Tsk! You must learn patience, my dear. All things in good time."

Though married but a few months, it certainly hadn't escaped Raelynn's notice that Jeffrey Birmingham could stand like a steadfast fortress when others' demands didn't meet with his approval. Nell had had to face his unyielding tenacity when she had tried to wheedle funds for her offspring both before and after the boy was born. For her effort, she had gained nothing. Nor did Raelynn believe that she could force her husband to comply with her wishes by simply making demands. Indeed, she'd be wiser by far not to provoke his intractability.

"As soon as you can manage," she beseeched in a softer, pleading tone and couldn't subdue another shiver as she thought of what ugly looking vermin might be crawling through her hair.

Jeff relented. "All right, my sweet. Sit down in the tub and hang your head over the side."

In her endeavor to submit herself entirely to his care, Raelynn faced away from him and complied with his directives, arching her back and leaning her head over the edge of the tub. Jeff began to comb the debris from the long strands, but as dedicated as he was to the task, he was inclined to feast his gaze liberally upon her lustrous bosom. In the flickering firelight her soft breasts glowed like luscious, golden melons. Though he yearned to taste their sweetness, he knew she wouldn't hold still for that, not when she was still debating his innocence or his guilt.

After raking the trash from her hair, he washed and rinsed the long strands. Then he toweled the sodden tresses vigorously before handing her another linen by which she could dry herself. As she rose from the tub and began patting the moisture from her body, Jeff squatted on his haunches for a moment and watched her. Such sights proved too much of a temptation, and he turned aside and began spreading the bedroll on the floor. When he checked the garments he had hung over the chairs, he found his shirt already dry.

"You can wear this for the time being," he said, tossing it to his wife. "I'll wash your gown and undergarments and hang them to dry before the fire. Then I'll see what I can do about rustling us up something to eat."

"Thank you," she murmured quietly, managing a tremulous smile as she glanced up at him. "You're very considerate to do all of this when it's usually the wife who should be doing the cooking and washing."

"As tired as you are, madam, you'd probably fall asleep while cooking our food, and I, for one, have no liking for burnt victuals. Besides, I'm probably more used to it than you are. Brandon and I had to fend for ourselves whenever we went hunting or camping in the woods. Believe it or not, madam, I'm not without experience."

"I'm glad one of us is capable of doing something," she murmured wearily. "I don't think I've ever been so exhausted in my entire life."

"A lesson to be garnered from your flight through the marsh, madam. Trudging through a swamp is definitely more challenging than traversing higher terrain." His eyes flicked down her naked body again as she slid her arms into the sleeves of his shirt. The garment all but swallowed her. The tail reached past her knees, and though she rolled the sleeves up several times, the shoulders fell almost to her elbows. Still, she seemed grateful to have something other than her sodden clothes to wear.

Jeff forced himself to look away from the winsome sight and, in an effort to set his mind to something less frustrating, began washing his wife's clothes. He'd do well to remember that she had all but condemned him as a murderer.

Raelynn was more appreciative of the shirt than she cared to let on. The manly essence that clung to it and the luxurious feel of the soft linen brushing across her naked breasts reminded her of the passion she had often shared with its owner and of his unswerving tenderness throughout their intimacy. Could a man who had given every evidence of being such a gentle, considerate lover actually turn so completely about-face in character and brutally stab a young mother to death?

Jeff finally lent his attention to the matter of food. After placing a griddle to warm on the rack above the fire, he set about slicing enough venison for the two of them. Soon he was ladling fritter batter into the thin layer of grease he had dribbled over the bottom of the skillet.

"Red Pete doesn't venture off very often," he stated without turning. "We can count ourselves privileged he invited us to make use of his cabin. He wouldn't do that for just anybody. When Brandon and I used to come hunting in this area as boys, we'd share whatever game we managed to bag with the old man. Perhaps this is his way of reciprocating."

An irresistible aroma drew Raelynn forward to the hearth, and she watched in rapt attention as bubbles began appearing first at the edges of the corn fritter batter and then in the center. She almost drooled in anticipation as she inhaled their delectable aroma. "I'm really starving, Jeffrey."

"You must be," Jeff murmured, flipping a cake over. "You didn't take any food along with you."

"I really didn't plan my departure very well," she confessed self-consciously. "I wanted to flee the house before you came upstairs."

Jeff had already figured out that much for himself. "You must think me an ogre, madam."

"For the most part, I have thought of you as my prince in shining armor, but there have been moments of uncertainty."

He slid the turner beneath a fritter and lifted it onto a plate. "Here, this will tide you over until the rest are done," he said, passing it to her. "Let it cool a bit."

The warning came too late, for Raelynn had already burned her fingers trying to pick the fritter up. She hurriedly blew on her seared digits as well as the food and then bravely took a bite. She found the flavor well worth the pain she suffered trying to chew it before it had sufficiently cooled. Closing her eyes in pure bliss, she made small noises of appreciation and then greedily took another bite, savoring it to the same degree.

Jeff cocked a brow above a lopsided grin as he peered askance at his young wife. "Guess Red Pete knew what he was doing when he made a fair-sized batch."

"You have the next one," Raelynn invited generously. Still, her eyes closely followed his progress as he broke off a portion and lifted it to his mouth. She licked her lips, relishing it for him, and was surprised when he reached out with a chuckle and popped it into her mouth. Giggling, she pressed her fingers to her lips and wiped away the spots of grease as she chewed. At length, she swallowed and smilingly complained, "You're going to make me fat."

"You were destined to face that fate ere I gave you the fritters, madam," he teased, stepping back from the heat of the fire. As she turned to face him, he reached down a hand and smoothed the shirt over her stomach. "Just wait a few months. You'll be waddling down the halls."

Raelynn's eyes lifted to his smiling face before they slipped downward over the length of him. Although she had been aware of the fact that her husband was tall, she had never really gotten a clear sense of his height until now. Perhaps the fact that he seemed as tall as a giant had much to do with the fact that his shadow stretched out behind him to the far side of the room and halfway up the vaulted ceiling.

Since they had been married in the heat of summer, she had never before had an occasion to observe him by the warm glow of a single hearth. His sun-bronzed skin seemed to glow with a radiance of its own as the bright flames highlighted the muscular expanse of his shoulders, the hard contour of his male breasts and the tautly fleshed ribs. As he loomed over her in all of his manly magnificence, it was somewhat like seeing a fabled god come to life.

Raelynn stepped away, troubled by the feelings he awakened within her even in the face of her suspicions. As he busied himself setting the food upon the table, she perused him with careful diligence, trying to discern some hint of the inner man. Although such manly perfection might well belong to a murderer, what of his character? Could a bright and noble temperament change with chameleon-like swiftness and, in a moment of rage, become something dark and tainted?

Jeff scooped up the last of the fritters and venison onto a platter and placed it on the table, announcing as he did so, "Dinner is ready, madam."

Raelynn stepped near. "Tell me what happened the other night," she pleaded in a whisper, finding it difficult to think of him as a depraved killer. "I mean, before I found you in the horse stall with Nell's body."

Jeff arched a dark eyebrow reprovingly. "Have you finally decided to give me a fair hearing, madam? Would it assuage your fears now that we're alone if you could find something in my claims of innocence to which you could give credence?"

Raelynn clasped a trembling hand to her forehead as she stated desperately, "I only know what I saw in the stable frightened me beyond anything I had ever experienced and that you were there, at the very core of that bloody scene."

"Our food is now hot, madam, but that fact won't last if you insist upon hearing the facts," her husband stated bluntly, pulling a chair out from the table for her. "And I, for one, am starved. If you aren't, then I have no doubt our child is."

Slipping into the proffered seat, she watched him move around to the opposite side of the table. "Are you going to tell me, Jeffrey?"

"Later perhaps. Right now, I don't want to ruin my appetite by remembering that gore. I'm sure you haven't yet considered the distress I suffered by being the one who discovered Nell. Believe it or not, madam, her murder bothered me, too. I can't think back on it without wanting to retch."

Raelynn understood completely and sought to find another topic. "Where are we going to sleep?"

"We'll have to share my bedroll unless you want to snuggle down in Red Pete's bed."

"I'd rather not." She abhorred the idea of sleeping in a strange man's bed. "I don't suppose you'd consider . . ."

"Not a chance. Red Pete swears there's no place in the Bible where it says that cleanliness is next to godliness. The tub I fetched for your bath had at least a week's worth of dust in it, and I'm not of a mind to bed down in another man's filth. I'm sorry, madam, but it looks as if you'll have to contend with my presence in the bedroll or roll yourself up in a wet blanket."

"You're not being very chivalrous," she complained mutedly.

Jeff snorted in disgust. "I don't suppose the fact that I let you dismiss me from your bed after I risked my life to rescue you from Gustav could be considered gallant," he retorted. "But, know this, I'm not of a mind to let it happen again. That much I've decided. We'll at least share a bed, madam, if nothing else."

"You would force me . . . ?"

"Hell and damnation, Raelynn, no!" he barked. "But neither am I going to let you throw me out of our bed or flee to another bedroom. I watched my brother agonize for months on end because he had distanced himself from Heather. I don't intend to be so foolish. As long as you live under my roof, madam, you'll share my bed."

"How easily you forget the conditions I set forth for our marriage," she retorted. "You agreed, then, to give me time . . ."

"That was *before* you yielded yourself to the idea of becoming intimate with me." Canting his head slightly, Jeff met her gaze at an angle. "Just tell me one damn thing, madam. What am I to you? Your puppet on a string, that I should dance at your bidding, and then, when you've grown bored or vexed with me, allow myself to be tossed into a shadowed corner of your life, where I must wait patiently until the mood strikes your fancy and you take me up again and expect me to perform for your pleasure? By damned, I'll not be at *any* woman's beck and call, not even yours, my dear! You'll either conform to this marriage or we will have no marriage at all."

Raelynn lifted her chin obstinately. "I failed to tell you, sir, that I was heading for Charleston when you found me."

The green eyes chilled as they met hers squarely. "You were heading for certain disaster in a sinkhole, madam. You'd have killed not only the mare but yourself as well."

"I shall yet go," she stubbornly declared.

"It's too late to consider an annulment," he rejoined tersely. "You're pregnant with my child, and if you don't want him . . . or her . . . then I sure as hell do!"

Raelynn clasped a trembling hand to her throat and stared at him in open-mouthed astonishment. "My-My baby will stay with me wherever I go, sir."

"You forget, madam. You're pregnant with *our* baby, not just yours. We'll have another seven months to settle our differences about where he shall live if you truly want to leave my house. Until then, I will urge you to consider his welfare. You're hardly able to make a living for yourself, much less support a child in a reasonable manner."

"I could work for Farrell Ives, just as Nell did," she protested. "I'm not without some skills in designing and making gowns."

An icy hardness came into those luminous emerald orbs, making her draw back slightly. Perhaps, she thought wildly, this was what Nell had seen just before he had stabbed her, a coldness so intense she was sure it could slice through metal.

"If that is your wish, madam. I'll not keep you married to me against your will."

Raelynn's jaw sagged another notch as she realized that she had been goaded into foolishly tweaking his temper. Indeed, she had cause now to think that this man, whom she had previously deemed so gentle and considerate, was definitely not the sort to antagonize. He had a mind and a will of his own and kowtowed to no one.

The handsome face was stoic as the cool green eyes flicked over her. "Until then, madam, you should try to eat something."

Raelynn sought to swallow the hard lump that had welled up within her throat. When she had left Oakley untold hours ago, she had been confused and frightened by what she had seen in the stable. She was still confused and frightened, but now her fears were far more complicated. Strangely, at the heart of them, there seemed to be a niggling apprehension that Jeff could actually bring himself to set her aside in a legal separation.

Perhaps he would be better off alienating himself from her, she thought grimly. Thus far, he had been served a brimming platter of grief, all because of her, and she could only wonder what next would follow. Since marrying her, he had been attacked, shot, accused of fathering a child out of wedlock and recently suspected of murder, mainly by her.

The verse from the Bible came back to haunt her. *She will do him good and not evil all the days of her life.*

". . . good and not evil . . ."

Raelynn started suddenly as she realized she had spoken aloud. In some chagrin she glanced up and found Jeff peering at her closely as if trying to discern her thoughts.

Her fingers trembled as she lifted a fork and broke apart a fritter. Dutifully she began to eat, but the silence between them had become a ponderous weight upon her heart. She hardly tasted her food, and if she could ascertain anything from the rigid muscles tensing in her husband's lean cheeks, she seriously doubted that he did either.

Time dragged sluggishly past as they finished the meal. In stoic silence Jeff cleared the table while Raelynn washed the tin plates and utensils in a wooden bucket. The griddle was the last to be cleaned, but it was near enough the fire to cause her to cry out in anguish when she took hold of it. Jeff was immediately beside her, grabbing her hand and thrusting it into a pail of cold water. After a moment, he withdrew it and slapped soda upon her fingers. He tore a long strip off the bottom of his shirt, wet the makeshift bandage and wound it around the seared digits before tying it off across her palm.

Raelynn winced as she clasped her bandaged fingers in her free hand. "I didn't realize the griddle was still hot."

"Obviously," Jeff retorted and threw a thumb over his shoulder, indicating his bedroll as he strode toward the door. "You'll be safe enough over there. I suggest you stay there and keep out of trouble."

"But where are you going?"

"Outside to get some more water from the well. Then I intend to take a bath." He settled a pointed stare upon her. "Any objections, madam?"

Raelynn closely inspected the frayed edge of his shirt. "I doubt that I'll be unduly shocked by the sight."

"You just might be if you stare hard enough," Jeff quipped without a trace of humor. "I still consider myself a newly married man."

Her voice was tiny. "I won't look if it will make you uncomfortable."

He grunted. "Uncomfortable is hardly the word for it, my dear. Aroused would better describe the way I'd be feeling."

"Even when you're angry with me?"

"I doubt that I'll ever be angry enough to ignore your presence, madam. You need only beckon with a finger for me to rise to the occasion."

"I'll dry my hair and wait for you in the bedroll," she replied quietly, seeing no other choice.

"No longer afraid of me?"

She wrung her hands, not daring to meet his gaze. "I'm still cautious."

"Oh."

The disappointment in his tone reluctantly drew a weak smile from her, but he had already turned away, and she found no need to do the same.

Seated upon the bedroll, Raelynn raked the tangles out of her hair, first with her fingers and then with his comb. Her bandaged hand made her attempts at grooming clumsy. Nevertheless, she made fairly good progress, at least until she happened to glance up at her husband. Then she forgot about her hair altogether. At the moment, he was silhouetted against the firelight with his back turned for the most part to her, with one knee drawn up nigh to his waist as he balanced on one foot. He had doffed his riding breeches except for one legging which he was presently in the process of tugging free. Never having observed him from this particular angle before, Raelynn felt her cheeks becoming inflamed with her own temerity as she eyed him surreptitiously. The sight was certainly more revealing than any she had yet seen, for the dancing flames vividly defined everything that was manly about him.

Upon ridding himself of the breeches, Jeff tossed them over a chair near the fire and faced her abruptly, naked as the day he had come into the world, in the process sending her eyes chasing elsewhere. Unconcerned with his lack of attire and oblivious to her gaze returning to him, he rummaged through his saddlebags once again, this time withdrawing a razor and a small, silvered glass.

"You have a mirror?" Raelynn cried in growing excitement. One day, she told herself, she'd just have to take a good, hard look at what he carried in those saddlebags of his; she just might be surprised at what she'd find.

"Some people venture into the woods better prepared than you did, my dear," Jeff gently taunted. "You can have the mirror *after* I've finished shaving unless you don't mind being scraped raw from my beard tonight. I was too anxious about you to even think of shaving."

"Thank you, I'll wait." Emboldened by his casual disregard of his nakedness, she flicked a meaningful glance toward his loins. It took no more than a brief inspection to put him on full display. As a result, she was prompted to inquire, "May I ask what you're going to wear tonight?"

When she finally lifted her gaze, his glowing eyes met

hers unswervingly. "As usual, madam, nothing more than my skin. "

"Perhaps tonight you should wear your breeches."

"Afraid of what I might do while naked?"

"Afraid of what you might do, period."

Jeff snorted cantankerously. "Tie the tail of my shirt snugly between your thighs, madam. It's the best chastity belt you'll be able to get your hands on here in this place, because I'm certainly not going to wear my breeches to bed just to suit you."

"Jeffrey!" she cried as he started to turn away.

Her husband threw up a hand impatiently. "Dammit, Raelynn, I'm not going to rape you, *if* indeed it can be called such a thing when it's between a husband and his wife. Now comb your hair and go to sleep. I won't bother you unless you invite my attentions."

Irritated with his young wife, Jeff returned to the matter of shaving and bathing. The linen towels he had given Raelynn to use had been left before the hearth. The fire was hot enough to allow them to be used again in similar service when he finally stepped from the wooden tub. He approached her, rubbing his torso vigorously.

"Are you sure Red Pete won't be back?" Raelynn asked, glancing toward the door worriedly.

"He's as good as his word," Jeff assured her, sweeping the linen behind him and scrubbing it across his back. "We're quite alone."

When Raelynn glanced back at him, immediately her gaze went chasing off again, but not before she had managed to store a mental image of the way her husband looked in the firelight, for it seemed as if water diamonds gleamed with a golden luster over his entire body.

"Where did you spend last night?" Jeff asked, snuffing the lamp.

In some chagrin, Raelynn admitted, "I spent it up a tree. And before you chide me for being so foolish, Jeffrey, be assured that I don't intend to ever do that again. I've never in my entire life suffered through a more miserable night."

Intent upon straightening the blanket over the bedroll, he made no attempt to look up as he asked, "What chased you up there, a snake?"

"How did you guess?"

His broad shoulders lifted casually. "Just figures. There are plenty of them around here. It hasn't been cold enough yet to send them into hibernation."

Raelynn turned her gaze apprehensively toward the door. "Please don't tell me that, Jeffrey. I hate snakes."

"Most women do, but not all snakes are dangerous. At least, you don't have anything to worry about in here."

"How can you be so sure?"

"Well, for one thing, they're more afraid of us than we are of them. Besides," he tossed her a grin, "snakes can't open doors."

"No, but the wily serpents can slip through almost any crack when you're not looking."

A soft chuckle briefly shook Jeff's shoulders. "Aye, they can at that, but if you're at all uneasy, stay close to me during the night. I promise to keep you safe in our lowly bed. Now come, madam, I'm tired and so are you. We need our sleep more than anything."

The wind chose that moment to rattle the door and pelt it with a sleeting rain, sending a chill shivering up Raelynn's spine. She was, in plain fact, beyond exhaustion. "Do you think it's going to storm again?"

"Could be."

"We won't be able to reach Oakley if it pours again like it did this afternoon."

"You needn't fret yourself overly much, madam. We'll be safe enough here until the weather clears."

"What if Red Pete comes back during the night?"

"He won't."

"Are you certain?"

"Aye, Raelynn. Now rest yourself." Jeff lay back upon the bedroll and, taking her into his arms, pulled her head down upon his shoulder.

Whatever protest Raelynn might have made was lost in the overwhelming sense of relief and safety that quickly settled down within her as he covered her with the blanket. It was dry and warm, doing much to chase away her shivers as the two of them nestled closely together. Jeff smoothed the damp hair away from her face and placed a doting kiss upon her brow. It wasn't long before the weariness of the past three terrible days claimed her, and Raelynn knew nothing more.

Nothing except the dream that came to her in the wee hours. In it, she was a child again, no more than three or four, playing in the garden beside her family's London estate. Everything seemed very large in her dream, but then, perhaps that was because she was so very small. The garden was buttressed by a brick wall, through which a tall, wrought-iron gate was the only passage. She could hear voices on the other side of the barrier, and then, suddenly, the gate stood open, revealing a young man who spoke to her with a thread of gentle humor in his tone. He handed her a flower, and she giggled as he swept her a courtly bow. A soft, gentle rain began to fall upon them, and though he strove to keep her dry, it washed away her dream. She tried desperately to hang onto it, but it slipped just like the silver droplets through her fingers.

14

*J*eff lay awake, listening to the low, disconcerted murmurings that now and then escaped his wife's lips. Though he drew her close within his arms and tried to soothe her and gently shush her ravings, he couldn't seem to penetrate the barrier behind which her mind wandered. Every movement she made, every whimper or whispered word she uttered in her sleep, he was aware of it.

Once, in rising fear, she even struggled against him and thrust her hands against his chest. Then, with a muted sob, she collapsed against him. Though she allowed him to draw her back within his encompassing arms, in a few moments he felt her stiffen again. Her head began to thrash against his shoulder, and when he tried to shush and soothe her, she gave a sudden wail and strained away from him as if he had become the devil himself. Jeff let her go immediately and rose up on an elbow to study her in the lingering glow of the fire. She was still asleep, that much was evident, but when she began to mutter again, he realized she was locked in the same nightmarish torment that had sent her fleeing in such a panic from the stables.

"Nell! Oh, noooo! Please, not Jeffrey! Oh, please, don't let it be . . . Please . . . Help me . . . There's so much blood. What am I to do . . . ?"

A feeling of dread swept over Jeff. It truly seemed his young wife had cast him as the villain in this dark, gruesome travesty. Yet, for the life of him, he could think of no way to assuage her fears and convince her of his innocence. Until the murderer was found and convicted, he was virtually helpless.

Must he give her ease of his presence? Jeff mentally groaned. As much as he loathed the idea, perhaps it was the only thing he could do for her sake. Tormented as she was, she'd never return to that place of free abandon within his arms until he had slain the demons that haunted her and proven himself completely blameless in her sight.

THE CONSTANT PATTER OF RAIN FALLING UPON THE roof finally ceased in the wee hours, and at length, the wind eased its vicious lashing of the trees. Somewhere within close vicinity of the cabin, a fox yelped. Raelynn's eyes flew wide, and a faint, indistinct murmur slipped from her lips, but she was still caught up in the throes of some dreadful nightmare. Jeff reached out for her, and she moved closer, instinctively seeking his strength and protection. Grateful that she would allow him to comfort her, he drew her within his sheltering arms. After that, she seemed to sleep more easily, allowing him to doze for a time, at least until he heard the horses whinny.

Jeff shook his wife awake. "Hurry, Raelynn! Get dressed! Someone's outside!"

Startled out of a sound sleep, she struggled to disengage herself from the blanket as Jeff leapt toward the chair where he had left her garments. He tossed them to her and wasted no time snatching on his riding breeches. He was just reaching for his pistols when the front door was kicked open, wrenching a startled gasp from Raelynn. The rough-hewn plank rebounded against the far wall as Olney Hyde limped through the portal with his left arm bound up in a poorly improvised sling, a long ragged rent flapping open in the left legging of his hide breeches, and an ominously large pistol clutched in his right hand.

"Drop yer weapons, dammit, or I'll put a hole through this bitch's head!" the young rogue barked, lowering the sights of his flintlock upon Raelynn, who sat frozen on the bedroll with the blanket clutched beneath her chin. She had barely managed to doff her husband's shirt and don her chemise before the door had been flung wide.

"I'm lowering them," Jeff stated, taking great care as he placed the pair of flintlocks on the table in front of him. "Now turn your pistol away from my wife."

"Not till ye lay yer rifle there, too, like a good lad," Olney replied, his voice taut with pain. He waited until Jeff had complied once again with his directive, and then thrust out his chin, indicating the lantern hanging from a peg. "Now, listen carefully so's I don't have ta repeat meself. I want ye ta light a lamp so's I can sees ye real good like. After ye do that, move yerself away from the table. An' if'n I were ye, I'd be very cautious 'bout what ye do, lest ye riles me temper."

Olney eyed his adversary warily until that one stepped around behind the girl. Then he limped forward to the rough-hewn table, slid the matched pair of pistols into his belt, tucked his own in the crook of his useless arm and then retreated slowly to the hearth where he lifted the rifle and settled it into the vacant hooks jutting outward from the stone. " 'Twill be safe there for the time bein', seein's as how I'll blow both o' ye ta smithereens if'n ye try anythin'."

Olney's yellowed teeth gnashed in a painful grimace as he took his own pistol in hand again and pressed the butt of it against his injured shoulder. Lifting bleary eyes to meet Jeff's, he rasped through his agony, "That damned fool mare o' yers scraped up against a tree whilst we was goin' at a run. Shaved me off'n her back just as clean as a woodcutter. Knocked me senseless, she did. When I come ta, the ornery beast had taken off. Lucky for her she did, 'cause I was in a mood ta cut her up in li'l pieces. She left me wit' me leg skint from knee ta crotch an' me arm hangin' useless, just like Mr. Fridrich's, 'ceptin' ye're gonna set mine back the way it was, *Mistah* Birmin'am."

"Me?" Jeff scoffed. "I'm not skilled at working dislocated joints back into their sockets. You'll have to search out Dr. Clarence to have that properly done."

"Too far an' too painful for me ta let the arm remain as it is 'til I find him. If'n ye don't mend it, I swears I'll part yer wife's hair wit' a lead shot."

The inducement was certainly enough to convince Jeff. "I'll do my best, Olney, but I must warn you that I have little experience or knowledge about such things."

"Then ye'd better do yer *very* best 'cause yer wife's life will depend on yer fixin' it. Do ye understand me?"

"But I told you . . ."

"*Well, I'm tellin' ye, Mistah Birmin'am,*" Olney railed back. "Ye set it right the first time or by heavens, ye'll be buryin' yer wife!"

"All right," Jeff agreed worriedly. "I'll just have to take my time working it back into place."

Olney took a gulp of air, as if relieved that he had crossed that hurdle, but he nearly writhed as a careless movement renewed his agony. Grimacing, he spoke through his pain. "I need somethin' ta deaden the pain. Got anythin' stronger'n water 'round here?"

"I haven't looked."

"Well, look!"

The rogue's bellow wrenched a start from Raelynn, who glanced in burgeoning alarm toward her husband. Nervously she returned her attention to the other man. "I'll see what I can find, Olney, if you'll just let me get my gown on first."

The man smirked through his pain, but gave her a consenting nod and then watched in wry amusement as she drew the blanket up over her head. She formed a protective tent around herself, securing it to the degree that he was forbidden even a brief glimpse of what she was doing. "Ye needn't be so timid 'bout showin' me what ye've got, yer ladyship. Ye can bet I've had me some o' what ye're tryin' ta hide, probably a damn sight more'n ye've had him."

Raelynn ignored his boasting as she yanked on her clothes. When she lowered the enveloping shroud a moment later, she held her gown carefully clasped together behind her back as she rose to her feet. "My husband will have to fasten it for me," she informed their captor. "Will you permit him to do so?"

"Guess I'll have ta, considerin' me arm is useless," Olney jeered, sweeping her with a prurient perusal. There was no real threat behind his inspection; he was in too much pain to think of appeasing himself with *any* wench, much less one Fridrich fancied for himself. It was one thing to satisfy fleshly cravings, but quite another entirely to court certain disaster.

Resenting his rude inspection, Raelynn struggled to subdue a shudder and to keep her expression carefully passive as she sidled toward Jeff. She dared no comment as she felt the lean fingers begin to work their way up the back of the gown. Apparently her husband wasn't shaking nearly as much as she was, for the task was completed without delay.

Once the placket was secure, Raelynn set about searching for a jug of whiskey or something of similar strength to placate the bully. She found such an item in a small, rough-hewn cupboard in the adjoining bedroom and hurried back to the main room where she poured the brew to the brim of an earthen mug. Olney promptly tossed down the contents and passed the cup back for a refill. As Jeff approached him, the scamp brandished his pistol.

"Wait 'til the pain eases," he bade and downed another swallow. "I ain't wantin'ta bellow me head off like Mr. Fridrich did in front o' yer wife. She might be o' a mind ta make one o' her nasty li'l comments again or do somethin' just as foolish. Then I'd likely lose me temper an' ye'd be out a wife. That might leave ye a mite reluctant ta fix me arm."

Jeff grew concerned over the rogue's ability to control his emotions. "I give you my pledge to be as gentle as I can, Olney. You've got to believe that. In return, I'd like your promise that you won't shoot my wife because you might become vexed with me."

"That's right gentlemanly o' ye, Mr. Birmin'ham, but ye've gotta know somethin'. Mr. Fridrich wants the wench real bad like, enough ta pay a weighty purse for her, an' thoughs I ain't in any shape ta take her wit' me now, ye can bet I'll be collectin' her fairly soon."

"Is that why you killed Nell?" Jeff prodded and heard Raelynn gasp in surprise. "You brought her out to my plantation, didn't you, probably hoping that by murdering her you could force a wedge between my wife and me? What I can't understand is why you took the mare and did so in such haste, not even bothering to put a saddle on her."

"Ye bastard! Don't go blamin' Nell's murder on me," Olney snarled savagely. "I brought out the li'l hussy, all right, ta make trouble for ye, so's I could get meself the thousand dollars what Gustav promised Cooper Frye. But I didn't know ye had it in ye ta kill the twit. She left me waitin' in the stables wit' her kid whilst she went ta yer bedroom ta speak wit' ye, mainly ta warn ye that if'n ye didn't own up ta fatherin' her li'l bastard whelp she'd be showin' all yer guests how much the babe looks like ye. That fool mare o' yers almost stomped me ta death when I tried ta slip inta her stall. She startin' kickin' up such a ruckus an' carryin' on, I had ta flee ta the next stall wit' Nell's kid under me arm. It got real quiet in the barn after yer man put her in the paddock outside, though, an' I figgered I'd be safe in her stall whilst I waited for Nell. Then I seen ye haulin' Nell out wit' yer hand clamped o'er her mouth an' yer high almighty self twistin' her arm behind her back nigh ta her shoulder. Good thing I scrambled up the wall an' dropped inta the next stall, 'cause ye took her straight ta the one where I'd left her kid."

"And, of course, you saw me kill her, too," Jeff jeered derisively.

"That's what I did, alright," Olney acknowledged with a sneer. "I was peerin' through the slats, thinkin' ye meant ta rape the li'l bitch, but then, I seen yer knife an' heard Nell's muffled scream when ye thrust it inta her gut." Raelynn gagged and clasped a shaking hand over her mouth, causing Olney to glance around. His lips curved in a taunting jeer before he faced Jeff again. "I don't recall what I did, maybe gasped or somethin', 'cause ye came a tearin' outa the stall after me. Guess yer long legs are good for somethin' 'cause ye were a lot faster'n I'da've e'er imagined. I was sure ye'd be skewerin' me just like ye did poor Nell. That's when I saw yer mare in the paddock. Takin' her seemed like me only chance ta live. I barely pulled meself astride afore ye were upon me, tryin' ta drag me off, but I gave the mare a hard kick, an' she took off. Cleared the fence wit'out so much as a stumble. I thought I'd lucked onto somethin' fine the way she raced off. As fast as we was goin', I had every hope o' reachin' Charleston in good time so's I could tell Mr. Fridrich o' yer murderin' deed. It would've made him real happy. But that fool animal threw me, an' here I be."

Jeff sneered. "Come now, Olney. You planned all this to entrap me in your foul deed so you could collect your filthy lucre, but it won't work. I sent Elijah out to track the murderer down, and he told Red Pete that he was chasing you."

"I knows all that," Olney growled irascibly. "Elijah followed on me heels 'til late last night. As much as I tried, there was no gettin' free o' the man. I got tired o' runnin' wit' me bad leg an' arm, so's I waited in the brush for him. Shot him in the leg, I did, an' sent him limpin' home on that ol' nag o' his."

"You seem very capable of disposing of anyone who gets in your way," Jeff retorted caustically. "Believe me, wounding Elijah will be one more crime for which you'll be held accountable. Once Sheriff Townsend catches you . . ."

"*If* he e'er catches me, I'll have a story ta tell 'bout ye killin' Nell," Olney snarled. "There was no mistakin' ye. Ye were all decked out for yer fancy ball. Can't says I'm overly fond o' black, not the way ye gents are, but then, it 'peared like ye were the only one wearin' it when I peeked inta yer window shortly after Nell an' I got there."

"Wait a minute," Jeff urged, a bit confused. "Let me get this straight. When you saw me in the stables, I was wearing black?"

"Yup."

"When I went out and discovered Nell in Ariadne's stall, it was about one in the morning. At the time, I was wearing a white shirt and tan trousers."

"No, it were more like half past eleven when ye stabbed her."

Jeff scoffed. "That's impossible. As many wounds as Nell had, she would never have lasted more than a few moments, much less an hour and a half."

"What're ye talkin' 'bout? I only saw ye knife her once."

"She was stabbed as many as three times."

"How do I know what ye did? Maybe ye went back later an' finished her off. All I know is what I seen ye do 'bout eleven or so."

"And you saw my face clearly at that time?" At Olney's crisp nod, Jeff squinted at him suspiciously. "Tell me, were there any lanterns burning in the stables? Normally there wouldn't be. There certainly weren't any lit when I went down. I took a lantern from the back porch when I heard Nell's scream."

"I could tell it was ye, alright. I didn't need no light."

Jeff arched a brow, clearly dubious of the man's claims. "So it was dark, and you couldn't really see my face in the shadows. So tell me, how were you able to identify me?"

"Ye're a tall enough bloke. No one could mistake you."

"You remember Sheriff Townsend, don't you? And Farrell Ives? What about my brother? Have you seen any of them?"

"Ye knows well an' good I did, the night all o' ye raided Mr. Fridrich's warehouse. The lot o' 'em were right alongside ye. But it weren't none o' yer cohorts. The one I saw comin' across the yard wit' Nell was tall and on the lean side. Some o' them others must weigh five stone more'n you. Another thing, the murderer had black hair, too. That much I saw in the moonlight."

"You sure it wasn't brown or auburn or something that would look dark or black at night?"

"I'm willin' ta swear it were as black as yers is now."

"I was dancing with my wife at the time you say the murder happened, Olney. I have witnesses to prove it."

Raelynn bit a trembling lip, not wishing to correct her husband in front of the brigand. Around eleven that night, he had gone outside to the privy. She remembered distinctly looking at the clock after he had left, wondering if she'd have time to run upstairs before he returned. If not for Farrell asking her to dance, she might have gone. Perhaps she would have even found Jeff with Nell in their room.

Jeff approached the younger man with measured care. "I'd better get to the business of setting your arm, Olney. By now, the whiskey should have had enough time to work." At the scamp's nod, Jeff gently stretched the injured limb toward him until the other's hand rested upon his shoulder. Olney's face paled at the pain it caused him, but he gritted his teeth against the heightening need to cry out in anguish. Having come this far without incident, Jeff mentally breathed a sigh of relief and began to work the arm around in a small circle. Even so minuscule a movement caused Olney to shudder, but he never once released his grasp on the pistol as he held its bore directed toward Jeff's midsection.

"I'm going to give your arm a slight tug," Jeff warned him. "Hopefully it will pop into place."

"And if'n it don't?" Olney asked thickly, his eyes glazed with pain.

"We'll continue working on it until it does."

Stepping near, Raelynn wiped the dappled sweat off the man's brow and offered him another sip of the strong brew, but he shook his head.

"Let's get it over with," he urged Jeff.

Clasping the other's shoulder in one hand and his wrist in the other, Jeff gave the latter a long, slow tug as he tried to guide the bone back into the socket with the hand that held his shoulder. Olney ground a curse between gnashing teeth at the agony he was being put through, but in the next instant he felt his arm slip into

the hollow. The pain faded almost instantly, allowing him
to breathe a sigh of relief.

"I think we've done it," Jeff announced, his tension
easing considerably.

Olney was panting as if he had just run a hard race.
"Aye, it doesn't hurt anymore."

"Nevertheless, I think I should bandage your arm to
keep it snug against your chest until the socket has a
chance to heal," Jeff advised.

"Do so. I don't want to have to go through that torment again." Olney glanced at Raelynn who hovered
near. "I need somethin' ta eat. I ain't taken any food
since I lit out on the mare."

"There's some venison and corn fritters left from last
night," she informed him.

"Anythin' will do, just as long as I don't have ta
skin it."

"How are you going to eat while you're holding the
pistol on my husband?" she dared to ask.

"I'm gonna send him across the room ta sit in a corner like a good li'l lad whilst I fill me gullet. Any more
idiotic questions, girlie?" he queried sneeringly as he
slanted a smirk toward her. Then he bellowed, *"Now get
me some food!"*

Miffed at his thunderous tones, Raelynn stalked past
him and began slapping corn fritters and venison onto a
tin plate. It would have pleased her immensely to add a
mound of salt or red pepper to cause the brigand some
grief, but she didn't dare, not when he was liable to start
blazing away with the three pistols in his possession.

After Jeff bandaged Olney's arm and tied it securely
against his chest, he was banished to a far corner where
he sat on his haunches while Olney supped. Though the
young rogue seemed ravenously intent upon devouring
the food Raelynn had brought him, the pistol lay within
easy reach of his right hand. Jeff made no effort to rush
his captor for possession of the weapon, for he suffered

no uncertainty that if he tried anything, Olney would dispense with him forthwith, leaving Raelynn at his mercy.

Emitting a loud belch, Olney got to his feet, patted his soft paunch, and settled a pointed stare upon Jeff. "Now, I'm gonna have ta borrow that there stallion o' yers, an' I'll be needin' ye ta saddle him for me. An' ye'd better mind yer manners whilst ye're doin' it, 'cause I'm gonna be keepin' me pistol on yer wife. Ye understand?"

Jeff responded with a singular nod. "Completely."

"Then get ta yer chores, boy. I ain't got all morn'n ta dally." Olney chortled at his own humor and rudely prodded Raelynn with the pistol. "Take yer time followin' yer man, girlie. I don't want ta have ta blow ye ta smithereens 'cause ye got too close ta him. Just remember, I'll be right behind ye, an' as li'l as ye are, a shot from this here pistol would make a bloody mess comin' out yer front side. Do ye kin?"

"I kin," she acknowledged, bestowing a glower upon him.

He chortled in amusement. "Ye're just as ornery now as ye were in Mr. Fridrich's warehouse, but that don't matter ta me, girlie. I ain't gots me heart on the idea o' sportin' wit' ye like the German. I enjoys the lustier ones meself."

"That's understandable," Raelynn quipped loftily.

The rascal's eyes narrowed. "What do ye mean by that?"

"Simply that you have the taste of a boar."

Jeff waved a hand, warning his wife to hold her tongue, but Olney's ire had already been set on end. He let out a horrendous roar as he raised an arm, fully intending to backhand her with the weapon. Jeff bolted forward to halt the blow, but the miscreant whirled upon him with the pistol cocked and threatening.

"Noooo!" Raelynn screamed, grabbing Olney's elbow. "Don't shoot him! Please! I promise, I'll be nice!"

Olney jerked his arm free of her grasp and eyed Jeff warily. His sullen expression made Raelynn tremble in trepidation, for she had no doubt that the brigand was capable of boring a hole through her husband just for the meanness of it. In a brief, sidelong glance, Olney met her pleading gaze and relented enough to lift the sights of the flintlock away from his adversary. "All right, girlie. Ye've saved yer husband's skin this time, but I'm warnin' ye, any more back-sass outa ye, an' ye might as well start diggin' his grave. Understood?"

Raelynn nodded contritely. "Understood."

The ruffian turned a sardonic smirk upon Jeff. "She likes ye a mite more'n Mr. Fridrich, that's for sure, but then, I gots ta admit, Mr. Fridrich ain't the easiest thing on a woman's eyes." He gestured with the pistol. "Now get yerself outside like a nice lad, an' maybe I'll let ye both go on livin'."

Jeff picked up the lantern and led the short procession outside to the lean-to where he had stabled the horses. Totally mindful of the pistol Olney kept leveled on Raelynn, he was on his very best behavior as he saddled Majestic. He even helped the younger man to mount and stood beside his wife as the fellow rode away, but when Jeff dropped a hand upon Raelynn's shoulder in relief, she bolted away from him and ran back into the cabin. He stared after her a long moment, and then cocked a brow at Ariadne.

"I don't know which one of you is more unpredictable," he muttered, causing the mare's ears to prick in alert attention. "Even as flighty as you are, I still think the lady has you beat. But then, you may claim the upper hand when the two of us try to ride you bareback all the way home."

When Jeff finally stepped through the front portal of the cabin, he realized his wife had already set up her defenses. She had placed herself at the far end of the table and was eyeing him warily. He had no need to ask what was bothering her.

"So!" They were right back where they had started before they had settled into his bedroll. "You actually believed Olney when he said he saw me kill Nell."

"I still have questions that need answering," she stated bluntly.

"Such as?"

"Such as where you went after you excused yourself about eleven or so the night of our ball. You said you were going out to the privy. Is that the only place you went? If it is, then it certainly took you long enough."

Jeff blew his breath out in a long, laborious sigh. He had forgotten about that particular trip, but his wife obviously hadn't. "I'm sorry. It slipped my mind."

"Deliberately slipped your mind?" she prodded. "If you're innocent of killing Nell, then why were you gone so long?"

"*Because*, madam, after taking a pee, I stopped to talk with some of my friends who were waiting their turn. Hell and damnation, woman, perhaps I should have gone behind the nearest bush and then scurried back to you. Would that have made you feel more confident of my integrity?" He snorted disagreeably and then snidely queried, "What are you going to do, ask my friends if they actually saw me relieving myself so your qualms can be mollified?"

"Don't be vulgar," she snapped.

"Madam, you just don't know how vulgar I'd like to be right at this very moment. Have you once considered that Olney could be lying to save his own neck or, quite possibly, to set us at odds with one another so he can collect the reward that Gustav promised Cooper Frye? Do you have so little regard for me that you'd willingly lend more credence to that rascal's claims of innocence than to mine?"

"All I know is that I saw you standing over Nell with a . . ."

Jeff flung up a hand to forestall her. "Spare me your repetitive declarations, my dear." His tone was snide. "I know well and good what you saw. I was there, remember? But only because I heard Nell's scream. Would you like to compare Olney's story to the real facts? Nell was stabbed three times, but he said she had only been stabbed once."

Raelynn shrugged. "Perhaps he just couldn't see well enough through the stall slats to really determine how many times she was stabbed."

"Ah, but, madam, if that be true, then how in the hell could Olney have been so unerring when he supposedly identified me? It was dark in the stables, he said. Have you ever been in the barn when there are no lanterns lit?"

Raelynn had no need to search her memory. "No."

"Well, perhaps you should venture out there sometime along about eleven or so at night when there are none burning, then you'd realize that even when there's a bright moon outside, you can only make out vague shapes inside and, with some difficulty, the difference between light and dark colors, but as I remember, there were clouds that night, so 'tis highly unlikely that Olney had the benefit of a moon by which to see."

"Olney said he saw you about eleven," she stated, fighting an onrush of tears, "and that's about the time you left the house."

"Nell couldn't have been stabbed that early," Jeff stated tersely. "If she had been, she'd have bled to death in half an hour or less. I heard her scream about one in the morning, and that's when I went out and discovered her dying in Ariadne's stall. She was barely alive when I reached her, and she begged me to pull out the knife and to hold her as if I really cared for her. I did both, madam, allowing her blood to soak into my shirt and for that, I've been condemned as a villain by the very one who should believe in me."

"We're naught but strangers," Raelynn stated obstinately and wrung her hands.

Jeff sneered. "Perhaps we are in *your* eyes, madam, but not in mine. From the first moment we wed I've considered you as the other half of me, my wife, my soul mate, blood of my blood, heart of my heart, but it's evident you don't feel the same way about me. Even in your dreams I'm considered the guilty one. Therefore, I think it would be best if you *do* go to Charleston . . ."

Raelynn's head snapped up, and she stared at him in slack-jawed astonishment. "Do you intend to seek a permanent separation?"

"Only time will tell, madam, but separation is definitely in order even if it's nothing more than you living in Charleston while I remain at Oakley. 'Twould seem beneficial for your well-being if I take you home first where you can rest for a day or two. During that time, I'll arrange for your stay in the city. I'm sure if you're talented as a couturiere, Farrell Ives will be delighted to have you working in his shop, but if I may be so bold to suggest, I think you should let a room in Elizabeth's house or, if you prefer, in Mrs. Brewster's. Both women could use the extra funds, which I'll naturally supply until that time you choose to distance yourself entirely from me. I must assure you at this time that I have a sincere interest in being a father to our child, but if you find that you're averse to that idea, then I'll relinquish all claims without contest so you needn't be unduly distressed by my presence in our offspring's life."

"You'll . . . let me . . . *go* . . . just like that?" For the life of her, Raelynn just couldn't manage to swallow the thickness that had risen into her throat. She turned aside, blinking against the sudden blurring of her vision, and after a moment, regained some semblance of composure. Perhaps it was just as well she separate herself from him.

Disaster seemed to come upon them whenever they were together.

Jeff released a pensive sigh. "I can't bear being looked upon as a murderer in my own house and by the very one who should trust me. You can be assured that I'll not send you away without some provisions for your comfort. You can take Tizzy with you to see after your needs, and of course, whatever you've been given since we've been married is yours to keep. Once I've arranged for your accommodations and spoken to Farrell about the possibility of hiring you on, Thaddeus can drive you in. Beyond that point, I won't burden you anymore with my presence."

15 ✑

$\mathscr{F}$arrell Ives leaned back in his chair and thoughtfully contemplated the glowing tip of the cheroot he normally allowed himself each morning before plunging into the maelstrom of designing fashions and appeasing ladies in their desire to dress well. Upon lifting his gaze, he squinted through the swirling smoke and fixed his gaze upon his early morning visitor, who perched nearby on an overstuffed arm of a leather settee, one of the many costly pieces furnishing his private apartment. "It's bound to strike folks as damned peculiar, Jeffrey, you staying out at Oakley while your wife lives with Elizabeth here in Charleston and works for me during the day."

Jeff lifted his wide shoulders in a perfunctory shrug. "I can't concern myself about what people may think, Farrell. I'm more interested in what is going on in Raelynn's head. I must give her the freedom and time to make up her own mind about me. Letting her go seems the best way to do that. You know better than anyone that we hardly knew each other before we wed, and though I'm firmly convinced we're well suited for one another, I can't force that premise on my wife. She must come to her own conclusions about me in her own time, at her own pace."

The couturier shook his head in utter bemusement. "Dammit, Jeffrey, what has happened between you two? Every time I've been around the both of you, Raelynn has given every indication that she's totally smitten with you."

Jeff met his gaze squarely. "When Raelynn came into the stables and found me standing over Nell's body with the murder weapon in my hand, the shock proved too much for her. She has yet to get over the trauma. It even haunts her dreams. I can only hope that by releasing her from any marital obligations and allowing her to come to know me as a man and possibly as a friend rather than a husband, she will eventually realize that I'm not capable of such brutality."

"How do you suppose that will happen while you're miles away and Raelynn is living here in Charleston? If you haven't realized it yet, my friend, it's no short jaunt from here to yonder," Farrell pointed out with satiric wit. He wasn't being unkind, just practical. "And what if Fridrich decides to masquerade as Attila the Hun again? Who's going to protect her?"

"I've considered all of that and have taken the initiative to speak with several trustworthy men who're willing to keep watch over her from a distance. Her safety naturally is of paramount importance to me. Though Elijah is presently hampered by his injured leg, he has agreed to keep a vigil from an upstairs window at the boardinghouse across the street from Elizabeth's house. I've spoken to Mrs. Murphy already about the idea of allowing me to rent a front room from which Elijah can watch. If there's any trouble, Elijah will send her chore boy to fetch me." Jeff chuckled briefly before adding, "I believe I saw a vindictive glint in that old woman's eyes when she assured me that it would be her greatest pleasure to be of service in that respect. It seems that she has no love for *Mr.* Fridrich after some of his men wrecked the furniture in one of her guest's rooms. It was their way of convincing her that she should pay the German for providing her protection. She showed me the weapon she fired behind his men when she sent them skedaddling, and I can understand why they've never been back. Believe me, it was closely reminiscent of a blunderbuss."

"That old woman has her fair share of Irish grit, that's for sure," Farrell stated with a deep chortle before growing serious again. "But, Jeffrey, have you considered the length of time it would take for someone to ride all the way out to Oakley to fetch you? Why, your wife could be taken, stripped and mounted before one of your men could reach you, and you know you'd never forgive yourself if Raelynn is ravished because you couldn't get to her in time."

"Actually, I won't be that far away. Unless I'm needed at Oakley, I'll be staying at a townhouse I'll be letting near my warehouse. I will endeavor, however, to keep that knowledge a secret from Raelynn lest she arrive at the conclusion that I'm spying on her."

Leaning forward in his chair, Farrell knocked the cigar ash into a glass receptacle residing on the table between them. "You're certainly going out of your way to protect her after giving her leave to enjoy her freedom, Jeffrey. You know, she could decide to dismiss you from her life entirely."

"I'm giving her every opportunity to do just that," Jeff admitted dismally. "She's the one who'll have to decide what she really wants, her independence or marriage with me. It wouldn't surprise me if she decides to sail back to England, but then, that's not a conjecture I enjoy pondering."

The occasion called for stark frankness, and Farrell had never been a man to withhold a decisive punch. "People will conclude the worst, Jeffrey. You know that."

"Aye, they'll think my wife left me because she believes I stabbed Nell to death."

Such bluntness made even the world-hardened ex-boxer flinch, but he made no effort to deny such speculation. On the contrary, he matched his friend's candor with more of his. "Jeffrey me dearie, have you given due heed to what that would mean if you're brought to trial for Nell's murder? The men who will sit on your jury may well have their judgment swayed by the knowledge that your own wife believes you're guilty."

"I guess I haven't reached that far in my thinking yet," Jeff conceded, his mouth twisting grimly awry. He didn't dispute Ives's supposition, but he couldn't allow himself to be influenced by it either. "Olney Hyde claimed that he was innocent of the deed and that he saw me stab Nell, yet he can't come forward into the open and accuse me, because Rhys would then be able to arrest him for making an attempt on my life. We both know Olney is capable of such a crime. He definitely meant to kill me before Raelynn was kidnapped, but it remains to be proven that he murdered Nell. The fact that he stole Ariadne clearly puts him at the scene of the crime when she was killed, but Elijah pointed out the fact to both Rhys and me that other footprints had scuffed up those that Olney had made. His footprints disappeared after he mounted the mare. The second set were obviously made by a pair of my own boots, which Cora found in my bathing chamber the morning after Nell was killed. Since I hadn't worn them for about a week, the fact that they bore fresh mud from the rain we had that night leaves me no other option but to conclude that Nell's killer wore them while murdering her. He might have even been one of our guests."

Farrell tamped the cheroot out in the dish. "Do you suppose Cooper Frye could have ventured out your way that night?"

"It's certainly possible," Jeff acknowledged. "He has as much to gain as Olney if he's the one to bring about Raelynn's final capitulation to Fridrich. From what Olney said, Fridrich offered Frye a thousand dollars to bring about our permanent disunion. What better way to perform that deed than arranging for me to be hanged for a murder I didn't commit? But if my memory serves me well enough, I'd say Frye wouldn't be able to wear my boots for the same reason Olney couldn't. I believe both men have fairly large feet."

Leaning back in his chair, Farrell made a steeple of his forefingers and pressed them to his lips as he eyed his friend's custom-made boots. "I seem to recall that none of us could wear your shoes, Jeffrey, which might not sit well for you if the culprit isn't caught. Your feet were always too narrow for any of us to wedge our toes in much less our feet."

"Well, that fact could certainly pin the blame on the murderer if we ever found him," Jeff countered.

Farrell came out of his chair with a frustrated sigh and began to pace about his parlor. He paused to look at his guest as he considered an alternative to the plan Jeff had come up with. "Have you asked Brandon if Raelynn can stay at Harthaven until you've proven your innocence? She'd be a lot safer out there with them than living here in Charleston, even with you residing several blocks away."

"Raelynn doesn't want to involve him or Heather in this matter."

Farrell couldn't subdue a flicker of surprise. "Given the gravity of the situation, Jeffrey, should your wife's preferences dictate the course of action you should take?"

"Not necessarily, but I consider myself a practical man. If I'm to win Raelynn's trust and regard, I must court her as a suitor. Having her ensconced in the midst of my family would seriously hinder her liberty to reject or to invite my attentions. In short, she'd find it difficult to dismiss me from my brother's house. As for Fridrich, if he really believes she has broken with me, he may be content to bide his time until I'm dispensed with in one fashion or another. Once the path is clear, he may think he can claim her without opposition." He jeered in rampant sarcasm. "As magnanimous as the man is, he'll probably suppose she has learned her lesson and will be grateful enough to accept his attentions. If she goes to Harthaven, he may well make another attempt to take her by force. My brother isn't going to stand for that without a fight, and considering the number of men Fridrich brought with him to Oakley, Brandon could be killed trying to protect her."

"Fridrich just may attempt that kind of force here if she's working on the premises," Farrell pointed out, not unreasonably. The possibility didn't concern him overmuch; he just thought his friend needed to be apprised of the hazards his wife could be facing outside his husbandly protection.

"If you're not averse to the idea, I could draw a couple of men from the lumber mill or one of my other businesses to watch over Raelynn here. She wouldn't be able to recognize them. Neither would Fridrich. Both would think you just acquired a few extra helpers."

"Business is certainly good enough to warrant some help," Farrell remarked drolly before casting a glance toward his guest. "I don't suppose you intend to send me someone who can actually thread a needle."

Jeff chuckled. "Well, if you're that much in need, I could send you experienced sailors who can stitch canvas with the best of them."

"Marvelous," Ives muttered, making much of his lack

of enthusiasm. "If Charleston's gentry suddenly takes to wearing sailcloth, my future will be secure."

&"I WILL BE HAPPY TO PROVIDE YOU WITH EMPLOY-ment, Mrs. Birmingham," Farrell Ives assured the young beauty a pair of days later after admitting her into his shop before opening time. Her maid was sitting quietly in the parlor, where she had a clear view of the area where Raelynn and he sat facing each other across the surface of his desk. Tizzy was there for the specific pur-pose of providing reasonable chaperone service to allay any rumors. Considering his bachelor's status and the fact that gossips were wont to enlarge upon his reputation with the most outrageous stories, the presence of the maid was most needful. If anyone had taken such tales seriously, then Farrell supposed that in the last few years they had credited him with siring half the city's infants, but to perform such a feat, he'd have been far too busy making babies to even think of carrying on his high fash-ion business.

Farrell swept his hand toward the tooled leather desk-top where he had spread Raelynn's drawings to better peruse them after Jeff had delivered them. It was a plain fact that the more he had studied them, the more he had become intrigued. "These fashion sketches of yours are marvelously animated, Mrs. Birmingham. They certainly leave no doubt as to your skill as a couturiere." Formality had come into play now that he could foresee them work-ing together. First names would no longer be used, but more than that, the lengthy appellation would serve to remind him that this very fetching lady was the wife of his best friend. As much as he might have enjoyed court-ing her had she been free, he was not about to endanger a close camaraderie that had been firmly established in his earlier youth. "Would it be possible for you to start immediately?"

"Immediately?" Raelynn was aghast. "You mean today?"

"Yes, of course. As I understand it, you'll be letting a room from Elizabeth from now on, and unless you have other things planned, I thought we could get you settled in here as well. Is that at all acceptable to you?"

Raelynn leaned back in her chair, totally taken aback. When Jeff had asked for the fashion plates, he had made it known that he would be leaving them with the couturier to allow him to consider her merits as a fashion designer, but Jeff had also warned her that if Farrell didn't think her contributions would come up to his standards, the man would likely find her other work to do in his shop. Relieving Elizabeth of some of the paperwork involved in keeping the accounts and records up to date for Ives's Couture had been an option, although one that Raelynn hadn't particularly relished, but having prepared herself for the worst, she had hardly expected the clothier to leap at a chance to hire her.

"Why, yes, I suppose it is, Mr. Ives. I mean, I can't see any harm in getting started this morning. In fact, it really doesn't matter when I begin. I have nothing else to do." Her voice caught, and she hurriedly turned her face aside lest she break down in front of the man. The fact that Jeff had handed her into the landau earlier that morning and, with a stoic frown, had watched them depart had left her feeling much the way she had after each of her parents had died, as if her heart had been suddenly laden with heavy, iron chains.

"Is anything the matter?" Farrell queried. He had thought that she'd be overjoyed with how well he liked her drawings. Yet, he was now inclined to think the lady was on the verge of tears. "You seem distressed about something. Does the idea of working for me disturb you?"

"No, of course not, Mr. Ives. I'm delighted that you like my sketches." Raelynn wrung her hands, wondering if she should be completely honest in her reasons for being in his shop. "You may think this strange, Mr. Ives, in view of the fact that I've made inquiries into the matter of my employment, but I wasn't at all averse to being Jeffrey's wife or, for that matter, Oakley's mistress. If I seem at all disturbed, then be assured that it has nothing to do with a reluctance to be working here. It's just that I realize that in the days and weeks to come, I will be disassociating myself from what I've come to hold dear. I really had no wish to alienate myself from my husband, but when I'm repeatedly haunted by grizzly impressions of him standing over Nell's body with a bloody knife in his hand, I have trouble sorting things out in my mind. I don't want to believe that Jeff is guilty of murder, yet I keep wondering, What if . . . What if . . .''

Farrell was relieved to hear her speak with such open concern about her relationship with her husband. It gave him some hope that in due time the difficulty between the couple would be resolved in a satisfactory manner. "You needn't fret yourself unduly about the matter, Mrs. Birmingham. Your husband has the greatest concern for your well-being and is allowing you this opportunity to come to terms with your fears. I've known Jeff for many years, and more than any of us, whether it's myself, Brandon, or Rhys Townsend, Jeff has a sincere fondness for most people. He's that way about animals, too, ofttimes to the sheriff's chagrin, but that's another story. I know what you saw in the stables shattered your trust in your husband, but if you'd give your mind leave to rest over the matter, I'm sure the true culprit will come to light in time, and you will be reassured that Jeff couldn't possibly have done such a deed. I should also like to add that if you think either Rhys or I are prejudiced in our friendship with your husband, then may I enlighten you by telling you that I once threatened Emory Dalton with serious mayhem if I ever saw him mistreating Elizabeth again. Though I didn't kill him myself, I actually felt a great measure of relief as well as a deep sadness when I buried him several nights later. Jeff's friendship means a great deal to me, but if I really thought he had killed that little girl, I'd be the first one to accuse him though it might well mean his hanging."

"Am I being a disloyal wife because I can't settle the matter of his innocence in my mind?" Raelynn asked in a tiny voice. Because she feared his answer, she turned her face aside and pressed a knuckle to her quivering lips, not wishing to glimpse any hint of his condemnation.

"Do you love Jeffrey?"

Her head snapped around, and for a moment she stared at her new employer as if he had taken leave of his senses. Then she lowered her gaze to the sketches on the desk and tried to swallow, only then realizing just how dry her mouth had become. Finally she bent her head forward in a disconcerted, jerky movement and uttered words that seemed distant even in her own ears. "Yes, I love him." Though she tried to blink away the moisture that rapidly filled her eyes, the tears began spilling freely down her cheeks. "I think I've loved him ever since he rescued me from that passing livery. He was so gallant, so noble . . . so incredibly wonderful. . . ." As she spoke, her head came up, and a surging joy began to well up within her and to overflow in a suddenly radiant countenance. Though it was an emotion she had begun to suspect mere moments before she had gone out to the stables, her present acknowledgment was as much to herself as to the couturier. Her whisper was barely audible, yet full of feeling. "Aye, I love him very, very much."

Amazed to find himself affected by her declaration, Farrell cleared his throat in sudden discomfiture and, feeling a need to move on to a less emotional subject, got down to the business at hand as he rose to his feet. "If you don't mind, Mrs. Birmingham, we'll find a place for you to work on your sketches and designs in the main hall. In there you'll be readily accessible whenever Elizabeth or any of the seamstresses have a need to speak with you about your designs or when our customers may wish to take a look at your drawings. I've settled on a few designs of my own for the spring season but not anywhere near the amount I'll be needing to appease everyone who'll be looking for something original. I'm hoping with your assistance that I'll be able to placate all our clients."

"I'll gladly give as much help as I'm capable of, sir."

"And I will likely be demanding a lot from you," Farrell warned with a grin. "Many of my customers expect no less than my personal attention, and the more customers there are, the less time I have to spend designing new gowns. Hopefully you'll fill in the gap."

Thoughtfully Farrell led her to the adjoining hall and scanned several possible areas where her desk could be placed. He went to stand in each location and, from there, considered the lighting, convenience, and the overall setting before finally selecting a place near the back of the corridor that permitted a view of a carefully tended garden, which, for his own relaxation, he took care of himself. Canting his head to peer at his newest employee over his shoulder, he gave her a grin. "Are you loath to being put on full display, Mrs. Birmingham?"

Raelynn smiled hesitantly, not knowing what mischief he was about. "I suppose I wouldn't mind as long as I don't have to answer impertinent questions about why I'm here, if I'm *truly* estranged from my husband and if he's *really* the father of Nell's babe."

A soft chuckle prefaced his remedy for that kind of situation. "I'll do my best to shush those nosy women with gushing compliments. You'd be amazed at how quickly some women will preen in pleasure when they're given a little manly attention."

Raelynn had no difficulty imagining the transformation that could occur in a lady's disposition when the one doing the complimenting was Farrell Ives. If not for Jef-

frey Birmingham, she might have been just as susceptible. "I suspect you've been blessed with the gift of blarney,
Mr. Ives."

His lips stretched into a wide grin beneath the neatly
clipped brush adorning his upper lip. "Aye, my dear
mother was as Irish as Dublin itself. I learned it well
from her, God rest her soul."

"You did at that, Mr. Ives," Raelynn readily agreed
with a chuckle.

Farrell stroked his beard musefully as he lent his attention this time to determining the best angle for situat-
ing her desk in the spot he had selected. He considered
the closest brass chandelier of a pair that hung from the
high ceiling and decided that if her desk was placed
slightly behind it, the fixture would cast more light on
her work. She would also be framed by the expanse of
windows overlooking the garden. "This is where I shall
put you, Mrs. Birmingham," he announced, stepping into
the spot to better mark it for her benefit. "A beautiful,
well-garbed woman will gain the attention she rightly de-
serves here in this charming setting. You'll have the windows overlooking the garden to your back, which will
offer natural light, while, in front of the desk, the chandelier will illumine your comely presence. None of our customers will be able to miss seeing you, and, of course, to
get to you, they'll have to pass the tables where all of
our most costly fabrics are displayed."

"You have quite a devious mind, Mr. Ives," Raelynn
averred in a voice imbued with amusement. "I'll have to
take care to guard my purse strings lest I fall in the same
enticing trap you lay for your customers."

Farrell gave her a devious grin as he whisked a finger
slyly beneath his mustache and waggled his eyebrows.
"My dear Mrs. Birmingham, you just don't know the half
of it." He leaned toward her as if to share a tantalizing
secret. "You see, you'll be the bait that lures the ladies

into my trap, for you'll soon be wearing some of my most stunning creations, as Mrs. Dalton does now."

Raelynn hated to dash the man's expectations, but she couldn't allow him to go to such expense and bother when in a month's time she'd likely be showing her pregnancy. A mischievous glow sparkled in her aqua eyes as she queried, "How are you at designing garments for expectant mothers, sir?"

Farrell's bearded chin dropped significantly to convey his astonishment. Briefly his eyes flicked downward to what seemed to him a perfectly flat stomach before he remembered himself and, in some chagrin, cleared his throat. "I'm sorry, Mrs. Birmingham, I didn't realize. Jeffrey didn't inform me of your delicate condition." He cocked a curious brow as he eyed her closely. "I assume you've told him."

"He's aware of my childbearing state," Raelynn stated carefully and thought it only fair to give Farrell a chance to retract his offer. "Under the circumstances, do you still wish to hire me on? I'll understand completely if you think your customers will be unduly shocked to find a woman in my condition working in your shop."

Farrell grinned devilishly. "Women in *your* condition, Mrs. Birmingham, will need beautiful clothes to mask some of their bulk. It's about time they had a source from which to procure such stylish garb, and I'm quite willing to supply them with gowns that will bring them out of hiding. If I can supply clothes for old spinsters and stout matrons, then I can only imagine how much more delightful it shall be to adorn a woman who has been truly appreciated by her husband."

Raelynn blushed significantly even as her effervescent laughter spilled outward in amusement. "Mr. Ives, you're positively perverse."

Grinning knavishly, Farrell flicked his eyebrows once again. "To be sure, Mrs. Birmingham, to be sure."

16

*W*ell before any of the other employees arrived, Elizabeth Dalton entered and approached Raelynn with a dazzling smile, readily conveying her eagerness to have the younger woman as a boarder in her home. "Your room is all ready for you, Mrs. Birmingham. Your coachman insisted upon taking your baggage upstairs, so if you'd like to send your maid over now, my Flora can show her to your bedrooms. Tizzy can start unpacking for you, and by the time we leave here this afternoon, everything should be done, and all we'll have to do is relax and enjoy supper. Flora normally has a meal ready and the table set by the time I get home, but I'm afraid for breakfast and weekends, you'll have to struggle through my cooking. I do what shopping needs to be done on Saturdays. Although I know there'll be things you'll be wanting to do on your own, Jake and I would love to have you accompany us whenever you'd feel up to it, Mrs. Birmingham. What I'd really enjoy is making you better acquainted with the city. I'm sure you'll come to love it as much as I do."

"Please, Elizabeth," Raelynn begged, bestowing a gracious smile upon the woman, "I'd be ever so much more comfortable if you wouldn't be so formal. Besides, if you continue calling me Mrs. Birmingham, it will arouse the customers' curiosity. They'll soon be gawking at me as if I'm an oddity in the shop."

Elizabeth laughed as she reached out and clasped the other's hand. "All right, Raelynn, you win. Of course, I should warn you that our casual address will likely cause Mr. Ives's brows to quirk at a higher level, but then, that's rather nice to see. Our employer looks diabolically handsome whenever he's crossed."

Both women broke into sudden giggles, drawing the couturier's curious attention even from where he was standing down the length of the hall. As the pair eyed him, his eyebrow shot up to a lofty height, evoking more laughter. Growing increasingly suspicious, he paced forward almost warily, sending the pair fleeing in opposite directions, Raelynn to her desk and Elizabeth to the first cubicle where she promptly began checking the prior days' progress of the seamstress who worked there. Farrell followed his winsome assistant as far as the open door and, tilting his head at a curious angle, peered intently at her ignoring back until Elizabeth finally deigned to glance back at him.

"Did you want something, Mr. Ives?"

Farrell was most appreciative of the enchanting vision she presented wearing one of his own creations, a fetching pink gown with a pleated collar that flared outward charmingly from beneath her finely boned jaw. The delicate hue favored her fair skin and rosy cheeks and, in like degrees, set off her lustrous dark hair, which today had been intricately woven into a heavy chignon at her nape. Confronted by the sudden realization of how her beauty affected him, Farrell had to jar his memory to even recall what had caused him to follow her. "Yes, well . . . ah . . . I was just wondering what you and Mrs. Birmingham found so amusing."

"Oh, nothing really." She wagged her head whimsically. "At least nothing you'd likely find entertaining. Just private observations, the sort women are wont to share in secret."

"Secret?"

When his eyebrow jutted sharply upward again, Elizabeth found her composure seriously threatened. Little spurts of laughter seemed destined to escape, finally driving her to mumble a hurried excuse and brush past him in her haste to flee the room. As she disappeared through the back door leading out to the garden and the outdoor convenience concealed from view by a collection of topiary, Farrell gave up his quest to have his probing inquiries assuaged, at least by that winsome lady.

Turning about on polished black heels, he fixed his cerulean blue gaze purposefully upon his newest employee and raised a querying brow when she suddenly busied herself shuffling through her drawings. One glance in his direction sent her giggling toward the same door through which Elizabeth had recently escaped.

Farrell set his jaw thoughtfully askew. Something was definitely going on between those two. He could feature a pair of virgins dissolving into instant sniggers at sight of a man, but these ladies were hardly that. So what in the devil had set off their twittering?

Inquisitively Farrell went to scan his long frame in the nearest floor-length silvered glass. He couldn't see that his cravat was askew or, more disastrously, that his trousers were too snug. In spite of the present fashion rage of slender trousers and closely fitting breeches, he had always been averse to defining his private parts by overly tight garb. Indeed, advertising one's manly possessions had always seemed the depth of crassness to him. He had always considered subtlety in good taste.

Cocking an eyebrow, he searched for some other flaw as he gave his image another critical inspection, but he could draw no firm conclusion from his appearance. Perhaps their amusement had nothing to do with him at all. Mayhap they had just been exchanging humorous comments about men in general, and without cause he had let their amusement unsettle him. What male wouldn't feel pecked apart when two hens started clucking together?

Musefully he lifted his bearded chin, wondering how best to cope with two ladies who seemed in complete accord about *heaven only knew what!* Ignoring them might be the answer, but then, he could hardly do that when he fully expected to garner valuable assistance from each. He might try chiding them for their undignified conduct, but that could backfire in his face. With their fine, beautiful noses lifted haughtily in the air, they'd resort to snubbing him, and then he'd be in more of a stew than he was now. Should he praise them as he did all those addlepated young fillies who thought they were the most fetching little things that this century had ever seen? He didn't know about Raelynn, but Elizabeth would definitely think he had taken leave of his senses, when, in her case, it would probably be the blooming truth. Best to go on as if nothing had happened, he decided. At least, then, he'd be able to keep his skin intact.

"HAS MR. IVES EXPLAINED WHY I'M HERE?" RAElynn asked Elizabeth hesitantly after they had returned from outdoors.

"He has informed me of your situation, but he hasn't seen fit to talk to the other women about it. If that contents you, then I see no reason why they should know.

You can be assured of Mr. Ives's discretion and, of course, my own."

"You're very kind, Elizabeth."

Gently smiling, the woman shook her head. "No, I'm merely a woman who has experienced some adversities of her own. Some night perhaps I'll tell you about them, but for the time being, let's have some tea. Then I'll introduce you to the other employees. I know they'll be curious, having seen you in here with Mr. Birmingham."

The five remaining seamstresses were well versed in discretion, having worked for Farrell Ives for a couple of years or more. Outwardly they betrayed only the slightest evidence of surprise at finding Jeffrey Birmingham's wife among the employees. In explaining the reasons for Raelynn's presence, Elizabeth chose to lighten the mood by relating an amusing exchange which had actually taken place.

"Once Mr. Ives learned of Mrs. Birmingham's enormous talent at designing lady's fashions, he asked her husband if he could steal her away from him." She laughed with the other women at the absurdity of such a notion and went on with her explanations. "In actuality, our business is flourishing, and Mr. Ives is hard-pressed to appease all of our clients. As you're well aware, some of them expect his personal attention, which leaves him less time to create. Therefore, as the wife of his best friend, Mrs. Birmingham has been gracious enough to consent to help him, at least for a time. We're fortunate to have such a talented employee with us for a time, do you not think?"

A combination of laughter and applause assured Raelynn that at least outwardly most of the seamstresses accepted the reasons that had supposedly brought her to the shop. Only one spoke obliquely of the real issue, a tall, older woman, with kindly gray eyes, who hesitated to speak, but finally seemed driven. "Such a terrible shame what happened ta poor Nell. I knew her widowed mother when Nell weren't no bigger than a wee mite. After her ma died, Nell went ta live with an aunt, but the woman was so busy raising her own eight, she didn't have much time ta spare for poor Nell. Whatever Nell's failings, no one can say she weren't a good mother ta her babe. He's such a winning li'l soul, he is, an' handsome as can be. I hope it won't be long afore a nice family takes him in. 'Twould be a bloomin' shame for the li'l tadpole ta grow up without lovin' parents."

Scarcely had the woman spoken than she looked horrified at her own temerity and clasped a trembling hand over her gaping mouth. Having overheard her comments, the other seamstresses, aware of the gossip that had claimed Jeffrey Birmingham as the sire, seemed clearly anxious.

Raelynn managed a smile and was further motivated to set them at ease by conveying a willingness to discuss the matter of the boy's welfare. "Presently Daniel is being tended by Mrs. Fergus, the wife of my husband's overseer. She seems to have a great fondness for babies, and it's obvious that he's thriving from her attention. Until his father can be located or a good family decides to take him in, the babe will remain with her." Raelynn's gaze never wavered from her audience of seamstresses as she deliberately added, "She'll give him the best of care which any orphan, who is found at Oakley and is thrust into similar circumstances, will receive. My husband has been very sympathetic to the child's needs in spite of the talk we both have heard, but he refuses to cast an orphan out because of such malicious rumors. He's too much of a gentleman for that."

Feeling relieved that she had gotten through such declarations with some measure of dignity, Raelynn found her tensions easing. Though the five women seemed to accept her claims, one could only guess what they were really thinking. In spite of her own qualms she had managed to voice her confidence in her husband's integrity, calmly refuting as merely rubbish such claims that he had impregnated Nell and had left the girl to whelp his bastard child in shame. She could only hope and pray that that was the truth.

Discretion notwithstanding, Raelynn had no doubt that her statement would be spread abroad throughout the whole of Charleston ere the sun lowered its face behind the horizon and that other conjectures would likely rise up just as quickly and be hopelessly mired in muddled confusion as the city's populace tried to determine why (if indeed she believed her husband innocent of siring Nell's babe and of other things which they dared not openly speak) she had left Oakley to work at an establishment belonging to a bachelor who was only one of a handful who rivaled the striking good looks of her husband.

᠍THE FIRST CUSTOMERS ARRIVED, AND THAT HERalded the beginning of a steady stream of ladies which did not ease throughout the remainder of the morning. During this heavy deluge of customers, Farrell hired a new seamstress, a janitor and a doorman. The latter two were burly, young fellows who seemed eager for the work. The more handsome of the two, who spoke with an Irish brogue and a twinkle in his eye, also seemed gifted with words and ever ready with a charming greeting. Farrell chose him to fill the doorman's position, for he had no doubt the ladies would come to adore the man. A nice cloth of a deep green hue to match the distinctive green door of Ives's Couture was found, and immediately a seamstress was given the task of making the fabric into a dapper uniform for him. The new doorman was then sent to Farrell's barber and favorite hatter, the latter place to be fitted for a top hat.

Much plainer apparel in matching green was bestowed upon the janitor, the more reticent of the two, but it soon became evident that this one enjoyed cleaning and working and that he was a perfectionist in his own right. He was promptly given several tasks, which included washing the square-paned windows stretching across the front and back of the building, polishing the large brass lanterns hanging on each side of the front door, and renewing the golden luster on all the brass fixtures adorning the front and interior of the shop, including the sign firmly affixed to the brick structure beside the main portal, which identified the shop and owner as *IVES'S COUTURE, Proprietor, Farrell Ives*. Farrell was no less than impressed by the man's capabilities and decided forthwith that if both fellows proved equally adept at their chosen tasks that it would behoove him to keep them on as permanent employees.

Into the midst of all this chaos of satisfying customers and engaging new employees came Mrs. Brewster, who bustled in virtually unnoticed until she confronted the couturier. Farrell had just finished showing a small collection of new designs to Isabeau Wesley, a recently widowed, comely young woman who had given every indication that she'd be dismissing her mourning weeds for more fashionable attire as soon as Ives's Couture could outfit her with a new winter wardrobe.

"Why, Mr. Ives," the plump, rosy-cheeked milliner coyly exclaimed in a sweetly chiding tone, "I didn't expect to find you outfitting Mrs. Wesley with new garments so soon after her husband's demise, but then, considering the advancing age of her dearly departed and the fortune she has recently inherited, I guess you and your designs have proven too much of a temptation for the young widow."

Farrell's smile was frail, at best. Barely had the comely widow left than he had found himself encountering another, but this one was neither youthful nor

handsome. In fact, she was a definite pain in the derriere.
"Good morning, Mrs. Brewster . . ."

"Thelma, please!" she interrupted, twittering with in-
gratiating laughter. Her eyelashes fluttered flirtatiously as
she swept her gaze away. As many times as she had insisted upon a less formal address, she had heard no similar request from him, but, of course, the man was ever-
so-busy he probably hadn't yet realized his oversight, and
she dared not hint that he should lest he think her forward.

Thelma Brewster was in the process of returning her
gushing attention to the handsome man when her gaze
swept past a familiar figure sitting at a desk at the far
end of the hall. Immediately her eyes returned, prompting her jaw to drop precipitously as she gaped in shock.
News of Nell's untimely death had reached the city and,
hard upon it, had flown rumors of Jeffrey Birmingham's
possible involvement in siring the girl's son and stilling
her tongue by taking her life. Since then, the city had
been hanging on tenterhooks awaiting further word.
Speculations ranging all the way from tales of Jeffrey's
arrest and subsequent confession to morbid stories of
Raelynn's own fate at Oakley had careened haphazardly
throughout the city streets. To see the lady sitting calmly
absorbed at some task did much to relieve Mrs. Brewster's
anxiety, but such a sight gave birth to a whole host of
new questions.

Mrs. Brewster's generous bosom expanded as she
marched in a straight line toward the end of the hall,
taking upon herself the task of assuring the young beauty
that all would be well, that the world she had entered
wasn't really as crazy as it truly seemed at times, and
that the true culprits (she dared not lay any names to
them) would be brought swiftly to their due reckoning.
Mrs. Brewster was ever-ready to help *anyone* in need, and
this *poor, poor* child was obviously in desperate want.

"Merciful heavens, child, what are you doing here so
early in the morning?" the milliner blurted and, when

Raelynn looked up from her work, hastened on with a volley of conjectures, giving no pause for the girl to reply. "My dear, are you well? Do you think you should be here? If you don't mind my saying so, you *do* look a touch pale. Of course, I can certainly understand that you have your reasons, what with all the recent goings-on at Oakley and everyone around these parts thinking that Mr. Jeffrey is as guil . . ."

Perceiving what the blunt woman's conjectures would be, Farrell leapt forward as if jolted by a bolt of lightning. "Tsk, tsk, Mrs. Brewster. You shouldn't believe all the rubbish you hear. Mrs. Birmingham has graciously consented to fashion some new gowns for me and, at this very moment, is hard at work at the task. If she looks a bit pale, perhaps it's because she's . . ." he glanced aside at Raelynn, who seemed both distressed and astounded by what had been on the tip of the milliner's tongue. He truly hoped she'd forgive him for revealing her secrets, but the milliner's thoughts had to be diverted from an outright accusation and censure of his best friend, "not feeling entirely herself these days, in view of her condition and all. . . ."

Thelma Brewster clasped a hand to her stout bosom and stared up at him with mouth agape. "You don't mean to say . . ."

In the face of her awestruck amazement, Farrell was immensely glad he could nod and answer in the affirmative. Yet when he thought of how fast word of Raelynn's pregnancy would spread from this one source, he almost cringed. "I mean, Mrs. Brewster, that Mr. and Mrs. Birmingham are going to be parents."

Now suddenly aflutter, the milliner lifted a plump hand and fanned her face as if she were about to swoon. "Oh, my, this is all too much for me. Mr. Jeffrey's wife working here at your shop while she's . . . Oh, this is highly irregular. What will people say?" The woman looked at him pleadingly. "Dear Mr. Ives, do tell me I'm dreaming. Why, I can't believe Mr. Jeffrey would actually allow this . . ."

"Oh, but he has, most graciously, in fact. Mrs. Birmingham is a very talented couturiere in her own right, and being a devoted friend of mine, her husband has allowed her to help me for a time."

The woman placed a hand to her brow as if faint from the wonder of it. "Did I say that it was early? Perhaps I'm still asleep and this whole affair is merely the peculiar workings of my imagination. You did say that Mrs. Birmingham would be working for you, didn't you, and that she's expecting a baby? And that Mr. Jeffrey knows and is permitting all this?"

"You're not dreaming, Mrs. Brewster," Ives assured her dryly.

"Not dreaming." The milliner slowly repeated the words as if in a daze. "Perhaps I should go lie down and consider this situation until I'm able to sort it out in my mind."

Farrell didn't want to seem overly eager for her departure lest he appear callous, but in good manner he lent as much assistance as he possibly could toward that end. Upon ushering her to the front door, he nodded, dutifully listening to her disjointed verbiage and entreaties not to work an expectant mother overmuch. When the portal was finally closed behind her, he turned to find a cup of coffee being offered him by his long-established assistant.

"You look as if you need this," Elizabeth observed with a sympathetic smile.

"Lord, save me from that woman!" Farrell muttered before draining the cup. Leaning near, he lowered his voice to an incredulous whisper. "Did you hear what that ghastly woman almost said to the wife of my best friend? Why, if left to her unruly tongue, Jeffrey shall soon find himself being strung up on the nearest tree."

His assistant smiled up at him. "You handled the matter amazingly well in spite of your annoyance, Mr. Ives."

Her softly spoken encouragement took the edge off his temper, and Farrell met her gaze with eyes glowing with something more than appreciation. "Thank you, Elizabeth. You've made me feel better already." He took her elbow. "Come, let us go do the same for Raelynn."

"Raelynn?" Elizabeth queried in surprise, looking up at him wonderingly. "Not Mrs. Birmingham?"

His large hand moved across her shoulders in a caress so light that it caused Elizabeth to wonder if she had imagined it. "Between the three of us, my dear, it will merely be Raelynn, Elizabeth, and Farrell. Our friendship allows us that privilege, don't you agree?"

Her soft lips curved upward approvingly. "Yes indeed, Mr. Ives."

"Farrell," he corrected warmly. "We've been through too much to bother with formalities, Elizabeth. Remember, I was there pacing your front porch like any anxious father when Jake was born."

"I've never forgotten that, Farrell," she confessed, looking at him with something akin to adoration. "In the years that have followed, I've realized that I never thanked you properly for what you did that night, and I'd just like you to know now just how grateful I was at the time to have you there. Emory wouldn't have been had he still been alive."

"Emory was a fool, my dear. I hated the way he abused you," Farrell replied and then instantly chided himself for being so frank. "I'm sorry, Elizabeth. I shouldn't have said that."

"No need to apologize, Farrell," she assured him mutedly, unable to meet his gaze. "You were always far kinder to me than Emory ever was. He tried so desperately to be wealthy and polished, mainly I think to prove that he was every bit the man you were. In his failure he made himself miserable."

The couturier carefully let his breath out in a pensive sigh and decided it was time to reveal a secret he had carefully hidden throughout the years he had known her. "If he was jealous of me, Elizabeth, then the converse was equally true."

For a moment, she gaped up at him, thoroughly confused. "But why? Emory couldn't even make a go of our farm, but you had everything. Why in the world would you have been envious of him?"

"He had something I desperately coveted."

Her darkly winged brows gathered in deepening bemusement. "What was that?"

"You."

Elizabeth searched his face with something closely akin to amazement. "Me?"

"I've been in love with you almost from the first." He now scoffed at his many attempts to dismiss her from his mind. "I sought desperately to be a gallant friend to Emory, so I said nothing to you before you married him. Afterwards, it was just too late to speak of it. I've often wondered if it wouldn't have been better for us all if I had just told you right off. Emory wasn't satisfied just to have you. He wanted the world besides. I'm not sure when he came to the realization, but he knew in the end how much I wanted you."

"You never said anything . . . even after he was killed."

"I couldn't bring myself to tell you because I thought you hated me."

"I've never hated you, Farrell. I was merely afraid of myself and what I might do if I relaxed my vigil." Elizabeth swallowed, trying to gather nerve to make an admission of her own. "You see, I've been in love with you since well before I married Emory."

Now it was the couturier's turn to be surprised. "You certainly kept it to yourself well enough."

"As did you."

His hand squeezed her shoulder fondly. "Don't you think it's about time Jake had a father? I've never stopped loving you, you know."

Elizabeth tilted her head aslant as she gazed up at him with a gentle smile. "Are you asking me to marry you, Mr. Ives."

"Aye, Mrs. Dalton. As soon as you're of a mind, whether it be this hour, this week, or this month, but I pray that I may not have to wait until next year."

"Are you sure?"

Farrell faced her squarely and, pressing her palms together, covered them with his own larger hands. "I would have asked you long ago if I would have had some inkling that you'd consider my proposal, but I was thoroughly convinced you'd turn me down."

Elizabeth's eyes caressed his handsome face. Had they been alone, she might have reached up and lovingly stroked his cheek. "Foolish, foolish man."

WHEN THE LAST OF THE SEAMSTRESSES, THE NEW EMployees, and the errand boy had made their departure for the day, Farrell Ives hung the *Closed* sign on the front door of his establishment and, with a sigh of relief, turned the key in the lock. It had been an unusually busy day, and Farrell had definitely had enough of mollycoddling spoiled, insipid little misses and haughty dowagers who thought they could control him by merely jangling their weighty purses in front of his nose. After a day such as this, he was wont to reminisce upon his good fortune during his boxing days, but of course, that pastime was better suited for younger men, not one who had passed a score, ten and three years of age and who, merely for pleasure now, only sparred with his friends.

Throughout most of the day, Raelynn had worked at her desk, out of the way of the normal flow of customers.

Though she hadn't actually conversed with any of the clientele, she had nevertheless recognized several who had attended the ball at Oakley and several other social events to which Jeff had escorted her in recent months, but the women seemed too embarrassed to make their way to her desk. From the brief snatches of whispered conversation that drifted to her ears, she had become mindful that word of her presence in the shop was already making its way about town. More than a fair sampling of ladies had apparently come to the shop for no other purpose than to settle in their own minds the question of whether such outrageous claims were actually true, for after espying her, they had left the shop in an excited dither, no doubt anxious to pass on the news. In view of the fact that she was married to the most handsome and exceedingly wealthy Jeffrey Birmingham, Raelynn could imagine that, for them, her presence might have been tantamount to the heroine of that quaint children's tale, Little Cinder, deciding she preferred the hearth near the ashes rather than a life of ease in the palace of Prince Charming. As for herself, nothing could have been further from the truth.

Grateful though she was that Farrell had allowed her to remain detached from the busy bustle of the place throughout the day, Raelynn knew her isolation couldn't continue. She was also of a mind to wonder how her presence might affect the couturier's business, especially once her figure began rounding out. When, at the end of the workday, her employer escorted Elizabeth to her desk and began leafing through her sketches again, Raelynn broached her concerns, yet the man put her at ease immediately.

"Don't worry about the clientele, Raelynn," Farrell replied. "We'll deal with them as the opportunity presents itself. As for these . . ." he indicated the drawings with a broad sweep of his hand, "I've never seen any quite like them. Your lines are exceptional." He held up one that he especially favored. "For instance, this gown would easily complement a woman of excellent figure, yet I believe it would also be kind to one less favored by nature."

"I hadn't really considered that aspect of it," Raelynn admitted, pleased by the man's enthusiasm. "I just thought the gown would flow better that way."

"Your illustrations come vividly alive, even on parchment." Farrell indicated another sketch wherein the figure, garbed in a ball gown, was caught as if in the midst of a waltz with the skirt swirling around the slender form and a meager glimpse of an ankle showing above an undulating hem. "This one doesn't just look like it's being worn; it gives one the feeling that it's actually being enjoyed."

Raelynn was aware that her drawings were different than other fashion sketches. Indeed, she had made a point of making them unique. Other artistic designers simply presented the front and back views of the garments they created without bothering to draw a figure of a woman, but she hadn't really cared for that bland way of drafting fashions and had sought instead to illustrate beautiful ladies in partial scenes and to incorporate a feeling of life within those sketches. "I simply thought it would be more interesting to illustrate gowns the way they might look actually being worn."

Farrell laid down the parchment and met Raelynn's gaze directly. "I like your idea of figures in various settings rather than the usual nondescript views. The drawings seem to bestir a wealth of stories right along with their great designs, as if the subjects have been caught in a particular situation, such as at a ball with a suitor nigh at hand. Kindly do more of the same. In fact, I may adopt this technique for use with all our designs."

He turned a smile upon Elizabeth who was peering past his arm to peruse the sketches. "Does that meet with your approval, my dear?"

His casual endearment brought a flush of color to

Elizabeth's cheeks even as her lips bowed upward at the corners. For too long she had envied other young ladies who had become the recipient of his attention, and she couldn't help but luxuriate now in a moment of secret pleasure beneath the warmth of his gaze. "I'm willing to predict that in the months or years to come such fashion plates will become the standard. They do seem to stimulate one's imagination about what wonderful things might be happening to the ladies in the sketches."

"You have an incredibly keen insight into such things, Elizabeth, which is only one of the many reasons I've come to admire you over the years."

The dark eyes searched his in smiling amazement. "I think you've been very secretive about a lot of things, Mr. Ives."

"Aye," Farrell acknowledged with a slanted grin, "but then, until recently you kept me virtually in a fog as to where I stood with you."

Raelynn's gaze flicked between the two. The magnetism between the couturier and his assistant was so strong she couldn't help but be inundated with memories of the breathless excitement that Jeff had always stirred within her. Just as quickly, a poignant regret over her loss pierced her heart, infusing within it a sadness so intense it seemed to constrict her chest. It was all she could do to stand there with a faint smile pasted on her lips and think of her drawings. It was as if the glow that had once lit her whole being with joy had darkened to a morose awareness of what she had previously possessed, but now had lost.

⮞ELIZABETH'S RESIDENCE WAS A MODEST, TWO-STORY, pale yellow house that sat off the street behind a white, wrought-iron fence and a well-maintained flower garden partially shaded by a huge live oak. All the trim, shutters and spindled railing adorning the front porch had been painted white, lending the place a fresh appearance. The interior was just as charming.

"It's absolutely enchanting, Elizabeth," Raelynn declared enthusiastically. What she saw was enough to convince her that the woman's talents were indeed vast and varied.

The brunette glanced around as if trying to see her home through another's eyes. "It wasn't much when I bought it, but I've been working for almost four years now, doing this and that in an attempt to improve it. Now I think it's pretty much the way I had first envisioned it."

"You did all the work yourself?" Raelynn asked in amazement.

Elizabeth laughed at such a notion. "I'm afraid if I had tried, I wouldn't have gotten very far. Farrell did the heavier refurbishing in exchange for some home-cooked meals, a routine cleaning of his apartment, and an ongoing agreement that I would make his shirts, all of which he now pays me for above my regular salary. As for papering the walls and the easier repairs, I did those myself."

A young boy about four years old ran through the kitchen on his way toward the back door, but with a laugh, Elizabeth caught his arm and brought him near for a hug, which she playfully administered with an exaggerated grunt.

"This is my son, Jake," she announced, settling her hands upon his shoulders as he turned about to face their guest. "He's four years old and can already count to twenty."

"Ya wanna hear me?" he asked, peering up at Raelynn with a sheepish smile.

"I do indeed," Raelynn replied, kneeling down to his level.

Proudly Jake recited the numbers and, at her praise, grinned with the same bashful timidity. He lifted large blue eyes to his mother to see her reaction and was rewarded by an affectionate smile.

"You're saying your numbers so well now, Jake, I think it's about time I started teaching you some more," Elizabeth stated, with gentle affection running her slender fingers through his sandy hair. "In fact, the way you're progressing, it won't take you any time at all before you're counting to a hundred."

The boy beamed with delight and hugged his mother's leg through her skirts before he scurried off to play. As Raelynn watched the youngster race toward the back fence, which at the moment another young boy was climbing over, she found herself thinking how nice it would be to have a son as fine as Jake and for that son to also have a father.

"Have you found it difficult being Jake's only parent?" she queried, struggling against the depression that never failed to sweep over her whenever she recalled her recent estrangement from her husband.

"At times, yes," Elizabeth admitted. "But I've also been fortunate having Farrell living so near. I can't account for all the times he has shared his time with the boy. He has truly been a good friend to us. On weekends, when I've been busy cooking or doing other things, he has taken Jake out fishing, riding or on some other kind of adventure men and boys seem to enjoy. Without him, Jake would have no fatherly influence at all in his life. In that respect, it hasn't been easy for the boy. Jake really wants a father and has often wondered why he doesn't have one when all his friends do. Once he even asked me if Farrell was really his father."

Raelynn looked at Elizabeth in surprise, realizing the boy had the same coloring as her employer. She dared not say as much, for she had no desire to pry into such matters.

Elizabeth lifted her shoulders in a casual shrug. "The idea was initially presented by an older couple during one of Jake's outings with Farrell. The people had paused to ask for directions, and before they went on their way, they told Farrell he had a nice-looking son. I'm not sure what Farrell's reasons were, but he didn't bother correcting the people. Perhaps it was nothing more than a brief exchange, but it had a lasting effect on Jake. He was terribly elated over the incident when he came home. Later that night he asked me if what the people had said was really true. As much as he wanted Farrell to be his father, I had to tell him that it just wasn't so."

Elizabeth sighed. "Jake is quite properly the offspring of my late husband. The boy takes after his late grandmother, Margaret Dalton, a dear sweet woman whose death left me grieving. She was someone I dearly loved and, even at her death, was still a handsome woman, although by that time her sandy hair had paled to white and her blue eyes had dulled, but they were just as kindly as always." Elizabeth cast her gaze downward in chagrin. "As for her son, I'm afraid I don't have many fond memories of him. Emory used to gamble quite a bit, and when he'd lose, which was quite often, he'd get mad and take his frustration out on me.

"Once, after witnessing such an event, Farrell threatened to kill Emory if he ever hit me again. Emory ignored his warnings, but I didn't dare let Farrell know for fear of what he'd do. He was so angry with Emory after witnessing his heavy-handed ways, he just might have carried through with his threat or, at the very least, given Emory a severe thrashing. Not many men can best Farrell in a sparring match even now." She laughed softly. "I've heard his friends complain about that often enough to be aware of that fact. Although that's all done pretty much in fun nowadays, Farrell was once a very proficient boxer." Elizabeth turned aside to hide a blush as she confessed, "The same night that Farrell issued his threat, I caught myself wishing Emory *would* die. There were moments when I actually thought I hated my husband for the pain he caused me. My wish came true a few nights later. I was so filled with remorse I couldn't bring myself to accept Farrell's assistance even when my labor started and my water broke. I fully expected to die in childbirth for daring to hope for Emory's death." Facing Raelynn again, Elizabeth forced a smile, but it was weak and tremulous as she met the other's sympathetic gaze. "As you can probably guess, I'm not very proud of that part of my life."

"I shan't tell anyone," Raelynn murmured reassuringly, dropping a hand upon the woman's arm.

"Thank you." Elizabeth patted the comforting hand and then heaved a sigh. "So now you know my dark, ugly secret, the *only* one who knows, I might add, but you seemed so distressed by your own circumstances, Raelynn, I thought it would help if you knew what I've been trying to hide these past few years."

"You're not the only woman who has wished for a man's death," Raelynn informed her. "When I thought Olney had killed Jeff, I wasn't in a very forgiving mood. I found myself wishing the same end for both Gustav and Olney. So you see, Elizabeth, I'm capable of having revengeful thoughts, too."

"It's not very heartening for a woman to realize she can feel so much hatred for a man that she can actually wish his death." Elizabeth managed a wavering smile. "At least you don't hate your husband."

Raelynn tried to laugh, but it came out sounding strained. "No, on the contrary, if Jeffrey were to banish me out of his life forever, I think my heart would probably shrivel up and die."

"Jeffrey seems immensely taken with you, Raelynn," Elizabeth ventured. "I can't believe he'd ever distance himself from you."

Raelynn could not bring herself to explain that he had done that very thing but in a smaller measure during the first two weeks of their marriage. "Only time will tell," she murmured dejectedly, "but if there's one thing I've learned in the short time I've been married to Jeffrey, then it's his utter lack of hesitancy to do the unexpected if the situation calls for drastic measures. He *will* set me aside in a divorce if we can't reconcile our problems."

Mentally casting off her gloom for her own sake as well as for her boarder's, Elizabeth assumed a brighter countenance. "Let's go upstairs, shall we? I'd like to show you the bedroom you'll be using while you're here."

~IN THE DEAD OF NIGHT, AFTER MUCH TOSSING AND turning in a pitch-black room, Raelynn finally gave up the battle she had been waging in her lonely bed and allowed her mind to drift back through her memories of Jeffrey. In whatever circumstance or mood, whether serious, sensual, angry or playful, he had never failed to demonstrate a gentle, chivalrous regard for her. He had likely saved her life in the swamp, and even in Red Pete's cabin, when he had known of her suspicions and, for a time, been angry with her, he had nevertheless nurtured her as a husband deeply concerned for her welfare.

One afternoon about a week after they had wed came to mind. They had been at a wedding reception for an old acquaintance of Jeff's. Male friends had drawn him away from her side to teasingly harass him for marrying without obtaining their permission. His ready quips had elicited boisterous laughter, prompting the wives of his companions to follow in growing curiosity, but by then, Raelynn had begun to sense that Jeffrey was keeping his distance, at least as much as circumstances allowed, and she hadn't felt the freedom to join the ever-expanding group, but had stood alone, self-consciously sipping her punch. Almost without pause, the vultures had descended upon her in the form of several former hopefuls who had crowded around her to ask snide questions, the most pointed being, "How in the world did you *ever* manage to entrap Jeffrey Birmingham in marriage?"

Perhaps her face had registered her deepening dismay, for it wasn't long before Jeff had left his friends to come to her rescue. With a debonair grin that had vividly defined the taut depressions in his cheeks, he had made a show of claiming her for the benefit of her antagonists, settling a hand possessively upon her waist as he bent near her ear and whispered much too softly for the other women to hear, "Would you like me to save you from these malevolent witches, my dear?" to which she had eagerly nodded and smiled.

His gallantry had extended itself in the form of kissing her hand before he had tucked it safely within the crook of his arm and turned to the other women to make their excuses. Had he been a knight in shining armor, he could not have looked more wonderful to her at that moment. Barely an hour later, when they had been about to climb into the landau, she had found herself once again the recipient of the inquisitive stares of the spiteful three. After handing her in, Jeff had taken a place beside her on the seat and had dropped the leather panels over the windows, ignoring the liberally accommodating gap that had been left between the frame and the shade. While the women had craned their necks to peer inside, Jeff had pulled her close and, to her utter amazement, kissed her in an overtly sensual fashion. In one way Raelynn had been entirely grateful for his favor and yet, in another, regretful, for the fires he had lit had been difficult to quench even after she had retired to her virginal bed later that night. But that task had hardly been as arduous as calming the tumultuous cravings now tormenting her. After tasting passion's appeasement to the fullest extent, she was now fully conscious of what she was yearning for, no less than her husband's amorous attentions.

Could a man who had been so caring and tender with her during that difficult period of abstinence turn so completely about face and callously murder a young mother with a baby at her side? The question flared without warning in her mind, as if to accuse her for her irrational condemnation of her husband. If indeed Jeff was capable of such a monstrous crime and some dark demon truly lurked behind that gallant facade, then wouldn't he be a man tormented by the wickedness lurking deep within him? Wouldn't she have glimpsed some evidence of those malevolent characteristics in him in some brief, carelessly unguarded moment? Was he such an accomplished actor that he could hide a vile nature so adeptly beneath a façade of gentlemanly refinement? Although he had ranted at Nell and expressed his desire to throttle the girl, was he more evil than other men who might have done the same thing in a moment of irritation without meaning a word of it?

Raelynn realized of a sudden that she had great difficulty rationalizing a man of Jeff's integrity being capable of such a despicable murder. That dark side just didn't seem to exist in the man. And she was an utter fool for ever doubting him!

17 ⬿

In the ensuing days Raelynn became more and more involved in discussions initiated by Farrell and Elizabeth as to what fabrics, trimmings, cordings, and other embellishments would go well with her designs. To some degree, the loneliness that assailed her throughout the long hours of night was assuaged during the day by her work. No one knew, of course, how desperately she yearned to see Jeff, yet she was beginning to think he didn't care to see her. If he had, then surely by now he would have done so. Indeed, the way things were beginning to look, it wouldn't be long before their marriage was over.

It was on a Friday afternoon when Raelynn glanced up from her work and espied Gustav Fridrich entering the shop with his usual disdaining arrogance. This he liberally bestowed upon the doorman who had stepped in behind him in an effort to question him. After all,

Fridrich was well known and unattached, which seemed primarily the cause for the cordial inquiry as to whether he had come to the right establishment. It was too late for Raelynn to hide, and with seemingly steadfast dedication, she bent her attention to her sketches.

Elizabeth drew Farrell's notice to the German's entrance, motivating the couturier to excuse himself forthwith from his customer, Isabeau Wesley. As he approached the doorway, he waved a hand to dismiss the doorman, but by that time, Fridrich had espied Raelynn in the adjoining hall and was already sweeping off his hat as he moved in her direction.

"Your pardon, Mr. Fridrich." Farrell's icy tone could have frozen both the Ashley and Cooper Rivers in the middle of summer. "Since this is a shop catering entirely to the fair ladies of our city, I must ask why you've come. I certainly hope it isn't to make trouble for Mrs. Birmingham again. I'd hate to upset my customers by a show of violence." He smiled stiffly before he added, "But if I must, I must."

Offended by the man's intimidation, Gustav peered up at the taller man, a feat that required a definite tilting of his bald head. His eyes were icy hard, his lips tightly compressed, and his nose pinched as if he smelled something putrid. "I do not zee vhy my visit should concern yu, but I vish to speak vith *Frau* Birmingham. Zhat is vhy I haf come. Now, please step out of my vay."

The German's haughtiness sorely nettled Farrell. He had definite limits as to the people he would indulge, and Gustav Fridrich was not one of them. "I'm afraid Mrs. Birmingham is presently working on some designs for a special customer of mine, and I'm reluctant to see her interrupted until they're finished."

"Vhat I haf to say to *Frau* Birmingham vill only take a moment if yu vill permit me to pass," Gustav stated crisply. Then, because he was himself well-versed in coercion, he warned the couturier, "I haf not come to of-

fend either *Frau* Birmingham or yu, sir, but I vill make
a scene if yu do not let me talk vith her."

Farrell's hackles rose. Quite willing to make a commotion himself, he almost caught the stout fellow up by
the scruff of the neck and the seat of his pants, but he
was brought up short by the realization that aggression
of that sort would likely drive the man to seek Raelynn
out after the shop was closed, and although Jeff had men
watching Elizabeth's house, Farrell still worried about the
time it would take for help to reach the women.

Thoughtfully he glanced down toward the area in
which he had ensconced his newest assistant. The burly
janitor had moved within close proximity to Raelynn, and
though the man had dusted the bookshelves and furnish-
ings in the area earlier that morning, he was presently
doing so again. In view of the fact that she had such a
capable protector near at hand, Farrell could hardly see
her coming to any harm by a one-armed man.

"I'll give you a moment to speak your piece with Mrs.
Birmingham," he informed the man brusquely. "And
then, Mr. Fridrich, I must insist that you make your departure as swiftly as possible." Inclining his head in a
curt nod, Farrell stepped out of the man's path.

Raelynn had decided that if she had to face Gustav,
she would feel much safer doing so behind her desk.
When the man halted before the massive piece, she lifted
her eyes with deliberate slowness to meet his gaze. Then,
without a flicker of an eye or a twitch of a lip, she returned her attention to the sketch she had been working
on. "Did you come here with some specific purpose in
mind, Mr. Fridrich?"

"Merely to see how yu are faring, *Frau* Birmingham."

"Why?"

The blunt question seemed to perplex the German,
and he struggled to find an appropriate reply. "I only
vished to express my zympathy for vhat happened to zhat
young girl on yur husband's plantation. It iz a terrible

tragedy zhat one so young vas killed zhere in such a merciless vay. I vorried zhat yu might come to zome harm, too, until I heard zhat yu had moved into Charleston. I can only commend yur decision to leave yur husband."

"My husband believes you had something to do with Nell's death." Raelynn peered up at the man to view his reaction as she asked outrightly, "Were you somehow responsible for her murder, Mr. Fridrich?"

The blue eyes flared, and for a moment Gustav blustered in hot indignation, "Yur husband iz only trying to cover his own foul deeds by casting zhe blame on me, but I am innocent."

Leaning back in her chair, Raelynn met his gaze directly. "Frankly, Mr. Fridrich, I believe you're far more capable of murdering a young girl than my husband is. You see, I haven't forgotten that you gave Olney tacit consent to shoot me after Dr. Clarence became incensed by the news that my husband was dead and refused to tend your shoulder."

"Oh, but zhat vas merely a ploy to force zhe good *dokter* to reconsider. I vould not haf actually let Olney kill yu, *mein Liebchen.*"

Tossing her head up with a derisive scoff, Raelynn derided, "If you really think you can make me believe that rubbish, Mr. Fridrich, then you're fooling no one but yourself. I have no doubt that you meant it."

Gustav clasped his hat to his breast in plaintive appeal. "I say to yu truly, *Frau* Birmingham, it vas merely a ploy to bring about zhe dokter's change of heart. How can I prove to yu zhat such vas zhe case?"

Laying down her quill, Raelynn lifted her slender shoulders in a casual shrug. "You could start by forgetting that I exist."

"Ho-ho-ho," Gustav tried his best to make light of her answer. "Yu are not so easily forgotzen, *mein Liebchen.* It vould be impossible for me to do so."

"Then there's no real reason to continue this discussion. I must get back to work," she stated bluntly, taking up her quill again. She leaned forward over her work and tried desperately to concentrate on the drawing she had been in the process of completing. "Mr. Ives is paying me to work, not to chat with people."

"Zhen may I haf yur permission to visit yu at yur new residence, *Frau* Birmingham?"

She never looked up. "I don't think that would be very wise, Mr. Fridrich."

"But vhy not?" He chortled and sought to convince her of the rightness of his request. "Yu are lonely, *Frau* Birmingham, and so am I. Iz it not right zhat zhe two of us should console each other in our solitary plight?"

Raelynn condescended once more to look up at the man. Bracing her elbows on the desk, she rested her chin on the slender fingers she had entwined to form a bridge. "Mr. Fridrich, may I remind you that I am a married woman. It would be highly inappropriate for me to accept a visit from *any* man as long as I'm wearing this ring." She fluttered the thin digits of her left hand, drawing his notice to the massive diamond that glittered there. Until Jeffrey asked for its return, she would continue wearing it in the hope that in the not too distant future all would be well between them. "Now, Mr. Fridrich, if you'll excuse me, I must get back to my work, so I'll bid you adieu."

Thus dismissed, Gustav marched irately away from her desk and was just approaching the entrance when the doorman swept open the door again, this time to admit Jeff. That worthy strode briskly into the shop without interruption.

It was a rare occasion for Jeffrey to be out and about in less than natty attire, especially when he came to Charleston, but at the moment he had all the appearances of having been interrupted from work, for he wore no coat or hat, his waistcoat hung open, and the sleeves of his shirt had been rolled up midway his forearms. What was more, ink splotched the second finger of his right hand. Nevertheless, Raelynn was struck by his sun-burnished good looks, much as she had been at their first meeting. She didn't quite understand the almost imperceptible nod he gave the doorman, but that broad-shouldered fellow reciprocated in kind and gently pulled the door closed behind the newest visitor.

Raelynn realized her heart was gathering speed with a rushing excitement and her cheeks were growing warmer by the moment. She fully expected Jeff to come to her desk, but he seemed much more intent upon claiming Gustav's attention. Settling his arms akimbo before the man, he lifted a dark brow in an unspoken question.

The German sneered in rampant distaste. "It vas a pleasure seeing yur wife again, *Herr* Birmingham, but I cannot say zhe zame for yu."

"The feeling is mutual, *Herr* Fridrich," Jeff managed to assure the man through a marked rigidity of his lips. It was the best substitute for a smile he could offer the man.

"Haf yu also come to visit yur vife?"

Jeff swept the man with a derisive perusal, and when his reply came, it was permeated with sarcasm. "If you were about to leave, *Herr* Fridrich, I wouldn't want to delay you *even* if I were to see a reason for explaining my business to you . . . . Now good day to you."

Jeff turned his back crisply upon Gustav and, in so doing, deliberately ignored the presence of his wife in the adjoining hallway. Jeff couldn't remember ever performing a more difficult task. The urge to go to her was so strong, and it was only by dint of will that he faced Farrell as that one came forward to greet him.

Raelynn's hopeful smile faded rapidly as her husband shook hands with the clothier. Bowing her head in a blend of embarrassment and shame, she stared at her sketch through blurring tears. In an effort to screen her face from the other occupants of the shop, she lifted a trembling hand to her brow, but that hardly helped to halt the flow of droplets that began to pelt her drawing.

Hurriedly rising from her chair, she turned aside and, with bowed head, brushed past the janitor as she hastened toward the back door. Never looking back, she remained incognizant of the green-eyed gaze that turned in her direction and followed steadfastly through the back window until she had gained the privacy of the tall garden hedge behind which the privy was located.

Only in the privacy of that cubicle did Raelynn dare release the flood of grief that nearly choked her. She sobbed harshly in overwhelming misery, feeling as if her life had plummeted into a dark crevice near the pit of hell. She had no idea what had brought her husband to the shop, but it was all too obvious that his business had nothing to do with her. He hadn't even felt inclined to offer a civil greeting.

Farrell had also witnessed Raelynn's departure, and he faced Jeff in deepening concern. "Don't you think you were a bit hard on her, Jeffrey? I may be wrong, but I think Raelynn was crying when she left."

Jeff released a troubled sigh. Though Raelynn's tears had caught at his heart and nearly driven him in the garden after her, it had only been by a firm resolve to remember his primary goal that he had managed to steel his emotions against any outward display. Still, watching her scurrying away in absolute misery had been much like having his vitals drawn out. The pain had wrenched him to the very marrow of his being.

"I must allow Raelynn to understand full measure what it will be like if we go our separate ways," Jeff replied with stoic control. "Quite simply, I have to let that become a reality for her, as painful as it may be for both of us. I'm afraid that a few days of my absence or reticence won't be as effectual in bringing that realization into fruition as a good fortnight or two would be. If not for Fridrich's visit, I would never have come here today."

"You certainly got here much sooner than I expected," Farrell admitted, having felt immeasurable relief when he had espied his friend. "How in the devil did you find out about that toad's visit so soon?"

Jeff allowed the couturier a spartan smile. "I have a whole league of men working for me, all the way from your shop to my shipping company. When the doorman signaled the vendor, the vendor whistled to the carpenter working several doors down, and so on and so forth until the livery that I've hired for the month came to fetch me."

"You sure are going out of your way to make Raelynn think you're taking this whole damned business rather casually, Jeffrey, when nothing could be further from the truth. You may cause her to think there's no hope for the two of you. Without some assurance, she may decide to sail back to England."

"Though as fearful as I am of that possibility, it's a chance I'll have to take."

"I swear you're the orneriest man I've ever come across, Jeffrey," Farrell retorted, and then stretched his own eyebrows upward briefly as he reconsidered. "Besides myself, of course."

"You can tell Raelynn I missed seeing her."

"You're going to leave, just like that, without talking to her?" Farrell asked incredulously.

"Yep."

Barely had Jeff issued that concise answer and made his departure than the doorman swept open the portal for another male, this one an English lord. Farrell immediately recognized his lordship as the one who had attended the ball at Oakley with Mrs. Brewster, but he had cause to mentally sigh, for he was beginning to wonder if he would *ever* get back to his customer.

"Good afternoon, my lord," he greeted graciously in

spite of his growing vexation. "May I be of some assistance?"

Lord Marsden inclined his head in a succinct nod. "As a matter of fact, I was hoping you'd consent to offering me some help."

Farrell was somewhat bemused. "If I'm able, my lord. How may I be of service to you?"

"If you'd be so kind as to share with me the name of your tailor, I'd be most appreciative, sir. I was no less than impressed by the fine clothing you wore at the Birminghams' ball." His lordship bounced on his toes as he stretched his chin upward in a museful vane. "Made me realize just how desperately in want my own clothes are. Indeed, sir, I wouldn't be at all reluctant to the idea of looking like a changed man once I return to England . . . in regards to my clothes, that is. Would you be of such a mind to help me, sir?"

"Certainly," Farrell replied and chuckled softly. Clothes might make a world of difference for the inner man, but they'd fall well short of enlivening the fellow's bland face.

Half turning, Farrell lifted a hand to claim Elizabeth's attention and made his request. "Could you please write out the name and address of my tailor for his lordship, my dear?"

The nobleman smiled in appreciation. "This is most gracious of you, sir. I shall never forget it."

"My pleasure to be of service, my lord."

Lord Marsden glanced inquisitively about the shop. "You seem to have a thriving business here, Mr. Ives. "The ladies certainly seem eager to see your latest creations. I overheard several talking at another table while I was having my lunch today. They were quite profuse with their compliments."

Farrell was having difficulty hiding his growing impatience. Helping his lordship was not as important to him as assuring a customer that he had not forgotten her. He could only wonder how long it would be before Isabeau Wesley would stalk out in an angry huff, never to be seen again.

Lord Marsden cleared his throat as he begged for another favor. "May I also ask, sir, if the same tailor makes your shirts? I noticed how well-made they are when you shed your coat and waistcoat before entering into an arm-wrestling match with the sheriff at the Birminghams' ball. Of course, your prowess at such a game impressed me as well."

"Thank you, my lord. You're very kind, but I must disappoint you in that respect. You see, Mrs. Dalton makes my shirts, and I'm afraid I keep her far too busy here in the shop to allow her time to make them for other men."

"Mrs. Dalton, you say," Lord Marsden's brows gathered thoughtfully. "Did I hear it rumored about town that Mrs. Birmingham was letting a room from a Mrs. Dalton?"

"Mrs. Dalton is my assistant here," Farrell replied without appeasing the man's curiosity and laid an arm about Elizabeth's shoulders as she came with the tailor's address. "She is also my fiancée."

Since no further explanation seemed to be forthcoming, Lord Marsden took the note from the brunette. "I shan't keep you any longer, Mr. Ives. I know you're busy."

"I do have a customer waiting," Farrell acknowledged, casting a worried glance over his shoulder at Mrs. Wesley. Elizabeth had been keeping the young widow's interest piqued by showing her the newest collection of sketches. Even so, he felt a pressing need to get back to her.

Lord Marsden lifted his head again to a lofty level and, as seemed his habit, bounced on his toes as he glanced around. "I say, I heard from several sources who know such things that Mrs. Birmingham is working for you in some endeavor. Under the circumstances, she might think me rude if I didn't pay my respects."

"I'm afraid Mrs. Birmingham is presently indisposed and won't be able to talk with anyone at this time. In fact, at this very moment she's not even in the shop."

"Then please give her my regards," Lord Marsden bade courteously and took his leave with, "Good day to you, sir."

Once the door had been closed behind his lordship, Farrell released a sigh of relief and returned to his earlier discussion with Isabeau Wesley. To his delight, he was informed that the widow had taken advantage of his absence and selected several more gowns from Raelynn's drawings.

Entirely engrossed in showing off the fabrics that would complement not only the fashions but the widow's beauty, Farrell remained oblivious to Raelynn's return. Only later did he notice that her eyes and nose still bore evidence of her weeping. He yearned to assure her of Jeff's deep concern for her, but in keeping with his friend's purposes, he could not bring himself to break such a trust. Instead, he strove to keep Raelynn busy and her mind well-occupied throughout the course of the day by urging her to finish several more sketches.

▬A FORTNIGHT PASSED QUICKLY FOR RAELYNN, MAINLY because Farrell was forever urging her to create more and more gowns, giving her hardly enough time to think about her depressing situation even when she climbed to her small bedroom at night. She had already completed a number of sketches that had elicited his praise and evoked the interest of his customers. This particular morning, after discussing a variety of fabrics that could be used for her newest designs, she had returned to her desk and had become absorbed in finishing another fashion plate when she heard a familiar feminine voice imbued with lighthearted mirth drifting from the front of the shop. Her heart rallied with sudden joy as well as an overwhelming sense of relief that she hadn't actually been ostracized by Jeffrey's family, a possibility that she had begun to suspect. Eagerly lifting her gaze, Raelynn found her diminutive sister-in-law almost hidden beyond the couturier's tall, broad-shouldered form. Despite her limited view, Raelynn could see that Heather's condition had been modestly masked by a light cape and that the winsome beauty was wearing a fashionable bonnet, the ribbons of which had been tied charmingly beneath her lovely chin. At the moment, its feathers were moving in a negative direction as Heather declined the man's hopeful inquiries.

"Absolutely nothing in my present condition, Mr. Ives," she replied, using the formality of proper names in spite of the fact that he was a close companion of both her husband and brother-in-law. While out and about where ears were wont to listen to every little tidbit and tongues were wont to wag and enlarge upon actual happenings, she had always maintained that it was far better to be discreet. "Thank you just the same."

"Then should I assume that you haven't come to engage my talents," he queried in a tone laced with fond amusement, "but to seek the company of your winsome sister-in-law?" Farrell felt a small surge of regret that lately far too much of his time had been spent dealing with petulant, avaricious women instead of enjoying the company of close acquaintances, at the foremost of which he counted the Birminghams. It wasn't to say that he didn't enjoy being around a goodly number of his customers. Had he not been fast friends with both Brandon and Jeff ere they wed, he knew he would've still been inclined to enjoy a casual association with their wives. In spite of the gossips who had branded Mrs. Wesley as brazen, he would have accepted her presence any day over Mrs. Brewster's. At least, Mrs. Wesley didn't let silly convention stand in her way when she wanted something badly enough. Still, it was a rare pleasure to encounter two utterly beautiful women who cared far more for their families than for the luxuries of life. In light of that, he wasn't at all surprised to find Heather Birmingham in his shop.

The petite woman dipped her bonneted head in a pert nod. "You assume correctly, sir, and if I may be so bold, I'd like to have a chat with Raelynn. She is here, is she not?"

Cordially Farrell swept his arm out to indicate the area which had become the domain of his newest assistant while she was in the shop. "She's there, awaiting your charming presence, madam."

Raelynn moved forward to greet her guest and was a bit surprised at her own nervousness. Still, she was of a mind to think that Heather bore her childbearing state with both an elegant grace and an unquenchable joy. Indeed, her beautiful face seemed to glow with a radiance that might have aroused more than a fair amount of envy from a number of ladies, not to mention bedazzling a few males who, often intrigued and yet bemused by the effervescence of some pregnant women, would have found it especially difficult not to admire this one.

Laughing gaily, Heather gave Raelynn an affectionate hug and then, upon stepping back, a quick inspection. She sighed, making much of her relief. "Thank goodness you bear no lasting marks after being dragged through the swamp."

Raelynn almost cringed when she realized her sister-in-law had been informed of her foolish flight. "I wasn't precisely dragged, Heather. It was a bit more genteel than that."

The sapphire eyes twinkled back at her. "I can imagine. Jeffrey has always been far more civilized than Brandon. I shudder to think how my husband would have reacted in a similar situation. I once ran away from him before our marriage, but I never got up enough nerve to do so afterwards. If I had ever dared wander off into the wilds like you, why, I have no doubt he would've given me a tongue-lashing that would have made a scourging with a cat-o'-nine seem tame." Heather feigned a shiver, certain her husband's formidable temper would have literally been torched if she had shown such reckless disregard for her own life. "But I'm curious to know what set you to flight in the first place, Raelynn, and I thought if you'd be of such a mind, we might venture off to a nice, quiet eatery and talk over sandwiches and a spot of tea."

Though her sister-in-law seemed blithely willing to ignore her status as a paid employee of Ives's Couture, Raelynn was hardly able to. "I'd love to go with you, Heather, but I must stay here and finish some new sketches I'm in the process of . . ."

"Nonsense," Farrell interjected, dropping what he had been doing nearby after overhearing her excuses. "I won't hear of you rejecting my favorite customer's request. It's the middle of the day, and as an expectant mother, you need nourishment. Otherwise you'll be giving your sister-in-law the impression that I'm a slavedriver. Why, my business would be positively ruined."

Heather's smile twinkled back at him. "At last, I know I'm appreciated."

Farrell gave her a roguish grin before jauntily executing a clipped bow. "Madam, may I assure you that you're always greatly esteemed. Without your beauty and grace complementing my designs, I wouldn't be where I am today. May I continue my boasting by saying that presently I have within my shop three of the most beautiful women in the Carolinas, each of whom, with their elegant taste in clothes, has attracted a legion of customers to my shop."

Heather eyed him in a teasingly aloof manner. "I'd feel much more honored by your praise, sir, if I didn't know you could charm the shoes off the little people. But being Irish myself, I can hardly be offended."

Chivalrously Farrell clasped a hand to his breast as if to pledge a solemn troth and gave her a clipped nod that sufficed as another bow. "I'm immensely relieved to hear that, madam, but be assured, with you as well as with these other two winsome ladies whom I greatly admire, I would dare make no such claims unless they be true."

Immediately he took both women by the arm and set himself to the pleasurable task of escorting them toward the entrance. Raelynn barely had time to seize her bonnet and cape before he was whisking the dark green panel open for them. "Enjoy yourselves, ladies."

"My heavens," Raelynn gasped as the heavy portal closed behind them. "I'd be of a mind to think he was trying to evict me from the premises if not for his alacrity in making up some of my designs." She checked the back of her gown, exaggerating her astonishment as she added, "It's a wonder he didn't catch my skirts in the door before he slammed it shut."

Heather laughed in amusement and linked her arm through Raelynn's as they began strolling in the direction of the tea shop. "I hope you don't mind if I lean on you a bit as we walk, my dear. I swear this baby is trying to push her way through before I'm ready for her, but I dare not tell Brandon, or he'll have me confined to bed."

Raelynn glanced at her worriedly. "Do you think it's safe for you to be so far away from Harthaven when you're nearing your time and feeling that way?"

"I may be taking a chance, true," Heather conceded, "but I had to talk with you about Jeffrey, and after the baby comes, it will be difficult for me to get away."

"Did Jeffrey urge you to come and speak in his behalf?" Raelynn asked, yearning for reassurances of his regard for her.

Heather was clearly astounded by her question. "Certainly not, my dear. If you knew your husband better, you'd be aware that he takes care of his own business in his own way, in his own time. He doesn't need me or his older brother to handle such matters for him. He's quite capable of dealing with his own affairs entirely bereft of any help from others," she flicked her brows upward in a tiny shrug as she added, "as much as we'd be amenable to offering our services."

"Then how did you know about my escapade in the woods?"

"Cora told me, dear. She also informed me that you're with child."

Raelynn groaned in chagrin and felt her own cheeks warm. "Just wait, she'll be telling the village crier next."

Heather's resulting laughter proved contagious, and soon the giggling women were drawing curious stares from passersby. But then, their passage had already been duly noted by more than a few residents of the city and the outlying area. Lofty matrons seemed overtly shocked and held their chins haughtily elevated at the idea of a woman in the latter stages of her pregnancy appearing in public. Others were cynical, especially after hearing conjectures about a murderer in the lofty Birmingham family being allowed to retain his freedom even in the face of irrefutable proof. A few seemed genuinely bewildered by the amiable dispositions of the pair when everyone was fully cognizant of the fact that Jeff and Raelynn had every intention of severing their marriage. Heather remained amiably unconcerned by the looks they were garnering, but Raelynn found the inquisitive stares far more difficult to ignore. After all, it was her marriage falling apart and her husband people were wont to condemn.

"Surely, Charleston is far too large and busy a place for its populace to have so narrow a range of focus," she mused aloud, evidencing her irritation as they entered the tea shop.

"Don't let them fool you into thinking they've singled

you out, my dear. They're just as interested in the newly widowed Mrs. Wesley, Farrell and Elizabeth, and a whole host of others, including Brandon and me. Most of the gossips enjoy so little excitement in their own lives, they must enliven others' difficulties with harsh rumors and vivid conjectures, all of which may be utterly false. You'll find their sort in every city of the world. As you've correctly ascertained, Charleston is unquestionably no exception."

The proprietress of the eatery greeted Heather in the friendly manner of a favorite patron, and soon they were being shown to a well-screened table in the back. Solicitously the owner offered the available choices and, when the selections had been decided upon, disappeared and, scant moments later, returned with a pot of tea and a small platter of dainty sandwiches.

Heather peeled off her gloves, laid them aside and then poured tea for Raelynn and herself. Choosing a turkey and cress sandwich to nibble, she eyed her sister-in-law with close attention until she could no longer maintain her silence. "If I'm not mistaken, my dear, you seem a bit unsettled about this whole alienation of affection idea. Is there something you wouldn't mind discussing with one who'd promise not to mention a word of it to another soul?"

Raelynn considered Heather's invitation a long moment as she took a sandwich onto her own plate. Making no effort to eat, she reflected upon what she should say and, at length, released a pensive sigh. "First of all, Heather, I'd like you to know that I'm very much in love with Jeffrey."

Heather's lovely brows lifted briefly. "That's not at all surprising, Raelynn. During the years I've been married to Brandon, I've heard rumors which have led me to affirm my suspicions that Jeffrey is now and always has been a favorite among the ladies. They absolutely adore him, old and young alike. Some women trip over themselves to indulge him. Mrs. Brewster gushes in nervous excitement in his presence and has been simply aswoon over the man for untold ages. She seems convinced that he can do no wrong, at least she was before that nasty business with Nell. In fact, I really don't know how Jeffrey has managed to escape being the most pampered man on earth." Heather met the other's gaze with a tender smile. "So tell me, Raelynn, what are *you* going to do about your state of affairs?"

Raelynn blinked as a sudden moisture blurred her vision. "I'm afraid if things continue the way they're going, Jeffrey will be asking me for a divorce. I can't sleep at night fretting about it."

The black-haired beauty grew a bit perplexed. "Now let's discuss this matter in more depth lest I become thoroughly bogged down in confusion. Cora said that you had run away from Oakley soon after Nell's murder, and though she wasn't aware of the precise details concerning your move to Charleston, she assumed it was your own idea. Now you're telling me you're afraid Jeffrey might seek to sever your marriage?" Heather bolstered enough courage to ask, "Under the circumstances, Raelynn, can you hardly blame the man?"

"He was the one who sent me away," Raelynn admitted in a small voice.

Heather's heart went out to the woman. Reaching across the table, she laid a hand consolingly upon the one that nervously fidgeted with a fork. "I'm sorry, dear, I didn't realize Jeffrey had done that. I thought you had left on your own accord. At least, that's what Cora had been led to believe."

"Well, actually I did, at first, into the woods, I mean, but that was only because I was caught up in a nightmare wherein I kept seeing Jeffrey stabbing Nell. After Jeffrey found me in the swamp, we took shelter from the rain at Red Pete's cabin. Olney Hyde held us at gunpoint for a while and claimed he had witnessed Nell's murder and that the murderer was none other than Jeffrey. What was I to think? After having my own life threatened by the scamp, I certainly had no doubt that Olney was capable of such a deed himself, yet he seemed genuinely convinced that Jeffrey had murdered Nell."

Heather had anticipated Raelynn's apprehensions and thought she should share some of her own experiences. "A few years ago, Brandon was suspected of killing Louisa Wells, the former mistress of Oakley. In fact, after her murder, Rhys Townsend actually came out and arrested Brandon. After living with the man for more than a year and coming to know him as a husband and the gentle, caring father of my son, I was sure that Brandon couldn't possibly have done such a brutal thing, even in a fit of temper. You and Jeffrey haven't had much time to become properly acquainted, but, for what it's worth, my dear, I'm convinced that Jeffrey doesn't have the temperament to kill someone unless his own life or some member of his family is seriously threatened. I *know* for certain he couldn't have killed Nell. It just isn't in the man. He's too noble . . ."

"Aye," Raelynn agreed dolefully, "and so confounded charming, handsome, understanding and . . . and . . ."

"So Jeffrey?" Heather suggested sweetly and patted the other woman's hand consolingly. "My brother-in-law has the most steadfast disposition of any man I know. He's neither boastful nor bashful, insecure nor arrogant, self-centered nor self-deprecating. If anything, he's equanimity personified. However," she added, lifting a slender index finger to make her point, "that's not to say that he isn't fully capable of making decisions that could turn us all on our ears. He's no saint nor, for that matter, a spineless whelp who'll take the worst of what you give him, contritely beg your forgiveness and coddle you while you're doing it. He has his pride, and if you can't bring yourself to trust him, then he'll let you reap the consequences. He's a man, after all, and he can be tough as

an ill-treated hide, but that only makes me love and admire him all the more."

Raelynn heaved a glum sigh. "Since we've been married, it seems as if I've brought him nothing but trouble.
I'm ever reminded that all of this started because of me,
because I couldn't bear to become Mr. Fridrich's little
doxy."

"Nonsense, my dear. Trouble began brewing when
Nell slipped into Jeffrey's bed, and that was long before
you ever put in an appearance."

Raelynn searched the beautiful face of her sister-in-
law and felt led to question her about the incident. "Did
Jeffrey ever explain how that came about?"

"He explained nothing."

"Then how . . . ?"

Heather smiled. "Cora confides in me quite often,
dear. She grew up at Harthaven. Jeffrey needed a housekeeper whom he could trust and who could take charge
in his absence, and of course, we had Hatti, reliable as
the salt of the earth. As for that particular night when
Nell forced her attentions upon Jeffrey, it seems that
nearly all the servants were awakened in one fashion or
another after he hauled the girl out of his room with
nothing more than a blanket draped about her. Kingston
was promptly sent out to fetch Cora, who was given the
task of finding clothes for the girl and packing her valise.
From what I understand, Jeffrey issued a series of orders
and returned to his room, from that point leaving his
servants to deal with Nell. Kingston helped her into the
waiting carriage, and from there, Thaddeus drove her
into Charleston where he secured a room for her at an
inn with funds Jeff had graciously supplied."

"Nell's babe favors Jeffrey to some extent," Raelynn
murmured softly.

"Oh, Raelynn, dear, it's got to be a coincidence,"
Heather argued. "Jeffrey would never have put on such
a performance merely for the sake of his servants. Cora

swore she had never seen him more outraged by an incident. She said that when she got to the house, Jeffrey was ranting something about 'that little slip of a girl should still be playing with dolls instead of men.' The story is that Nell woke him up out of a sound sleep, so there's no telling what she actually did to provoke his rage after she slipped into his bed, but I rather suspect that she didn't limit herself to just kissing him."

Raelynn couldn't bring herself to even entertain the possibility that Cora had lied to Heather. Indeed, the housekeeper had probably reported the incident just as it happened. Then there was Kingston, whom Raelynn had heard harshly chiding Nell for what she had done close to a year before. The butler had laid the blame solely at the girl's feet, not Jeffrey's.

Raelynn also imagined that when a man was as handsome and looked as enticing in clothes as her husband did, a girl like Nell, who had obviously nurtured a deepening obsession for him, might have proven herself quite brazen after launching her seduction. Since it was Jeffrey's habit to wear no clothes to bed, Nell might have liberally indulged her fantasies, at least until that moment he woke.

Of a sudden, Raelynn felt a sizable measure of regret that she had ever allowed Nell to alienate her from her husband. "I'm ashamed to admit it, Heather, but I haven't been a very trusting wife. I allowed the girl's accusations to come between Jeffrey and me, just as I allowed myself to believe he could be a murderer. Now that I've had some weeks to reflect back upon that bloody scene in the stables, I realize I never gave Jeffrey a chance to explain anything before I took off. He has a perfect right to feel offended by my lack of trust."

Heather laid a gently consoling hand upon the other's. "At one time, I thought I hated my husband. I definitely feared him for a while."

Raelynn looked up in shock. She had presumed the

couple's marriage had been idyllic from the beginning. When the two seemed so much in love now, it was impossible to entertain any notion that they might have once been dissatisfied with each other. "I had no idea."

"Even after marrying him, I thought Brandon was no less than a tyrant," Heather acknowledged, a distant smile curving her soft lips. "But by the time we had sailed from England to Charleston, I was wont to think he was the most magnificent man the world had ever created. Though I was hopelessly in love with him by then, pride continued to hinder us. In fact, it wasn't until almost a full year after Beau had actually been conceived that we finally let down our barriers. Now, you and Jeffrey are having problems just as serious as we once had. I really hope that this kind of thing doesn't become a family tradition." She drummed her fingers lightly upon her distended belly. "If it does, I pity the ones who'll follow in our wake."

Raelynn almost shuddered to think what their offspring could reap if their woes were visited upon them. "Let us trust that none of those whom we hold dear will be suspected of murder as Jeffrey and Brandon have been."

Heather murmured her agreement before moving swiftly on to a less distressing topic. "I truly wish, Raelynn, that you'd consider coming out to stay with us at Harthaven until this rift between you and Jeffrey is mended. You'd be entirely welcomed to remain as long as it takes for both of you to work out your differences."

Touched though she was by the invitation, Raelynn shook her head. "Thank you, Heather, but I just can't. I don't think Jeffrey would feel comfortable visiting you while I'm there. Besides, I'm loath to involve you and Brandon in this matter."

"But we're family, dear. We're already involved."

"Of course, you are, but it just wouldn't be right for

me to put myself between Jeffrey and his family," Raelynn argued.

Looking decidedly downcast, Heather muttered dejectedly, "Brandon said you'd refuse, but I just had to
try."

18 ✑

"Miz Raelynn! Miz Raelynn!" Tizzy cried in an anxious dither as she scurried into the clothier's shop late one afternoon three days hence. "Mr. Brandon's coachman jes' arrived at Miz Elizabeth's, an' he says dat Miz Heather's gone inta labor an' dat she's askin' if'n yo'd be o' a mind ta come out an' help her through de delivery."

Raelynn rose to her feet without delay and was just turning to search out Farrell to ask for his permission to leave when she saw him striding hurriedly toward her.

"Just go!" he urged, motioning her toward the door. "Don't worry about cleaning up your desk. Elizabeth can put everything away. Stay as long as you're needed. If something comes up that won't wait, we'll know where to find you. Now go, get yourself ready. You have a long ride ahead of you."

"I done packed a valise fo' yo', Miz Raelynn, jes' in case Miz Heather's baby takes its own sweet time gettin' here," Tizzy informed her. "It's already in Mr. Brandon's carriage. If'n ye're o' such a mind, ye can leave right now."

"Thank you, Tizzy," Raelynn said gratefully, already scurrying. She snatched her cloak from the coat tree and dragged it on as she ran.

In a moment she was slipping out the front portal which the doorman was holding open for her. The coachman had pulled alongside the boardwalk in front of the shop and, in anticipation of her arrival, was there waiting at the open door of the conveyance.

"Aftahnoon, Miz Raelynn," he greeted, tipping his hat. "Ah hope yo' don't mind rushin'. Mistah Brandon was fit ta be tied, worryin' o'er his li'l darlin'. Befo' I left, he said ta get yo' dere as fast as I could whip de horses inta a frenzy."

"Thank you for coming all the way to Charleston to fetch me, James. I want to be there." She placed a hand in his massive, gloved paw and accepted his assistance into the landau. Her slippered feet barely touched the coach steps as she made a hasty ascent. Settling back into the seat, she felt the carriage lurch as the servant climbed to his seat, and soon they were on their way.

Once they left the outskirts of the city, James displayed a definite urgency as he cracked his whip time and again above the heads of the four-in-hand. The horses' hooves were nearly churning up the winding road, yet the servant gave no signs of relenting. Obviously he had taken his master at his word.

Twilight had settled over the land before James turned into the long lane leading to Harthaven. At the far end of the oak-lined drive, the blazing lights of the large house cast a welcoming ambience. Soon the landau was drawing to a halt before the steps, and Raelynn caught sight of Brandon hurrying across the porch to meet the approaching conveyance. When she scooted forward on the seat, he was there to swing open the door and give her a hand down.

"I'm glad you were able to come," he murmured, obviously relieved that she had seen fit to do so. Settling a hand beneath her arm, he whisked her across the porch. "Heather said something about you two being sisters almost as much as Jeffrey and I are brothers. She got it in her head that she wanted you beside her, and there was no denying her request." He chuckled softly, but it lacked a carefree tone. "I told James to drag you forcibly into the carriage if need be, but he only laughed and assured me that he'd bring you back without going to that extreme."

"Heather is not in any danger, is she?" Raelynn queried anxiously, glancing up at her brother-in-law as he opened the front door for her. Perhaps it was only because she had been away from Jeffrey for more than three weeks, but at the moment she was struck with a keen awareness of just how tall her brother-in-law really was. But then, she reminded herself, he was no taller than Jeffrey.

"Hatti says everything is going along as it should be," Brandon informed her, but in the brief pause that followed, he released a wavering sigh. "Since that could mean a whole plethora of things, her statement is hardly very soothing."

Heather was in the grip of a painful contraction when they arrived at the master bedroom. Even so, she managed an anguished grin for the new arrival. When she finally could relax, she dropped her head back upon the pillow and, regulating her breathing again, rested a moment before reclaiming a genuine smile. In spite of the crispness of the weather, her hair was damp and a tiny dappling of sweat shone on her face. Yet she seemed oblivious to that and the pain she had just endured as she stretched forth a slender hand, inviting Raelynn to come near. "I'm sorry I couldn't greet you properly just now, but this baby has a way of demanding my full attention. My labor started some hours ago, so I don't imagine that it will be too long now before I give birth."

Raelynn clutched the woman's thin hand fondly within her own and managed a wobbly smile. "James made sure I got here as soon as I could," she replied and, in spite of her concern, tried to sound amused by it all as she added, "I don't believe I've ever experienced a swifter ride."

Heather groaned in mock chagrin. "I didn't mean for him to scare you to death, dear. I would've been content to wait another half hour if need be."

"Our offspring might not have waited that long," her husband interjected, moving around to the opposite side of the bed. Lifting a knee upon the mattress, he settled beside his wife and gathered her free hand within his much larger one. "You were having hard contractions when I sent James to Charleston to fetch Raelynn, and now they're coming with greater frequency. Frankly, madam, I don't know how much more of this I can stand."

Heather and Raelynn smiled at his dry wit before his wife reached up to run a hand lovingly along his upper arm. "You'll do fine."

"Doesn't help knowing I promised to stay with you until the end," Brandon confessed. "My knees are already feeling a little weak at the idea."

"That was your suggestion, not mine," Heather accused sweetly. "I can manage without you."

Brandon laid a gentle hand over the sheet that covered her distended belly. "Who's responsible for this baby?"

"We both are," she acknowledged with a smile.

"Then we'll both be here when she's born," he assured her, his green eyes gazing into hers. He brought her hand to his lips for a doting kiss. "Now tell me, my sweet, how are you feeling now?"

"I'm doing fine," she assured him, threading her fingers through his. She lifted sapphire orbs and perused his face with wifely concern. "How about you?"

Briefly Brandon held out his free hand before her as he boasted, "You see? Steady as a rock."

"Aye, and I'm my mother's uncle," Heather replied, chuckling as she caught the large extremity within her grasp.

Barely a half hour later, a servant softly rapped on the door and, when Brandon went to open it, a young black woman announced in soft tones, "Mistah Jeffrey's downstairs, suh. He jes' arrived."

"Thank you, Melody. Tell him that I'll be down directly."

Brandon closed the door as the servant left, and when he turned, he found himself meeting Raelynn's gaze. It seemed to him that she looked suddenly unsure of herself, but he had no idea how to put her at ease. He lifted his shoulders in a lame shrug. "Farrell must have sent word over to him."

"All the way to Oakley?"

"Probably at Jeff's townhouse in Charles . . ." Brandon broke off abruptly, realizing he had just betrayed his brother's confidence. Seeing Raelynn's deepening confusion, he offered an excuse that was no real exaggeration of the truth. "Jeff has had a lot to do lately at his shipping company. He didn't want to have to ride in every day, so he let a townhouse from a friend."

Raelynn opened her mouth to speak, but then closed it again just as quickly, realizing she was on the verge of tears. In view of the fact that Oakley was about an hour's ride from Charleston, she had consoled herself that her husband had had no time to come in to see her when he was so busy tending to his many business affairs. If, however, he had been in the city all this time, then she could only believe he had been deliberately avoiding her since she had started working at Farrell's.

In fear of betraying her crumbling reserve, Raelynn cleared her throat and dared to put forth a question. "Has he been there long?"

"I'm not exactly sure how long it has been now. Only a couple weeks or so, I think. I've lost track." It seemed a trite excuse Brandon offered, but true. While he had been so wrought up worrying about what Heather would have to face during the birth of their child, he hadn't hardly thought about anything else.

"Brandon," Heather called from the bed.

"Yes, my love?" he answered, moving to her side. He was grateful for her interruption, yet he also sensed she had something on her mind that didn't necessarily involve him.

His wife clasped his large hand against her bosom and smiled up at him gently. "Go downstairs with your brother. I'd like to talk with Raelynn alone for a few moments."

Brandon perceived that she intended to lay out the complete and honest truth before their sister-in-law, and that it would be better for all concerned if he removed himself. He did so willingly, preferring to leave rather than witness the tears that would likely be forthcoming. "Don't do anything while I'm gone now," he urged with wane humor. "I said I'd be here with you to the end, and you know I always keep my word."

"Even if you pass out doing so," Heather teased, lifting her face to receive his doting kiss.

"Me?" Brandon straightened and turned a pointing finger toward his own chest in an attitude of wide disbelief. At her grin and nod, he feigned a bruised countenance, "Why, madam, shame on you. I wouldn't do anything like that."

"Of course not," she sweetly agreed and squeezed his lean fingers before letting him go.

When the door closed behind him, Heather beckoned Raelynn around again to the left side of the bed, near the spot where she lay. Raelynn readily complied, but at Heather's sudden grimace, she reached out and clasped the delicately boned hands.

"Can I do anything to ease your discomfort?" she asked anxiously, amazed by the small woman's tenacious grip.

Unable to answer, Heather strained downward a lengthy moment until at last the contraction eased. Then she blew out a long breath, and once more slowly inhaled. Regaining her composure, she smiled up at Raelynn. "It won't be too much longer now."

"You wished to speak with me," Raelynn asked gently.

"Yes, dear. I just wanted to assure you that the reason Jeffrey is staying in Charleston has everything to do with you."

"Me?" Raelynn laughed at the absurdity of such a notion. If not for the fact that she was so completely distraught, her actions might have seemed to mimic Brandon's earlier protestations. "But I haven't hardly seen him since I left Oakley. He came to Farrell's shop briefly, but he didn't even glance at me."

"That doesn't mean Jeffrey hasn't been concerned about your welfare. All along he has had men watching over you to ensure your safety, mainly from Gustav. I haven't been informed of just where his men are located, but I believe they're fairly close to the areas where you're working and living. Jeffrey is staying in Charleston in case there's trouble."

"It seems he's just as honorable as always," Raelynn replied stiltedly. "Or is he just using me as bait to catch Gustav?"

"Raelynn, dear, I truly believe Jeffrey cares for you. Otherwise . . ."

"If that is true, then why hasn't he come to see me?" Raelynn interrupted, her voice weakening. "If you ask me, it's just a matter of manly pride. He can hardly be accused of leaving me to my own defenses if he has men watching over me when Gustav decides to come calling again with his ruffians."

Heather tensed and pressed her hands against her stomach as another contraction rent her restraint. After a moment, she gasped, "You'd better call Hatti. I think the baby's head is beginning to push through."

Raelynn tore from the room and rapidly descended the stairs, calling for the black woman. Brandon charged out of the study like a man possessed, and as he bolted for the stairs, Raelynn stumbled to a halt, her eyes falling on the tall, handsomely garbed figure entering the main hall.

As their eyes met, Jeff nodded a greeting and leisurely advanced to the stairs, there placing a booted foot upon the first step. Though the hall had suddenly come alive with servants rushing to and fro, carrying bundles of linens and buckets of water, Raelynn remained unaware of everything but her husband until she realized of a sudden that Hatti had passed her some moments ago.

"Heather will be wondering where I am," she gasped. Whirling, she caught up her skirts and raced back upstairs. She didn't realize just how much she was trembling until she had closed the bedroom door behind her and leaned back against it. Of a sudden, her knees felt so weak they seemed incapable of bearing her weight. If not for the fact that she had clenched her teeth, she had no doubt that they would have been chattering by now. Chiding herself for allowing her husband to dismantle her reserve so completely, she forged an unsteady path to the bed, totally amazed by his debilitating effect on her. But that was not the worst of it, by any means, for her heart was thudding chaotically against the wall of her chest, as if she had run a fierce race.

At present, Heather was straining hard to thrust her child into the world. Brandon was beside his wife, his long fingers entwined with hers, appearing every bit as stalwart as his physical bearing conveyed as he murmured encouragements and dabbed at her glistening brow. Only Raelynn noticed that the large hand, which gently wiped Heather's brow, was shaking far more now than it had been. Indeed, it nearly matched the tremor in her own.

"Yo' doin' fine, honey chile," Hatti encouraged as she busily prepared the bunting for the new arrival.

Heather's head fell back upon the pillow as the spasm passed, and for a moment she panted as if thoroughly spent. Then she let out her breath in a sigh, composed herself, and glanced around, only then noticing her sister-in-law standing near the end of the bed. Heather held out her free hand invitingly, and Raelynn seized it, fighting anxious tears. Between Jeffrey and Heather, she didn't know if she'd ever be the same.

"It's all right," Heather soothed, managing a brave smile. "It will all be over very, very soon. No need to fret now, dear. I'm doing fine."

In another moment, Heather was grimacing and bearing down hard again. The baby's head finally pushed through, and immediately a muted, angry squall was heard, evoking laughter from all who heard.

"Ain't got de volume Mistah Beau had," Hatti commented with a white-toothed grin. "Dis one sounds mo' like a dainty li'l girl ta me. Very shortly, ah 'spect, Miz Heather, yo' gonna be havin' yerself a looksee at your li'l daughter."

Heather's head came up off the pillow again as she strove through the throes of childbirth. It wasn't long before the black woman was cackling in glee.

"Sho nuff, a fine black-haired, li'l girl. An' she's a real beauty, too."

"Oh, she is," Raelynn agreed, laughing. Of a sudden, she felt as if her heart would soar.

Hatti placed the squalling infant upon her mother's stomach and dispensed with the rest of the necessities involved in child-bearing. Much awed by the miracle of birth he had just witnessed, Brandon thrust a finger through the tiny, bloody fist of his new daughter and immediately the baby stopped her crying and started making a sucking noise.

"Well, we know what our new little darling will soon be wanting," her father said with a chortle.

Hatti took the newborn to a corner of the room where she cleansed and swaddled her. Within moments, the tiny girl was lowered into her mother's arms.

"She's absolutely gorgeous," Raelynn observed proudly.

Heather gazed down upon the small, wrinkled face and laughed. "Only a loving aunt would be so kind."

Brandon rose from the bed and, crossing to the door, grinned back at his wife. "I'm going down to fetch Beau and Jeff. They'll be wanting to see Suzanne, too."

Heather was absorbed in inspecting her new daughter and making sure that everything was as it should be. Hatti and Melody were tidying up the bedroom and repositioning the cradle near the bed. In the confusion, no one noticed Raelynn slipping out of the room and hastening down the stairs. She left through the back of the house just as quietly and hurried out to the privy, diligently seeking the privacy it afforded. She really didn't want Jeff to see her while she was so wrought up. At the merest thought of confronting him again, she had started shaking enough to make the trip to the privy a requirement. With her pregnancy came the necessity, and she *definitely* needed to go.

She hardly expected Jeff to be waiting just outside the cubicle when she opened the door. She flushed red in embarrassment, as if he had never seen her scurrying toward a chamber pot in their bedroom. Nervously she smoothed her skirts. "I'm sorry, I didn't realize you were waiting to use the convenience."

"I was waiting for you, madam," Jeff corrected. "I was informed that James brought you out from town, and

I was wondering if you'd care to share my carriage on the return trip to Charleston. It would save James the trip in."

Put that way, Raelynn couldn't see how she could refuse. "Tizzy packed a valise for me just in case I'd be staying overnight. I'll have to fetch it."

"James gave it to me some moments ago, madam. It's already in my carriage," her husband informed her. "Once I pay my respects to the newborn and her mother, I'll be ready to leave. Will that be acceptable to you?"

Raelynn couldn't decide whether she should feel offended because he had taken her reply for granted, or if she should be pleased that he had gathered her belongings with his usual punctilious competence. "Yes, perfectly."

Not daring to touch her for fear of what that would lead to, Jeff swept his hand toward the narrow path leading to the house. "After you, madam."

Raelynn hurried along the well-worn trail, even in the moonlit shadows feeling his unrelenting gaze following her. His long legs had no difficulty keeping up with her, and when she arrived at the door, he was there to swing it open.

"Thank you," she replied, glancing up nervously. She was so intent upon eyeing him that she failed to notice where she was walking until her head met the sharp ridge of a doorjamb, the hard way. She stumbled back, completely stunned by the impact, and wished in mortifying chagrin that she had fallen into a bottomless pit somewhere.

"Are you all right?" Jeff asked solicitously, lifting her chin with a knuckle to see the damage.

She stood blushing furiously with a hand clasped over the swelling knot on her forehead, telling herself that it was perfectly sane for a woman to wish the earth would open and swallow her up. Her husband was trying to pull away her hand in a quest to see her battle scar, but she was too embarrassed to let him. "I'm fine! Just leave me be, Jeffrey."

"You're not fine," he argued. "There's blood dribbling through your fingers."

Startled by his announcement, she yanked away her hand and stared at it in shock. It was indeed bloody, but what was even more disturbing was the fact that droplets began plummeting onto her bosom. "Oh, my gown! It's going to be ruined."

"It's a wonder your head isn't," Jeff quipped, gently dabbing a clean handkerchief to the small cut on her brow. He swabbed up the blood there and then, with husbandly familiarity, proceeded to her bodice.

His diligent swipes across her breast immediately caused Raelynn to forget her throbbing head, for she could feel her nipple drawing into a tight little nub beneath his casual ministrations. She lost any semblance of a ladylike poise and clasped a hand over her breast, unable to ignore the hungrily throbbing peak. "Please, Jeffrey, just leave me be!"

"Your head needs tending, madam," he reasoned, "and at the moment everyone is busy in the house, so I'd be grateful if you'd just let me take care of it."

"I can take care of myself."

"You can't even see your head."

"Oh, all right!" Much like a petulant child, she plunked herself down upon a stool near the rear door and leaned her head back, still holding her breast within her hand. "Tend me!"

Jeff drew a bucket of water from the well, poured a small amount into a tin cup that hung from a hook, and brought it near. "You needn't act so offended, Raelynn," he rebuked gently, wetting the handkerchief. "I've done a lot more than handle your breast."

It dawned on Raelynn that she probably looked more than a little ridiculous sitting there with a hand clasping the womanly fullness. Shifting uncomfortably, she lowered her arm to her lap. Just as quickly she caught the glance her husband shot toward her bodice and looked down at herself, curious to know what had provoked his interest. Her nipple was still tightly puckered, and with a mortified groan she crossed her arms, drawing a low chuckle from Jeff.

"It isn't as if you haven't seen such sights before," she fussed.

"My memory needs refreshing." Jeff gave the excuse with a grin. "It has been awhile."

She wanted to quip something appropriately tart, but nothing came to mind. As it was, she endured the careful cleansing of her head wound, allowed him to bandage it, and then sought the covering of her cloak before following Jeffrey upstairs to the master bedroom.

When they arrived, Beau was sitting on the bed beside his mother, peering inquisitively at the little creature his father was holding within his hands. The boy was asking numerous questions about where his new little sister had come from. Finally Brandon settled his tiny little daughter in one hand and, reaching across with the other, laid it on the blanket covering his wife's stomach, which was now noticeably flatter.

"That's where Suzanne and you both came from, son."

Beau pondered this a moment, before looking up inquisitively. "But how'd we get in there?"

Jeff pressed a knuckle against his lips to subdue a chuckle as his brother looked at him with a pained expression. The elder Birmingham turned back to his wife and, clasping her hand, finally gave an answer. "Love put you and your sister there, son."

"Love?" Beau asked, his voice imbued with an incredulous tone. "You mean the way Hatti loves fried chicken?"

A hoot of laughter came from Jeff, who threw his head back and guffawed to the ceiling. His amusement proved contagious, and soon the whole room was filled with sounds of hilarity.

✒DARKNESS HAD SETTLED OVER THE LAND BY THE TIME Jeff and Raelynn bade their farewells to the family and settled into the landau for the long ride to Charleston. Raelynn yearned for the trip to be shortened by an invitation to stay the night at Oakley, but it soon became apparent that her husband was not inclined to make such an offer.

Though at first she felt tense and nervous sitting beside Jeffrey, the day's events had taken a decided toll upon her energy. Soon she was nodding off. She hadn't donned her bonnet for fear of ruining the ribbons with a fresh flow of blood from her head, which left her bruised brow rather vulnerable when it brushed up against the interior wall of the carriage. She came awake with a jerk and, in deepening mortification, straightened herself upon the cushioned seat, well aware that her maddeningly stoic husband was watching her with unrelenting persistence through the moonlit gloom.

Only a few more miles had been traversed before Raelynn's eyes were drooping closed again. She never knew exactly when Jeff lifted her onto his lap and nestled her brow against his throat, for she had ceased her struggle against an encroaching sleep. She was just as oblivious to the kiss he placed upon the top of her head.

Sometime later Raelynn became vaguely aware that she was being borne along through an area of darkness. She heard the sound of a door closing, and then muted voices seemed to drift upward from a deep well. A glowing lamp moved somewhere beyond her, casting elongated shafts of light and shadows across ceilings and corridors. A door's hinges creaked as a portal was opened and then closed. When a moment later she was placed

upon a bed, she recognized a familiar squeak. She tried
to wake when she heard Tizzy's sleepy voice, but much
deeper tones banished the girl to her own room. Gentle
hands plucked open buttons and other fasteners, and
with a contented sigh Raelynn turned her face upon the
pillow as her baby rolled within her womb. The movements seemed obscure and distant, as if she only dreamt
them, much like the inviting warmth of a large hand resting upon her cool stomach. She felt a nightgown being
drawn over her head and, at long last, a blanket being
tucked in around her. Then a lantern at the end of a long
tunnel was snuffed, and darkness closed in around her
as she sank deeper into a dreamy vortex from which she
had no desire to rise.

19

*N*earing closing time on a Friday a fortnight later, a tall, dapper figure of a man pushed open the distinctive green door of *Ives's Couture* and swept off his top hat as he approached the lone desk near the back of the seamstress's corridor. Raelynn was just tucking the last of her drawing supplies into a drawer when a manly shadow, cast from the hanging fixture overhead, fell upon her. She glanced up, fully expecting to find her employer with some question about one of her designs. Several moments earlier he had taken Elizabeth upstairs to search for some new fabric samples he had left there, one which he especially liked and was considering using for a gown that Raelynn had finished sketching earlier that afternoon.

When her gaze lit upon her own husband, Raelynn was struck by an avalanche of impressions closely reminiscent of those that had been instrumental in leading her to accept his proposal of marriage less than an hour after their initial meeting. His manly good looks were just as stirring, his smile with twin depressions in his cheeks just as engaging, his green eyes just as luminous as they had always been. The only detectable difference was within herself. She couldn't remember her heart beating as chaotically, even after he had scooped her out of the path of the onrushing coach, as it now did. Surely no fear could have stirred such giddiness. Neither could that emotion have warmed her cheeks to the extent that she could actually feel them glowing.

"We didn't have a chance to talk when I brought you back from Harthaven," he murmured, "and I've been wondering how you've been feeling. Is your head better? I see no sign of a scar."

Jeff swept his gaze down the length of her as she moved around the end of the desk. Though she wore a charming, dark green and blue plaid frock that served to conceal her condition, it was obvious nevertheless that she was with child, but then, when he had stripped her for bed after carrying her up to her narrow room at Elizabeth's house, he hadn't been able to mistake her small, rounding belly. He had noticed small movements there, motivating him to lay a hand over the gentle roundness and to feel his child moving within her womb.

"No, as you can see, it's just fine now," Raelynn murmured, trying to curb her elation. "And I'm feeling remarkably well myself." More than a month ago she had departed his house, but there had been times since then when it had seemed like a year. Through all of her past debates over his guilt or innocence, she hadn't realized just how desperately she would come to miss her husband until a goading worry began to assail her, leaving her fearing that she might never see him again. That dread had taken deep root in her heart, and she had learned a harsh lesson about what it feels like to vainly pine for a man. If Nell had brooded over Jeffrey's aloof-

ness as much as she had done within the agonizing weeks
of their separation, then Raelynn could definitely understand why the girl had felt driven at times to demand
his recognition.

"None of the usual discomforts that accompanies
pregnancy?" Jeff asked solicitously.

"Nothing of any significance, only a lethargy that still
makes me want to sleep at odd and sundry times, but I
can't very well do that while I'm working here."

"No, I don't suppose you can."

"How is Heather and the baby doing? I've been meaning to hire a livery and go out to see them, but we've
had so many customers ordering spring wardrobes that
the three of us have hardly had time to take a deep
breath."

"Heather and the baby are fine," Jeff replied. "Suzanne has even managed to sleep from dusk to dawn
several times, which of course delights her parents. Nursing a babe every four hours night after night can wear
on a body after a while, I suppose. But then, that duty
falls entirely to the mother, regardless of a husband's efforts to help."

Hesitantly Raelynn approached a subject that had
been worrying her of late. "I understand from recent
comments I've overheard in the shop that we've now become the prime interest of gossipmongers," she ventured,
tracing a finger along the arm of a small, French fashion
mannequin which resided on her desk. She dared not
meet his gaze as she probed, "I've even heard people
saying that you've spoken to your lawyer and have initiated the termination of our marriage."

A derisive snort attested to Jeff's feelings about that
particular bit of hearsay. "Don't believe everything you
hear, my dear, or, for that matter, only bits and parts of
what you see. I'd never do that unless it became your
desire." He tilted his head thoughtfully aslant as her eyes
slowly lifted to meet his. "Has it?"

"No, of course not," Raelynn hastened to assure him with an uncomfortable little laugh. "I was just afraid it might be true, considering how vexed you were with me before I left Oakley."

"Afraid?" Jeff repeated, wondering at her choice of words.

"Concerned, afraid, anxious, they all mean about the same thing," she stated gloomily.

"I agree, Raelynn, but are you telling me that you were actually concerned enough to be afraid?"

A wavering sigh escaped her lips. Jerkily she nodded. "Yes."

"Does this mean that you're suffering some doubts about my guilt in Nell's death?"

His blunt question brought tears to her eyes. Diffidently she met his searching gaze. "I haven't been able to come to any definite conclusions about what happened that night, if that's what you mean. At times, it seems utterly foolish to even suspect that you could have had anything to do with that kind of brutality, and then I wake up from a recurring nightmare in which your appearance changes before my eyes. The demon you become makes me quail in fright."

Jeff certainly hadn't been able to forget the night he had lain beside her at Red Pete's cabin and had heard her tormented ravings. Rather than stir up past hurts, he considered it wiser by far to change the subject. "I came here, madam, to ask you to have dinner with me."

"At Oakley?" Did he truly mean to break his self-possessed reticence and allow her to enter his home again? Hardly daring to breathe, she awaited his answer as if she were about to receive a sentence somewhere between life and death.

"At a restaurant here in the city," he informed her and immediately wondered if the gentle radiance in her eyes had dimmed a slight degree or if it had only been a trick of his imagination. "If you're at all acceptable to the idea, we can have dinner out, and then afterwards, I can escort you back to Elizabeth's. I'll hire a livery to take us there if you're not up to walking. At the moment, I'm without the landau. I had to send Thaddeus back to Oakley to do some errands for me."

Raelynn wished fervently she would have had enough foresight to have donned a more elegant gown earlier that morning. "I should tidy my appearance."

"Nonsense, my dear, you look as ravishing as always."

His magnanimous claim did much to buoy her mood. Even so, it evoked a dubious laugh. "Hardly that, Jeffrey."

He glanced around. "Do you have a cloak? It seems unusually moist and breathless outside, which leads me to surmise that a fog may be rolling in before too long."

Raelynn indicated the coat tree where she had left her woolen wrap. "The cloak is Elizabeth's, the cape is mine." From a nearby chest, she swept a pert cap that had been made on the order of a Scottish bonnet and went to stand before a tall, silvered glass where she proceeded to don it. Settling it upon her head at a cocky angle, she glanced at her husband again to reassure herself that he was still there and ready and willing to be seen with her in public. He was there all right, looking back at her as he lifted her cape from the hook. Suddenly asmile, she gave no heed to what she was doing as she thrust a long hatpin through the deep blue velvet. She promptly regretted having diverted her attention as she rammed the point of the pin into her forefinger. Her startled cry quickly brought Jeff back to her side, but by then, she had dislodged the stickpin and dropped it on the floor to clasp her bleeding finger in the palm of her hand before the tiny droplets could mar her gown.

"That was clumsy of me," she fretted, grimacing in pain.

"Let me see what you've done this time," Jeff urged, brightening her cheeks to a vivid hue. Mentally she groaned in discomfiture. Why, in heaven's name did she have to be so inept when he was around?

Taking her hand within his, Jeff drew her to a nearby washstand, which had proven a necessity for Raelynn when she sketched in charcoal. There he poured a small amount of water into the bowl. After soaping and rinsing her hand, he withdrew a clean handkerchief from his coat and wiped the slender digits dry as he gently implored, "You should be more careful, Raelynn."

' Vividly aware of his tall, neatly garbed presence so close at hand, Raelynn pressed a trembling hand to her brow in an attempt to hide her flushed cheeks. Her clumsiness as well as her finger 'had been all but forgotten in the face of her heightening awareness of his all-too-manly presence. She was rather shocked to find that she was actually becoming physically stimulated. Her nipples tingled with a hungry yearning to be caressed again, not only by his hands and mouth, but by the slow, rhythmic strokes of his furred chest during the intimate rites of love. It was all she could do to ignore the throbbing urgency in her loins as she yearned to be joined with him and to soar once again to those lofty heights to which he had taken her so often, but, of course, that was nothing more than foolishness. *Best to cool your blood*, she rebuked herself. *If he had wanted you in that way, he'd have been around long before now.*

Jeff's features were sharpened with his own burgeoning desire to gather his wife up close against him and to kiss her with all the passion he had been holding in check since her departure. Only he knew of the agony he had suffered during their separation, but he heard Elizabeth's rapid footfalls drifting from the corridor leading to the upstairs apartment and, close behind her, those of Farrell's. The approach of the couple left him with no other choice but to smother the awakening fires that had been so quickly and easily ignited.

"What happened?" the brunette asked worriedly as

she hurriedly entered the corridor and came toward them. "Raelynn, are you all right? I thought I heard you cry out."

"I just stuck a hatpin into my finger," Raelynn confessed shamefacedly. "Thankfully Jeffrey is taking care of it."

"Well, he certainly doesn't need our help," Elizabeth replied cheerily as she noticed a pink blush infusing her friend's cheeks. Struggling not to smile, she quickly retreated and, behind her back, motioned for Farrell to do likewise. "We'll just take ourselves back to where we came from."

Jeff turned to meet the widow's sparkling gaze. "My wife and I will be having dinner out this evening, Elizabeth. You needn't wait up for her. It may be rather late before we return."

"Oh, of course." The buoyant lilt in her voice evidenced her delight. "Don't worry about a thing. Just have a good time."

"We'll endeavor to do such a thing," Jeff pledged with a grin.

In the couple's absence, Raelynn rose on tiptoes to whisper near her husband's ear, "Elizabeth invited Farrell to supper tonight, and the way they've been mooning over each other lately, I'm definitely relieved to have someplace else to go. I would've felt like a third thumb."

"Even if I'm your escort?"

A smile curved Raelynn's soft lips as her sparkling eyes met his. "I wouldn't have gone with anyone else, Jeffrey."

NIGHT FELL QUICKLY OVER CHARLESTON AS THE BIRminghams wended their way along the city streets. Thin wisps of fog had begun to drift up from the wharves into the narrow lanes and byways through which they passed.

Soon it began rolling up around stately edifices and twining ghost-like through formal gardens. What post lights and lanterns could be seen in the distance were nothing more than vague auras of light glowing in the mists.

Jeff had chosen an elegant French restaurant at which to dine, and though the couple drew the shocked attention of nearly everyone they passed as the *maitre d'* led them to a secluded table near a window at the back, this time Raelynn was much more receptive to the stares. Swept forward on her husband's arm, she graciously nodded to those who gaped at them in wide-eyed astonishment.

"Does this meet with your approval, Mr. Birmingham?" the *maitre d'* inquired solicitously .

"Very nicely indeed, Gascon. Thank you."

The headwaiter stood patiently aside as Jeff removed Raelynn's cape. Upon receiving it, the man hurried away. After assisting his wife into a seat, Jeff took a chair close upon her right and, when the waiter appeared, ordered a bottle of wine and an appetizer. He had just taken his wife's hand to speak of an affair dear to his heart when a tall, dark-haired man dared to intrude upon their privacy.

"Your pardon, Mr. Birmingham. I don't know if you remember me from your ball, but I'm Lord Marsden." The man indicated the vacant place on Raelynn's left. "Would you mind if I sit a spell with you and your lovely wife and discuss a matter which has brought me all the way from England to the Carolinas?"

Jeff had had every intention of courting his wife, but in good manner he could hardly refuse his lordship's request. Hiding his annoyance, he swept a hand to invite the man to join them. "Please, be my guest."

The waiter arrived with the wine and was promptly sent for a third goblet. After sampling the choice vintage and a sizable portion of the timbales of shrimp and spinach, which Raelynn had shared with him from her plate, his lordship complimented his host for his excellent taste in wine and food. "It must be a rarity to find a libation of this quality here. I certainly haven't been able to find the equal."

"It depends on where you go and whom you know, my lord," Jeff replied. "But then, my ships import a lot of the wines this city serves."

His lordship chortled. "No wonder you're so knowledgeable about where the best of it is located. Yes, indeed. Aside from their marvelous wines, I'm particularly fond of French cuisine. The sauces they use to enhance their dishes are simply superb. I became indoctrinated with everything French when I served as a royal courier to that country some years ago, but, of course, that was before their horrible revolution. When the peasants overran the country, they destroyed everything I enjoyed about it. Now France has a First Consul who means to become emperor. Napoleon will be satisfied with nothing less. No sooner did we get a treaty of peace with him last year than we're back at war. Bloody confident, he is, and it's no wonder, what with the scuttlebutt about there being spies in our camps, even near his majesty's throne. Do you hear much about that sort of thing here in the colonies, sir?"

"Carolinas, you mean?" Jeff corrected, managing a brief smile. "We no longer consider this a territory under English rule."

"Yes, of course. A slip of the tongue, as it were."

"As to your question, we seem to be entirely removed from the happenings of the English court and the intrigue going on there."

"But I understand your wife is English. Has she not heard of the deceit practiced near the throne by some men?"

"She has suffered mightily because of that very thing, your lordship," Jeff informed the man, reaching across the table to take Raelynn's hand. He wasn't surprised to feel it trembling within his grasp. "I believe it's still very much a painful subject for her. You see, her father was falsely accused of treason and died in prison awaiting his trial."

"Oh, I'm dreadfully sorry," Lord Marsden replied. His dark brows gathered in deep concern as he conveyed his regret to Raelynn. "I hope I haven't offended you by speaking out of turn, madam. If I have, I humbly beg your forgiveness."

"You could hardly have been cognizant of my distress, my lord," she murmured graciously, managing nothing more than a wan smile. "After all, you only know me as Mrs. Birmingham. My late father was James Barrett, Earl of Balfour."

Lord Marsden fell back in his chair, his jaw sagging in surprise, but he quickly recovered and hastened to assure her, "My dear, although I knew your father distantly, I had great regard for him. At the time of his arrest, I was unable to equate the charges against him as anything having solid basis. The man was admired and respected by his peerage . . ."

"Nevertheless," Raelynn interrupted with quavering tones, "there were those among his peers whose guileful subterfuge brought about his demise. My father was confident that the culprits would be exposed by the very thing that he had within his keeping once he came to trial, but alas, he died in prison before he ever had a chance to reveal them as the deceitful men they were."

Shadows moved behind Raelynn's eyes as she recalled the final, haunting days of her father's imprisonment. He had been concerned for his family's safety and, for that reason, hadn't wanted them to visit the prison where he was being held. There was much at stake, he had claimed, and had charged them to keep to themselves and to secure their safety in obscurity. Yet her mother had finally gone to see him, a rare incidence in which she had disobeyed the husband whom she had honored and cherished. On that occasion, James Barrett had appeared wan and weary, yet in tolerably good health. Less than a day later, he was dead. His widow was simply told that he had taken a chill, believable enough in the dank confines of his cell, and had died of an inflammation of his lungs.

"But, surely, even after his death, you could have established his innocence with such evidence as he had in his possession," Lord Marsden said.

"My father's integrity and loyalty to King George will be brought to light in time, my lord," Raelynn said, confident of the axiom that good is eventually victorious over evil. "There will come a day of reckoning, of that I have no doubt."

"Well, I've certainly turned the festive mood of this occasion into a morose declaration of noble platitudes," Lord Marsden observed dryly. "Again, forgive me for bringing up the subject of England's difficulties with France. I must remember where I am, here in the Carolinas where neither French nor English is the standard."

"Aye, we have our own ways of doing things in this country," Jeff affirmed and leaned forward to inquire, "Now, your lordship, if you wouldn't mind my asking, what is the nature of the matter you wish to discuss with me?"

"Yes, of course. I nearly forgot my business in musing over my country's difficulties with France." He swallowed and began afresh. "Perhaps you might remember that I was looking for an estate to gift my daughter upon her marriage. The nobleman to whom she is engaged has no hope of claiming his father's title and, for that reason, has decided to venture to the Carolinas where his youngest brother has settled. I would have visited you sooner about this matter, but, as I discovered, you've been out of the way for quite some time, sir, and I haven't been able to make it to your shipping company as I had hoped. Might you be able to help me in my endeavor?"

"Why don't you come around to my shipping company on the morrow," Jeff suggested. "I could take you over then and introduce you to some men who'd have more knowledge of properties that are presently available in the area."

"Of course, Mr. Birmingham. As for this evening, would you and your wife consider being my guests for dinner? I should be honored by your company."

"Thank you, my lord, most kindly, but I was actually looking forward to enjoying some privacy with my wife while we dine."

"Oh, of course, how stupid of me." The Englishman rose hastily to his feet, more than a little offended by his host's rejection. "I shall endeavor to enjoy my dinner just as well alone."

Raelynn grimaced slightly as she watched the man stalk pompously away. "I think you angered him, Jeffrey."

Her husband glanced toward the rapidly departing figure. "I really didn't want our evening ruined by his presence. Had he invited us some days ago, I would've been inclined to accept his invitation, but I wasn't especially fond of the way he imposed himself upon us tonight."

"You probably won't be seeing him again," she warned.

Jeff lifted his shoulders in an indolent shrug. "Matters not a whit to me, madam. His title carries little weight here in the Carolinas, and I need not feel obliged to kowtow to his wishes just because he's a lord." Reaching across, he plucked free a curling wisp of hair that had found its way into her banded collar. Smiling, he rubbed the strand between his thumb and forefinger, admiring its silken texture. "Like I told him, my dear, I was looking forward to enjoying your company entirely alone."

Warmed by the deep huskiness of his voice, Raelynn felt as if she were melting from the inside out. Espying the curl twined through his fingers, she swept it upward out of his grasp as she tried to smooth her hair. "I must look a sight with my hair falling where it wills."

"Aye, madam, that you do," Jeff murmured and swept smoldering eyes over her face and bodice, drinking in her beauty. It seemed like an eternity since he had last seen her. The lengthy separation certainly wasn't due to some gnawing reluctance to seek her out. On the contrary, he had oftentimes found himself pacing the confines of the townhouse as he tried to remind himself of his goals and bolster his will against an almost overwhelming need to see her. From the very first, it had been his plan to keep his distance for extended periods of time, in so doing allowing her to come to an awareness of what her true feelings were toward him, yet knowing all the while that he was playing a dangerous game of chance wherein he could lose her forever. By dint of will, he had held to his resolve, but the lengthy wait had made him unwilling to accept *any* infringement, even by an English lord.

Dinner was exceptional, the company more so, but Raelynn's pleasure hit its peak when a small plate of bread pudding, liberally dribbled with chantilly sauce, was placed before her. The combination was no less than heavenly, and with each spoonful, she closed her eyes in sheer exaltation, eliciting chuckles from Jeff, who hadn't been at all desirous of partaking in a dessert. He indulged himself instead in watching the winsome antics of his dazzlingly beautiful, young wife.

"Our baby will be too fat to come into this world, madam, if you continue eating the way you've done tonight," he warned.

She tossed him a coy pout. "You shouldn't tempt me beyond my ability to resist, Jeffrey. This is all your fault. You bring me to a place where every morsel is a delight and then chide me because I make a glutton of myself? I suppose now I'll have to starve tomorrow to make up for tonight."

"Perhaps I should stay away if I'm such a bad influence."

Her expression turned glum. "You've stayed away far too long as it is, Jeffrey. I was beginning to think I would never see you again."

Detecting a telltale quaver in her voice, Jeff allowed himself to savor a measure of hope for their marriage. Nevertheless he spread his hands and gave a convenient excuse. "I'm sorry, madam, but I've been busy."

"Obviously. Too busy to bother yourself about seeing your wife." Raelynn heaved a sigh and pushed away her unfinished dessert, having lost her appetite as well as her elation. Struggling against an overwhelming urge to cry, it was a moment before she gained enough aplomb to glance up at him. "I'm ready to leave now if you're of such a mind."

Immediately Jeff snapped his fingers, gaining the waiter's attention and requested the check. When the man returned, Jeff briefly glanced at the bill and tossed down enough to bring a wide grin to the fellow's lips.

"Thank you, Mr. Birmingham. Thank you very much."

Soon Jeff was escorting his wife outside. Just beyond the door, he paused to snuggle the cape up close around her neck before he glanced around at the wall of fog surrounding them. It had definitely thickened, to the degree that he couldn't see much beyond the length of his own arm.

"This reminds me of London," Raelynn commented with a shiver.

"I'm glad I know the area well. This stuff is as dense as the chantilly sauce you just had with your bread pudding."

Jeff drew her arm through his and strolled along the boardwalk at a leisurely pace. Now and then footfalls seemed to echo back at them as they passed other busy restaurants and coffeehouses. Once they had left that particular area behind them, Jeff paused to listen for a brief moment and then began to quicken his pace.

"Jeffrey, why are we walking so fast?" Raelynn asked, having difficulty keeping up. His legs were much too long for her to hope to keep up with his long strides. "I'm going to be winded by the time we reach the next block."

"We're almost to the corner," he encouraged, unrelenting of his long strides.

Raelynn strained to see through the whitish murk, but it seemed like a wall now encompassed them. "Are you sure?"

"Aye, madam. Trust me." They reached the division just as he had said. Raelynn almost stepped into the street, but Jeff snatched her back against him. As she turned to inquire as to his reason, he pressed his fingers against her lips, urging her to be silent. Leaning down, he pressed his face near her ear. "There's a wagon coming up behind us. Can you hear anything else?"

Canting her head to listen, Raelynn recognized the jangle of harnesses from the approaching wagon and, on the cobblestones, the slow clip-clop of horses' hooves. Did she also hear hurrying footfalls following behind them? Or was that merely an illusion created by the fog?

She became aware of Jeff's distraction and, in heightening dread, moved closer. The driver of the wagon had set his steed to a faster trot and came at a fairly good clip around the corner where they stood, paying no heed to them as he nudged the horse with the end of his whip.

When the vehicle had finally passed, Jeff clamped an arm around Raelynn's waist and wrenched a gasp from her as he lifted her off her feet and sprinted across the street. Once there, he pushed her back against the wall and braced himself in front of her as running footfalls rapidly approached them. Out of the hazy shroud, a tall, ominously hooded figure seemed to soar toward them on the wings of a widely flapping cloak, setting the eerie vapors aswirl. As he advanced, this darkly shrouded demon from hell lifted a large, gleaming blade high above his head and, with a strange hissing sound, charged her husband.

Raelynn's scream quickly faded in the thick, dank air, but Jeff was just as nimble as his attacker. Stepping forward to meet him, he grasped the other's wrist and wrenched it behind the fellow's back, evoking a sharp yowl of pain from him before the blade clattered to the ground. The devilish fiend twisted free and, thrusting a hard elbow into Jeff's midsection, drove that one back against the brick building. Jeff barely had time to recover his breath before a backhanded blow slammed him once more against the wall, momentarily stunning him. The cloaked one scurried to fetch the knife and was just reaching for it when Raelynn snatched the long, ornate stickpin out of her cap and went flying toward him. It had become frighteningly clear that their assailant's intention was to kill either one or both of them, but she wouldn't take what he was dealing out without handing out some of her own.

Her forward charge gave her impetus, and the pin sank to the tip of its ornate hilt into the fleshy part of the man's buttock, tearing a scream from the fellow and bringing him abruptly upright. Now incensed, he whirled upon her with knife in hand, his breath slashing outward through the holes of his hood.

"Your end has finally come, bitch!" he hissed. "After tonight, we'll have no more worries about what you may find."

Having shaken free of his daze, Jeff recognized the threat to his wife and sprang upward from a crouch, hitting the culprit squarely beneath the ribs with a well-muscled shoulder and driving him back upon the cobblestones. Immediately a fierce scuffle ensued for possession of the knife as Raelynn circled them, watching for an opening to lodge her stickpin once again into their attacker.

Intent upon their struggle for survival, none of them

noticed the approach of swiftly running footfalls until a loud bellow boomed through the fog, "What the hell's going on here?"

Instantly Jeff recognized the voice as one belonging to a friend. "Rhys! Help us!"

Though Jeff reached out to seize the cloaked form, the man clasped the butt of his knife and brought it around with a powerful sweep of his arm, striking Jeff's chin and sending him flying backward into the lamppost. His head hit the metal pole, and he slithered unconscious to its base.

Espying Raelynn near at hand, the villain flipped the knife around in his gloved hand and stepped toward her as he lifted the weapon high for a downward thrust into her breast. She screamed in terror, but in the next instant a shot from an exploding pistol sent the blade flying out of the hooded one's hand. The scream that tore free from the assailant's lungs was enough to cause Raelynn to cringe. The hooded one grabbed his now bleeding hand, looked at her as if considering another attempt, and then swung his attention around to bear upon the sheriff who was just raising the sights of a second pistol. The cloaked man promptly got down to the business of escaping down the street. Rhys gave chase, leaving Raelynn to look after her husband. A moan of despair escaped her as she gathered his head into her lap and, with the skirt of her gown, wiped away the blood that trickled down his forehead.

Several moments passed before Sheriff Rhys Townsend came back and collapsed to his knees beside Jeff. There he sat, gasping for breath. "The beggar's fast. Outran me in a wink," he explained, breathing hard from his exertion. Looking up at Raelynn, he found tears streaming down her face and hurried to soothe her fears. "Don't you cry now. Jeff has a head as hard as granite."

Even so, he pressed a pair of fingers alongside his friend's throat and was quickly reassured by the slow, steady pulse. Turning on a knee, Rhys pressed those same two digits into his mouth and gave forth with a piercing whistle, wrenching a start from Raelynn. Soon the same horse-drawn wagon that had passed them earlier emerged from the fog. Upon halting beside them, the brawny driver peered down at them.

"Ye got a wounded man there, Sheriff?"

"Yeah, Charlie, help me get Mr. Birmingham loaded in the wagon."

"Ye want me ta drive him all the way out ta Oakley?" the driver queried worriedly.

"No," Raelynn answered for the sheriff. "You can take him to Mrs. Dalton's house, and then, if you'd be so kind, I'd appreciate it if you'd fetch Dr. Clarence for him."

20 ∽

"*G*ood heavens, Raelynn," her employer exclaimed after swinging open the front door of Elizabeth's modest house and finding his newest assistant leading an unusual procession. Close upon her heels came the bewhiskered deputy who had each of Jeff's knees tucked through his elbows. The sheriff followed, having locked his own arms across their friend's chest from behind. The way the unconscious man's head was lolling against Rhys's chest, Farrell wasn't at all sure if Jeffrey was alive or dead. "What the devil happened?"

Stepping aside, Raelynn allowed the two men to precede her as she worriedly supplied the information. "Jeffrey and I were attacked, and in the scuffle Jeffrey was thrown against a lamppost. He hit his head and has been unconscious ever since."

Subduing the urge to burst into frightened tears, Raelynn rushed after Rhys, who by then was closely following his deputy up the stairs. She regained enough control over herself to call after them in a steady voice, "My bedroom is upstairs and to the left."

Once they reached the door to her bedchamber, she swung it open and ran ahead to whip down the covers on the bed. After spreading a clean linen protectively over the pillow, she stood aside as the men eased their burden back upon the bed.

"Careful now," she urged, hovering near. Her husband was so tall that his hair brushed the headboard and the soles of his boots pressed against the footboard. Until now, she had been of a mind to think that it was a fairly large bed. It had certainly seemed enormous when she had huddled in it in lonely solitude.

Pausing to catch his breath, Rhys finally instructed his deputy. "Go fetch Doc Clarence, and be quick about it."

As the man scampered out, Elizabeth came to the door with Farrell and asked solicitously, "What can I do to help?"

Raelynn faced the woman, thankful for her offer. "Dr. Clarence will likely be needing bandages after he closes the gash on Jeffrey's head. If you possibly have some clean linens that have outserved their usefulness, Tizzy can tear them up into bandages."

"No need to wake Tizzy," Elizabeth rejoined. "I can do that easily enough. It won't take me any time at all."

The brunette promptly left, and in her absence, Farrell approached the bed and gestured to the sheriff who stood on the far side. "Jeffrey will be more comfortable without his clothes, Rhys. Help me strip him."

As the men lent themselves to that particular task, Raelynn poured water into the washbasin and placed the bowl on the bedside table. Then she went downstairs to fetch some medicinal herbs and ointments from Elizabeth. By the time Raelynn returned to the room, Jeffrey had been disrobed and covered with a sheet and a blanket.

Farrell sought some answers as she gently cleansed the gash in her husband's head. "Who did this thing, Rae-lynn? Do you know?"

"I haven't a clue to the man's identity." Her voice shook as she described his appearance. "Our attacker was fully cloaked and had a black hood over his head. He spoke, but in a low, rasping hiss that seemed strangely exaggerated. He seemed tall, maybe Jeffrey's height or even taller."

"He outdistanced me in short order," Rhys interjected from the chair into which he had settled. "Leads me to think the man not only has a lengthy stride, but long enough legs to lend him a definite advantage over most men. I have a feeling he enjoys running, because when he got to a safe distance ahead of me, he turned and taunted me about my inability to keep up. Then he said, 'You young men have no heart to run fast.'"

"Doesn't sound like Fridrich or Hyde," Farrell concluded.

"No, this man was much taller than either of them, and if he called me young, then I would assume Hyde would be but a babe to him."

"But why did he attack Jeff and Raelynn?" the coutu-rier pressed.

Raelynn gained their full attention by offering a sup-position of her own. "I may be mistaken, but I have a feeling the man's real intent was to kill me."

"You? But why?" Farrell demanded.

She lifted her shoulders in a diffident shrug. If indeed she had been the principal target, the supposition that her husband might have suffered once again because of her offered little comfort. "I haven't the faintest idea. When the man first threatened me with his knife, he told me that my end had come and . . .I remember this part distinctly . . . he said, 'After tonight, we'll have no more worries about what you may find.' When he said that, he had every hope of killing me."

"He was certainly trying to accomplish that very thing when I shot the knife out of his hand," Rhys affirmed.

"Actually that was the second time he tried to knife me. When the man initially launched his attack, he seemed resolute about killing Jeffrey, but it just might have been that demon's way of removing obstacles to get to me. In any case, Jeffrey and I will have to be far more wary of venturing out along dark, lonely streets until our assailant is caught."

"Excuse me for asking," Rhys said a bit hesitantly. "I know he's supposed to be your uncle, but by any chance, could it have been Cooper Frye who did this thing?"

"No, I'm certain of that," Raelynn replied with confidence. "Cooper Frye is much heavier and a lot clumsier than our attacker. And if it's any relief to you, I don't consider him any uncle of mine."

"Aye, I remember you telling me that once, but I didn't know if you had possibly changed your mind since then," Farrell replied.

When Elizabeth returned with the newly made bandages, Dr. Clarence was close upon her heels. After the physician examined Jeff's most recent wound, he rumbled, "Is this some more of Fridrich's doing?"

"No, sir," Raelynn answered in a voice fraught with emotion. "This assailant was infinitely more dangerous than Gustav. He had every intention of killing us and might have succeeded if not for Rhys coming to our rescue."

Dr. Clarence raised his eyes above his spectacles and, fixing them on the sheriff, gave him an appreciative nod. "It's always reassuring when we hear that our lawmen are watching over the people of this fair city. But then, I've never doubted Rhys's dedication to that task."

The sheriff finally offered more insight into his timely

intervention. "My deputy was making his rounds when he espied a cloaked form following the Birminghams. He immediately came back to fetch me, but Charlie got turned around in the fog and couldn't locate them immediately. I struck out on foot, leaving Charlie to search elsewhere with the wagon."

"Charlie likely saved Jeffrey's life," the doctor replied. "If he hadn't been so wary, you'd probably never have found them in time, and Jeff would be dead now."

"And Raelynn," Rhys added and, when the old man's bushy eyebrows jutted upward in surprise, went on to explain, "The assailant tried to take her life, too. I shot a knife out of his hand during one attack, but Raelynn has just informed me that was his second attempt." The lawman shrugged. "I don't know if my shot wounded the man that seriously, but just in case, be on the lookout for anyone who might come to you or some other doctor sporting a hand wound."

"I'll spread the word around, but the scoundrel may well tend his hand himself. Something more serious might have brought the cad in screaming for us to save his life."

When Dr. Clarence finished wrapping a bandage around his patient's head, he concluded soberly, "There's nothing more now that can be done. 'Twill only be a matter of waiting to see if Jeffrey regains consciousness. He has had a hard blow to the head and is likely suffering a concussion. Hopefully, it's only a mild one if he is, but in any case, he may be out for a while. Once he comes to, he'll be inclined to think the top of his head is about to come off, but, with due rest, the headaches should eventually ease . . . at least that's my hope." He faced Raelynn and lifted a crooked finger as he instructed her. "If you can, keep Jeffrey in bed. Don't let him chase after your attacker as he did with Gustav, and *don't* be taking him to Oakley where I can't reach him in time if something happens. If Elizabeth doesn't object, let him stay just where he is. Give him plenty of water to drink. If the pain becomes too intense, slip him a little laudanum that I've left on the table there, but mind you, girl, not too much."

"I understand, Dr. Clarence," she answered mutedly. "I really appreciate the fact that you came out to tend him." She moved toward the chest where she had left her handbag. "If you'll wait just a moment, I'll pay you."

The physician held up a hand to halt her attempt. "No, child. Jeffrey can do that once he's on his feet again. I don't take payment until I know I've helped someone." He waved farewell. "I can see myself out."

The sheriff hefted his bulk out of his chair. "Charlie and I will take you back, Doc."

The physician paused in the doorway. "Thanks, Rhys. My eyes don't work as well at night as they used to, and most definitely not in this blasted fog."

Rhys followed Dr. Clarence out, but as Farrell moved to the door, he paused to speak with Raelynn. "Jeffrey requires your attention here, so you needn't worry about coming to work in the morning. As much as I may need your help at the shop right now, I'd feel a far sight better knowing you're taking care of him."

"Thank you, Farrell. So would I." Choking up, she turned aside to hide the tears that promptly sprang forth. Her voice was heavily imbued with misery as she added, "Even if I went to work, I wouldn't be able to concentrate while fretting about Jeffrey. I pray no real harm has been done."

"Shh, don't cry, Raelynn. Jeffrey is going to be just fine," Farrell murmured consolingly, laying a gentle hand upon her shoulder. He sincerely hoped what he predicted would come to fruition and that he wasn't just letting his confidence in his friend's unswerving tenacity cloud his thinking. "There's not much that can keep your husband down. I know that from experience. We've been friends too long for me to doubt his fortitude. Why, he'll likely be hale and hearty on the morrow."

Raelynn sniffed and, with a dainty handkerchief, hastily swiped at the wetness trailing down her cheeks. "I hope so," she muttered thickly, finding it difficult to speak. "I know my heart would surely die should he succumb."

"You don't have to fret about any of that. Jeffrey's not going to die. And right now, you're the best balm for him. So stay and take care of him."

A wavering sigh escaped her lips as she turned to him. "I wish now that I would have stuck a knife instead of a hatpin into our assailant's behind."

Farrell blinked in confusion as he sought to assimilate her statement in the realm of what a proper young lady would do under similar circumstances. "Excuse me, Raelynn. Perhaps my ears were playing tricks on me. Could you repeat that again?"

Her cheeks reddened beneath his inquisitorial regard. "Never mind, Farrell. It was nothing of any great import."

"But you said something about sticking a hatpin in your attacker's backside," the couturier pressed, his lips curving teasingly.

Mortified, she beseeched him, "Please don't tell anyone."

Laughter invaded his voice as he denied her request. "Oh, but, Raelynn, this is too humorous to keep a secret. I commend you for your spirit." Obviously this was one lady who had enough grit to help her man out when he was in danger. "Not many women would have resorted to that precise method of revenge, but take heart. Only our closest friends will know. Now, if you'll excuse me, I must go down and catch Dr. Clarence before he leaves. 'Twill do the old man good to hear about this. He'll surely laugh over it all the way home."

Raelynn responded with a mutinous pout. "Looks like you're making every effort to be our next town crier."

"Most assuredly, madam, most assuredly," Farrell managed through his guffaws.

Raelynn felt like slamming the door behind him, but she dared not, for fear of discomforting Jeffrey with the noise. Instead, she quietly closed the portal and began to undress. Perhaps it was foolishness on her part, but she donned her prettiest nightgown, a garment that she hadn't worn since leaving Oakley. Heaving a disconcerted sigh, she turned the wick down in the lamp until the room was once again entirely enclosed in a flinty blackness. Then she crawled beneath the covers.

For a time she lay upon her back, staring toward the ceiling through the ebon darkness as she struggled to subdue an urge to snuggle against her husband. It soon proved a temptation she could not resist. Turning on her side, she pressed close against his long, male form and, as had once been her wifely custom, lifted a sleek limb to rest across his hardened thighs. Her fingers swept upward along a corded arm, across a shoulder, and brushed a male nipple all but hidden amid crisp, black hair. His breathing remained unchanged, and she grew bolder still, slipping a hand downward over his taut, flat belly until she took possession of the torpid fullness.

If she had held aspirations of awakening her husband from his stupor in such a manner, then Raelynn quickly realized that such an idea was no less than foolish. Heretofore, even from the deepest sleep, Jeff had always awakened fully roused in response to her explorations. But that was too much to expect in his present state. His mind was held bound in a place where it couldn't be reached, and that worried her exceedingly.

A sudden trembling took possession of her as she became inundated with all the heart-rendering possibilities. He might die, he might never wake from his stupor, he might become a raving lunatic . . . and on and on and on.

"Enough of this!" Raelynn hissed angrily in the impenetrable gloom. "My husband will live! He *must* live!"

∽SHE WAS A CHILD AGAIN. THE TALL, GLASS-PANED doors of her father's study stood open just behind her, and in the enveloping serenity of the carefully tended garden, she could hear her parents' muted voices, comfortably close, drifting out to the marble step where she sat playing with her dolls. Nearby birds were flitting from bush to tree, well out of the reach of her cat, Mischief, who cocked its head curiously as it watched them intently.

Gathering her dolls in her arms, she tottered out across the granite terrace. Mischief followed along beside her, playfully pouncing here and there, fiercely attacking some leaf or bug it found along the way. The path led to a stone bench residing in a restful spot under a tree, and she crawled upon it to play. She called for her cat, wanting to dress it in doll's clothes, but Mischief wouldn't come. Sliding off the bench, she tottered along the lane, following to where she had last seen the fuzzy animal. Just ahead of her loomed the lofty, ornate wrought-iron gate that bordered her family's property. There was something behind it, something she especially sought. But what?

The gate was unlocked; it squeaked open as she pressed her face between the bars. With an elated laugh she dashed through and found herself in another garden. A butterfly fluttered past. She lifted her hand and ran after it. Bejeweled with color, it soared very high and swooped just as low, but always just out of the reach of her fingertips.

A deep voice, laden with laughter, came from nearby. "You'll never catch them like that, little miss."

She turned, meeting emerald eyes and a grin that

awed her. Entranced by the black-haired young man, she approached and leaned her head far back to meet his smiling gaze. Like the gate, he loomed so tall above her that he seemed to reach to the sky.

"Here now, let's get you home before your parents come looking for you." Strong arms swung her up and settled her onto his shoulder. Her perch was so high she squealed in fright and grasped a handful of his hair for security, but his hand held her tightly as he strolled along toward her home.

It began to rain again, a gentle misting rain that dampened her curls and the black hair through which her fingers were entangled.

DRIFTING UPWARD FROM HER DREAMS, RAELYNN became vaguely aware of a large hand searching upward beneath her nightgown. She thought she was still dreaming until her thighs were gently urged apart and the explorations deepened. Her heart soared with joyful relief as gentle fingers moved with tantalizing slowness over her softly swelling flesh, eliciting within her womanly being a quickening excitement.

Nothing but total darkness greeted her when she turned her head on the pillow. "Jeffrey?"

"Aye, madam," a familiar male voice answered huskily. "I'm here."

"How do you feel?"

"Horny."

She giggled. "I was talking about your head."

"I wasn't." He patted upward in search of her hand and, drawing it downward, enclosed it over the engorged flesh.

"I see what you mean," she crooned, nuzzling his neck. "You feel very nice . . . very warm, in fact."

"So do you," he breathed as his long fingers continued to ply her silken flesh, "but you have too many damned clothes on for my liking."

Raelynn readily sat up and shifted from hip to hip as she dislodged the tail of her nightgown. Whisking the garment up over her body, she dragged it off her head and, with an outward sweep of her arm, banished it into the sea of blackness beyond the bed.

"Better," her husband muttered against her throat after resetting her close against him. Her fingers threaded through the hair at his nape as his lips traced downward, and he heard her gasp in delight as his open mouth found a nipple. Hungrily he devoured the soft peaks, tasting their sweet nectar, licking, teasing, evoking small, quickening tremors that seemed to shake her whole body.

Jeff braced on an elbow above her, prompting Raelynn to complain, "This bed squeaks, and Elizabeth's bedroom is just down the hall. What if she hears us?"

"Elizabeth is a widow, my sweet," he breathed, in the dark void searching out her mouth with his own and murmuring against it. "She'll understand a husband's need after so long a wait."

Raelynn curled her tongue into his consuming mouth, sliding it over, around and under his in a slow, sensual dance, all the while tasting the essence of the wine he had earlier quaffed. She turned upon her side to face him and mentally groaned when the bed protested her movement. She retreated from his kiss to ask, "How can I face Elizabeth on the morrow, knowing she'll likely be aware of what we're doing together tonight?"

Jeff sighed in frustration and sank back upon his pillow. The heavy draperies were tightly closed over the windows, forbidding even a minuscule ray of moonlight to penetrate the sooty darkness. It was impossible for him to see his wife's face, and he had no way of telling whether this was a true concern she voiced or nothing more than a lame attempt to reject his advances. "Do you want me to stop, Raelynn?"

"No! Never!" she whispered emphatically, lifting a leg over his hip. Her heel pressed between his buttocks as she anchored her now vulnerable softness against the lengthy shaft. "I want you! I want to be your wife, your lover, your mate for life. I want to feel you inside me, to be one with you, to bear your children, to possess you as you possess me, to touch you as often as I wish, and to feel you quicken in my grasp. I need you, Jeffrey, most desperately."

She slipped a hand downward between them and, in a fierce grip, closed it over the manly flesh, causing Jeff to catch his breath at the sweet, brutal intensity of her possession. Her open mouth teased his in provocative invitation as she began a slow, methodical seduction upon his body, plying every skill he had taught her until the warm flesh was nearly throbbing for want of more. Indeed, it was all Jeff could do to keep himself from being swept away by his growing ardor as she worked her will upon him.

His lips merged with hers in a rapacious kiss that soon had them straining against each other. His hand returned to her womanly softness and found no resisting barrier, only a wifely eagerness to accept his intrusion and to comply with his rutting urges. Soon she was arching her back, thrusting her breasts upward as an offering, and nearly writhing with the ecstasy of the tumult he created within her as he teased the sensitive swell and, with slow, purposeful deliberation, caressed the silken flesh.

"Oh, I've missed you so much," she gasped in a whisper, unable to bear the rushing excitement another moment without feeling him inside of her. Rising above him, she guided the hardened shaft into the moist cleft and settled down upon him, sucking in her breath at the heady bliss that began sweeping upward from the core of her being. Lifting her face to bask in this all-consuming ecstasy, she paused in quiescent stillness to luxuriate in the feeling of being one with him. She felt his long, beautiful hands moving over her naked body with mesmerizing slowness, but ever so much more pleasurable was the stirring warmth of him deep within her.

"You feel even nicer than I remember," she crooned, sweeping her hands upward over his chest.

"You can sit upon my lap any hour or day you have a mind to, my sweet," he replied huskily.

She brought his hands up to her breasts and pressed the fullness into his encompassing palms, nearly shivering in delight as his thumbs thrummed across her nipples. Rising up from his pillow, Jeff buried his face between her breasts as he clasped the soft orbs tightly against his lean cheeks. In the next moment he became like a man driven by an insatiable desire, with predacious greed taking each nipple in turn into the warm, moist cavern of his mouth. Her slender fingers kneaded his shoulders as her hips began to move with slow, undulating strokes. Then his hands were clasping her buttocks, giving her driving momentum as he pressed her down upon the hardened shaft. A soft moan escaped her lips as his throbbing warmth began to surge upward within her, and she began to shudder as waves of bliss began to wash over her. Vaguely she was aware of the bed protesting their movements, yet there was no stopping now. Darkness became infused with myriad flashes of light that seemed to burst all around them, exploding in sharpening, scintillating ecstasy as they soared far beyond the galaxy into another universe entirely.

Reality came winging slowly back, well after their awe over what they had just experienced together began to wane. They lay side by side, their fingers entwined, his knee bent and tucked beneath her thighs, her head resting upon his stalwart shoulder.

"I love you," Raelynn whispered.

Jeffrey lay as if frozen, hardly able to believe what he had just heard.

"And I've missed you so very, very much."

"Will you come back to live with me at Oakley?"

"Oh, yes, just as soon as you're able."

"I'm able now, madam."

Rolling toward him, Raelynn laid an arm about him and rubbed her nose against his corded neck. "Dr. Clarence said you shouldn't be moved right now."

"I can move myself," Jeff protested.

"Nevertheless, we'll remain here until I know for certain you won't suffer any repercussions after being waylaid."

"It was that damned post that waylaid me!" he argued.

Raelynn giggled. "Now that you've become my captive, dear husband, I don't intend to let you go. You'll serve my purposes here in this bed until you can't wield your little finger much less anything else."

Jeff grinned into the blackness looming over them. For a man who had oft been teased about his backbone of steel, he gave in to his wife's coercion with an alacrity that evidenced his eagerness to submit himself entirely to everything she threatened and a lot more besides. "We could stay for a day or two, at least until we've entirely exhausted this poor bed. Indeed, by the time we're finished with it, Elizabeth will be of a mind to buy another."

His wife snuggled contentedly beneath his arm. "I thought you'd eventually reconsider."

For another half hour or so their silence remained unbroken, allowing Raelynn's eyelids to sag closed.

"Raelynn?"

Drowsily she stirred against her husband, making every effort to open her eyes. "Yes, Jeffrey?"

"I love you, too." He waited for an interminable length of time, listening for some response. He hardly expected to hear a tearful sniffle. Rising above her, he pressed his hand gently alongside her cheek and, feeling the moisture trailing down it, asked in amazement, "Are you crying, madam?"

"Yes," she choked through gathering tears.

"But why?"

"Because I'm so happy."

Jeff fell back upon his pillow, dumbstruck by the oddity of her declaration. Would he *ever* understand this beautiful creature he had married well enough to recognize the difference between weeping for joy and crying in sorrow?

—"OH, ELIZABETH, I'M SO VERY HAPPY FOR YOU," Raelynn assured the woman in her kitchen on Saturday morning a pair of days later. Raelynn felt especially honored that the dark-haired beauty had thought enough of her to give her the news before revealing to another soul the fact that she and Farrell would be getting married. Already Raelynn was beginning to consider Elizabeth as dear a friend as her own sister-in-law, Heather. "Have you given him a date?"

"No, not as yet. I had to discuss it with Jake first. He really likes Farrell, but one can never predict how boys will react when their mothers decide to remarry, especially when they're only four, but I'm hoping we can be wed fairly soon. We've spent all this time apart, thinking the other didn't care. It's time we made up for all the lost years."

Elizabeth was even more convinced of that particular rationale after waking several times to the distant, rhythmic squeaking of her guests' bed. Suffering through those titillating episodes with a heightening perception of her own cravings had made her yearn for instant appeasement, and she had wondered how best to approach Farrell about the matter. Although he had said it would be up to her to set a date, he hadn't made any mention of that since. Presently she was of a mind to think that they shouldn't plan anything at all, just simply get married, but as yet, she hadn't gotten up enough nerve to suggest a hasty wedding.

"We want it be a private affair, just intimate friends, you understand. Farrell holds Jeffrey in the highest esteem and will want him to stand up for him as best man, and, of course, I'll want you as my maid of honor."

"I'd be delighted," Raelynn answered happily. Perhaps she was coming to know Elizabeth as well as she knew herself, but she sensed her friend wasn't entirely comfortable with the delay. Mentally acknowledging the possibility that she was being tempted to speak out of hand, Raelynn bit her lip and almost refrained from doing so. Still, the woman's distant expression led her to be bolder. "Elizabeth, do you really want to spend all that time planning a wedding when you and Farrell could be enjoying marriage tonight?"

Elizabeth gave a little groan as she collapsed into a chair at the kitchen table. "How in the world can I tell Farrell that I want to be married right away?"

"Don't you think he's eager for that, too? I've seen the way he looks at you, as if he could devour you half a room away. If you'd like, when Jeffrey wakes up, I could ask him if he'd talk to Farrell about moving ahead with the wedding."

"Are Jeffrey's headaches easing any?"

"The laudanum helps him sleep through them, but I have to slip it to him in his food. Otherwise he'd be as stubborn as an old bull about taking it. He was in such intense agony this morning, he barely got his breakfast down. I mixed some of the laudanum in his eggs, and I had to threaten to sleep on the couch before he'd finish them, so don't pay him any mind if he complains about your cooking. We're hoping to go home tomorrow, but we'll just have to wait and see if Jeffrey is up to the drive. He has been sleeping so much after his injury, there's no telling how he'll feel once he gets on his feet again."

"I'll miss you."

Raelynn gave her a puckish grin. "Not if Farrell is in your bed."

Elizabeth pressed slender fingers to her lips in an effort to subdue her amusement and then cast a shining glance askance at her friend as she flipped the end of a dishtowel toward her. "You should be ashamed of yourself, suggesting such a thing."

Raelynn chuckled, feeling incredibly happy now that she and Jeff were together again. "I may be married, Elizabeth, but I'm certainly not blind. Farrell is as nicely proportioned and handsome as my own Jeffrey."

The brunette was in full agreement and was led to recall an incident that even now brought a vivid blush to her cheeks. It was odd the freedom she felt with Raelynn, as if she could tell her *anything* without being condemned. "Aye, there have been many times when I've caught myself thinking how handsome he is, and yet I was afraid of being around him. I certainly didn't want to find myself acting like some of those addlepated fillies who'd come into the shop just to gawk at him. I had my chance at doing that very same thing about six months ago when I went up to Farrell's apartment to tidy up. At the time, I was under the impression that he had gone out for an appointment with a textile merchant, but I soon learned the hard way that the meeting had been canceled. The door of Farrell's bathing chamber was standing open, and I entered without realizing he was at home. He was just stepping out of the tub, reaching for a towel when I barged in. I was so astounded, I couldn't move. I just gaped at him."

If Elizabeth's cheeks weren't hot enough, they fairly flamed as she confessed, "My late husband didn't have much to sport with in bed, but I was an innocent and didn't know . . . ah . . . that some men have more in their breeches. I finally collected enough of my wits to flee, and though I later got up some gumption to apologize for my intrusion, Farrell was gentlemanly enough to brush it aside and say that it was all his fault for not warning me that he was there when it was my normal cleaning day. He acted as if nothing untoward had happened. Yet to this day, I haven't been able to forget that morning."

Raelynn grinned back at her. "Which is only one more reason you shouldn't delay your marriage. If you do, you both may find yourselves in bed together, and think of the eyebrows that would raise if anyone found out."

"Mama! Mama!" Jake cried, running into the kitchen where the two women had been icing a cake. "There's a mean-looking man standin' in front o' our gate."

Elizabeth and Raelynn faced each other in sudden alarm, both suffering sudden apprehensions that another assailant had come. Elizabeth hurriedly pushed herself to her feet while Raelynn caught up her skirts and dashed toward the front of the house.

"Gustav!" Raelynn gasped upon arriving at the front window and peering through the lace panel. The German stood before the gate with a bouquet of flowers clasped in his good hand.

Elizabeth groaned. "I think Mr. Fridrich has come courting." There was more concern in her tone than the like of such a simple declaration might normally have elicited. She beckoned Jake to her and immediately gave him instructions. "Go upstairs and tell Tizzy to run over and fetch Mr. Farrell, and to be quick about it!"

"Yes'm," the boy hurriedly replied and charged out of the hall, his high-topped shoes nearly flying over the rugs in his haste to comply.

Raelynn clasped a shaking hand to her throat as she watched Gustav swing open the gate, step through, and then pause to pull it closed behind him. "What should we do? He's coming in."

Trembling, Elizabeth grasped Raelynn's arm. "I have Emory's flintlock upstairs." She could issue nothing louder than a strained whisper. "I could hold him off until Farrell comes."

"Do you have it in you to shoot a man?" Raelynn glanced at her worriedly.

Elizabeth made a lame attempt to appear confident about performing such a task, but had to confess, "I've never had the need."

"Get it," Raelynn urged, trying hard to keep her teeth from chattering. "Knowing what the man is capable of if he isn't stopped, I think I could do it."

Gustav had gained the front porch by the time Elizabeth arrived back with the pistol. She passed it to Raelynn who immediately looked it over in some confusion.

"How can you tell if it's loaded?"

"At least *I* know that much," Elizabeth chided, grabbing it out of her friend's hands. "I loaded it before I came down here. Now get behind the door where he can't see you. Perhaps he'll go away and leave us alone if I discourage him."

Upon stepping near the portal, Gustav tucked the spray of flowers within the crook of his useless arm before reaching out to knock. Only after doing so did he take his hat off, set it aside on a porch chair and retrieve the colorful cluster within his grasp.

Cautiously Elizabeth swept the pistol behind her skirts before she reached out and swung the door open. Forcing a smile, she met the man's unwavering ice-blue gaze and felt a cold shiver sweep through her. "Mr. Fridrich, I believe," she said, her tone unusually high. Lifting a hand, she indicated the nosegay and cleared her throat before making another attempt to speak. "To what do we owe this occasion?"

"I haf come to present my respects to *Frau* Birmingham," he announced officiously.

"Is she expecting you?" Elizabeth inquired impertinently.

"I vish to speak vith her." Gustav thrust his chin outward briefly as his eyes glinted with icy shards. "Fetch her for me."

"I'm not sure that Mrs. Birmingham wants to see you," Elizabeth boldly stated. She thought perhaps if she could just stop shaking, she'd get through this thing without revealing just how frightened she really was. "After all, you did kidnap her from her husband's home. How do we know that you won't try something like that again?" Elizabeth had noticed the pale blue eyes hardening progressively, but she was hardly prepared for his roaring bellow, which drew a sudden start from her.

"Get zhe *Frau* Birmingham before I lose patience vith yu, yu stupid woman! Get her now!"

In the face of such flaring rage, Elizabeth retreated precipitously until she collided with Raelynn, who had come out of hiding. The resulting collision promptly sent the brunette stumbling forward again. Managing to stiffen her resolve as well as her spine, Elizabeth opened her mouth to speak and found to her abashment that her voice had fled. She cleared her throat sharply and tried once more. "Mr. Fridrich, I will allow no man to shout at me in my own home. Calmly restrain yourself or I shall have you removed posthaste."

The German smirked at such a silly notion. "Who vill do zhat task for yu, *Frau* Dalton? Zhe man of zhe house?"

"Possibly," a male voice boomed behind the women, startling a gasp from each. Striding forward to the door, Farrell stepped past Elizabeth and nearly filled the modest doorway as he faced the German and settled his arms akimbo. Though Farrell hadn't competed in a boxing tournament in more than six years, he had nevertheless kept in prime condition sparring with his friends and was confident that he could send this arrogant intruder flying without undue effort if worse came to worst. "What do you want this time, Fridrich?"

When Jake had heard the strange man yelling at his mother, he had scurried behind a chair where he had then crouched in trembling fear, but Farrell's presence did much to bolster his courage. Leaving his hiding place, he slipped past their tall protector and proceeded to give the shorter man a swift kick in the shin.

"Go away!" the boy demanded. "We don't like you."

"Yu little guttersnipe!" Gustav railed, sending the boy stumbling backward with widened eyes. "I vill cut yu up into little pieces and feed yur carcass to zhe sharks! Zhey vill gobble yu up as zhey do a tiny morsel."

Reaching out, Farrell laid a comforting hand upon the lad's shoulder and drew him back against his leg. When the youngster glanced up in wide-eyed trepidation, the couturier tousled his sandy hair and grinned down at him. "Don't let that mean old man frighten you, son. Not as long as I'm around."

Whirling, the boy wrapped his arms about Farrell's thigh and held on tightly.

The sound of angry voices had awakened Jeff. Not knowing exactly what was transpiring, he had donned his trousers and hastily made his way down the stairs, bereft of shirt and shoes. When he espied Tizzy nearly jumping up and down in great agitation in the hallway, he inquired, "What's going on out there?"

"It's Mistah Fridrich, Mistah Jeffrey," she hissed furtively and silently pointed toward the front entrance as Jeff strode forward. "He's out dere on de porch, lookin' all spruicified, jes' like some gentlemon caller. Ah 'spect he's done come ta pay court ta Miz Raelynn."

"Oh, he has, has he?" Despite the dull throbbing in his head, Jeffrey was more than willing to deal with this antagonist. It didn't matter that he was insufficiently dressed for the occasion, considering he had nothing more than his trousers on. His fighting spirit was definitely primed. Indeed, he now understood exactly what Brandon had felt like when he had nearly thrashed a man for forcing a kiss upon Heather shortly after Beau was born.

Raelynn caught her husband's arm as he sought to step past her. When he paused and looked down at her, she beseeched him, "Please, Jeffrey, let Farrell handle this. You're in no condition to get into a set-to with Gustav."

Giving her a smile, Jeff took her hand within his grasp and lifted it to his lips for a loving kiss as his eyes melded with hers. "No need to fear, madam. I'll be careful."

Elizabeth backed away to give Jeff room to pass as he neared the door. Farrell caught sight of him out of the corner of his eye and moved out onto the porch, allowing his friend to follow him, but Farrell wasn't about to leave this conflict to be decided by a man who had just suffered a concussion and was barefoot besides.

A thin eyebrow jutted upward as Gustav swept his foe with a sneering perusal. "I zee zhat zhe good sheriff haf not yet zeen fit to do his duty by arresting yu, *Herr* Birmingham. No one had as much reason to kill Nell zhan yu. Once more, everyvone knows she vas killed in yur stables, but here yu are, free as zhe wind. Being friends vith Sheriff Townzend has its rewards, *ja?*"

"And I see that you still have aspirations of claiming my wife for yourself, *Herr* Fridrich. What will it take to convince you that she belongs to me?"

Gustav jeered as his eyes passed derisively over his enemy's long, half-garbed form. Birmingham was not only younger, taller, and more muscular, but also trimmer. It didn't help that the man's waist was lean and taut and bore no evidence of a paunch, a problem he had been battling since the age of a score and ten. "She'll be a vidow fairly soon, *Herr* Birmingham, right after zhey hang yu for killing Nell."

An abortive laugh escaped Jeff. "Don't hold your breath while you're waiting for that event to happen, Fridrich. You could descend into the netherworld before your time."

"It iz yu, *Herr* Birmingham, who vill go to hell, not me! I do not kill anyvone."

"No, you wouldn't soil your clammy white hands doing that kind of dirt. You'd just let your henchmen do it for you. I was told you offered a thousand Yankee dollars to both Hyde and Frye if they'd dispense with me in one way or another so you could have a clear path to my wife. It would be interesting to see which one of your two henchmen killed Nell in an effort to bring that about. Perhaps you were even responsible for the attack upon me the other night." Jeff snorted sneeringly. "Don't be too surprised if Sheriff Townsend comes calling upon you to ask you a few questions about that particular incident. I'd certainly be interested in hearing what you have to say about that myself."

The idea of the sheriff nosing around his warehouse again sent the German into a blustering rage. "I haf done nozhing!"

"You've done plenty," Jeff flung back, "not to mention frightening the women and the boy. In my way of thinking, that's more than enough reason for me to send you on your way."

"I came here to pay court to Raelynn, zhat is all."

"*She's married!*" Jeff barked. "To me! Now get your filthy boots off this porch before I dust its planks with your broad backside!"

The German's upper lip drew up in a caustic sneer. "I'm a patient man vhen I haf to be, Herr Birmingham. I can vait till yu are dead to claim Raelynn for my own, and zhat I vill most assuredly do. As zhey say, I vill have her over yur dead body."

The man chortled at his own humor and then, with another haughty sneer, flung the flowers at Jeff's feet. Snatching up his hat, he settled it upon his bald pate and, pivoting about face, stalked off the porch and down the walk. He didn't bother closing the gate behind him but raised his able arm and hailed a waiting livery down the street. When it halted before him, Gustav climbed onto the step, shook his fist at Jeff for one last time and then settled himself in the interior. The conveyance rumbled past the house, but Gustav glanced neither right nor left.

"I'm glad that's over," Elizabeth sighed in relief, letting the hand clutching the pistol fall to her side.

The two men came inside, and when Farrell caught sight of the flintlock his fiancée held, he lifted her wrist and gently plucked the weapon from her grasp. "You won't need to worry about having to defend your household from now on, madam. If you have no objections, I'm going out right now and find a preacher so the matter of our marriage can be settled once and for all."

An ecstatic cry escaped Elizabeth as she flung herself into his arms. The fact that she nearly choked him in her eagerness drew a strangled chuckle from him.

"Good heavens, woman, let me breathe," he begged.

"Oh, I'm sorry," she whispered in blushing chagrin and stepped back, but only momentarily. Unable to resist the nearness of his lips, she rose to the tips of her toes and brushed a quick, furtive kiss upon them. Then, in some embarrassment at her temerity, she sought to turn aside, but found his hand between her shoulder blades, pressing her against him once more as his mouth descended upon hers. Since his proposal, Farrell had carefully maintained his reserve, knowing only too well that once he started kissing her he'd be tempted to do much more. Only in that way had he persevered through his growing desire for her, but it had hardly prepared him for the tumultuous barrage presently going off within him as their lips merged in fervent hunger.

Jeff cast a twisted grin toward them as Raelynn came into his arms. He was greatly tempted to follow suit, but he had already noticed Tizzy's jaw hanging aslack. No telling where it would be if he kissed his wife with equal fervor.

"I suppose this means that you're in agreement?" the couturier inquired softly as he and his fiancée drew apart.

"Oh, yes, Farrell. Yes! Yes! Yes!" Elizabeth cried exuberantly.

His white teeth gleamed in a broad smile. "Then I'd better be on my way." He placed a lean knuckle beneath her chin and lifted it. "Put on your prettiest gown while I'm gone, my love, and pack up whatever you may need to tide you over for the night. I'm sure Raelynn and Tizzy can watch after Jake until we return on the morrow. As for now, I'll be back as soon as I can."

"But where are we going tonight?"

He winked back at her. "To my apartment, madam, where else?"

Pausing beside Jeff on the way out, he urged, "You'd better get some clothes on if you're going to stand up as my best man, Jeffrey me dearie. I've never gotten married before, so I'm not entirely certain about the normal protocol, but it seems to me that you should be garbed in something more appropriate than just trousers."

Jeff realized of a sudden that his headache was gone. "I'll see what I can do, Fancy Man. You wouldn't happen to have an extra clean shirt at your place, would you?"

Raelynn slipped an arm through his. "No need for that, dear. Tizzy washed and ironed yours. It's upstairs in our room."

"I'm feeling a little woozy." The twin grooves in his cheeks deepened with an unquenchable grin as he offered the excuse. "I think I need some help getting to our room and dressing myself."

Leaning her head upon his shoulder, Raelynn looked up at him with softly glowing eyes. "I suppose I could lend you some assistance if I find that it's warranted. 'Twill hardly be any trouble when I'll be dressing for the occasion, too."

"Yo' gonna need my help, Miz Raelynn?" Tizzy called from the hall.

"Only with my hair, Tizzy. In the meantime, you can lend whatever assistance the bride may require. Miss Elizabeth may enjoy having you arrange her hair especially nice for the ceremony." She glanced at her friend and received an eager nod. Raelynn laughed. "See there, Tizzy, you're in high demand in this house. I'll call you when I'm ready for you."

Raelynn climbed the stairs under her husband's encompassing arm. Once they entered the bedroom upstairs, she was drawn into Jeff's embrace as he leaned back against the door. His kiss was long and thorough, and by the time he let her go, she was feeling a little woozy herself.

"You can't possibly imagine how much I've missed you during our separation, madam," he whispered above her mouth. "I wanted to run to you every day and beg you to come back to me, but I was afraid you'd draw away from me again, just like you did that night at Red Pete's place."

"Oh, Jeffrey, I don't think there was a night during our separation that I didn't cry myself to sleep, worrying about what was happening between us. You seemed so angry because of the doubts I suffered about you, and you had a right to be. I should have believed in your innocence, but I was so confused. On one hand, I was afraid you'd sever our marriage, but on the other, I was haunted by the possibility that you weren't as noble and honorable as you seemed." She laid her palm alongside his cheek. "It seems unthinkable now to imagine that I could truly, deeply love a man who's capable of such a ruthless murder."

"I should have been more patient with you," he

breathed, lowering his opening mouth toward hers. "You had a terrible shock."

"That's all over now," she murmured before his lips covered hers in demanding fervor. Slipping her arms close about his neck, she rose on her toes and strained up against him, aware of his hardening maleness and the hungry throbbing in her own loins. Her nipples grew taut against his steely chest and throbbed for his attention as she pressed ever closer.

"We'd better get dressed, my love," Jeff muttered at last. "Knowing Farrell, he'll be back here in short order, and if we continue with what we're doing, I'm going to make that old bed squeak like it has never squeaked before."

A small, frustrated groan escaped Raelynn as she drew back, but she began unfastening her bodice, at least until her husband pulled her close again and slipped a hand within her chemise. Encompassing a round breast, he stroked a thumb across the softening peak, drawing it up into a tiny nub again. Raelynn smiled up at him questioningly, quite willing to continue the interlude, but when she leaned into him again, he sighed and shook his head.

"Enough of this, woman," he whispered huskily. "If we don't hurry, Farrell will be here pounding on the door."

Though Jeff was feeling in dire need of a deep, warm soak in a large tub, he realized that a basin bath was the only thing he had time for. His muscles were still a bit sore after his confrontation with the masked man, but more than that, he would have enjoyed involving his wife in a good lavation as well. Many times while they were apart, he had reminisced on those moments wherein she had lain back against him in their tub. During their separation that singular, recurring vision had nearly brought him to his knees before her. It was a relief to know there would be more baths in the future to equal those he had stored in his memory.

Raelynn laid out her husband's clothes as he began to bathe and had just settled into a chair to don a pair of stockings when she happened to glance up and found him standing stark naked before the shaving stand. It was a sight that normally awakened her admiration, but today she was especially intrigued. It wasn't long before she had gained Jeff's undivided attention.

"Have you acquired a fetish for my baser parts, madam?" he teased. "Truly, if you stare much longer, I won't be able to hide myself underneath my trousers."

"Jeffrey, how would you compare to other men?"

His brow jutted upward quizzically. "What brought that on?"

"Curiosity." She lifted a grin to him before she raised a leg and smoothed her stocking over her calf. Considering the many explicit conversations they had been involved in, many times after making love, she wasn't the least bit abashed about discussing his manly attributes. During their foreplay he certainly had never displayed any timidity about instructing her in what pleased him or, with rousing dedication, demonstrating the places where she was most sensitive to stimuli. "Well, are you going to tell me?"

Jeff chuckled at his wife's inquisitiveness. "I've never gone around mentally measuring myself against other men, madam, if that's what you mean. That never fell into my realm of interest." Bending closer to the small, round mirror on the shaving stand, Jeff plied the straight-edged razor along his cheek, scraping whiskers away as he did so. After whisking away the last of the white froth, he scrubbed a hand over his face to check for areas still in need of smoothing and then wiped his face with a warm, wet cloth. Finally he tossed a glance toward Rae-lynn and realized from the playfully baleful gleam in her eyes that she was not about to desist until he had completely appeased her curiosity. "All right, my dear. You can sheathe those blue daggers. I'll tell you what I know."

Like a child who had anxiously pleaded for a story, Raelynn scooted up to the edge of her seat and waited, thoroughly captivated with the subject of their conversation. Jeff couldn't help but chuckle as he took pleasure in the utterly fetching sight. She perched like a prim maid on the stool, yet her scanty attire utterly destroyed any idea that she was priggish, for she wore nothing more than a dainty chemise that left her rounded bosom nearly overflowing its shallow bodice and the soft, pale peaks of her breasts straining against the gossamer cloth.

"If only Gustav could see you now, my love. He'd run me through with the nearest sword just to have you for himself."

"Oh, don't mention that cad's name. I dislike him intensely." She lifted a hand and fluttered slender fingers to hasten her husband back to their original topic. "Go on, Jeffrey, I'm waiting."

"Aye, that you are, my sweet." He sighed, relenting to her winsome urgings. "When I was a youth, I had to endure a lot of ribbing when I went skinny-dipping with my friends. We used to swing out over the water on a long rope tied to one of the branches of the tree that grew alongside the stream. Sometimes it evolved into a contest to see which of us could sail the farthest before letting go and plunging into the creek. A few of us had more than the average handle, and there were many humorous suggestions as to what our companions could do if the rope ever broke. Their recommendations amounted to me or any like me climbing up in the tree as a replacement for the rope. Their hilarity was as vast as their imagination, for they wagered that since our members would have some flexibility, everyone would be able to fly farther. Otherwise, they claimed there'd be little difference between us and the rope."

"Didn't their teasing make you feel ashamed?"

Grinning, Jeffrey raised a hand and, with a finger, scratched his cheek reflectively, very near the intriguing cleft made visible by his grin. "Considering that a few of them had nothing more in their breeches than what amounted to a spit in a pot, I decided I wasn't so unfortunate after all. At least no one ever mistook me for a girl."

"I like the way you look."

Feeling himself responding to her ogling stare, he offered a suggestion. "I don't suppose you'd consider taking a moment to sport with your husband, would you? I could offer excuses for our tardiness downstairs."

Raelynn could imagine the curious stares they'd receive upon returning downstairs. "The bed squeaks too much, Jeffrey. They'd know without a doubt what we were doing."

Her husband snorted. "I'm going to take you home where the bed *doesn't* squeak, madam, and then I'm going to keep you there until you plead for me to let you go."

Her countenance brightened as she dimpled. "Promise?"

He winked at her. "You have my word on it, madam."

21

Gustav Fridrich strode down the street, oblivious to anyone who was foolish enough to get in his way. Although his shining, round face had become a mottled scarlet from his exertion, and his breath wheezed harshly from his stout chest, he never once considered slowing his pace. Pausing to rest would have been a weakness he despised almost as intensely as the world in which he found himself.

His upper lip curled derisively as he observed the relaxed passage of several elegantly garbed couples on the street. *"As if zhey haf no care in zhe vorld,"* he mentally jeered. *"Fools! Veak, despicable fools!"*

In his opinion, Charleston was a cesspool of languid self-indulgence and careless gaiety deserving only his contempt. Despite the fact that his many smuggling exploits and business affairs in the city and the surrounding area had made him a very wealthy man, he loathed the populace. People here seemed much more interested in enjoying the simple pleasures of life and being hospitable to their friends and neighbors rather than striving and working hard in a serious quest for fortune. He especially disliked its sheriff. If not for Rhys Townsend, he'd still own Raelynn. Possessing her would have served as sweet succor for his useless arm. He had never had a woman the likes of her before, and he was gut-wrenching tired of the jaded strumpets who eagerly bellied up to any man for a coin or two. Those he had attempted to ride after his shoulder had been shattered had left him writhing in shame and frustration. He had sent them fleeing in wide-eyed trepidation before the lash of his savage tongue and his bellowing rage.

But with Raelynn, it would be different, he consoled himself. The merest thought of bedding her kindled that part of him which the harlots, with all their knowledge and experience, hadn't been able to stir from its limpness. Enchantingly beautiful, well-bred, and elegant, not to mention sufficiently young to be easily held underneath his thumb, Raelynn would have proven a delectable morsel in his bed.

It didn't help knowing that his insatiable desire for her had already resulted in a horrible impairment, one which grieved him unmercifully. Now he couldn't even bear to look at his own reflection, the girth of which was growing with each month's passing. The dead weight of his useless arm, much like the one in his crotch, was a constant reminder of why he utterly loathed Jeffrey Birmingham. The constant awareness that the sheriff hadn't yet seen fit to arrest the man for Nell's murder only served as another sharp, nettlesome thorn in his flesh.

Dwelling on his grim musings, Gustav turned crisply into an alley to take advantage of a shortcut to the area where he had left the livery waiting. Oblivious to the two sailors, who, after exchanging a nod, followed him into the narrow lane, he strode angrily on, absorbed in his own violent musings and hatred.

Of a sudden, his good arm was seized, and he was shoved face-first against a wall, causing him undue pain as the force of the impact nearly broke his nose. He tried to look behind him, but a stout forearm wedged up close against the back of his neck.

"Here now!" Gustav barked. "Vhat iz zhe meanin' of zhis outrage!"

A chuckling breath left him gasping in a cloud of fetid stench as a hoarse voice rasped near his ear. "Give o'er yer money, gov'na, or I'll cuts yer throat here an' now." To emphasize his willingness to perform such a deed, the sailor pressed a large blade to his victim's stout neck until a thin trickle of blood oozed from a newly inflicted cut.

The other sailor wasn't up to wasting time with mere threats to get what he wanted. Kneeling beside the German, he started rifling through his pockets. When he could find no suitable amount of coin, he began searching upward underneath their victim's coat. A bulge around the man's waist made him whisk out his own gleaming blade. He made short work of the man's suspenders, and soon he was dragging the trousers downward over taut hips. Once free of the ham-like buttocks, the pants dropped forthwith around Gustav's ankles, leaving naught but the tails of his coat and long underwear covering his heavily muscled legs. The ties of the money belt were severed, and soon it was slung over a brawny shoulder.

"This should tide us o'er for a winter or two, mate," the fellow boasted with a chortle and clapped a hand upon his companion's shoulder.

"What do we do wit' him?" the latter queried, looking to his companion for guidance.

"Slit his gullet, what else?"

Accustomed as he was to inflicting rather than being a casualty of fear, pain and death, Gustav was literally paralyzed by fright at the thought that he'd be murdered by a pair of lowly tars. His heart thudded against the inner wall of his rib cage, and his harsh breathing was now reduced to sharp gasps. As much as he loved money, he gave no tiniest thought to it at the moment. What loomed before him was his life in retrospect, the men he had ruined, the ones whose deaths he had arranged for his own gain, the women he had used in the foulest way possible, the elderly he had swindled and left to beg on the streets, the children he had kicked out of his way or the beggars he had backhanded and sent flying. A few of his victims had been pawns in his climb to wealth and power, others useless entities he had trod upon without regret after reaching the lofty height to which he had once aspired. Now, as he balanced on the precarious precipice between life and death, the faces of his victims came back to haunt him, at the forefront of which loomed Nell. Hadn't he promised a thousand Yankee dollars to see Jeffrey Birmingham removed as an obstacle between himself and Raelynn? And what had followed but the death of the young mother!

Not my fault! I didn't know! his mind screamed to the black-shrouded judge whose skeletal visage towered above him. The gavel came crashing downward. *Guilty, by all intents and purposes! The sentence is death!*

Not having prayed since the tender age of six, Gustav struggled to remember just how to go about it when a groan suddenly broke from the tar who held the knife wedged against his throat. The other sailor raised his arm with a gleaming knife clutched in his hand, but abruptly gasped in surprise. A long, bloody blade slipped free of his gut, and then, quite slowly he doubled over with a muted groan.

"Ye can pull up yer breeches now, Mr. Fridrich," a familiar voice informed him. "These here tars ain't never gonna do ye no more hurt."

"Olney?" Gustav struggled mightily to drag his trousers up over his long underwear.

"Aye, it's me all right."

Facing the younger man, the German finished tugging the waistband up over his buttocks and began buttoning the flap as he settled a glower upon the scamp, totally dismissing from mind the fact that Olney had just saved his life. "Vhere haf yu been? I expected yu back veeks ago."

"I've been tryin' ta save me arse. Me arm was busted an' I had ta wait till it healed afore I dared come outa hidin'. If 'tweren't for Birmin'am's hired men snippin' at me heels an' the sheriff trackin' me wit' his men, I'da've been able ta get some rest here and there. But they nearly drove me inta me grave tryin' ta escape 'em. Me temper got plumb sour, it did. I ain't had me a real bath or bedded a wench in o'er a month. Considerin' everythin' I'd been through, I decided I had enough o' runnin' through the swamps an' woods an' could just as well hide out at that there cat house where I found Ol' Coop the last time. Yes, sir, I'm gonna have me a taste o' them fancy women they've got there. In fact, that's where I was headin' when I seen ye an' yer friends here turn inta the alley." He canted his head curiously. "What's happenin' wit' Birmin'am, anyway? He been arrested yet?"

"Nein! Zhat stupid sheriff refuses to do anyzhing about Nell's murder! Yu killed her for nozhing!"

Olney laughed caustically. "I didn't kill the li'l wench! Birmin'am did! I saw him do it!"

"Yu're lyin', Olney. Yu took her out zhere, promisin' to make trouble for Birmingham. Zhen I hear she vas killed. Vhy vould he bother to murder Nell vhen he has such a beautiful vife?"

The curly-headed man lifted his brawny shoulder. "Maybe Birmin'am flew inta a rage after Nell went into his house durin' his fancy ball an' threatened to expose him afore all o' them friends o' his. She said she was gonna tell 'em he were the one what filled her belly wit' that 'ere li'l bastard she whelped. The ways I figgered it,

Birmin'am didn't want ta suffer the shame o' his friends thinkin' he'd knocked up the li'l twit an' then sent her packin'. Some men are like that, carin' more 'bout their reputations than they do 'bout keepin' themselves respectable an' safely wit'in the law. O' course, the two o' us don't e'er have ta worry about that none, do we, Mr. Fridrich?"

Though he sensed the question was spoken in derision, Gustav ignored the insinuation to his life of crime as he considered the viability of his foe being a murderer. "As much as I vould like to have it so, I haf trouble believin' Birmingham vould be so foolish," Gustav muttered. "Perhaps yu vere mistaken, Olney. Maybe yu saw zhe real murderer an' just thought it vas Birmingham."

"I'd almost be willin' ta swear afore a judge that it were Birmin'am himself, but that ain't hardly gonna happen, 'cause the minute I show me face, the good sheriff'll arrest me. Huh! He'll probably tell all kinds o' nasty things ta the jury just to see me locked up for the next brace o' years. A measly thousand dollars ain't worth the trouble I'd be gettin' meself inta, so if'n that's what ye're expectin' me ta do ta get it, ye can be keepin' what ye promised me."

The ice blue eyes narrowed calculatingly as Gustav considered what would tempt the rogue. "Vhat about zhree zhousand?"

Olney snorted. "The only way I'd do it is if'n ye give me the use o' yer lads ta spread the news that I'm back in town an' that I saw Birmin'am kill Nell. Yer men would have ta go 'round town, stirrin' up the people against Sheriff Townsend an' accusin' him o' bein' partial ta his friends. Then they'd have ta follow me ta the sheriff's office, along wit' the people they riled, an' be 'ere ta heckle Townsend when I turns meself in."

"I can haf my men do zhat easily enough. Vhen do you vant zhem to start?"

"I'll need a bath, a couple of hours with a wench an' ten thousand up front."

"Zen zhousand! Yu must be mad! I vill never pay yu so much!"

Olney lifted his shoulders, blandly unconcerned. "Suit yerself, Mr. Fridrich, but I'm not doin' it for anythin' less. I may have ta spend a few years in prison, an' I wants a nice tidy sum ta invest afore I'm taken in so's I can live like a Birmin'am once I'm set free."

"Vhat yu ask iz highway robbery!"

A derisive chuckle came from the younger man. "Well, me grandpa was a highwayman, so's it must be in me blood somewheres, but if'n 'ere's a thief betwixt the two o' us, Mr. Fridrich, then I'm lookin' at him. Ye pay me wages, remember? I'm an honest, hard-workin' gent who knows how ta barter when the time's right. Three or more years in prison is too long a time for me ta even consider the measly pickin's ye're willin' ta dole out. In short, I ain't acceptin' anythin' less'n what I asked for."

Gustav peered at him narrowly. "Yu guarantee Birmingham vill be arrested if I agree?"

"I guaran*tee*."

"Zen zhousand zhen for his arrest. If yu fail, yu vill be found in zhe river vith yur throat cut. Zhat much I promise yu."

&"GOOD AFTERNOON, SHERIFF."

Rhys Townsend spun around in quick reflex, his hand reaching for his pistol. He hadn't been able to forget that voice, not by any stretch of the imagination. It had haunted him night and day through all of his efforts to figure out just where that wily rat, Olney, had lit out to. He surely hadn't expected the scamp to come prancing himself across the threshold of his office like some dandified gent in garb that could've crossed one's eyes. But there Olney stood, big as life, leaning cockily against the doorjamb and wearing a loudly checked frockcoat, a red shirt, and the bottoms of his tan trousers stuffed into overrun, deer-hide boots that had seen better days.

"What the devil are you up to, Olney?" Rhys barked, flicking his gaze out the window at the crowd of people collecting in front of his office. His hackles fairly prickled. Something was up all right. He could feel it in his vitals.

Making no effort to curb his grin, Olney sauntered forward with an air of a man who had the world by the tail with a downhill pull. His thick shoulders came up in a casual shrug. "I just thought it were time I came ta pay me respects, Sheriff. Any objections?"

As the younger man ambled past him, Rhys wrinkled his nose and turned his face aside in sharp repugnance as if he had just gotten a strong, downwind whiff of a polecat. "You smell like a perfume factory, boy."

Olney threw back his head and loudly guffawed, snatching awake the deputy who had been dozing in a nearby cell. The older lawman stumbled to the bars and stared bleary-eyed through the barrier as he mumbled sleepily, "Wha's happenin'?"

"Go back to sleep, Charlie," Rhys bade tersely, sending the deputy tottering back to the bunk. Rhys cocked a brow at the sly, young fox who was doing everything but swishing his tail across his nose.

"Don't ye like me new duds, Sheriff?" Olney inquired, tossing back a taunting grin.

"A bit gaudy for my taste, Olney, but then, I'm not you. How'd you get the money from Fridrich to buy them?"

"There ye go again, Sheriff, always supposin' me integrity's for hire."

Rhys scoffed in rampant amazement. "What integrity?"

"Don't ye worry none 'bout that, Sheriff," Olney retorted hotly, coming around in a huff and thrusting a forefinger beneath the lawman's nose in an effort to dismiss his jeer. "I gots meself plenty o' that."

"Yeah? You and who else?"

Olney sighed heavily and shook his head as if sorely lamenting his visit. "Here I be, ready ta help ye solve a murder ye can't unravel, an' ye ain't even willin' ta be nice ta me." He flung a hand toward the thickening throng milling about in front of the sheriff's office. "I'm sure all o' 'em folks out 'ere would be eager ta hears what I has ta say on the matter o' Nell's murder, even if ye ain't."

Rhys strode thoughtfully to the barred window and gazed out. He had a good memory for faces, and some of the men he saw looked very much like the same ones who had been in Fridrich's warehouse the night he and a whole host of friends and deputies had barged in with guns blazing. "I don't know why it is, Olney, but I have a gut feeling that your friends out there already know what you're about. In fact, I think you're just itching to tell me the name of the man you claim is a murderer. Would you like me to guess the one you're going to blame?"

Tugging on an earlobe, Olney mauled a smile as he considered the sheriff's offer. "I suppose I can allow you one guess."

Rhys jerked his head toward the street. "Considering all those people you've brought with you on your mission of goodwill, no doubt with the idea of forcing my hand, I'm of a mind to think that you'll be naming none other than Jeffrey Birmingham as the murderer."

Chortling softly, Olney scrubbed a forefinger beneath his nose. "Ye know, Sheriff, at times ye plumb surprise me. Ye don't seem nearly as daft as I've been led to believe."

"Thank you, Olney," the sheriff rejoined dryly. "I'd

accept that as a compliment, but I must consider the source."

"I seen Birmin'am do it, Sheriff! I ain't lying!" the brigand insisted irately.

Rhys's gaze skimmed the rascal's gaudy attire. "I assume from your new clothes that Fridrich has already paid you for submitting yourself to my authority so you could reveal this information to me."

"Ye might say that, Sheriff, an' ye just might be right. Knowin' how eager ye've been ta lock me up, I wouldna've even considered wanderin' o'er here if'n I hadn't gotten enough booty ta make it worth the time I'll have ta waste in jail. As it stands now, I can looks forward ta something real nice when I gets outa prison. When I told Mr. Fridrich what I seen, he thought I'd give meself o'er ta ye just ta let justice have its due." Olney snorted derisively at such a farfetched notion. "That'll be the day, for sure. Took ten thousand ta make me cross yer threshold today. So, here I am, Sheriff, ready ta confess all, my sins as well as those o' yer friend's."

"You know, Olney, I can usually tell when a body is lying. I get this funny feeling in my gut that just won't settle down until I finally come to the realization that I can't swallow what's being told me. Some people lie for the sheer pleasure of it 'cause they've got this black rot eating 'em up inside. Preachers might be wont to say that's the devil taking hold of 'em. Now, we know that the devil has you already tied up and in his bag and is looking for another sucker to catch. What I'm getting at, boy, is if you have any hope of fooling me in this matter for very long, you might want to save your breath, 'cause eventually it's not going to do you one bit of good. I'll be catching the murderer in due time with or without your help."

"I knows what I seen, Sheriff," the scalawag stated flatly, his eyes purposefully dull as he fixed a level stare upon the sheriff. "An' it's the truth whether ye wants ta believe it or not. Now, are ye gonna lends an ear ta hear what I has ta say? Or should I go inform those people out 'ere that ye don't want ta listen ta anything mean an' ugly 'bout yer rich, precious friend?"

"Oh, I'm not against hearing your version of the story, Olney. But know this, I'll reserve my judgments about Birmingham until I have better proof than your word. Just consider this, if you would. Your conclusions may well be the truth in your opinion, but that may not necessarily be the way things stack up in the long run. Now, if you would, I'd like for you to tell me one thing before you give your eye view of what happened. Can you positively identify the man who chased you out of Birmingham's stable that night after you witnessed Nell's murder?"

Olney gaped back at the sheriff in surprise. "How the devil did ye know 'bout that?"

"I've got my sources," Rhys assured him with a bland smile. "You stole Birmingham's mare to get away from the murderer, didn't you?"

Olney's jaw had fallen slack with awe, but sudden suspicion made him squint at the lawman. "Birmin'am say anything ta ye 'bout that?"

"I haven't talked with Birmingham about this matter since the day after Nell's murder." Dropping his gaze to the floor, he contemplated the brigand's scruffy footwear and smiled wryly. "You left tracks in the paddock outside Birmingham's stable that were as obvious as a plodding cow's. If you haven't noticed before, Olney, you've got very wide feet and you have a habit of running your boots over on the sides. There's no mistaking your footprints."

Wary skepticism still troubled the face of the curly-headed rogue as he continued to eye the sheriff. "So how do ye knows I was chased out there?"

"Another set of prints made from smaller, fancier boots followed yours at a run, scuffing up your tracks in the paddock. Yours stopped in the spot where you hauled yourself astride the mare. From there, you took the mare over the fence to get away. The other footprints turned back and reentered the stables. You saw Nell's murder all right, Olney, and then you lit out on the mare as if your tail had been scorched. Elijah said the mare threw you off in the woods, which left you afoot for a while. You did a lot of stumbling around, like you were in a lot of pain." His eyes raked the younger man. "Obviously the mare crippled you in some fashion."

Olney had thought he'd have the upper hand once he faced the sheriff, but the bloke had turned the tables on him. It was evident the man relished lifting the hair off his nape by telling him what he had seen and done, as if he had been a mouse in a corner of the stable that night. It was damned disconcerting to be the one now standing with jaw hanging aslack.

Olney shook himself, managing to flatten only a few of his hackles, and finally muttered, "Yeah, I took the mare. Damn near killed me, too, she did. Tore me arm out o' the socket when she scraped me off'n her. Later I found Birmin'am at Red Pete's place. He an' his missus were 'ere all by their lonesome till I come upon 'em. Forced him ta fix me arm, I did. He tried ta tell me it weren't him what killed Nell, even said she'd been knifed three times." The scamp scoffed. "I only seen her stabbed once."

"Birmingham wasn't lying to you, Olney," Rhys informed him. "Nell *was* stabbed three times."

"Then he must've gone back ta finish her off, 'cause I only seen him do it ta her once."

The sheriff sought to confirm in his own mind what Olney was telling him. "If the murderer actually returned to stab her twice more, then you're saying it happened after you had lit out on the mare."

"I'm sayin' that, all right."

"Did you happen to see the murderer's face clearly at any time before your departure?"

"I seen meself a man what were all duded up in fancy evenin' clothes an' more'n a half head taller'n me."

"And though you never saw his face, you can swear without a doubt that you can identify him?" Rhys pressed.

"I'da've known him anywhere, Sheriff. It were Birmin'am, hisself," Olney answered emphatically. "He nearly scaredt the livin' daylights outa me, comin' after me the way he did. He almost caught me too, he did. If not for that fool mare bein' there when I needed her, I'da've been a goner just like poor Nell. I ain't ne'er seen me a man what runs that fast, an' here I be, 'bout ten years younger than that 'ere bloke."

Rhys shot him a glance that was a mixture of surprise and dawning perception. "You say the man was very tall?"

"Yeah, I say the man was tall, 'bout as tall as Birmin'am hisself," Olney rejoined acidly, growing vexed with the lawman's dogged persistence. "About as tall as ye an' that other fancy friend o' yers, the one what makes ladies' dresses." He curled his lip contemptuously. "Guess he likes frilly clothes so much he had ta start makin' 'em so's he could hides out in his fancy 'partment whilst he's wearin' 'em."

Rhys settled an incredulous stare upon the balmy fellow. "Lest you continue in your foolish assumption about Farrell Ives, boy, let me inform you that he not only retired an undefeated boxer, but for the last ten years running he has also been the best marksman in this area. At sixty paces, he could blow your eyeballs out of their sockets without fluttering your lashes."

"Ye sure are defensive 'bout yer friends, Sheriff," the rapscallion challenged with a sneer. "*Now*, are ye gonna hear what I have ta say 'bout Birmin'am or not?"

~"I'LL GET THE DOOR, TIZZY," RAELYNN called to the back of the house where the young black woman had gone to bathe Jake. "Just continue what you're doing."

"Yas'm, Miz Raelynn."

Raelynn stepped first to the window and cautiously looked out to make sure the visitor had a friendly face. Upon espying the sheriff, she hastened to pull open the door in some surprise. "Rhys, what are you doing here?"

Then her eyes swept past him to the street in front of the house and widened perceptively as she saw the people who had gathered there, at the forefront of which was Olney with his wrists shackled. Of a sudden, she knew why the sheriff had come. Olney had finally come forth to accuse her husband.

"Jeffrey didn't do it, Rhys," she declared, not even pausing to debate the question in her own mind anymore. She was now firmly convinced that Jeff couldn't have done such a horrible deed. He was just too upright and noble to kill anyone in such a dastardly fashion. "I know he didn't!"

"I'd like to talk to him, Raelynn," Rhys said in a solemn tone. "Is he here?"

"Yes," she replied reluctantly, drawing the door open all the way and stepping back to admit the large man into the hallway. "Jeffrey had another bad headache a few hours ago, and I gave him some laudanum in his food to make him sleep. It should be wearing off by now."

"I'd really appreciate it if you'd tell him that I'm here?"

"Come in and have a seat in the parlor," she invited reluctantly.

"Thank you, Raelynn."

Once he had entered the house, Rhys glanced around. "Is anyone else here?"

"Just my maid and Jake. Elizabeth and Farrell got married this afternoon, and they're spending the night at his apartment."

A wide grin spread across Rhys's lips. "I'm happy to hear that. They should've done that long time ago."

"I'll get Jeffrey up. You may have to wait a few moments before he comes down. He'll need to get dressed."

"I don't mind, Raelynn. I'm not going anywhere."

By the time Raelynn arrived at their bedroom, Jeff was already up and splashing water on his face. As she came in, he threw a thumb over his shoulder toward the front window, from which he had drawn the heavy draperies aside.

"What's going on out there?" he asked, drying his face. "What are all those people doing in front of the house?"

"I think if you'd care to take note more closely, my love, you'll find that one of them is Olney Hyde. Rhys Townsend is waiting downstairs to talk with you. Though he hasn't said as much, I'm afraid he has come to arrest you."

Jeff sighed wearily and tossed down the towel. "I'd better get some clothes on."

She swept her gaze down his long, naked body, but her eyes lacked the usual twinkle of admiration. "I think you'd better. Rhys wouldn't be unduly shocked if you came downstairs that way, but Tizzy certainly would."

"Can you have her make me some coffee? I'm still feeling a bit groggy." He scrubbed a hand across his brow, as if seeking to banish a lingering stupor. "I don't know why I'm sleeping so much lately."

Raelynn dared not reveal the reason. "I learned how to make coffee while working for *Ives's Couture*," she informed him quietly. "I'll make you some just the way Farrell likes his. Strong."

A few moments later Jeff came downstairs suitably attired in shirt, trousers and ankle-length boots. He entered the parlor where Rhys awaited him and exchanged a brief greeting with the man before facing his wife who was just emerging from the dining room with a tray upon which resided a china coffee service and two brimming cups of coffee sitting atop daintily flowered saucers. Feeling in great need of the coffee's stimulant to clear his muddled thoughts, Jeff stepped forward and helped himself to a cup from the tray. The coffee was still scalding hot, and he had to sip it slowly as Raelynn moved past him to the sheriff.

"Would you care to have some coffee, Rhys?" she asked graciously, presenting him the tray.

"I drink mine black, just like Jeffrey," he announced, taking up the remaining cup and saucer before leaning back in his chair.

Jeff settled on the settee, an arm's length away, and silently patted the cushion beside him as he caught Raelynn's eye. Giving him an answering smile, she placed the tray on the narrow table in front of them and settled into the seat beside him.

Rhys took a sip of the brew and then bobbed his head in approval. "Good coffee. Just what I needed."

"Thank you," Raelynn murmured, forcing a smile. It was difficult to appear relaxed when in another few moments she might well be facing Jeffrey's arrest. "Elizabeth taught me how to make it."

Rhys glanced up with a grin. "You two can make coffee for me anytime. In fact, I just might bring you both over to my house so you can instruct my Mary. She makes it too weak to my way of thinking. She's always trying to save a coin here and there, no matter how weak the coffee may taste afterwards. The frugality of her Scottish blood can leave a man vexed for want of a darker brew."

The tense silence of the Birminghams made it evident that they were waiting for him to state his purpose for being there and that no amount of easing into the subject could ease their qualms. Rhys cleared his throat and finally got down to the foul business that had brought him. Peering at his friend, he jerked his head toward the street. "I assume, Jeff, that you've seen the crowd outside," he ventured and took another sip of coffee, loathing the task he was about. "Olney made sure of his reinforcements before he ever came to see me. He swears you were the one who killed Nell . . ."

"I know what he *thinks*, Rhys, but he's mistaken," Jeff protested. "I didn't kill Nell. I told you what happened, and it was the truth."

"Jeffrey couldn't possibly have killed that girl, Rhys," Raelynn stated once again with conviction, evoking her husband's amazement. Readily yielding her hand to the larger one that reached out to clasp hers, she pressed on with unswerving dedication. "You've been acquainted with him longer than I have. You ought to know better than anyone that he's just not capable of such a thing."

Rhys raised a hand to forestall them. "Please, Jeff, Raelynn, let me finish. Let me assure you both that I have another suspect in mind, but to keep you safe from that mob out there, Jeff, I've got to take you with me. If I don't arrest you, those people out there might decide to lynch you. Fridrich's men have incited them to the point that they're firmly convinced that I haven't been doing my duty merely because you're my friend. Now, what I'd like for you to do at the moment is to tell me if you noticed anything at all about the man who attacked you and your wife. We both know that he's tall, fast, and if he was able to knock a man of your size into a lamppost, he's obviously very strong. Can you think of anything else about him that may have slipped your mind? Did you happen to notice his feet?"

Jeff stared at his friend as if he had taken leave of his senses. "You asked me the same question about Olney's feet, and the answer is still no. I was trying to stay alive and keep that butcher from killing my wife." He frowned at the lawman curiously. "Was there something noteworthy about his feet that gained your attention?"

Rhys lifted his heavy shoulders. "I never got that close to him. I was just wondering if you might have noticed whether or not he had small enough feet to wear your boots."

Jeff leaned back against the settee, a look of wonder sweeping over his face. "You mean the muddy boots that Cora found in my bathing chamber while you were there looking into Nell's murder?"

"Exactly."

"Why would the man who murdered Nell try to kill me?" Jeff asked, unable to think too clearly even yet. "It seems more likely that someone killed her to implicate me." In growing frustration, he scrubbed a hand along-side his temple. "I'm sorry, Rhys, but I'm having trouble putting all this together. I'm beginning to think that blow on my head has left me permanently impaired."

"Oh, I wouldn't worry yourself about that, not while you're being given laudanum. That blame stuff can make a body nigh sense . . ." Rhys halted abruptly, realizing what he had just spilled. Grimacing over his blunder, he met Raelynn's worried gaze and silently begged her forgiveness.

Jeff wasn't so confused that he missed the visual exchange between the two. In response he turned to his wife. "You gave me laudanum?"

Beneath his incredulous stare, Raelynn scrunched her shoulders, very much like a child drawing into a tiny shell of herself. "I had to do something to ease your head-aches, Jeffrey. They were making you nauseous."

"But I told you I didn't want to take that stuff," he pointed out. "I prefer the headaches over the lameness of my brain. Right now, I can't even think clearly enough to consider everything that is being said."

"I'm sorry, I won't do it again," she promised, lifting soulful eyes to his.

All of Jeff's exasperation rapidly dissipated before his young wife's obvious contrition. "Lord, madam, you could steal the heart from the devil himself," he murmured in awe. Locking an arm in a fierce embrace about her shoulders, he pulled her close against him. After agonizing through the weeks of their lengthy separation, the last thing in the world he wanted now was to cause her more anguish. Dropping a kiss upon her head, he whispered against her sweetly scented hair, "Don't fret now, love. Please, I can't bear it."

Rhys didn't even attempt to curb a grin as he considered the pair. He did, however, help himself to another cup of coffee. "I suppose this means that everything is all right in your home camp, eh, Jeff? I mean, other than the fact that I'll have to arrest you for a time." His gaze dipped to the gentle fullness beneath Raelynn's skirts, which in all the excitement the other night he had overlooked. "I see you're going to have your hands full as new parents next year. My Mary and I will be busy in the same way, but I rather suspect ours will be coming before yours. First thing you'll know, Jeff, we'll be having grandchildren."

"Whoa!" Jeff cried, and gave a brief laugh. "Let me enjoy siring a few more before marrying off this one, Rhys. I'm not that old yet."

"No, I guess you're not, considering you're two years younger than I am. Mary has her heart set on having a large family, but she'll either be having one every year for the next eight years, or I'll still be siring them into my fifties. But then, Mary will always be young, at least in my eyes."

"Let's get back to the man who attacked us the other night," Jeff urged. "I'm wondering what you may have learned about him since then and why you think he may have murdered Nell?"

"Olney said the man who chased him out of the stables was very fast, and it caused me to recall my own amazement over how quickly your assailant left me behind. Of course, I can't rightly say for sure if there's *any* connection between the two incidents, but it seems mighty peculiar the way Olney and I were both awed by the swiftness of the men with whom we had each come in contact, the murderer whom Olney saw, and the man who attacked you the other night. Now, I know you're no slowpoke, Jeff. I remember the races we used to run as boys, and you won your fair share of them, but you never impressed me as being *overly* fast, I mean, to the point that you'd leave people agog. I can only think . . . and hope . . . that the man who murdered Nell is the same one who attacked you. If it is, that would definitely make my job a lot easier. Then I'd only be searching for one man instead of two."

"But as yet, neither you nor Olney have a clue what he looks like," Jeff pointed out. "Olney was under the misguided idea that it was me, but that assumption might have come about because the murderer brought Nell out after she had gone into my bedroom supposedly to have a talk with me. Olney said the man was tall, dark-haired and dressed in evening garb, which at the time fit my description. How are you going to find a man like that among all the people living here in Charleston when I can't even tell you which of my guests matched that report that night?"

Rhys pursed his lips and blew out a long breath as he pondered that question. "That, Jeffrey me dearie, as our friend, Farrell, would say, is a matter that would snarl any cat's tail."

A knock on the door prompted Rhys to lift a hand to urge Raelynn back into her seat. "No doubt that'll be Charlie wanting to tell me those folks out there are getting a little anxious to see me do my duty."

Pushing himself to his feet, he moved from his chair and went into the front hall where he opened the door. "Yeah, Charlie?"

"Sheriff, Olney is gettin' those folks out there riled up. Ye want me ta gag him or somethin'?"

Rhys muttered a curse beneath his breath and, in an impatient tone, bade, "Tell 'em to hold on to their shirt-tails, Charlie. Mr. Birmingham and I are coming out shortly."

Returning to stand beside his chair, he faced Jeff directly. "We'd better be going now or Olney will have that crowd out there storming this place."

"Why in the devil did you bring that scamp along with you, Rhys?" Jeff asked in vexation. "You should've known he'd make trouble."

"Well, as usual, Charlie took his own sweet time about repairing a few things around the office. This time it just happened to be the new cell doors that were supposed to be put on several days ago. He'll have to get that chore done as soon as we get back so we won't have Olney disappearing on us again. As long and as hard as I've been chasing after that rascal, I don't want him slipping through my fingers again."

Leaving the settee, Jeff approached the sheriff and reluctantly stretched forth his wrists. "Those people out there will expect to see me in shackles, Rhys. You'd better do your duty."

The lawman snorted. "I've got news for 'em, Jeffrey me boy. They're not going to see it, at least not while I'm sheriff."

"I'll get my wrap," Raelynn choked, struggling hard not to break down as she moved around the table.

Jeff faced her and shook his head, causing his wife to look at him in stunned disbelief. "I don't want you to come out with me, Raelynn. There's no telling what that crowd may be tempted to do once they see me, and I don't want you getting hurt. Please, for my sake, just stay in here where you'll be safe."

Her eyes grew bright with brimming tears in the midst of their doleful pleading. "But, Jeffrey, I want to be with . . ."

"No, my love, I cannot allow it," he stated, his own voice fraught with emotion. "You're staying here inside the house where you'll be safe, and that's final."

Rhys cleared his throat uncomfortably as Raelynn, blinded by the wetness welling upward over her lashes, stumbled toward the dining room. Jeff muttered a curse, annoyed by the whole situation, especially by the fact that he had to leave his wife alone in the house with no greater protection than Tizzy and Jake. He followed her to the adjoining room and, as he came up behind her, laid an arm around the small of her back as he swept her far beyond the door to a spot where Rhys couldn't see them. Turning her about to face him, he crushed her to him as his lips plummeted down upon hers. Her lips tasted salty from her tears, but they parted eagerly beneath his ravaging mouth and questing tongue. She answered him with a zeal to match his own, and soon she was straining up against him as if beset with a desire to become totally merged with him in both body and spirit.

When Jeff finally drew away, Raelynn's limbs were shaking uncontrollably and seemed incapable of providing her support. Weakly she leaned against him and squeezed her eyelids tightly closed, causing tiny rivulets to spill freely down her soft cheeks. His lips pressed against her brow for a long moment until he heard her sniff, and then, with a tender smile, he stepped back and fished into his trouser pocket for a clean handkerchief. Like a father with a child, he dried her eyes and gently bade her to blow her nose. She complied and looked up at him through a blur of fresh tears.

"I'll get your coat," she muttered thickly. "It has turned nippy outside."

Some moments later, Sheriff Rhys Townsend escorted his lifelong friend down the front walk, out through the white gate and toward the waiting wagon. Most of the rabble were strangers to both Rhys and Jeff. If their clothes were an indication, then they were from the poorer section of town, which left open the possibility that at least some might have been paid to come out as part of a vigilante group. They harassed the sheriff in sneering tones, accusing him of favoring his rich friends and taking sides against an ordinary working man like Olney. As for Jeff, they were not above calling him names like "child-molester" and "filthy murderer" and spitting at him as he passed. Beneath their hateful, jeering slurs, even his deeply bronzed face darkened to a ruddy hue.

Raelynn stood at the window, making no effort to restrain the flood of tears streaming down her cheeks and along the pale column of her throat. Well over a month ago she had been dismayed by the sheriff's lack of action in arresting her husband. Now she was filled with a burgeoning resentment that he had allowed this particular situation to occur. He had literally been forced to arrest Jeff in spite of the fact that he believed him innocent of the crime.

When Jeff reached the wagon, Olney was already sitting in its bed under the watchful eye of the deputy who perched on a side rail. Although Jeff sought to join Olney in the back, Rhys promptly summoned him to the front of the buckboard, a seating arrangement that gained more sneers and catcalls from the crowd.

"Ye gonna let him go as soon as ye get him outa town, Sheriff?" a deep voice heckled from the crowd as the sheriff climbed into the buckboard.

At this taunting, Rhys slowly turned to scan the faces of the people who were closing in around the conveyance. He met many eye to eye. "You think you've forced my hand to arrest a murderer," he rumbled, gaining their silence. "Well, you're wrong. I'm merely making sure Jeffrey Birmingham comes to no harm from you or others like you. I don't think he's guilty of Nell's murder . . ." Sudden jeers prompted Rhys to lift a hand to halt the interruption. Though some were still muttering, he continued speaking, forcing them to fall silent. "In time, you'll be able to recognize that what I now say is true, but until then, mark my words well. If you should cause

anything of a violent nature to happen here in this neigh-
borhood or anyplace else in this city tonight, I'll be coming after you. I've seen your faces, and I'll hunt you down
to the last man if need be. I won't abide a lynch mob
taking control of either this city or this matter. I've already sent for reinforcements from neighboring towns to
guarantee that law and order is respected here." His gaze
swept the uplifted faces. "You think you're right, but I
know you're wrong, and I'm going to make every effort
to prove that in the next several days. Until then, I'd
suggest you take my warning. My friend, Jeffrey Birmingham, has never killed anyone . . ." Rhys allowed the
silence to drag on a lengthy moment for emphasis before
he smiled tersely and completed his statement, ". . . but
I have."

As Rhys sat down beside Jeff on the front seat and
took the reins in his hands, Charlie settled into the bed
of the wagon beside Olney. He had no complaints with
the sheriff; he had learned years ago that people were
better off not getting into a squabble or trying to butt
heads with Rhys Townsend. The man had his own way
of doing things, and for some strange reason, they always
seemed to turn out right.

22 ✍

*C*ooper Frye braced a shoulder against the heavy wooden plank and shoved through the main door of Gustav Fridrich's warehouse. He saw the German immediately on the far side of his office, sitting behind his massive desk where he could usually be found nowadays. His lame arm apparently had made him reluctant to endure the tawdry surroundings and noisy bedlam of the cat houses where on a frequent basis he had once been inclined to spend hours wallowing in prurient activities and women, in his case half a dozen at a time. The German's wealth had bought the harlots cheaply enough, but it certainly hadn't helped lately to ease his dark moods. Nevertheless, Frye had come for the specific purpose of relieving the man of a small measure of his riches.

The ice blue eyes lifted slowly from the ledgers and settled upon the Englishman. During his short association with the Englishman, Gustav Fridrich had at times found it amusing to hear what Cooper Frye had up his sleeve, for the man was immensely clever when his brain wasn't pickled by hard liquor. He was also a crook through and through. Of that, there was no doubt. Gustav hadn't forgotten that it had been Frye's sly tricks that had cost him Raelynn and, in a roundabout way, the loss of his arm. One day he would make the Englishman rue his deception.

Leaning back in his massive chair, Gustav tapped the feathered end of his quill against the finely tooled leather surface of his desk as he smirked in wry amusement. "So, Cooper Frye, to vhat do I owe zhis occasion? I rarely zee yu zober, so it must be zomezhing important. Vhat iz it zhis time? Zomezhing different altogether? Or iz it money as usual? Zince zhat is nearly alvays zhe case, I can only vonder vhat yu're villin' to do for zome coins zhis time?"

Cooper settled himself without invitation into a chair across the desk from the German. "I've been keepin' me ears open an' stayin' abreast o' the happenin's an' goin's on in an' around Charleston. This very afternoon I heard Jeffrey Birmin'am had been arrested for Nell's murder. Since he has, I thought ye'd feel obliged ta give me what ye promised the last time we talked."

"For vhat?" Gustav demanded in wide skepticism. "Vhat haf yu done zhat iz vorth zhis interruption? Can yu not zee I am vorkin' on my accounts? An' yu should know from past experiences zhat I dislike being disturbed vhen I'm involved in my vork."

Cooper gave the German a facial shrug. The man's dislikes didn't bother him overmuch. "If I hadn't killed Nell, Jeffrey Birmin'am wouldn't be in jail now, an' as I remember it, ye promised me a thousand Yankee dollars if'n I'd cause a split betwixt me niece an' that there fancy bloke she married."

The German shot to his feet in rapidly rising fury and slammed his palm down flat upon his desk. "Yu are lyin'! I spoke vith Olney earlier. He told me zhat he saw

Birmingham kill zhe girl, so vhat are yu trying to do? Claim my money for zomezhing yu did not do?"

Frye sneered in rank distaste at the mention of his rival's name. That young scamp was always trying to undermine his efforts to get a few coins. "Olney is mistaken, as usual. Birmin'am didn't kill Nell."

Gustav's eyes blazed as they met the man's bland stare. "Vhy don't yu tell me just vhat in zhe hell happened out zhere zhat night. I hear vone zhing from Olney. Now yu tell me another. I vant to know vhich vone of yu iz really lying and trying his best to cheat me."

"I suppose I can appease yer curiosity," Frye allowed. He had never liked Gustav, and if not for the man's wealth, he'd have found a way to be free of the tyrant. "Ye sees, I gots wind that Olney was gonna take Nell out ta make a ruckus at Oakley durin' the Birmin'am's ball if'n my nephew by marriage didn't cooperate, as it were. So's I decided ta go have a looksee 'round 'ere meself, 'ceptin' I hads me a foul time findin' meself a horse, what wit' all the liveries hired out ta escort guests ta the affair. Humph, by the time I arrived, the shindig was o'er. Still, I looked 'bout the place real careful wit' a lantern burnin' real low like, jes' ta see what might o' happened, an' that's when I come across Nell lyin' wit' a gut wound in a horse stall. There she was, just her an' her babe. She was in pain, all right, but it 'peared ta me like she was gonna make it through just fine once she got herself a li'l help from a doc.

"At first, I thought Olney mighta've stabbed her wit' the knife I saw lyin' nearby, but Nell told me some stranger had done it ta her. She said she'd gone lookin' for Birmin'am ta warn him one last time 'bout the shame he'd suffer if'n he didn't meet her demands. When she slipped inta his bedroom, she said it weren't Birmin'am 'ere atall, but a stranger who'd been pryin' on a box on Birmin'am's desk. Nell said she tried ta leave real quick like, but the bloke caught her, put a knife ta her throat an' threatened ta slice it open if'n she screamed. After

the rain, it was real muddy outside, an' he didn't want ta
get his fancy shoes dirty, so's he hauled her ta the bed an'
sat on her whilst he put on a pair o' Birmin'am's boots."

"Vhy didn't just he kill her in *Herr* Birmingham's bedroom? He could haf saved himself a lot of bother."

"What wit' him bein' a guest, I suppose he didn't want
a hew an' cry made o'er her body whilst he was still in
the house."

Gustav thrust his chin out musefully as he considered
the man's conjecture. Then he waved his hand officiously. "Continue."

"The fella took her out ta the barn an' stabbed her.
He was gonna knife her again, but accordin' ta Nell, he
heard a noise, an' that's when Olney ran out o' the next
stall. The gent raced after him, but Nell figgered Olney
took off 'cause she then heard a clatter o' hooves rattlin'
off inta the distance. The stranger came back ta see 'bout
Nell, but she played real dead like. Guess he fell for her
game, 'ceptin' she weren't dead. That's when I started
thinkin' ta meself. Here ye'd gone an' promised me a
thousand dollars ta split the newlyweds, an' 'ere a
stranger were ta blame for it all. That's when I decided
ta finish Nell off meself." He laughed shortly. "She
screamed when she saw me intent, but it did her little
good. Still, me timin' was off a bit. I seen a lantern comin'
from the house an' quickly snuffed out me own. I hide
meself in another stall, an' that's when Birmin'am himself
come out ta have a looksee 'round the barn, 'ceptin' he
didn't get no farther than poor Nell. She was still alive
when he reached her, an' she mewled on 'bout her lovin'
him an' how sorry she was for e'er lyin' 'bout him sirin'
her babe. A short time later, me niece come out searchin'
for him, an' from the way things looked, she got it inta
her head real fast like that Birmin'am had killed the girl,
'cause me niece went flyin' back inta the house like
someone had torched her petticoats."

"So, Frye! Yu are satisfied zhat yu vere zhe vone vhat

put a vedge between Birmingham and yur niece, except she vas in zhe same house vith him vhen I vent to *Frau* Dalton's."

"No matter that." Frye waved his hand, dismissing the importance of that bit of information. "What matters is the fact that Nell would still be alive if'n 'tweren't for me, an' Jeffrey Birmin'am wouldn't be in prison now 'cause Nell would've told everybody he were innocent o' stabbin' her an' gettin' her wit' child. She were kinda love-sick o'er that 'ere rich gent, an' ye can bet she wouldna've let him suffer more'n a day's time in jail afore she'da've spilled out the truth, maybe e'en as ta how I'd put her up ta claimin' Birmin'am as her kid's pa."

Gustav made no effort to hide the sneer in his tone as he voiced a conjecture. "I take it, zhen, zhat yu vant payment for vhat yu did."

"A thousand Yankee dollars, just like ye promised, Mr. Fridrich. Otherwise, I'll have ta send word ta the sheriff that me niece's husband ain't the bloke he wants, that he should be lookin' for a fancy stranger who attended Birmin'am's shindig."

Gustav's mouth twisted downward as he considered the Englishman's threat. He had already given Olney ten thousand for Birmingham's arrest, and that deed had been accomplished. Considering the unfavorable sentiment that event had already been evoked against his rival, Gustav had every hope that before too much time elapsed Jeffrey Birmingham would be hanged for Nell's murder, which would leave Raelynn a bereaved widow. Once that happened, then he'd be able to collect everything he wanted from her. However, Frye could muddle up everything before the hanging, but Gustav wasn't about to stand for that.

"I vill pay yu zhe zhousand dollars to keep yur mouth closed, Frye," Gustav agreed at last, bringing a cocky grin to the Englishman's face. The German drew out a small strongbox from his desk, unlocked it, and counted out the necessary gold coins. "If I don't give yu zhis, I know yu vell enough to be assured zhat yu vill keep yer threat and haf Birmingham set free."

"His wife is me niece, after all, an' as they say, blood is thicker'n water." Frye collected the coins in a leather bag and then jauntily returned to the front portal, where, with a casual salute and a succinct smile, he took his leave.

"Damnation!" Gustav roared, slamming his fist down upon his desk. Pivoting about face, he stalked through the dark halls of his warehouse. "Vhere iz everybody? Morgan? Cheney? Muffat? Vhere are yu?"

No answer came, and he strode deeper into the structure until he could hear men grunting as they stacked wooden rifle boxes.

"Morgan, vhere are yu?"

"Here, sir, loadin' the rifles like ye told us ta do for shipment upriver."

"Forget zhat for zhe moment," Gustav commanded sharply. "I haf more important vork for yu to do now. Cooper Frye left here moments ago. He has become a hazard to our business ventures. I vant yu to . . . ah . . . How shall I say it? Put him out of his misery? Frye has a bag of coins on his person. If yu three lads do avay with him, then zhat vill be revard. Yu may share in it evenly or zeparately. It does not matter to me vhich vone of yu do it as long as Cooper Frye iz zilenced permanently. Yu understand?"

∽COOPER FRYE STROLLED AWAY FROM THE WARE-house, feeling very cocky with a thousand Yankee coins in his possession. It had been a while since he had had his mind clear of the dulling intoxicants he was wont to liberally quaff, and at the moment he was convinced that he could do no wrong. In fact, he had already planned his next venture to enlarge his wealth, possibly by as much as a few more thousand. It entailed arranging a meeting with an old acquaintance whom he had diligently been avoiding. This fellow was exceedingly more dangerous than the German, but if he kept his wits keen and clear, he had no doubt that he'd come out the victor. After all, this was his lucky day.

It was a rare occasion indeed when Cooper Frye sauntered down Meeting Street to the best hostelry in town and crossed its threshold. It wasn't that he disliked being in such a place. His reluctance to enter the establishment was simply due to the fact that he normally couldn't afford anything that was worth having on the premises and that, when he came in, the manager, along with almost everyone on his staff, looked at him as if he were something tainted that had just been washed up from the sea. Previously he had always left the place feeling the throes of deep depression, which had only driven him to imbibe all the more. At least now, he had money in his purse, but sorrowfully not enough to abide overlong where the taste of luxury was so pronounced and far too tempting for him to ignore.

A small bribe of a coin paid to a fetching maid, just slightly past her prime, left him reasonably assured that his note would be given to the occupant of the suite his acquaintance was letting. Even so, he followed covertly until well assured that the delivery had been made to the specified room. The maid had given the missive to the man's steward and then bustled back toward the area in which she had been working, humming happily to herself until her breath was snatched inward in shocked surprise as a large hand clapped rudely between her buttocks. She whirled with eyes blazing and, before Cooper Frye could stumble back to a safe distance, clamped a hand to his crotch, catching his manly possessions in a fierce grip that made him soar to the tips of his toes.

"Don't e'er do that again, ye blackguard!" she hissed through gnashing teeth. "If'n ye do, I'll tear 'em out, so help me I will. Do ye ken?" To make her point, she increased the pressure until Frye began to mumble all sorts of pleas and promises. *"Do ye ken?"*

He nodded speedily, affirming the fact that he'd do *anything* if she'd just let him go. Finally she condescended to turn him loose and did so with a satisfied chuckle. Cooper's breath left him in a relieved "whoosh" as she stepped back and dusted her hands, as if intimidating him had been all in a day's work.

"Bitch!" Cooper mumbled none too loudly and glowered after her as she pranced off with skirts swaying from stem to stern. His face contorted in a grimace as he twitched and tugged at his breeches, trying to right everything. What he feared most now was that he had been permanently shriveled.

Frye gradually collected his aplomb and straightened his clothes, shoddy as they were. Assuming an air of one who had immense wealth, he returned to the lower foyer and strolled out into the crisp, late afternoon air. He had no doubt that his associate would keep the appointment; it was certainly in the man's best interest to comply. Of course, Cooper Frye had been careful to arrange a meeting where the two of them would be well in sight of people. It was much safer that way.

"DAMMIT, RHYS, YOU'VE GOT TO LET ME GO," JEFF demanded hotly as he whirled to face the lawman, who, at the moment, was leaning back in his chair with his feet propped on his desk. "By now, most everyone in Charleston knows I've been arrested, and that knowledge will surely mean danger for my wife. Whether it's Gustav or the miscreant who attacked us, they'll likely see her as a bird in hand while I'm conveniently locked up and out of the way."

"You're not locked up, Jeffrey," the sheriff pointed

out, not unreasonably. He swept a hand toward the only occupied cell in the jail. Now that the doors were on both cells, he could even feel confident about keeping his young prisoner. "Olney is locked up. You're free." He indicated the wide area in which his guest was striding irately about, as if that one needed a reminder that he was roaming about the office unhindered and of his own accord. "In fact, if you don't stop pacing about, you're going to wear a damned hole through my floor."

"I'd like to wear a hole through that thick pate of yours, my friend. Maybe then you'd be able to understand what I'm talking about," Jeff retorted, pivoting about. "Can't you understand that my wife is virtually alone in Elizabeth's house, with only her maid and a four-year-old boy to come to her aid if something happens? Gustav has already been there, pressing his case to have her for himself. And no telling what that hooded demon who attacked us might be tempted to do in my absence. I tell you, Rhys, you've got to let me go!"

"Now, now, Jeffrey, I've got everything under control," the sheriff assured him. "I've spoken to Elijah, and he'll continue to watch over your wife. If anything happens, he'll let me know."

"That's not nearly enough to satisfy me!" Jeff argued. "Not now! Not while I'm in here!"

Rhys heaved a sigh, growing a bit frustrated with the unyielding persistence of the man. "Look, Jeffrey, why don't you just go lie down in your cell for a while and take a nap or something," he suggested. "Maybe then you'll calm down and see my point. If I were to let you go, then you'd likely be strung up, and what good would you be to your wife then?"

Pausing, Jeff set his jaw thoughtfully aslant and considered his situation, giving Rhys justification to think that he intended to be more reasonable now. That supposition was served quick death when Jeff stated his deductions. "I could just as well walk out of here. You haven't arrested me, and you know damn well that I'm innocent. So, I guess basically that leaves me a free man." Seriously testing that theory, he grabbed up his frockcoat and strode toward the front door. "I'll see you later, Rhys."

"Charlie!" Rhys barked, overturning his chair in his haste to get to the portal first. He did so, but only barely.

"I'm here, Sheriff," the deputy replied, shuffling in from the back room.

Rhys met the glaring emerald eyes that were level with his own, and though he never wavered before them, just the same he felt the hackles rise on the back of his neck. He faced a man equal to his own height and, though lighter by a couple of stone or more, was still very much in prime physical strength. Jeffrey Birmingham could be damned pleasant, as Rhys well knew, even easygoing, but there was no doubt about it, steel formed the core of his backbone. It didn't take but a moment for Rhys to realize just why the Birminghams were considered dangerous men to rile. If those deep green shards couldn't stab a person to the heart, then it would be the men who possessed them who'd continue the fight until the last foe and culprit was hung. "Handcuff Mr. Birmingham to his cot."

"What?!" Jeff cried in spiraling rage. "Dammit, Rhys, you're not going to do that to me, not when my wife may be in danger!"

The sheriff pushed a hand against the hard, muscular shoulder, trying to shove his friend back away from the door. "Get in your cell."

"No, dammit!" Jeff snapped, coming around with a clenched fist.

It wasn't much more than a tap on the head, but after his recent concussion, it was definitely enough to send Jeffrey buckling to the floor and into the realm of oblivion. Rhys beckoned for Charlie to come help him, and between the two of them, they managed to get the unconscious man into the cell where they stretched him out upon the cot.

"That should keep Mr. Birmin'am quiet for a while, eh, Sheriff?" the deputy remarked with a rueful grin. "Ye still want me ta handcuff him?"

"No, just leave him be. He's going to be mad enough when he wakes up without adding mayhem to folly. We'll just lock the door to make sure he stays in here once he comes around." Rhys shook his head ruefully. "If we come through this thing with our hides still intact, Charlie, it certainly won't be because Mr. Birmingham won't be trying to skin us."

"Hey, Sheriff?"

Rhys turned toward the occupant of the other cell. Presently the curly-headed rascal was lounging upon his cot, looking for all the world like he was enjoying himself. The young rogue took great delight in harassing him. Indeed, he just wouldn't give up. "What do you want, Olney?"

Scratching his chin, the scamp turned his head on his pillow and grinned back at the lawman. "Ye afraid o' Birmin'am? If'n ye ain't, ye sure act like it."

Rhys sighed heavily. "Be quiet, Olney."

⌐◦COOPER FRYE WAITED AT THE PROVOST DUNGEON, an old custom house which the British had used to lock up prisoners during the war, until half an hour past the time he had specified in his note. Considering everything, he had thought it a befitting place to meet, but he now decided that it would do him little good to stay around any longer. Obviously the man wasn't going to come.

Leaving Exchange Street, he turned north toward Market Street and, after entering that area, bought himself an apple to munch. He had just braced a shoulder against the trunk of a tree when an elongated shadow fell upon him and stretched out across the ground beyond him. In the next moment he felt a knife prodding in the area of his ribs.

"Aftahnoon, Coop," a husky voice greeted near his ear.

"Morgan?" Cooper Frye tried to turn, but the point of the blade gave him another goading, reminding him to keep still. "What are ye doin'?"

"Ye made Mr. Fridrich real mad this time. Me an' the boys were sent out aftah ye, but I founds ye first, so's I'm supposin' that means I can keep the reward all ta meself."

"What reward?" Cooper's eyes cut to the left as he strained to catch a glimpse of the man.

"The reward ye're carryin' on ye. I'll take it if'n ye don't mind."

"I gots it in me shirt, but if'n I tries ta give it ta ye now, people'll think ye're robbin' me an' call the law."

Morgan thought about that not more than a moment. Fridrich wouldn't like Sheriff Townsend involved in this matter, and neither would he. "Let's go closer to the bay where there ain't as many folks what'll be around ta watch us." As Frye hesitated, the blade nudged the flabby roll around his waist. "Get goin' afore I lose patience wit' ye."

Cooper Frye reluctantly complied. When they were well out of sight of witnesses, he began dragging off his coat. It was still attached to one hand when he brought it around with a vengeance, striking Morgan hard across the face and sending the knife flying and its bearer stumbling backward with eyes smarting. In the next instant Cooper scooped up the weapon and plunged into the soft paunch of his would-be assailant. When it was drawn out again, Morgan gave a gurgling sound and collapsed to his knees. Frye smirked in satisfaction for barely a moment as the man crumpled in a knot at his feet, and then he glanced about, finding the way entirely unencumbered with people. Lucky day, it was indeed, he thought as he made good his escape.

꙳BARELY HAD COOPER FRYE DOSED OFF THAN HE WAS snatched abruptly awake by a weird, low, caterwauling wail that sent shivers spiraling up his spine. His eyes popped open and warily he rolled them about their sockets until his gaze lit on something huge and monstrous looming above him. It had no face, only a loose blank mask of deep blackness from which sunken cavities served as eyes. At first, he was convinced that he was dreaming. His second conclusion was exceedingly more terrifying. He was a man with little conscience, that being a poorly stunted nubbin which had never troubled him overmuch. He did, however, have a vivid imagination and a deep dread of spirits, which he was still convinced had haunted his grandfather's house where he had grown up, upon the property of which a later discovery had found a boarded up well filled with the skeletal remains of nigh to a dozen men. The shape that hovered above him now had all the same appearances of a specter from hell.

". . . G-ghost!" Frye screamed in a whisper, the best his constricted throat could issue forth. He thought of Morgan right away. After all, it had happened only two or three hours ago. Or was it some dreadful spirit from a past encounter during which he had deemed the taking of a life in his best interest? A whole host of names had long been forgotten from such incidents.

Then, if the visitation wasn't frightening enough, Frye's fumbling brain fell upon a prospect that was far worse. Had the darkly cloaked form come to herald his death?

Frantically clawing his way up against the headboard,

he croaked, "Are ye' a banshee? I thought I heard ye' howl."

"Wake up, man. You heard nothing more than a tom-cat yowling outside your window," a cold voice jeered. A soft, merciless chuckle deepened Frye's descent into a terror of the unknown. "Of course, there are some who've been led to think that I'm a messenger from Satan, and to be fair, I must allow that they have had just cause to think that way."

Even as Frye tried to sort this out in his sleep-dulled brain, a new panic surged upward within him, chilling his heart as a shaft of moonlight glinted on the length of a gleaming blade. A strangled sound emitted from his tightening throat as he felt its deadly edge press against his windpipe.

"I suggest that you try not to shake overly much," the apparition cautioned in a tone of exaggerated concern. "I have a remarkably steady hand, but even so, accidental slips have a way of occurring."

Frye croaked a response which amounted to little more than a hastily babbled agreement.

The intruder chuckled again. "Tell me," he urged, "have you any idea who I am?"

Frye nodded frantically. Much to his sorrow, he knew exactly who was here with him, the very one who had first stabbed Nell.

"And do you know why I've come?"

"I . . . I left ye a note askin' ye ta meet me, mate, but ye ne'er showed up."

"I'm not one of your sniveling mates, so don't call me that again," the abrasive voice snarled as the edge of the knife encroached menacingly.

"Wh-What w-would ye like for m-me to call ye, milord?"

"That's better." The knife was withdrawn ever so slightly. "How did you know I was here in the colonies and where I was to be found?"

Frye could hardly think when his every thought was focused on the sharpness of the weapon grating against his whiskers. Though the constraint had eased to some degree, it still remained precariously close to a vital vein. "Please, I'll tell ye if'n ye give me room ta breathe."

An evil, jeering hiss was emitted from the dark mask as the pressure lessened some slight degree. "Think before you speak, Frye. I will tolerate no lies."

"I know, milord. Well, for one thing, Nell was still livin' when I found her in the stables. I helped ye out, I did, by finishin' what ye'd started, but afore I did, Nell told me she'd come 'pon a stranger whittlin' on me niece's coffer in Birmin'am's bedchamber. I figgered it could only be one o' three blokes interested in that 'ere box. An' since ye're a man o' taste, I decided ye'd be at the best inn in town. Then, too, I thought yer friends would be o' a mind ta send ye ta take care o' business, seein's as how ye were the most . . . ah . . . efficient."

"Barrett's daughter is not your niece, you uncouth bastard, so don't put on airs with me. You'll never be part of the nobility. You're just a common tar who has a fair memory when he's sober and once had the good fortune to become mates with the real Cooper Frye before he was swept overboard and drowned."

The aging seaman chortled. "Aye, young Coop always liked ta talk 'bout his family, he did. Worked ta me advantage right nicely, too. I knew his stories 'bout his home an' folks well enough ta fool his own sister, I did."

His lordship laughed caustically. "Yes, and much to our regret, you talked her into sailing here to the colonies."

"I al'ays had a hankerin' ta settle down in this here part o' the world, but e'ery ship I signed onto took me anywheres but where I wanted ta go. Convincin' Lady Barrett o' the merits o' livin' here wasn't too hard, considerin' the ridicule she an' her daughter 'ad fallen prey ta after Lord Barrett keeled o'er. 'Twas certainly the best way I could think o' ta get meself o'er here, so's I pleaded poverty till she agreed ta loan me money for me passage."

"In so doing, you left me and my companions wondering if we could trust you. I decided forthwith that we couldn't, so I followed. After all, I was the one responsible for letting the missive fall into Barrett's hands. It was my fool luck that my servant mistook Barrett for the one he was supposed to meet, and it was Barrett's greater folly to be at the wrong place at the wrong time, but, of course, it didn't help that the courier to France had been delayed. But that is neither here nor there. Barrett is dead, thanks to you, and right now, all my companions and I have to worry about is the whereabouts of the information he sequestered in his resolve to present it at his trial. Considering all the transfers up the scale of individuals responsible for passing it on to the king, I suppose he had a right to feel wary of it falling into the wrong hands. After what we had done to the man, one could hardly blame him for being cautious, even about those who tried to help him. He refused to see anybody until you came along. Indeed, if not for your chicanery in claiming to be his wife's brother, Barrett would have presented his evidence, and my companions and I would have been arrested. For that I must be grateful, but I can only wonder what you're up to now. If you've found the message and intend to use it against us, be assured, I have ways of dealing with men like you. So I'll ask you outright, what do you want from me?"

"I did find the message, gov'na, just as ye thought, an' after takin' a looksee at it, I can understand why ye were so afraid o' what ye'd loose if'n it fell inta the wrong hands, yer life at the very least. No doubt, it would've served England's enemies well, what wit' it reportin', amonst other things, the weaknesses in his majesty's military defenses. Too bad it bore the signatures o' ye an' yer two companions. If not for that, ye needn't have gone ta so much bother tryin' ta get it back."

"Such knowledge could bring about your death, Frye," the gravelly voice warned.

"Oh, aye! I knows that for sure, gov'na. That's why I haven't talked ta another soul about it until now, milord."

"You certainly took your own sweet time getting the news to me. Nell has been dead for over a month."

"I had ta work up me courage, gov'na, seein's as how I left London wit'out tellin' ye, an' all. I was afraid ye'd cut me up wit' that knife o' yers, but I finally decided ta take me chances an' tell it ta ye outright, like the honest man that I am."

Lord Marsden laughed disparagingly. "Somehow I just can't believe you, Frye. You know as well as I do that you're not very honest at all."

"Now would I seek ye out if'n I didn't mean ta give ye the parchment?"

Though his lordship was suspicious of an ulterior motive, he was nevertheless curious. "Where did you find the missive? In Barrett's personal coffer as I had once thought it might be?"

"Aye, gov'na, but it took more'n just openin' the lid ta find it. I scratched me noggin many an hour puzzlin' o'er that box, but then, I had time on me hands sailin' all the way from England. If'n ye hadn't suggested 'ere might be a hidden compartment in the box, I'da've given up long afore I found it. Nearly took me two an' half months ta finally figger out how ta get inta the damned thing, but 'ere it were, just like ye'd said, right in the bottom o' the box, the very same ye tried ta get inta afore ye stabbed poor Nell."

The cloaked form turned aside to gaze upon the moonlit scene stretching out beyond the window. "I thought it would be there," he murmured thoughtfully, "but after framing Barrett on treasonous charges and having my claims deemed ludicrous by many of his peers and those in much higher places, I was afraid to even go near his estate for fear his friends would be watching. You were my last resort, and of course, when you managed to get into Barrett's cell with claims of being his brother-in-law, I had high hopes that you'd be able to find what we were searching for." Once again the menacing figure faced the shaggy-haired fellow, but now his hissing voice was imbued with a caustic sneer. "I never expected you to bungle your visit and kill him before you had the missive well within your grasp."

Frye protested. "How was I ta know the poison would work on him as fast as it did? I thought I'd have plenty o' time ta question him. I gave it ta him in a little wine just like ye said, an' then, followed yer directions ta the letter by informin' him o' what I'd done an' promisin' him an antidote if'n he'd give me the paper or, at the very least, tell me where it were ta be found, but the poison barely hit his belly an' then he was gone." Frye snapped his finger to lend emphasis to his declaration. " 'At fast, damn him!"

"No, 'tis you who'll likely be damned, Frye, for being the conniving scoundrel you are," the hooded one countered. "You not only turn on your foes, but your friends as well. My companions and I didn't realize you weren't to be trusted when you overheard us talking and offered us a solution to our dilemma. You took our money and then you turned right around and encouraged Lady Barrett to leave England. Now I've heard enough of your feeble excuses . . ."

"She was gonna flee the country anyway," Frye declared in an anxious rush. "She couldn't bear the jeers o' e'en the common folk livin' 'round where she'd taken a cottage. I knows that for a fact. One o' 'em threw a cabbage at me whilst I was visitin' the Barretts an' nearly knocked me cross-eyed. I did everythin' a bloke could've done in a situation like that. Didn't I convince Evalina Barrett that I were her own brother? Do ye think that were easy?" Frye got himself so worked up in exaggerating his excuses, tears of misery sprang into his eyes. His knobby chin even quivered. "I've been livin' as Cooper Frye so long now sometimes I don't e'en remember me own name!"

"By the way, what is your real name? We never got around to that."

"Fenton . . . Oliver Fenton."

It mattered not a whit to the man who heard it. "Well, Fenton, where is the missive now?"

Oliver Fenton still had a card he hadn't played yet. "Seein's as how ye an' yer friends were so anxious ta get it into yer thankful li'l grasp months ago, I thought we could come ta some kind o' new agreement 'bout what ye'd be willin' ta pay ta get it back."

"Be warned, Fenton," the visitor rumbled. "I'll not tolerate being skimmed by the likes of you again."

"When have I e'er . . . ?"

"You took payment from me and my friends, Prescott and Havelock, and we trusted you to find the letter that had fallen into Barrett's hands. We paid you a goodly sum and promised you more." His voice hardened. "The first portion you guzzled down in England in spite of the fact that you produced absolutely nothing to appease our fears. Now I can only wonder what more you may be wanting."

"Only what ye promised me, milord, an' a li'l bit more ta allow me ta buy a proper pub . . ."

"What?" The darkly cloaked one scoffed in rampant disbelief. "For you to drink up all the profits? Where is the message you found?"

"In safekeepin', milord."

The knife pressed against Frye's throat again, this time drawing blood. "Tell me where it is, damn you."

"If'n ye kill me, milord, ye'll ne'er find it. It's in someone else's safekeepin' an' should they hear o' me death, they'll be takin' it ta the Barrett girl . . . or, as she's known now, Mrs. Birmin'am."

"The devil, you say!" Marsden barked. "Why would you have it sent to her? From what I hear, she and that Yankee husband of hers forbade you to even set foot on their plantation, much less allow you to approach them here in Charleston."

"Ye could say I owes the girl one for poisonin' her pa an' lettin' her ma starve. Besides, after I'm dead, it won't matter ta me anymore that I don't have any money. That'll be the only good I'll be leavin' behind me." The seaman chortled. " 'Sides, she an' her mister ain't likely gonna be the ones what'll kill me. Fine, up-standin' people, they are."

Lord Marsden saw the logic in the man's reasoning and sensed that this time Fenton wouldn't be moved from his stand. And why should he? In this case, he had the upper hand. If the girl received the missive, she would definitely see that it was carried swiftly back to England by reputable barristers, and they, in turn, would set about clearing her father's name and condemning those guilty of not only framing him but of treasonous acts against the crown.

Abruptly Marsden removed the knife. "So, Fenton! How much more do you want, and how do you intend to carry out this trade so each of us can be assured that we won't suffer the consequences of trusting the other?"

"I want at least five thousand more."

A long silence answered him as his lordship limped slowly away. His rasping voice spoke from across the room. "Go on."

"Now I knows if'n I don't keep me end o' the bargain, ye'll be comin' after me, lookin' for blood. That, so to speak, will warrant me good behavior. As for meself, I want ye ta send yer servant wit' the five thousand Yankee dollars ta the name o' the cat house what I'll be directin' ye ta. Once there, yer man will be given further instructions as ta where ta go. After I have the money in hand, he'll receive the message in a wooden box that'll be sealed ta keep yer secrets secure. Then I'll send yer steward home ta ye in a carriage."

"That really doesn't guarantee that I'll be getting the missive after you get your money. There must be a better way to handle this matter."

"I knows what ye can do wit' that 'ere knife o' yers, gov'na, an' I also knows other things ye can do, like runnin' for the sheer pleasure o' it. Now, ta tell ye the truth, I ain't ne'er seen that afore. But then, I guess that's what keeps ye fit an' happy, likin' peculiar things like that." Fenton laughed briefly. "Ye can bet I ain't gonna be around long after I receives me money. An' just ta keep ye satisfied it's been a fair trade, I'm gonna keep me word for a change. Maybe then ye won't be o' a mind ta comes after me wit' that big knife o' yers."

The grating voice finally responded. "You may live beyond this night after all, Fenton. Just be careful to do exactly as you have said. Otherwise, I won't rest until I've seen your carcass buried in a slime pit."

The door closed behind the darkly cloaked visitor, and Oliver Fenton finally slumped away from the headboard and let his breath out in a long sigh of relief. Throwing himself from the bed, he poured himself a stout drink and tossed it down with a flip of his wrist. He lit a lamp and, for a moment, considered his shaking hands. One thing was for sure, he was getting too damned old to be scared out of his wits.

Stumbling footfalls in the hallway made him stiffen in sudden apprehension. He could only think that his lordship had had a change of heart and would be concluding the matter with a murderous deed, but the voice of the fellow passing the room was slurred from heavy imbibing.

Fenton released his breath for a second time in so many minutes, deciding it was only a drunk searching for a vacant bed in the boardinghouse. He had no wish to endure the presence of another in his rented room, and, to forestall such a possibility, stepped to the door, opened it and peered out. He had closed it again and was about to lock it when the plank was shoved suddenly inward by a brawny shoulder. Stumbling back with a gasp of surprise, Fenton gaped at the two men who approached him with knives drawn. He let out a blood-curdling scream as he was seized, but the sound was effectively silenced by a deep slit across his throat. His eyes widened as he realized it hadn't been his lucky day after all. He gulped, gurgling up blood, and then toppled forward to the floor.

In the yard outside, a cloaked form came around with a start as a shriek of terror filled the night. His eyes searched out and found the room in which he had just visited, and as he watched in gathering dread, two men immediately began crawling out through the windows. They scrambled across the roof and as one paused to throw down an object that looked very much like a knife, the other one dropped to the ground below. Both left as quickly as they had appeared.

A woman's scream pierced the stillness of the night. "Fetch the sheriff! Cooper Frye's been killed!"

The dark shade turned and hurriedly limped into the trees. He knew where he must go now.

23 ❧

The garden was damp with the morning dew. Behind him the house his uncle owned was silent as a tomb. After a midday Sunday feast, his relatives had retired to the drawing room to play whisk. Personally he had never had too much interest in those card games and looked in on his older brother, who had ensconced himself in the library. No entertaining diversions to be found there, he thought. Finally he wandered out into the garden to have a look around the mansion that had been handed down through a long line of ancestors. A wrought-iron gate separating the neighboring grounds lent strong evidence of an abiding friendship between the two landowners. Beyond it, he had occasionally glimpsed a little, auburn-haired girl playing with her dolls and cat in the adjoining garden. The animal was ever wont to come slinking through the ornate gate to investigate the neighbors' softly tilled soil. Appearing quite large with its gray, puffed fur nearly standing on end, the feline usually poked its pink nose into this and that until she found a suitable spot. Today, the cat came to sniff around his polished riding boots. Rubbing herself against the fine leather, she purred as if pleading to be picked up. Willingly he complied and scratched her behind the ear just as he had always done with the cats back home. Upon hearing the creak of metal, he glanced up to find the little girl, with a tentative smile upon her face, standing near the open gate as she peered about inquisitively. A butterfly soared close overhead, and squealing in glee, she held out a hand as she chased after it.

He chuckled at her efforts. "You'll never catch them like that, little miss."

The girl seemed startled by his voice and, looking around, gazed up at him with a curious frown. She saw her cat in his arms, and her aqua blue eyes twinkled back at him, as if that made him acceptable.

"Here now, let's get you home before your parents have to come looking for you," he gently admonished, sweeping her onto his shoulder. She gave a little cry, as if afraid of being so high, and grabbed a handful of his hair to secure her lofty perch. An auburn ringlet tumbled down around her lace collar as she looked down at him. She managed a hesitant grin and then a nervous giggle.

It began to rain, a gentle misting rain that dampened her curls and his uplifted, smiling face.

૭ᴊᴇғғ BOLTED UPRIGHT, ABRUPTLY SNATCHED FROM his dreams. That's when his head exploded. "Damn!" he muttered in agony and clasped the heels of his hands to his temples as he bellowed, *"Rhys! What the devil did you do to me?"*

A soft chuckle from nearby made Jeff squint against the glare of the lantern that hung in the aisle between the cells. His eyes probed the gloom beyond the circle of light until he espied the young rapscallion who had started all of this.

"Afternoon, Birmin'am," Olney greeted with a cocky grin. "How ye feelin' this evenin'? Maybe ye don't know it, but ye've been out for quite a while. In fact, the sheriff was of a mind ta think ye were gonna sleep clean through till morn'n. Guess he figgered it was safe ta leave ye."

"Be quiet, Olney," Jeff snapped. In spite of the throbbing in his head, he swept his gaze carefully about the confines of the jailhouse and found it empty save for Olney and himself. Though he was sure his head would likely come off, he staggered to the cell door and reached out to shove it open. Much to his amazement, it wouldn't budge. Angrily he shook it and then, leaning his forehead close against the bars, peered down the narrow corridor leading to the back of the building. "Dammit, Rhys, come open this door!" he railed at the top of his lungs. "You have no reason to keep me locked up in here!"

The curly-haired scalawag sniggered in amusement and, lying back upon his bunk, folded his arms beneath his head and crossed his stockinged ankles. "The sheriff an' his deputy went out a while ago. Someone came flyin' in here, sayin' a man had gots his throat cut at some boardin'house. 'Ere's just ye an' me here now, Birmin'am. Yep, the ways I figures it, Sheriff Rhys wanted ta keep ye for a spell, maybe just ta show ye who's boss."

"I'll show him who's boss," Jeff promised with a snarl, eyeing the ring of keys hanging on a lofty hook across the narrow hall. He stumbled back to the cot, picked it up and promptly smashed it to the floor, breaking off a wooden leg. Flipping it over, he proceeded to kick off the rest of the supports and then used one to break apart the frame.

All of this was enough to make Olney sit up on the side of his bed and chortle. "I always knew ye had a bad temper, Birmin'am."

"You haven't seen the half of it yet, Olney," Jeff assured him, finally freeing a side frame from the cot. It was just about the right size, slightly longer than he was tall.

Jeff took up the rail and stepped back to the bars of his cell. Sliding the piece of wood through the iron barriers, he grasped one end firmly and, slipping his free hand through another section of bars, maneuvered the end of his makeshift pole until he had positioned it just beneath the ring of keys hanging from a peg on the far side of the corridor. Fishing around until he had the end of the shaft in the circlet, he took his time easing the ring off the dowel. He grinned broadly in satisfaction as the metal loop slid downward along the wooden shank, right into his grasp.

Olney had watched in rapt attention for the last few moments. Now he closed his mouth, realizing it had plummeted open in surprise. Perceiving some hope for his own escape, he approached the bars of his cubicle as Jeffrey unlocked his cell door and stepped out. The rascal licked his lips, already tasting the freedom that could be his if he could only get the other man to comply. "Eh, Birmin'am, how 'bout lettin' me out, too. I really didn't do anythin' deservin' o' bein' locked away for years ta come . . ."

"What about attempted murder?" Jeff asked curtly. "As my butler can attest, you tried to kill me when you and the rest of Gustav's brigands forced your way into my house."

"Oh, but that were just a bloomin' accident, Birmin'am," Olney cajoled and reached out a hand imploringly, hoping the man would relent. "Please, ye've gotta understand. I didn't mean ta shoot ye. Me pistol just went off by itself."

Jeff clasped the ring of keys in his hand and, taking aim, sent them sailing back to the peg from whence they had come. Then he settled his hands on his lean hips and shook his head sorrowfully as if sorely lamenting his perfect bull's-eye. "Now I really didn't mean to do that, Olney. I'm sorry. They just landed there by accident."

Olney snorted, sounding much like a bull elephant. "Yeah! Sure! An' ye're a black-hearted liar, Birmin'am."

Realizing his headache had eased, Jeff decided he felt remarkably well and content with himself, at least enough to toss a grin toward the young miscreant as he strode past his cell. "Like you, Olney?"

❦HER CAT BOUNDED ALONG BESIDE HER AS SHE TOTtered past flowers taller than she. Musicians were playing in the neighbor's yard where a number of guests had collected, luring her ever onward to the garden gate. Through the ornate filigree adorning the iron barrier she espied several couples swirling about the marble terrace adjoining the elegant mansion. Entranced with a childlike fascination for fairy tales, knights in shining armor, and beautiful ladies, she watched the graceful dancing, her small body swaying to the music. Her cat purred as it brushed against her skirts. Inquisitively the animal turned to peer into the adjoining garden, and then, with lithe grace, leapt through the bars. The feline paused to investigate a recently tilled flower bed near the opening before sauntering leisurely onward to other areas, by slow degrees nearing the cluster of people who sat in a group near one corner of the terrace.

Suddenly a loud barking rent the peace, and a large dog raced across the lawn toward the cat, who hissed in sudden fear and scurried to the safcty of several large, encompassing shrubs, through which the canine could not readily pass. Frantically searching for an opening, the dog raced back and forth in front of the bushes until a loud whistle drew his attention. A tall, young man with short-cropped black hair strode into view and issued a brusque command, sending the dog lumbering back toward the house where a servant put him on a leash. The nice man squatted near the shrubs and coaxed the cat out of hiding until it came into his arms where it purred contentedly beneath the long, slow, gentle strokes of his hand.

Tossing a glance toward the gate, the gentleman broke a flower from its stem and came forward with a grin. Smiling into the aqua-blue eyes that watched him intently through the bars, he swung open the iron portal and stepped through. He whisked the animal to the ground and then, with a gallant bow, offered the flower to the little girl.

Smiling timidly, she accepted the young knight's gift and sampled its fragrance. The petals tickled, and she wrinkled her nose as she giggled. Leaning her head far back, she peered up at the one who loomed over her. The early afternoon sun shimmered behind his head, and the brilliance of the halo around his dark head made her squint and rub her eyes. Yawning, she dropped her head and fingered the petals as she examined the pretty flower.

"Looks like it's your nap time, little miss," the handsome knight remarked with a chuckle. "Perhaps I should take you back to your parents before you fall asleep out here."

Bending low, he lifted her up into his arms and followed the winding trail back toward the neighboring mansion. After another yawn, she began to sing a tune her mother had taught her. Her tall knight joined her. He had a nice, soothing voice, and soon he was waltzing her along the path, evoking more giggles.

Once they gained the clearing near the place where her mother had been gathering flowers from their garden, the young man sat her to her feet and was about to turn away, but she caught his hand and grinned up at him until he squatted down. Throwing her arms about his neck, she kissed him on his cheek and then ran laughing to her mother, who had turned in time to witness the exchange. Smiling, her parent invited the man in for a cup of tea, but his uncle had invited guests over to meet them, he explained, and hurried back along the trail.

Tilting her head from side to side, she began to chant a singsong ditty as the sun smiled down upon her and a butterfly flitted past.

RAELYNN CAME AWAKE WITH A START, NOT ENTIRELY sure why she had been snatched so abruptly from her dreams. She lay for a moment, trying to discern what was wrong, all her senses keenly attuned to the sounds of the house. A distant thump intruded and, in trembling apprehension, she waited to hear more, hoping it had come from a neighbor's house.

Another thud and a chair scraping over a bare floor downstairs brought Raelynn out of bed in an instant. Shaking uncontrollably, she searched down the length of her bed, patting her hands over the rumpled covers as she sought to locate her robe. She found it near the foot and donned it in frantic haste. She stumbled over her slippers and slid into them, all the while mentally sorting out what she must do. If the noises had indeed been created by a human, then she could entertain no hope that it was her husband returning. Before departing, Rhys Townsend had taken time to assure her that he would be keeping Jeff locked up for his own safety. Nor could she believe that it was Elizabeth or Farrell returning. When the newly wedded couple had left, they had said they wouldn't be coming back until Sunday night at the earliest, still a good many hours away.

Cautiously Raelynn crept through the impenetrable blackness until she reached the door. Once there, she turned the doorknob ever so carefully and eased the portal open. She was thankful for the shaft of moonlight streaming through the windows at the far end of the hall, for it allowed her to see her way clearly. A concern for Jake and her servant drew her down the corridor toward Tizzy's room. Slipping within the cubicle, she paused within the door to let her eyes adjust to the dense shadows until she could make out the girl sleeping soundly in her bed. Raelynn approached and, leaning across, pressed a hand over the maid's mouth.

Tizzy came upright with a muffled gasp and searched about with widened eyes, until her gaze lit on her mistress. The spark of fear shining in her dark eyes ebbed as her brow gathered in confusion.

"Don't make a sound," Raelynn whispered, leaning near the girl's ear. "There's someone moving around downstairs, so listen very carefully, and please, please don't make any noise. Slip into your robe, wake Jake up, and wait for me at the landing. I'm going to fetch Miss Elizabeth's pistol from her room, and then, if I can, I'm going to try and lure the intruder away from the kitchen. Make sure the path is clear before you slip downstairs, so watch and listen very carefully to determine where the man may be. You're to leave by the back door. Go directly to Mr. Farrell's apartment, and tell him that I'm here by myself and that there's a prowler in the house. Do you understand?"

"Yes, Miz Raelynn," the girl whispered back worriedly, "but if'n it's Mistah Fridrich downstairs, yo' gonna be in mo' trouble than ah'd be if'n ah stayed. Why don't yo' let me draw him 'way from de back door whilst yo' leave an' take Mistah Jake ta Mistah Farrell's. Dat way yo'll be safe an' sound."

"No argument, Tizzy. Just do as I say," Raelynn insisted. "Mr. Fridrich won't kill me. He wants me too much. You, he might. Now get yourself up, and hurry! If I get a chance to slip out the house, I will, but I've got to make sure you and Jake are safe before I do."

Tizzy heaved a reluctant sigh, but she had no other option. She had to obey. She set about fulfilling the behest as quickly as possible and, some moments later, waited at the top of the stairs with a cautious hand over Jake's mouth as her mistress began a cautious descent.

Raelynn winced as the step upon which she had cautiously lit popped beneath her weight. In the next instant, she heard a bump in the dining room. In Elizabeth's absence, the draperies of the front parlor had been left open, and one glance confirmed that there was no one in the room. In a rush Raelynn completed her descent and flew to the parlor from whence she dared to call out, "Who's there?"

No verbal answer came, only another thump.

"I know someone's here in the house!" she cried in quavering tones. "Now who are you?"

A strange scrape, much like a foot being dragged across a section of floor, made her start and clasp a trembling hand to her throat. If she had had any doubt before, then her suspicions were now thoroughly confirmed. There *was* an intruder prowling around.

"Gustav, is that you?" she called in a faltering voice and tried desperately to pluck up her courage. "If it is, you'd better be warned. I have a loaded pistol in my hand, and I'll use it if I must."

Out of the corner of her eye, Raelynn saw Tizzy and Jake scurrying into the hall. Lest the man hear them moving about, she continued talking. "You shouldn't have come, Gustav. Sheriff Townsend will see your intrusion into this house as reason enough to arrest you. This time you won't be able to claim innocence."

Another scrape of a chair almost sent Raelynn flying back upstairs in spiraling trepidation. By dint of will, she held her ground even though it took every effort for her to remain where she was. If not for her shaking, she might have felt a lot braver about the situation.

A large dark shadow emerged from the dining room,

and Raelynn gasped as she realized it wasn't Gustav at all, but their cloaked and hooded assailant. She screamed, totally forgetting about the pistol she clasped, and raced into the hallway. She fully expected to be caught by a man whose swiftness had aroused the sheriff's awe, but much to her bemusement, he lumbered after her, as if impeded by some unknown hindrance. Indeed, he seemed to be dragging a foot behind him.

Now recognizing an imminent threat to her life, Raelynn darted into the dark kitchen and tore around the huge hearth in an anxious quest to get to the back door, only to cry out in sudden alarm as she went flying over an overturned chair, an obstacle that had been deliberately placed in the shadows across the path to the back door where it wouldn't be readily seen. No doubt Tizzy had been creeping cautiously through the kitchen when she had come upon the chair, but Raelynn had been too caught up in a frenzy to escape to notice.

Tumbling forward, Raelynn made every effort to spare her baby injury by twisting to the side. Alas, she forgot about the large crock that stood at the far end of the brick hearth. Her head caught the brunt of the impact, leaving her senses jarred.

Dazed but still determined to find safety, she forced herself to keep moving and managed to crawl beneath the table where she huddled in the shadows near the far corner. Barely a moment later, the darkly clothed shade stumbled into the kitchen and then came to a halt, evidently mystified by her whereabouts. Very slowly he crept to the back door. He snatched it open abruptly, wrenching a surprised start from Raelynn, but she clasped a trembling hand over her mouth, stilling herself for that moment when he would turn and start searching the kitchen for her.

Hardly daring to breathe while her assailant was so near, Raelynn waited in heightening anxiety, her heart thudding wildly in her chest as she crouched in a small knot within the gloom. She became increasingly mindful of the man's laborious panting and considered that very odd indeed for one who could run so swiftly. Indeed, he wheezed as if afflicted with some strange malady. Considering the physical prowess he had already exhibited, the man should have displayed no exertion at all, especially from so simple a task as walking into the kitchen, but that didn't appear to be the case at all. Then she recalled that moments earlier she had heard him lumbering behind her. That memory certainly didn't conform to Rhys's premise that their attacker enjoyed running. Perhaps she had been mistaken about this being the same man who had launched his attack upon them in the fog, Raelynn thought. But then, the hood and the cape were the same, weren't they?

Crouching in her lowly hiding place, Raelynn debated her chances of reaching the dining room door before the man became aware of her hiding place and blocked her path. The way he was plodding along, she just might be able to do it.

In the waiting silence, Raelynn heard the front door open, bringing her to alert attention. The visitor's footsteps were too quickly muffled by the hall rug to allow her any hope of recognition, but her eyes widened in sudden apprehension as she saw the darkly cloaked intruder draw a knife from the enveloping shroud he wore. Turning, he advanced toward the dining room with a rapid, but halting gait.

Raelynn's mind flew. Tizzy hadn't been gone long enough to allow any possibility that the new arrival was Farrell. So who, other than Jeffrey, was making his way into the house?

Finding no other name but her husband's to lay to the one who had just entered, Raelynn scrambled out from underneath the table and, behind the man's back, dashed through the doorway leading to the hallway, trying desperately to cock the weapon she clasped as she ran. Such a task proved much harder than she had supposed, and she cursed the foul thing as a tool of Satan as she raced with all of her heart and strength in a frantic effort to outdistance the masked prowler. When she reached the parlor door, the culprit was just leaving the dining room.

Rhys Townsend glanced in her direction, having heard swiftly racing footfalls approaching from down the corridor. Oblivious of the intruder entering the parlor, he never saw the knife hurtling toward him.

"Rhys, look out!" Raelynn screamed.

The lawman threw himself to the side, but much too late. He gasped as the blade sank into his chest and staggered unsteadily as his legs slowly gave way beneath him. In the next moment he collapsed against a chair and then slowly slid to the floor where he sat, feebly trying to clasp the hilt of the weapon.

Intent upon this murderous game, the villain advanced upon the sheriff with an awkward hop and a skip. Raelynn gnashed her teeth in fierce determination and drove the side of her palm downward upon the firing mechanism. It clicked into place just as the man jerked the knife from Rhys's chest, wrenching an agonized cry from the lawman. The assailant drew back his arm, fully intending to plunge the knife in again for good measure. In the next instant the pistol exploded, sending a lead ball through the culprit's hand. The devilish demon roared in pain as the blade went flying out of his grasp. Clutching the wounded extremity, he seemed to writhe in agony as his breath slashed harshly through the air holes in his mask. Then he stumbled about to face Raelynn, and the moonlit glow streaming through the parlor windows glinted off the eyes hidden beneath the slitted openings, making the hooded beast seem truly demonic as he rasped in guttural tones.

"Bitch! I'll kill you yet!"

Lurching toward her, he snatched a handkerchief

from a pocket in his cloak and wrapped it about his bleeding hand. Then he put into play his hitching gait that, though clumsy, seemed far too fast for her to escape.

Raelynn's hands still stung from the force of the exploding pistol. Had she been given enough time to reload the weapon, such a feat would have been difficult, for now she was shaking uncontrollably. Gritting her teeth to still the tremors, she raised the useless flintlock behind her head and threw it at her adversary. It caught him alongside his darkly garbed cheek, causing him to curse and bat it away with his good hand.

The moonlight touched upon his hooded head, illumining the cloth to a midnight gray while darkening the eyeholes to a flinty black. His gaze now seemed centered unrelentingly upon her as he hobbled toward her.

Raelynn whirled, knowing full well where she was going this time. Out! Spurred on by the realization that the man would kill her if he caught her, she raced for her life, back over ground she had covered moments earlier. Already breathing heavily from her attempt to reach the parlor ahead of her assailant, she was nevertheless desperate to get away. That goading fear put swift wings to her feet.

In the kitchen she fairly sailed over the same chair that had brought her down earlier. In the next moment she was yanking open the back door and flying across the roofed porch. Hearing swiftly lumbering footfalls following in her wake as she ran into the yard, she threw a fearful glance over her shoulder to find the man crossing the porch in hot pursuit. An instant later her breath left her in an audible "Ooph!" as she ran full bore into something very solid. A tree trunk might have gained the same results, but this solidity proved all too human as long arms came around her, wrenching a scream from her. In her panic her mind settled on the obvious. There was not only one madman after her; there were two!

"Raelynn!"

The familiar voice was the last she had expected to hear, but it was definitely the most welcomed. Still, there was a demon with a knife behind them, seeking to reap a grim harvest. The man would kill them both if he could.

"Jeffrey, look out! He knifed Rhys!"

Jeff had left the jail without a single weapon in his possession. Still devoid of one, he pushed Raelynn behind him and braced himself to meet this oncoming foe bare-handed and head-on. His adversary lifted the blade high for a downward thrust into the chest of this new threat, but Jeff grasped the front of the black mantle and, with a hard-driving knee to the groin, brought the knave crumpling forward with a half-wheezing, half-gagging groan. For good measure, Jeff repeated his assault with every hope of crushing any little pebble that remained in the other's loins.

The cloaked miscreant collapsed in a billowing heap of writhing torment upon the ground at Jeff's feet. That worthy snatched the hood off with such force that the culprit's head lolled loosely around his darkly clad shoulders. Jeff was intent upon rendering the fellow his just due and once again seized the front of his cloak. Hauling the man upright, he slammed a hard fist into his jaw, jerking that one's face about. He wasn't above turning the other's cheek with another driving blow. Indeed, he proved unrelenting as he slammed another right into the now sagging jaw and followed it with several more blows until their would-be assassin drooped unconscious within his grasp. Jeff finally relinquished his hold and allowed his opponent to collapse in a dark heap upon the ground. Only then did Jeff reach down and turn the other's face to the meager light of the moon.

"None other than Lord Marsden," he sneered.

"Marsden!" Raelynn gasped, stepping beside her husband. "But why, Jeffrey? What did we ever do to him?"

"The key to this, my love, may well be what *he* did to your father. He's an English lord, is he not? And he said he knew of your father's trouble, so undoubtedly he came from England fairly recently, perhaps on your heels. Let us even suppose that he didn't come for the purpose of acquiring land for his daughter, but on a definite mission to find something of great value or importance, possibly even a letter that verified your father's innocence, which, at the same time, might have proven Marsden's guilt in the matter. If he had thought your father had sequestered such evidence in his coffer, then that would explain why someone, perhaps even Marsden himself, tried to pry open the secret compartment. When I discovered it, it held nothing at all, but that's not to say that Frye didn't steal what it contained when he had it within his possession."

"You found such a niche?" Raelynn asked in amazement.

"Aye, I did, the night you ran away from Oakley."

Raelynn searched her mind. "Perhaps, as you say, Cooper Frye discovered the compartment during the voyage and took whatever it contained."

"We'll have to ask him about that. As for Lord Marsden, he was at our ball. Perhaps he was even in our bedroom when Nell came to the house to threaten me. He may have killed her just to keep her quiet. As we're both aware, this man is partial to knives."

"He stabbed Rhys, too."

At that precise moment, Deputy Charlie came huffing and puffing around the corner of the house with a large pistol clutched within his grasp. Becoming suddenly aware of the pair of shadowed forms in the yard near the house, he settled into a stance with legs splayed and then clasped the butt of his weapon in both hands, taking aim. "Hold there!"

"Put that damned thing down, Charlie, before you blow somebody's head off," Jeff barked.

"Mis-Mis-ter Bir-ming-h-ham?" the deputy stuttered in

confusion, letting his arms drop to his sides. "I-I thought w-we left ye locked up at the jailhouse."

"I let myself out," Jeff informed him succinctly and indicated the unconscious man on the ground. "Tie this bag of bones into a bundle, Charlie. I'm going into the house to see about Rhys. My wife said this devil knifed him."

"K-Knifed S-Sheriff Townsend?" Charlie's voice held a note of weakness that conveyed his sudden concern.

Jeff gestured toward the senseless man. "If this heap of dung moves while you're watching him, kindly lower the butt of your pistol upon his head with enough force to send him into the netherworld. You'll be doing us all an enormous favor."

Half-turning, he laid an arm about his wife's shoulders and drew her close against his side. "Tell me, my love, are you all right?"

"Yes, just a bit shaken, that's all." It was so very nice to be safe within her husband's arms once again, but she couldn't hold back the sobs as she fell against his chest. "Oh, Jeff, that horrible man . . . he . . . he would've killed me if you hadn't come. I tried to warn Rhys after he came into the house. I had a pistol in my hand, but by the time I managed to get it cocked, it was too late. Lord Marsden threw a knife at Rhys, and I saw it sink into his chest. He might even be dead now."

"Let's go see about him, my love," Jeff urged thickly and then hurriedly cleared his throat, trying to force back the emotion that welled up within him. It threatened to rise to the surface again as he thought of the close camaraderie he had enjoyed with his childhood friend throughout the years. He knew Rhys's death would be a hard loss for him to bear.

Jeff solemnly closed the kitchen door behind Raelynn before stepping ahead to pick up the fallen chair. Settling a hand upon the small of her back, he guided her toward the dining room door by way of the meager glow radiating from the small, flickering fire in the kitchen hearth. Moonlight streaming through the parlor windows aided their progress around the dining room table. They were just stepping beyond that piece when a familiar voice bellowed from the parlor.

"*Damnation, where is everyone?*"

In the shadowed gloom, Jeff and Raelynn looked at each other in surprise. Curiosity spurred them on, and they rushed into the front parlor where Rhys had managed to prop himself up against the arm of a chair.

"You're alive!" Raelynn cried with a joyful laugh.

"Of course, I'm alive!" Rhys rumbled, clasping a hand to a bloody area below his shoulder. "Though no thanks to that fellow who knifed me." He turned a suspicious squint upon Jeff. "How the blooming devil did you get out, may I ask? I left you locked up hard and fast!"

"Not so hard and fast," Jeff countered with a chuckle. "I'm here to prove that."

"That damn fool Olney get away, too?" Rhys demanded angrily.

"Nope, he's safe in his cell. At least, he was when I left, and unless he's a contortionist, I would imagine he's still there."

"Good thing for you. I'd have chewed your as . . ." Catching himself abruptly, he eyed Raelynn through the meager light and cleared his throat sharply before rephrasing his threat. "Chewed your head off, that's what I would've done."

"How bad is your wound?" Jeff asked in anxious concern, kneeling beside him.

"Bad enough to have thrown me on my rear," Rhys grumbled and then winced sharply as Jeff sought to remove his coat. "Don't be in such an all-fired hurry to see the damage! It'll still be there even if you take your time gettin' to it."

"Sorry," Jeff murmured in chagrin and proceeded more slowly.

Raelynn had fetched swabbing cloths and towels for Rhys's wound and then hastened to light several lamps in the parlor. She placed one on the table beside Rhys as Jeff eased the sheriff's coat off and spread the bloody shirt to examine the wound. The puncture was located beneath the lawman's shoulder, safely away from his heart and lungs, but deep enough to require a physician's care.

Jeff sat back upon his heels and grimaced. "Doc Clarence will have to tend to this, Rhys. Did you bring anyone besides Charlie with you?"

"Yeah, there should be a few more deputies out front somewhere. At least, that's where I left them when I came inside to check on things here in the house. The rest of my men are at Fridrich's warehouse. That's where I was when Elijah finally located me. After seeing a cloaked man entering through the front door of this place, he rode out to find me, but he had to follow my trail from the jail. If not for the man who had gotten his throat slit at a boardinghouse, I'd have been here a damn sight sooner." Remembering the kinship between the dead man and the young woman, he lifted an apologetic gaze to her. "I'm sorry to tell you this, Raelynn, but the man who was killed turned out to be your uncle."

Jeff and Raelynn both stared back at Rhys in stunned surprise. Finally Raelynn managed to clear her throat enough to ask, "Cooper Frye, you mean?"

"Aye, Cooper Frye. I had a gut feeling Fridrich was somehow connected with his murder. Earlier in the afternoon one of Fridrich's men turned up dead, and after finding Frye, I figured some chicanery had been going on, like maybe Fridrich had sent his men out to finish Frye off. Going on that premise, I swore in some deputies and launched a raid on the warehouse. This time we caught the bald-headed demon red-handed with crates of stolen rifles and supplies in his possession, which we cheerfully confiscated. Now we have all the proof we need to hold him on several charges, at the forefront of which will be the murder he arranged for Frye. Lord only knows how many more he has had killed for this reason or that, no doubt for his own gain. As for the smuggled firearms, it seems that he has been selling them to various customers with bad reputations for some years now. I saw that much from Gustav's records." Rhys chuckled. "The man just happened to be working on them when we broke in, so there was no hiding them this time. After what we've already discovered, we'll be able to send Fridrich to the gallows in short order."

"In the meantime, Rhys, we'd better send someone over to fetch Doc Clarence for you," Jeff insisted, pressing a towel over the wound. "Hold this tightly in place while I go find someone to send."

Taking a lamp with him, Jeff stepped to the end of the porch just as a shirtless Farrell came sprinting up the walk on bare feet. It was rare indeed to see the couturier dressed so casually. Only when he was involved in a little boxing practice did the man dress down. This time apparently he had considered his appearance far less important than Raelynn's safety.

"Jeff!" he cried, coming to an astonished halt on the front steps. "Tizzy said you had been arrested and that Raelynn was here by herself with an intruder in the house. Is she all right?"

"Aye, but Rhys has been wounded."

"What the hell happened?"

"Our cloaked assailant returned, tried to do away with my wife, and knifed Rhys instead."

"Is Rhys seriously hurt?" Farrell's voice had lost some of its strength.

"According to Raelynn, our hooded adversary, Lord Marsden, tried his best to kill him, but Rhys should be all right once Doc Clarence closes the wound."

"Lord Marsden," Farrell said in stunned amazement. "Why . . . ?"

"It's a long story, and I'll tell it to you when I've got more time."

"Did Marsden get away again?"

"No, this time he got caught. Charlie's watching over him in the backyard. I've got to send somebody back to relieve him and another rider to fetch Doc Clarence for Rhys. His men are supposed to be out here someplace. I hope they'll be showing their heads as soon as they recognize us."

Farrell waved Jeff back into the house. "I can find them. Just go back in there where you're needed."

"Thanks, friend."

A PAIR OF HOURS PASSED BEFORE CHARLIE DROVE DR. Clarence, his bruised lordship, and a bandaged Rhys to the jailhouse. The latter had refused to go home until he had made sure that everything was as it should be at his office. By the time they arrived, the other deputies he had recruited had locked Gustav Fridrich and his men, including the pair who had killed Frye, in the cell Jeff had earlier vacated. For the sake of his own skin, Olney had chosen to keep his distance from Fridrich, but he was nevertheless wide-eyed with curiosity as Rhys and Charlie entered with their newest prisoner. Another bunk was brought in from the back room and placed in Olney's cell. It was upon this that the still dazed Lord Marsden carefully reclined before Dr. Clarence bent to the task of treating the cuts and bruises that marred his face.

"Find another place for those keys to hang, Charlie," Rhys bade his deputy. "I don't want Fridrich or any of his men pulling the same trick that Mr. Birmingham did." Grinning, he peered at Gustav as he drawled, "Though I can't rightly imagine that whole company of brigands having anywhere near the wits my friend has."

Gustav snorted in rank disgust at the situation in

which he found himself. "Yu're the *dummkopf*," Sheriff Townzend, if yu zhink yu vill keep me here. I am a very rich man. I vill hire zhe best lawyers . . ."

"Considering what you've stolen, Mr. Fridrich, most of your money will go toward reimbursing your victims. You won't be allowed to keep it."

Gustav showed his yellowed teeth in a snarl of rage. "Yu cannot do zhat to me!"

"Oh, I wouldn't be doing it to you myself, but I'm sure the judge shall, once I give over all the evidence that's now in my possession. In fact, if you're still living past the end of this year, I'll be surprised."

The normally florid tones of the German's face waned to a much paler hue, and shakily he went to a corner of the barred cubicle where he lowered himself with some difficulty to the floor. It was the only place where one could sit . . . and *think*.

Turning, Rhys pressed a hand to his injured shoulder as he allowed himself a grimace of pain. He went to his desk where he poured himself a small draught of whiskey from a small jug he kept handy for the purpose of flushing minor wounds and easing the pain of injuries, of which he had had his share throughout his years as a sheriff. Opening a side drawer, he fished through its contents until he found what he sought and closed his hand around the small item that he had placed there for safe-keeping a number of weeks ago. He winced again at the searing discomfort in his shoulder and realized that his strength was fading and that he wouldn't be on his feet much longer. Still, there was one more thing he had to do before he went home.

Making his way to Olney's cell, he waited outside the door until the deputy who had entered with the doctor came to unlock it. Then he crossed to the cot where his lordship was presently being treated. "How's your newest patient, Doc?"

A perplexed frown creased his brows as the physician straightened. "I don't know, Rhys."

"What do you mean, you don't know? His lordship has a few bruises and scrapes on his face. What's so confusing about them?"

"Lord Marsden is running a high fever."

"You mean he's sick?"

"It appears so."

"Too bad," Rhys replied blandly.

Detecting the lawman's sarcasm, Lord Marsden cocked a split and swollen brow at him, but winced in sudden regret. "Have you come to gloat, Sheriff?"

"Whatever makes you think I'm gloating?"

His lordship snorted in disbelief. "You were wounded by my hand, were you not?"

"Yep."

"And you *are* Birmingham's friend, are you not?"

"That I am." the sheriff acknowledged, immensely proud of that fact. "The very best, you might say."

"Why wouldn't you gloat?"

"You've got a point there," Rhys rejoined.

Marsden sneered. "You colonials are all alike. Addlepated bastards, the lot of you."

Dr. Clarence and Sheriff Townsend exchanged a meaningful look before Rhys quipped, "I suppose that's a site better than being an arrogant dunderhead."

Lowering his gaze thoughtfully to the floor, Rhys grew suddenly intent as he peered at a spot. Though it cost him much pain, he bent down and made a pretense of scooping something off the floor. "What's this?" He held the item up for the doctor to see. "This yours, Doc?"

Lord Marsden snatched the snuffbox from the sheriff's grasp. "That's mine, you callous oaf. I must have dropped . . ." Suddenly realizing his error, he stuttered and reached out to return the porcelain box to the lawman. "I'm sorry, I was mistaken. It isn't mine at all."

"Oh, but it is, your lordship," Rhys countered with a

wry grin. "You dropped it in Birmingham's bedroom the night you took Nell out to the stables and stabbed her."

Dr. Clarence gasped in surprise and looked at the Englishman in sudden distaste. Coming to alert attention, Olney sat up on his bunk.

"Not him," the younger man argued. "He can't even walk straight, an' he's slow as molasses in a hard winter."

"Perhaps he is now," the sheriff agreed, "but several weeks ago he was fast enough to almost catch you when he chased you out of the stables." He gestured casually to the older scab on the man's hand which was very close in size to his most recent wound. "You see this? I gave this to him when he was trying to knife Mrs. Birmingham almost a week ago, so this is the same rogue I tried catching. He was certainly fast enough to leave me in the dust, but since then, he has been more or less hindered by a wound inflicted upon him by Mrs. Birmingham."

A look of sudden dawning swept over Dr. Clarence's face as he remembered Farrell laughing his head off about the long hatpin that Raelynn had jabbed into their assailant's backside. Lowering a frown upon the man, he urged, "If you're having problems with that injury, my lord, you'd better tell me now. A tainted sore may be what is causing your fever, and if not treated, you could die."

In swiftly advancing alarm, Lord Marsden shrank back upon the bed. His voice had dwindled to barely a whisper as he acknowledged, "My hip is swollen."

"Any known reason why it should be?" Dr. Clarence prodded.

"I sat on a pin," his lordship snapped.

Dr. Clarence made no effort to deny the man's claims. "Would you mind letting me see your backside?"

Marsden reluctantly complied by loosening his trousers and very carefully turning facedown upon the cot. He did so with a great measure of discomfort, not knowing at this point which gave him more anguish, his front side or his backside. The Birminghams had left him extremely tender in both areas.

Dr. Clarence pulled the man's pants down and smothered a gasp of surprise when he saw the red streaks flowing outward from the blackened, pus-filled wound. On further examination he found that the man's right buttock and thigh were noticeably larger than his left. Indeed, from all appearances, the doctor had little choice but to believe that the infection was of a serious nature. In his years as a doctor, he had amputated many a limb, but severing a buttock was something he had never done before.

"We'll have to put a poultice on your hip to try and draw out the poison," the doctor mused aloud. "But I must warn you, it may be too late."

"You've got to do something!" his lordship insisted. "You can't let it continue to fester. Why, I could die!"

"I'll do what I can, my lord, but I can't promise anything."

Rhys was on his last legs and wearily bade Charlie to take him home. By the time he was ready to leave, Dr. Clarence had finished applying a poultice to Marsden's rump. That was all he could do for the time being and begged a ride home. When they stopped at Rhys's house, he went in to assure Mary that if her husband's wound didn't fester, he would be going about his duties in a week's time, whereupon Rhys promptly told the physician that he didn't have that much time to waste. It was the soft-spoken Mary who quietly promised the doctor that Rhys would rest as much as was required to expedite a proper healing.

⌘IT WAS MIDMORNING BY THE TIME THE HARLOT, Trudy Vincent, found her way to Elizabeth's residence and delivered a small packet to Raelynn Birmingham.

Amid tearful sniffles, she explained to the dumbfounded girl, "Yer Uncle Coop told me if'n somethin' bad happened ta him, I was ta give ye this here package ta ye an' ta tell ye he found it in yer pa's coffin or some such place, an' that by rights, it belongs ta ye. He said somethin' 'bout the missive bein' able ta clear yer pa's name an' convict the real scamps what did him dirt."

Raelynn clasped the precious envelope to her bosom. "Thank you most kindly, Miss Vincent," she replied, tearing up from sheer joy. Begging a gold coin from her husband, she paid the woman for her trouble. It was the very least she could do for such a wonderful gift.

The strumpet had never earned a gold coin in her life and, though she hadn't been of a mind to be generous with her information when she had first arrived, she was now grateful enough to relate the rest of the message that the man whom she had known as Oliver Fenton had bade her to give to the girl. "He also said ta tell ye that it were Lord Marsden what killed Nell an' that yer real Uncle Coop was drowned at sea when he were but a mere lad. Ol' Coop sailed wit' him then. That's why he knew so much 'bout him. He'da've written all this down for ye himself, but he weren't especially handy wit' quill an' ink. He did all right when he had ta, but writin' out words weren't somethin' he was especially fond o'."

Jeff was feeling especially benevolent himself after hearing what the woman had to say and gave her another gold piece for good measure. "My wife and I both thank you, Miss . . ."

"Just call me Trudy, gov'na," the harlot replied with a buoyant grin. " 'At's what everybody calls me." She clutched the coins to her bosom. "I'm the one what should be thankin' ye both for these here coins. Ol' Coop . . ." She shook her head and began again. " 'At is, Oliver Fenton an' me, we got on real good together. Afore he were killed, we were plannin' on goin' north an' startin' us up a pub. He said it weren't safe livin' here wit' Mistah Fridrich an' others always tryin' ta do him hurt." She heaved a sigh. "I 'spect truer words weren't ne'er spoken, seein's as how he got his throat slit by that ol' carp's men. That Marsden fella guttin' Nell were nigh as bad."

Trudy sighed, deeply lamenting the girl's death, before she peered up at Jeff again. "I knew Nell real good. Ye could say we were e'en friends. Once I tried ta talk some sense inta her 'bout followin' ye 'round an' a-moonin' aftah ye. If'n 'tweren't for her thinkin' herself in love wit' ye, Mr. Birmin'am, she might ne'er've let that 'ere Irish sea cap'n take her inta his bed whilst they were stayin' at the same inn. She said he looked a powerful lot like ye, but he had ta sail off a couple o' days later. What wit' the short time he were humpin' Nell, bet he don't know he left his kid growin' in her belly. One day maybe he'll sail 'round this way again an' I can tell him what a fine li'l boy he an' Nell made together."

Raelynn extended a hand in friendship to the woman. "Thank you for coming here today, Trudy," she murmured as the harlot accepted her offering in some amazement. "Thus far, you've managed to enlighten us far better than anyone has managed to do. I'm immensely grateful, so much so I doubt that I could fully explain. Though at odd and sundry times I've perceived some of what you've told us to be true, I never knew the whole of it until now. I'm immensely relieved to discover that there is actually someone who is cognizant of the truth and can explain it in detail. Thank you for everything."

"Ye're kindly welcome, Miz Birmin'am."

Jeff was not above asking the strumpet, "If my wife and I escorted you to the sheriff, would you be willing to relate all of this to him? It would make his investigation easier."

Trudy thought about it briefly and then nodded. "I can do that, Mr. Birmin'am." She shrugged. " 'Sides, I'd like ta see all o' 'em murderin' rascals locked up for a change instead o' roamin' free an' doin' their dirt ta right fine folk like ye an' yer pretty missus."

⮞OAKLEY WAS THE SAME AS RAELYNN HAD REMEMbered it, but in many respects, she came home a changed woman. She now reveled in a newfound wealth of aspirations and expectations. She was fully confident that once barristers delivered Marsden's document to trustworthy noblemen within close proximity to King George of England that in the not-too-distant future her father's name would be cleared, whereupon Marsden's accomplices, Lords Prescott and Havelock, would be arrested and brought to trial for treasonous acts against the Crown.

Thanks to Trudy, rumors were now making their way throughout the city of Charleston, carrying the news that Lord Marsden was Nell's murderer, not Jeffrey Birmingham as many had supposed. Trudy was also letting it be known that an Irish sea captain had sired Nell's son, and that here, too, Jeffrey Birmingham was totally innocent of the deed some had been wont to lay to him.

All of these revelations pleased Raelynn immeasurably, but she was also infinitely gratified that no question now remained in her own mind as well as others that she was Oakley's mistress and beloved wife of Jeffrey Lawrence Birmingham, gentleman planter and entrepreneur *extraordinaire*. She was thrilled that she was going to bear him a child and fully confident that in years to come they would have many more. If providence proved kind, they would eventually grow old together and have grandchildren. At the present moment, however, she was thoroughly content to enjoy her happiness just as it was.

A few days after arriving home, the couple had gotten word that Rhys Townsend had returned to work, still suffering some from his wound, but nevertheless hale and hearty. Lord Marsden, on the other hand, had lapsed into a feverish coma brought on by a deepening infection. At the moment, Gustav Fridrich and his men were still sharing the same cell at the sheriff's office, and Olney was still ensconced across the hall from them with the ailing Lord Marsden. It seemed that Olney was not willing to trust his life to his former employer or to be anywhere within vulnerable contiguity to him. He was ten thousand dollars richer now, having turned himself in to Sheriff Townsend to bear witness against Jeffrey Birmingham, erroneous though his story had been. Still, as far as Olney was concerned, he had earned the money, for he could have gone to parts unknown and retained his freedom. He could expect to spend a few years in prison for wounding Jeffrey Birmingham, whereas Fridrich would likely hang for all the murders he had bade his men to commit, none of which Olney had taken part in. The tars he had knifed in Fridrich's defense, he kept to himself and fervently hoped the incident had been forgotten by the German, who had never been one to give much heed to favors he had been granted. Still, he could have pleaded self-defense, for at least one of them had tried to kill him. Fridrich, of course, had nothing more to lose by telling all, and if he remembered the incident, he would surely cause Olney trouble. After all, others' lives meant nothing to him, which of course made Olney all the more willing to tell what he knew about the man and his operations, at least while he was privately sequestered with the sheriff.

The newlyweds, Farrell and Elizabeth, had come out to visit Jeffrey and Raelynn and had made a proposal that the latter could hardly resist. If Raelynn continued to supply them with an appropriate number of new fashion designs for the changing seasons, which she could work on at her leisure at Oakley, the couple would be happy to provide her, after the birth of her child, with complete wardrobes for every cycle of the year for as long as she cared to sketch new gowns for them. Not only would they benefit from her designs, but she would be a walking testament to the beautiful quality of clothes they made in their shop. Jeff allowed his wife to make the decision, drolly quipping that if she accepted, then he would be able to keep his money and still appease his desire to see her dressed in the height of fashion. Raelynn was delighted to take the couple up on their proposal. It was definitely work that she enjoyed, and as long as she could stay at Oakley where she was happiest, then it definitely seemed that she would be favored with the best from both worlds.

It was shortly after supper on a quiet, warm, early November evening that Kingston came into the dining room where the couple were lingering over their tea and coffee and announced that several wagons had stopped in front of the house. He went on to explain, "Dey be foreign folk, Mistah Jeffrey, Gypsies, I think dey call demselves. Anyways, dey be wantin' ta know if yo'd be o' a mind ta let 'em camp on your land tonight. Dey says dey's on their way ta Georgia an' doan means ta do yo' or your land any bother, but earlier today, a couple o' dere chilluns got sick from eatin' fermented berries an' de motion o' the wagon is jes' makin' dem chillun dat much sicker. Dey says if'n yo' be o' a mind ta let 'em stay, they'd play some music fo' yo' befo' dey goes a ways off an' makes camp. Dey's wantin' yo' ta knows, too, suh, dat dey's honest folk, not given ta stealin' or hurtin' others. Dey makes a livin' playin' music, suh, an' dat's all."

"Oh, how nice," Raelynn warbled, taking her husband's hand. She turned a smile upon him. "Would you be of a mind to let them stay, Jeffrey?"

Her husband readily yielded himself to her sparkling plea as he drew her from her chair. "I see no harm in letting them, madam, providing it's only for one night."

Slipping an arm through his, she laughingly bade, "Then come, Jeffrey. Let's go outside on the porch where we can listen to their music."

Arm in arm, they strolled out into the hall where Kingston awaited them with a shawl for his mistress. Jeff settled it around his wife's slender shoulders and once more gallantly presented his arm as they stepped out onto the portico. To their amazement they found almost a dozen musicians with instruments in hand collecting on the front lawn. Only one spoke well enough to be understood, but even then, his efforts confused them. However, the melodious strains of his violin and the accompanying guitars, flutes and other violins transported the couple into a realm of rare pleasure. The music fell as silk upon their listening ears, stirring their hearts with joy and admiration. Whether lively or soothing, the tunes evoked pleasure, so much so that Raelynn soon found herself in her husband's arms, being waltzed around the length and breadth of the porch.

Stars twinkled through the leaves and the gracefully sweeping limbs of the huge live oaks that encompassed the grounds. The fragrance of fall was in the air, eliciting a headiness that neither man nor woman could deny. They were happy, content and feeling wonderfully alive.

"My goodness, sir, you do go to a lady's head," Raelynn remarked in breathless wonder. "I haven't been this entranced with a man since I was about three."

"What happened when you were three, my love?"

"I can't remember all of it, but I can recall being in a garden with my cat and my dolls and it started raining. We rarely get a downpour in England, just a soft, gentle rain. That's the reason English gardens are so lovely, I suppose." She laughed suddenly and shook her head at her whimsical memories. "Sometimes I wonder if I have just dreamed it all."

Her husband's eyes gleamed back at her as they caught the glow of the huge lanterns burning beside the front door. "My uncle had an estate in London, and when I was much younger, we used to visit him as a family. I remember being surprised by how cool it was there, at least compared to here. It rained almost every day."

"That's true," Raelynn agreed with a soft laugh, and then stopped suddenly, caught by memory. "It's odd but I think I've been dreaming about that lately." She fell silent again, chasing a fleeting vision, really just a sensation. She was a child again, very small, in a garden, someone had lifted her high . . .

"Strange that you should say that, my love," Jeff murmured.

"How so, Jeffrey? We dream about all sorts of different things."

"True, but what you mentioned was somehow . . . familiar." His brows gathered as he tried to recall what it was exactly. "I think I may have been dreaming about London recently myself."

"Did it make such a great impression on you?" she asked teasingly.

"I liked it well enough, I suppose. I remember that my uncle's estate had a walled garden our mother always raved about. She even brought a few of the plants back to Harthaven when we returned."

"We had a walled garden on my father's estate. It was my favorite place. I had the most wonderful adventures there, searching for elves and pixies." She giggled. "I even met my Prince Charming."

Jeff shot her an amused glance and laughed. "Should I be jealous, or was he some gallant squirrel, perhaps?"

"You have cause to be envious," she goaded sweetly, dimpling. "I fell in love with him."

Jeff's brow jutted sharply upward as a lopsided grin turned his lips. "So tell me about this errant rogue who stole your heart. Was he as handsome as I?"

"Very princely in both manners and good looks."

"What traits did you like best about this dandified coxcomb?"

Raelynn braced an elbow on his shoulder and musefully laid a finger alongside her cheek. "He had black hair, I think. An iron gate provided a passage through our walled gardens. I wandered into his one day, possibly in search of my cat. He saw me and took me back to my home. I remember feeling a little frightened when he lifted me onto his shoulder. They were very broad, as I remember." Her smile deepened at her childhood fantasy. "And in case you're wondering, it started raining."

Jeff was now staring at her most peculiarly, so much so that Raelynn rushed to assure him, "He wasn't really my Prince Charming, Jeffrey, but when I was so young, he seemed that way to me."

In slow deliberation Jeff asked, "Did this Prince Charming ever give you a flower?"

Raelynn stared up at her husband in surprise. "How could you possibly have known that, Jeffrey?"

"Because many years ago, during a particularly rainy London spring, I met a beguiling elf who kept wandering into my uncle's garden. She was such an endearing little thing that I could hardly mind her visits, but I did try to convince her to stay closer to home. She agreed most prettily that she would on condition that I would . . ."

"Dance with her," Raelynn completed in awe, stunned almost beyond words. "You picked me up. I sang a song and you joined me, and then we danced. It was a glorious time, a memory I've held dear all these years. But after that, you went away, and I never saw you again."

"My uncle died, and we no longer had any cause to return to London," Jeff replied softly, in his mind's eye seeing once again the little girl she had been.

Raelynn stared at him. From that time forward, he had been her beau ideal, the chivalrous Prince Charming for whom she had unknowingly longed throughout the years and miles that had separated them. "Do you actually think we were meant for each other from the beginning?"

Jeff smiled. "My heart never found ease with another

woman, and yet, when you ran into my life that day in Charleston, it was as if you had stepped from a dream that I had been nurturing all these years. I was utterly swept away by joy at the idea that I had found my beloved at last."

Her softly glowing eyes delved into his as she, in some awe, whispered through sweetly smiling lips. "Jeffrey, you have been the only man I've *ever* loved. You were my princely knight when I was but a child, and now, as my husband, you are the joy of my life. I am so pleased to be your wife."

"Excuse me," a deep, male voice bade from the narrow lane in front of the house.

Startled from their shared revelry, Jeffrey and Raelynn broke apart and looked around. A tall, broad-shouldered, good-looking man swept off his hat and came forward to the steps leading to the porch.

"Are ye Mr. Birmingham?" the man asked with an Irish-infected brogue.

"Aye, I am Jeffrey Birmingham. I also have a brother, Brandon, who answers to that name." Jeff motioned in a westerly direction. "He lives several furlong away."

"I believe ye be the one I've come ta talk wit', sir."

"And your name?"

"Captain Shannon O'Keefe. Trudy sent me ta ye."

A look of wonder swept over Jeff's face. "Are you Daniel's father?"

"I believe I am that, sir. Nell were an innocent when I took her inta me bed, an' I have no cause ta think she'd have gone ta another man's bed in so short a time."

"Have you come for a visit?"

"I've come ta claim me son, give him me name, an' let me sister, who's barren, raise him as her own. She's been pinin' her heart out some years now for a wee babe ta call her own, an' since I've no wife o' me own, 'tis fittin' I let Bryden care for him whilst I pay his board an' keep, at least 'til he's old enough ta go ta sea wit' me."

Jeff crossed the porch and stretched forth a hand in friendship. "We're delighted to see you, sir. We've been worried about the boy, wondering what kind of future he'd have without his father's name. It's a relief to know he'll be cared for and loved."

⟋⟍RAELYNN SNUGGLED CLOSER AGAINST HER HUSBAND until her head was resting beside his on his pillow. "Have you thought of whether you'd like a son or a daughter?"

Jeffrey swept the curve of her belly. "If given a choice, I'd like to have at least one of each."

"Not at the same time, surely," she protested, giggling. She grinned at him and traced her fingertip over the tiny half-moon scar at the side of his mouth. "I'd like to have a son who looks like you."

"Beau certainly looks like Brandon," Jeff mused aloud, flicking his brows upward in a shrug. " 'Twould seem that there is a strong likelihood of that being the case. But then, I think we should have a daughter who looks like you."

Raelynn pressed his hand over the place where their baby was moving in her womb. "Do you feel him?"

"A busy little squirrel, isn't he?" her husband commented with a chuckle.

"I don't mind," Raelynn replied and sighed contentedly. "It reassures me that all is well."

Jeff placed a doting kiss upon her brow. "Aye, madam, all *is* well. You are in my arms, where you've always belonged."

"The world is truly a fine place when we're together, isn't it, Jeffrey?"

"It is indeed, madam. It is indeed."